SUPERMAN ADVENTURES

the man of STEEL

Written by:

Mark Millar

**Evan Dorkin
and Sarah Dyer**

Illustrated by:

Aluir Amancio

Terry Austin

Bret Blevins

Colored by:

Lee Loughridge

Marie Severin

Lettered by:

Phil Felix

Superman created by **Jerry Siegel** and **Joe Shuster**

SUPERMAN ADVENTURES VOL. 4: THE MAN OF STEEL
Published by DC Comics. Cover and compilation copyright © 2006 DC Comics. All Rights Reserved.
Originally published in single magazine form as SUPERMAN ADVENTURES #35-39. Copyright ©
1999, 2000 DC Comics. All Rights Reserved. All characters, their distinctive likenesses and related
elements featured in this publication are trademarks of DC Comics. The stories, characters and
incidents featured in this publication are entirely fictional. DC Comics does not read or accept
unsolicited submissions of ideas, stories or artwork.

CARTOON NETWORK and its logo are trademarks of Cartoon Network.

DC Comics, 1700 Broadway, New York, NY 10019
A Warner Bros. Entertainment Company.
Printed in Canada. First Printing.
ISBN: 1-4012-1038-4   ISBN 13: 978-1-4012-1038-0
Cover illustration by Rick Burchett and Terry Austin.
Publication design by John J. Hill.

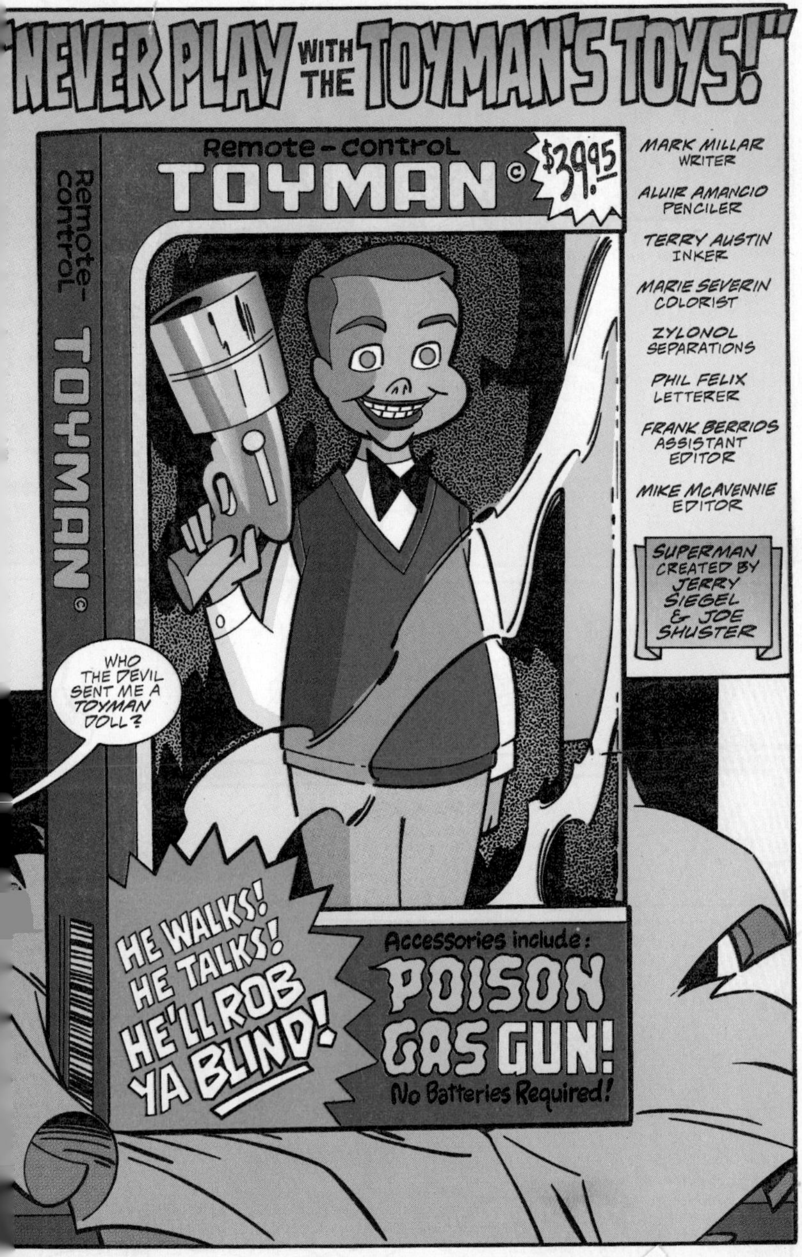
"NEVER PLAY WITH THE TOYMAN'S TOYS!"
Remote-control TOYMAN ©
$39.95
Remote-control TOYMAN ©
MARK MILLAR WRITER
ALUIR AMANCIO PENCILER
TERRY AUSTIN INKER
MARIE SEVERIN COLORIST
ZYLONOL SEPARATIONS
PHIL FELIX LETTERER
FRANK BERRIOS ASSISTANT EDITOR
MIKE McAVENNIE EDITOR
SUPERMAN CREATED BY JERRY SIEGEL & JOE SHUSTER
WHO THE DEVIL SENT ME A TOYMAN DOLL?
HE WALKS! HE TALKS! HE'LL ROB YA BLIND!
Accessories include:
POISON GAS GUN!
No Batteries Required!

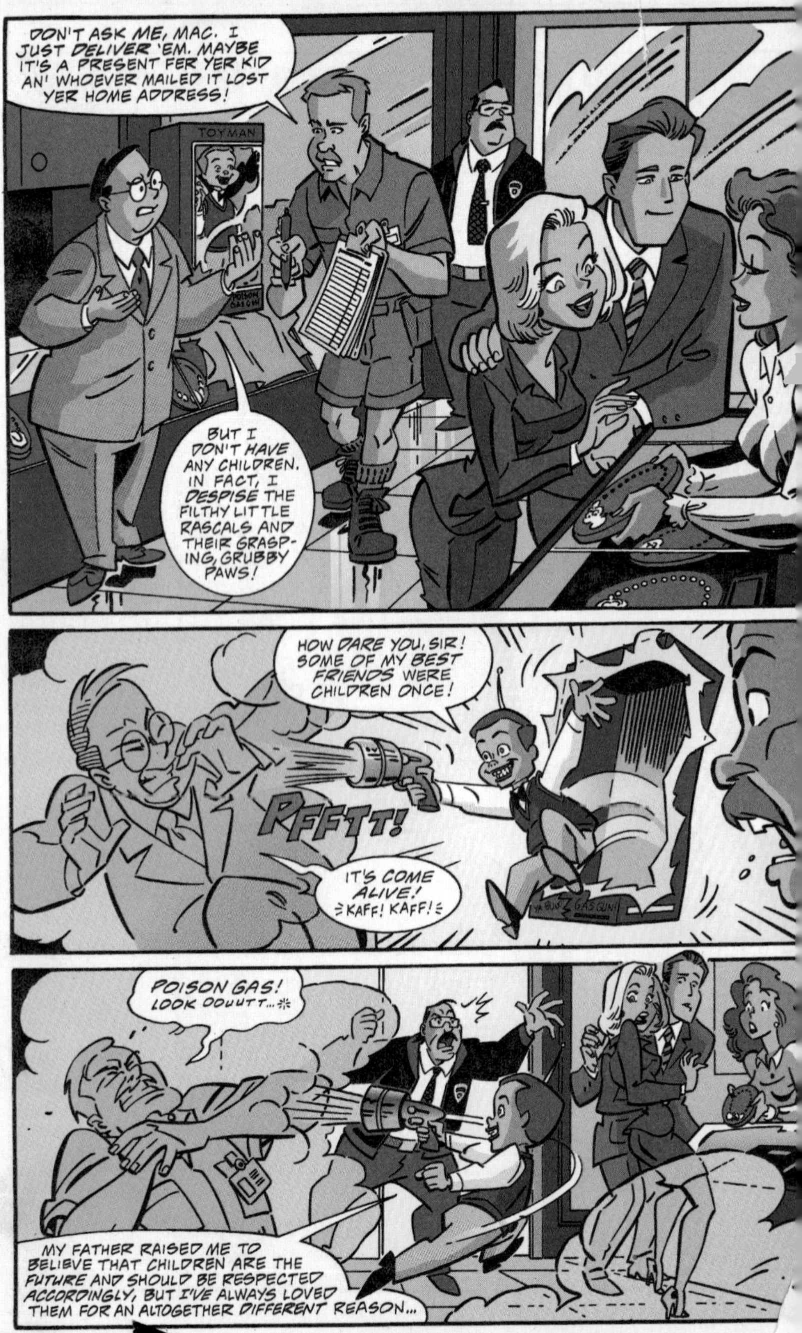
DON'T ASK ME, MAC. I JUST DELIVER 'EM. MAYBE IT'S A PRESENT FER YER KID AN' WHOEVER MAILED IT LOST YER HOME ADDRESS!
TOYMAN
BUT I DON'T HAVE ANY CHILDREN. IN FACT, I DESPISE THE FILTHY LITTLE RASCALS AND THEIR GRASPING, GRUBBY PAWS!
HOW DARE YOU, SIR! SOME OF MY BEST FRIENDS WERE CHILDREN ONCE!
PFFTTT!
IT'S COME ALIVE! KAFF! KAFF!
POISON GAS! LOOK OOUUTT...
MY FATHER RAISED ME TO BELIEVE THAT CHILDREN ARE THE FUTURE AND SHOULD BE RESPECTED ACCORDINGLY, BUT I'VE ALWAYS LOVED THEM FOR AN ALTOGETHER DIFFERENT REASON...

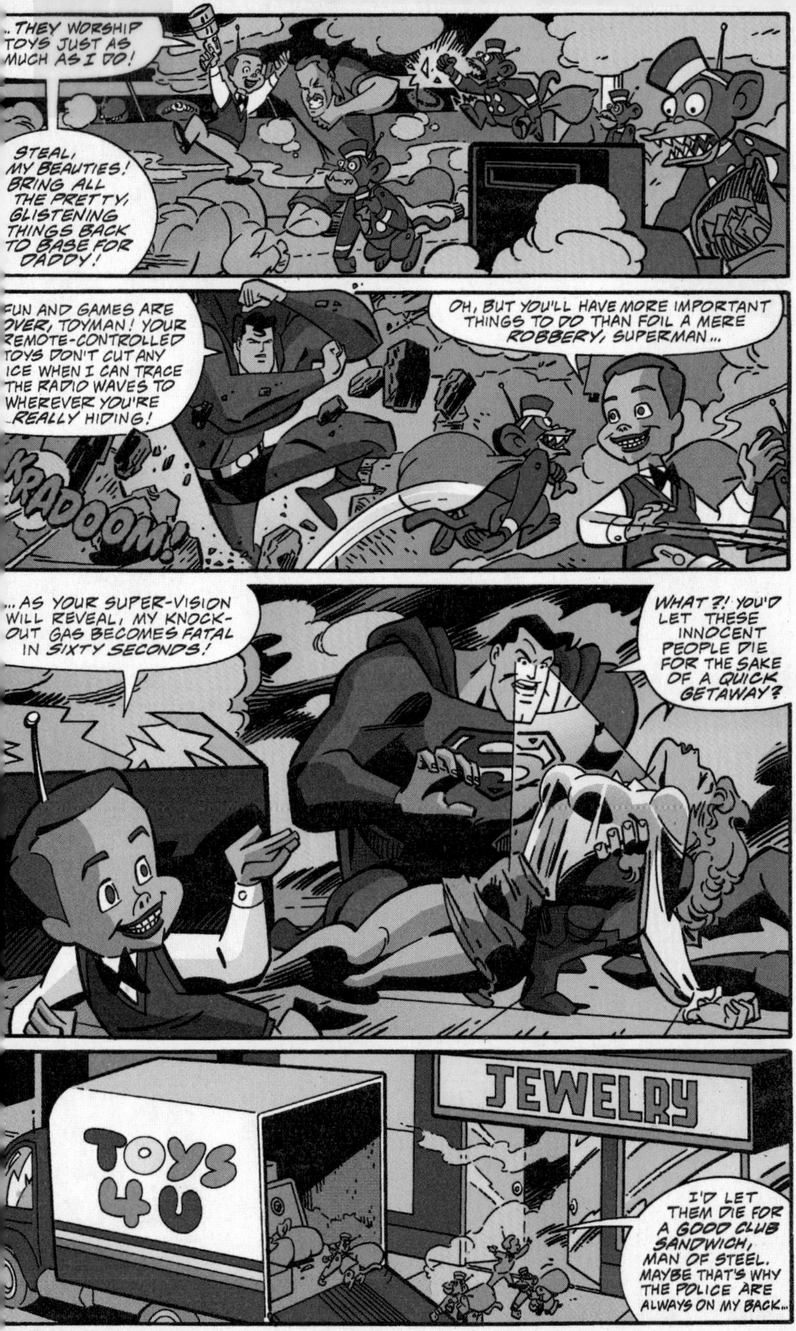
..THEY WORSHIP TOYS JUST AS MUCH AS I DO!
STEAL, MY BEAUTIES! BRING ALL THE PRETTY, GLISTENING THINGS BACK TO BASE FOR DADDY!
FUN AND GAMES ARE OVER, TOYMAN! YOUR REMOTE-CONTROLLED TOYS DON'T CUT ANY ICE WHEN I CAN TRACE THE RADIO WAVES TO WHEREVER YOU'RE REALLY HIDING!
OH, BUT YOU'LL HAVE MORE IMPORTANT THINGS TO DO THAN FOIL A MERE ROBBERY, SUPERMAN...
KRADOOOM!
...AS YOUR SUPER-VISION WILL REVEAL, MY KNOCK-OUT GAS BECOMES FATAL IN SIXTY SECONDS!
WHAT?! YOU'D LET THESE INNOCENT PEOPLE DIE FOR THE SAKE OF A QUICK GETAWAY?
TOYS 4 U
JEWELRY
I'D LET THEM DIE FOR A GOOD CLUB SANDWICH, MAN OF STEEL. MAYBE THAT'S WHY THE POLICE ARE ALWAYS ON MY BACK...

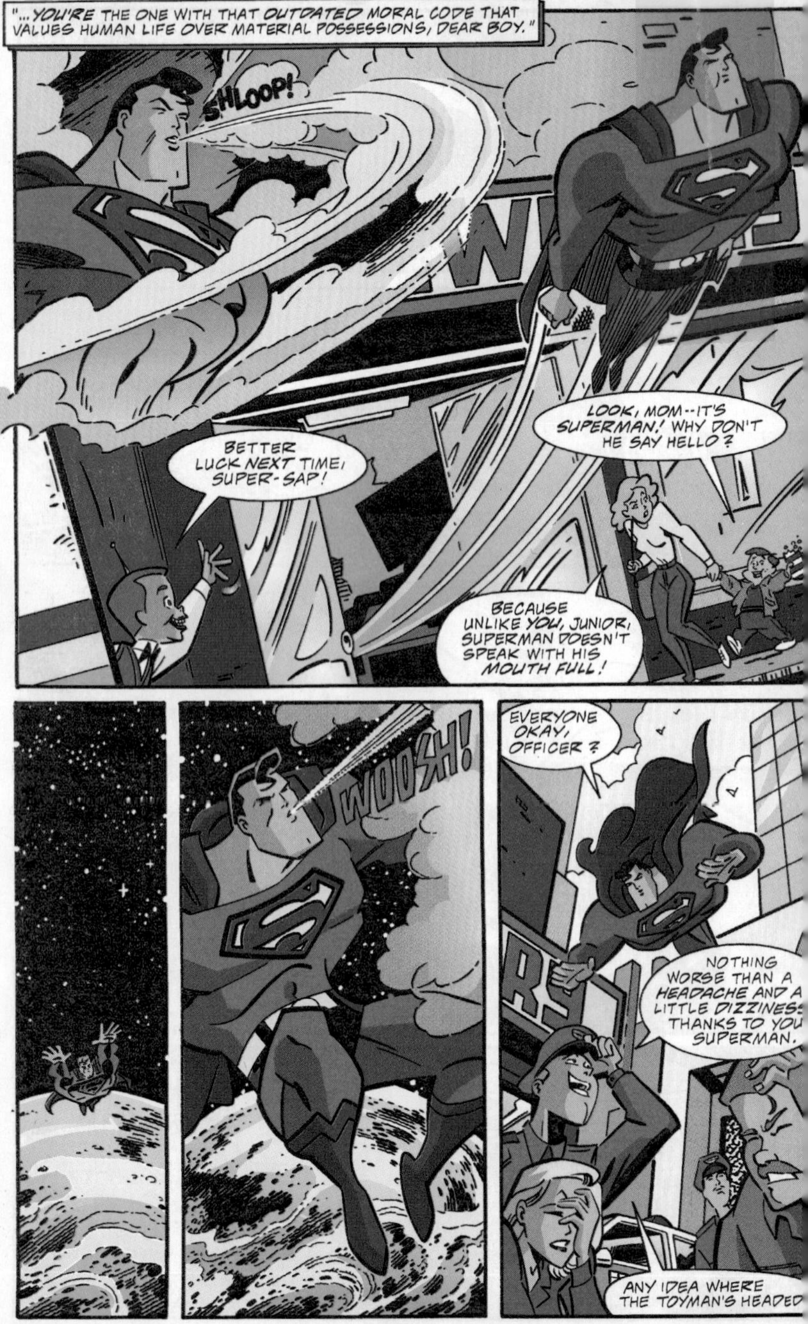
"...YOU'RE THE ONE WITH THAT OUTDATED MORAL CODE THAT VALUES HUMAN LIFE OVER MATERIAL POSSESSIONS, DEAR BOY."
SHLOOP!
BETTER LUCK NEXT TIME, SUPER-SAP!
LOOK, MOM--IT'S SUPERMAN! WHY DON'T HE SAY HELLO?
BECAUSE UNLIKE YOU, JUNIOR, SUPERMAN DOESN'T SPEAK WITH HIS MOUTH FULL!
WOOSH!
EVERYONE OKAY, OFFICER?
NOTHING WORSE THAN A HEADACHE AND A LITTLE DIZZINES THANKS TO YOU SUPERMAN.
ANY IDEA WHERE THE TOYMAN'S HEADED

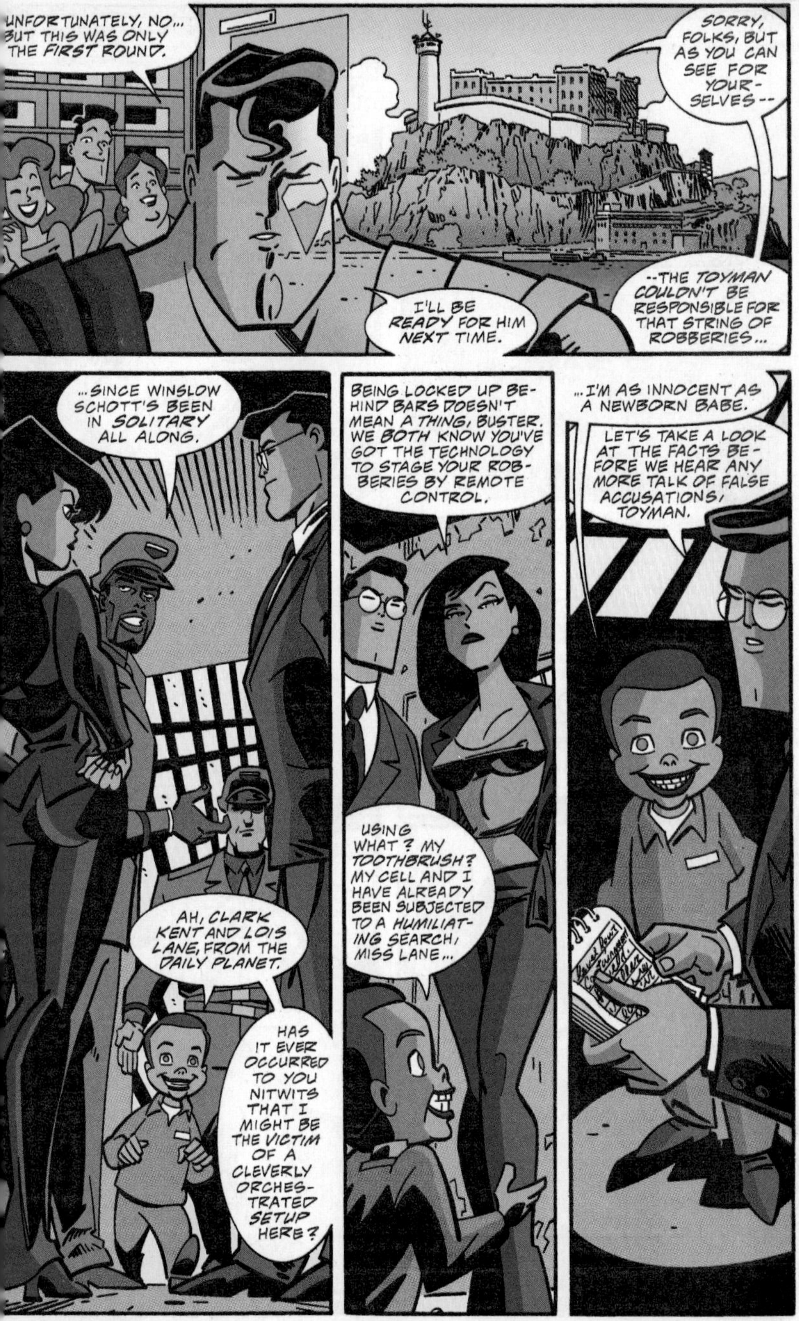

UNFORTUNATELY, NO... BUT THIS WAS ONLY THE FIRST ROUND.
I'LL BE READY FOR HIM NEXT TIME.
SORRY, FOLKS, BUT AS YOU CAN SEE FOR YOURSELVES--
--THE TOYMAN COULDN'T BE RESPONSIBLE FOR THAT STRING OF ROBBERIES...
...SINCE WINSLOW SCHOTT'S BEEN IN SOLITARY ALL ALONG.
AH, CLARK KENT AND LOIS LANE, FROM THE DAILY PLANET.
HAS IT EVER OCCURRED TO YOU NITWITS THAT I MIGHT BE THE VICTIM OF A CLEVERLY ORCHESTRATED SETUP HERE?
BEING LOCKED UP BEHIND BARS DOESN'T MEAN A THING, BUSTER. WE BOTH KNOW YOU'VE GOT THE TECHNOLOGY TO STAGE YOUR ROBBERIES BY REMOTE CONTROL.
USING WHAT? MY TOOTHBRUSH? MY CELL AND I HAVE ALREADY BEEN SUBJECTED TO A HUMILIATING SEARCH, MISS LANE...
...I'M AS INNOCENT AS A NEWBORN BABE.
LET'S TAKE A LOOK AT THE FACTS BEFORE WE HEAR ANY MORE TALK OF FALSE ACCUSATIONS, TOYMAN.

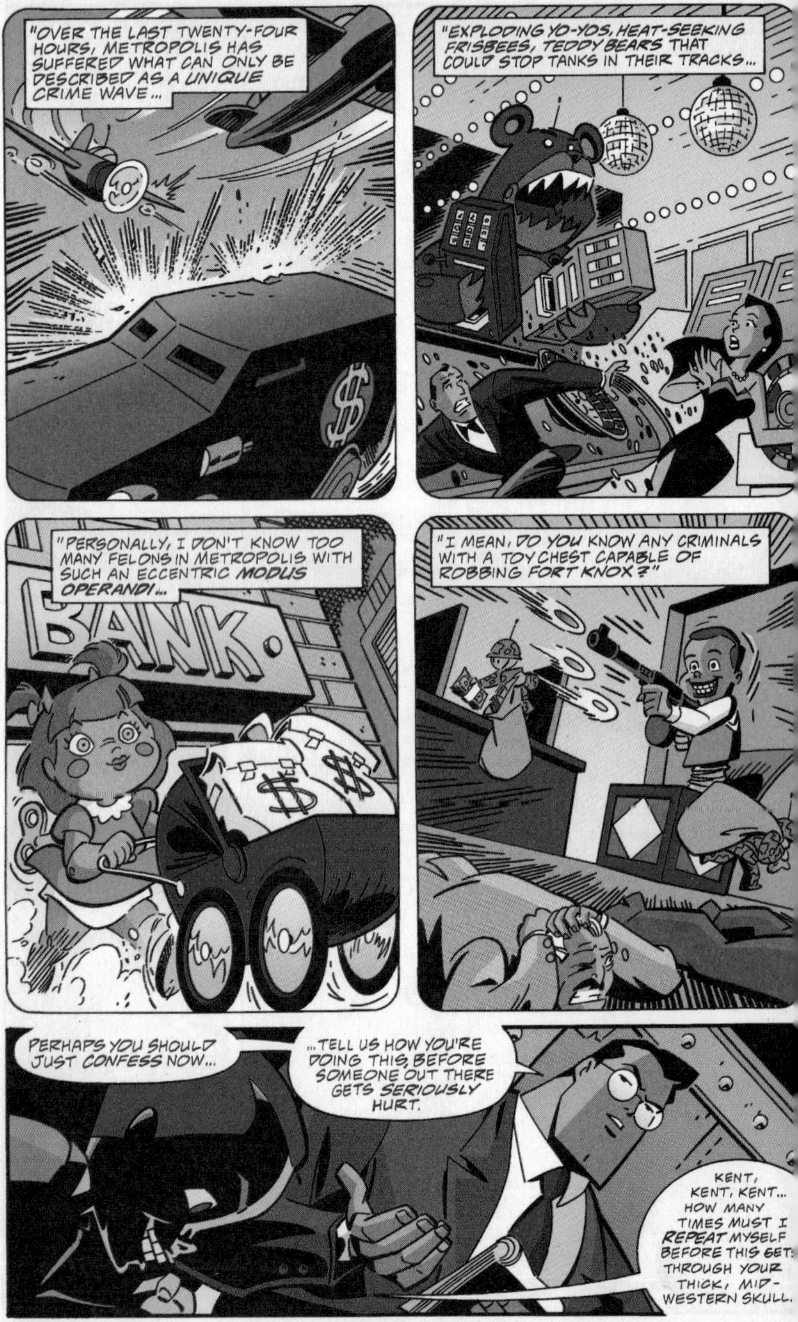
"OVER THE LAST TWENTY-FOUR HOURS, METROPOLIS HAS SUFFERED WHAT CAN ONLY BE DESCRIBED AS A UNIQUE CRIME WAVE...
"EXPLODING YO-YOS, HEAT-SEEKING FRISBEES, TEDDY BEARS THAT COULD STOP TANKS IN THEIR TRACKS...
"PERSONALLY, I DON'T KNOW TOO MANY FELONS IN METROPOLIS WITH SUCH AN ECCENTRIC MODUS OPERANDI...
BANK
"I MEAN, DO YOU KNOW ANY CRIMINALS WITH A TOY CHEST CAPABLE OF ROBBING FORT KNOX?"
PERHAPS YOU SHOULD JUST CONFESS NOW...
...TELL US HOW YOU'RE DOING THIS, BEFORE SOMEONE OUT THERE GETS SERIOUSLY HURT.
KENT, KENT, KENT... HOW MANY TIMES MUST I REPEAT MYSELF BEFORE THIS GETS THROUGH YOUR THICK, MID-WESTERN SKULL.

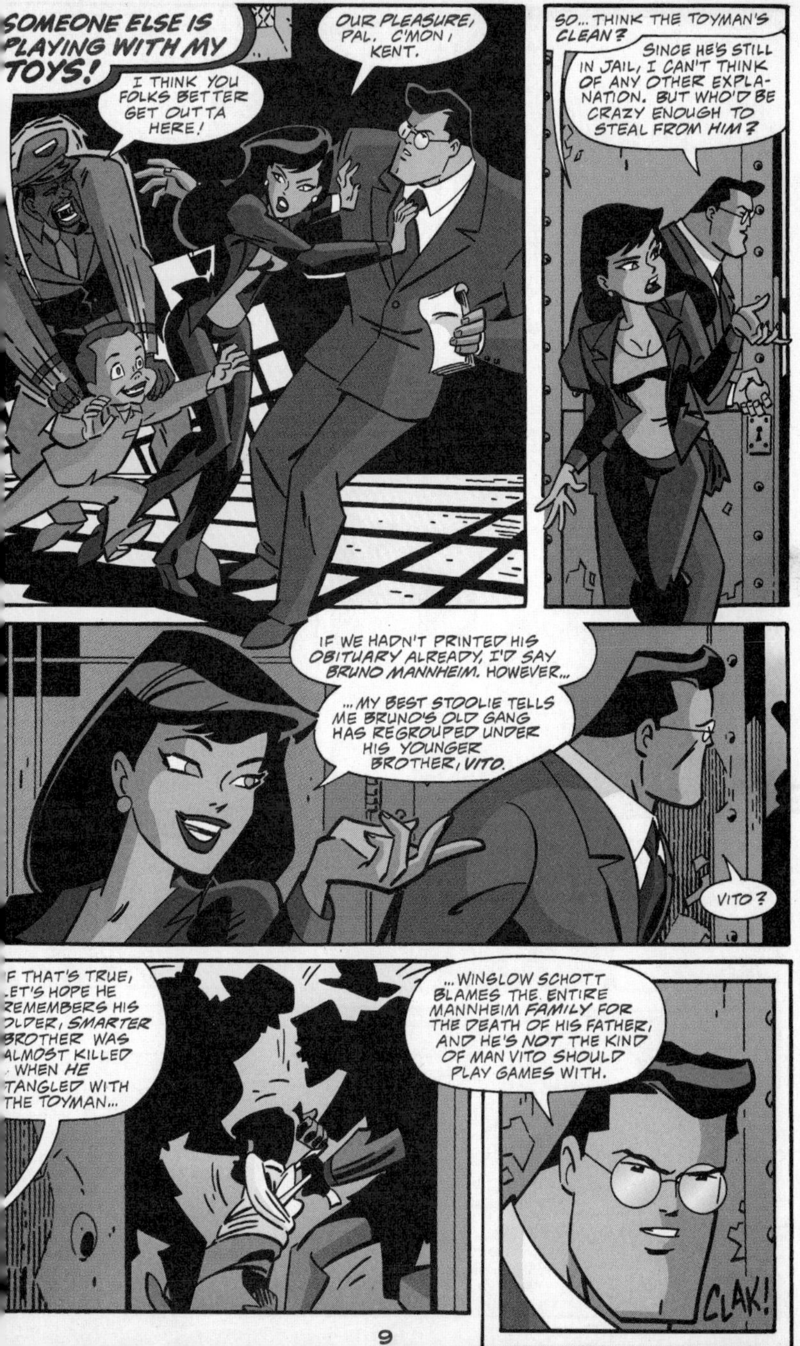
SOMEONE ELSE IS PLAYING WITH MY TOYS!
I THINK YOU FOLKS BETTER GET OUTTA HERE!
OUR PLEASURE, PAL. C'MON, KENT.
SO... THINK THE TOYMAN'S CLEAN?
SINCE HE'S STILL IN JAIL, I CAN'T THINK OF ANY OTHER EXPLANATION. BUT WHO'D BE CRAZY ENOUGH TO STEAL FROM HIM?
IF WE HADN'T PRINTED HIS OBITUARY ALREADY, I'D SAY BRUNO MANNHEIM. HOWEVER...
...MY BEST STOOLIE TELLS ME BRUNO'S OLD GANG HAS REGROUPED UNDER HIS YOUNGER BROTHER, VITO.
VITO?
...WINSLOW SCHOTT BLAMES THE ENTIRE MANNHEIM FAMILY FOR THE DEATH OF HIS FATHER, AND HE'S NOT THE KIND OF MAN VITO SHOULD PLAY GAMES WITH.
CLAK!

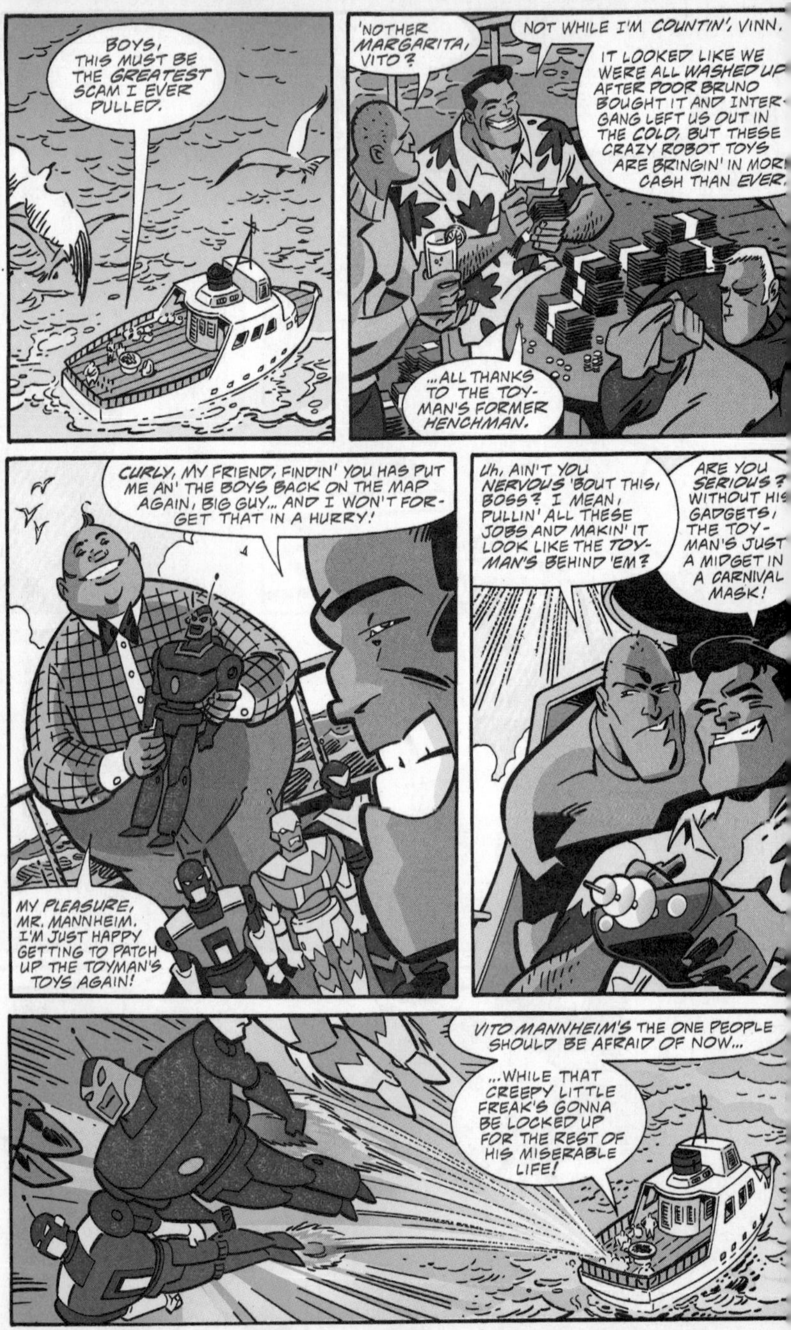

BOYS, THIS MUST BE THE GREATEST SCAM I EVER PULLED.
'NOTHER MARGARITA, VITO?
NOT WHILE I'M COUNTIN', VINN.
IT LOOKED LIKE WE WERE ALL WASHED UP AFTER POOR BRUNO BOUGHT IT AND INTERGANG LEFT US OUT IN THE COLD, BUT THESE CRAZY ROBOT TOYS ARE BRINGIN' IN MORE CASH THAN EVER.
...ALL THANKS TO THE TOYMAN'S FORMER HENCHMAN.
CURLY, MY FRIEND, FINDIN' YOU HAS PUT ME AN' THE BOYS BACK ON THE MAP AGAIN, BIG GUY... AND I WON'T FORGET THAT IN A HURRY!
MY PLEASURE, MR. MANNHEIM. I'M JUST HAPPY GETTING TO PATCH UP THE TOYMAN'S TOYS AGAIN!
UH, AIN'T YOU NERVOUS 'BOUT THIS, BOSS? I MEAN, PULLIN' ALL THESE JOBS AND MAKIN' IT LOOK LIKE THE TOYMAN'S BEHIND 'EM?
ARE YOU SERIOUS? WITHOUT HIS GADGETS, THE TOYMAN'S JUST A MIDGET IN A CARNIVAL MASK!
VITO MANNHEIM'S THE ONE PEOPLE SHOULD BE AFRAID OF NOW...
...WHILE THAT CREEPY LITTLE FREAK'S GONNA BE LOCKED UP FOR THE REST OF HIS MISERABLE LIFE!

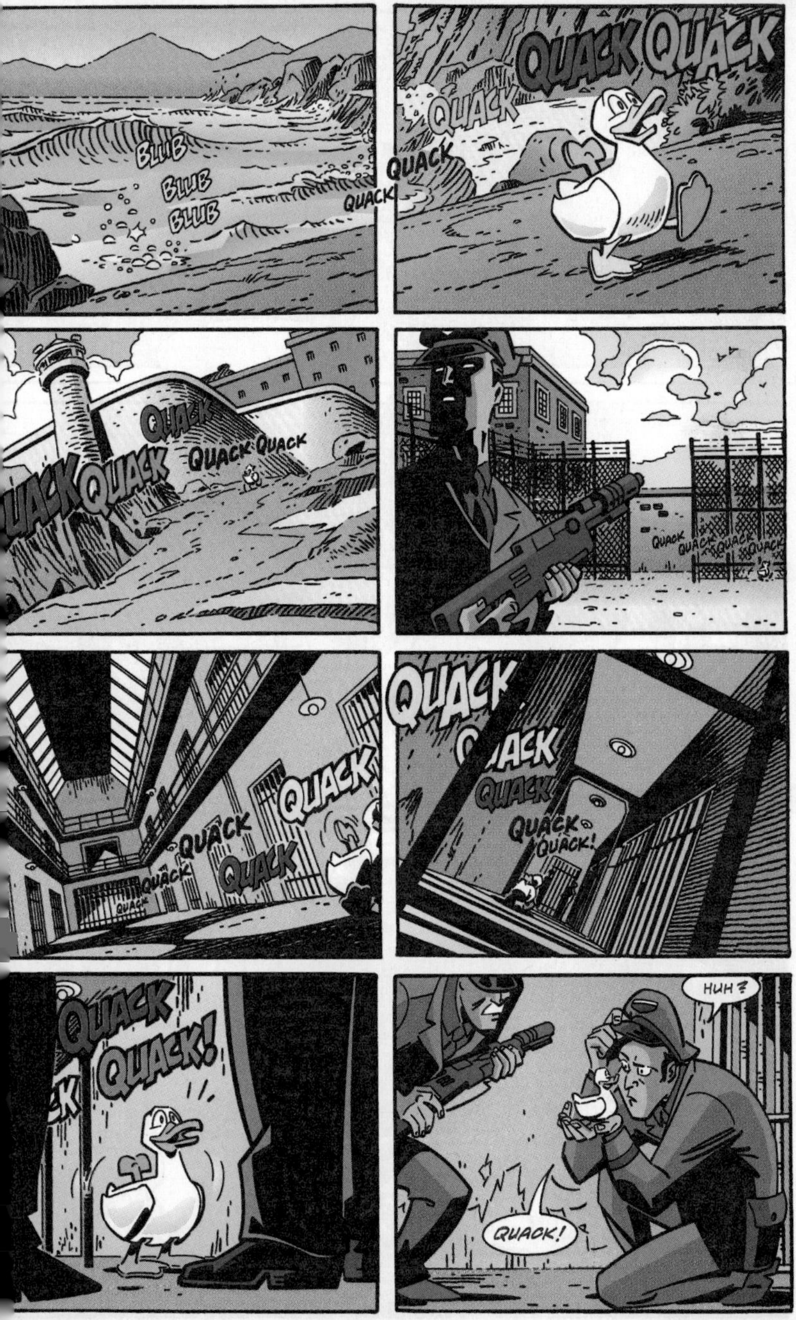
BLUB
BLUB
BLUB
QUACK
QUACK
QUACK QUACK
QUACK
QUACK
QUACK
QUACK QUACK
QUACK
QUACK
QUACK
QUACK
QUACK
QUACK
QUACK
QUACK
QUACK
QUACK
QUACK
QUACK
QUACK
QUACK!
QUACK
QUACK!
HUH?
QUACK!

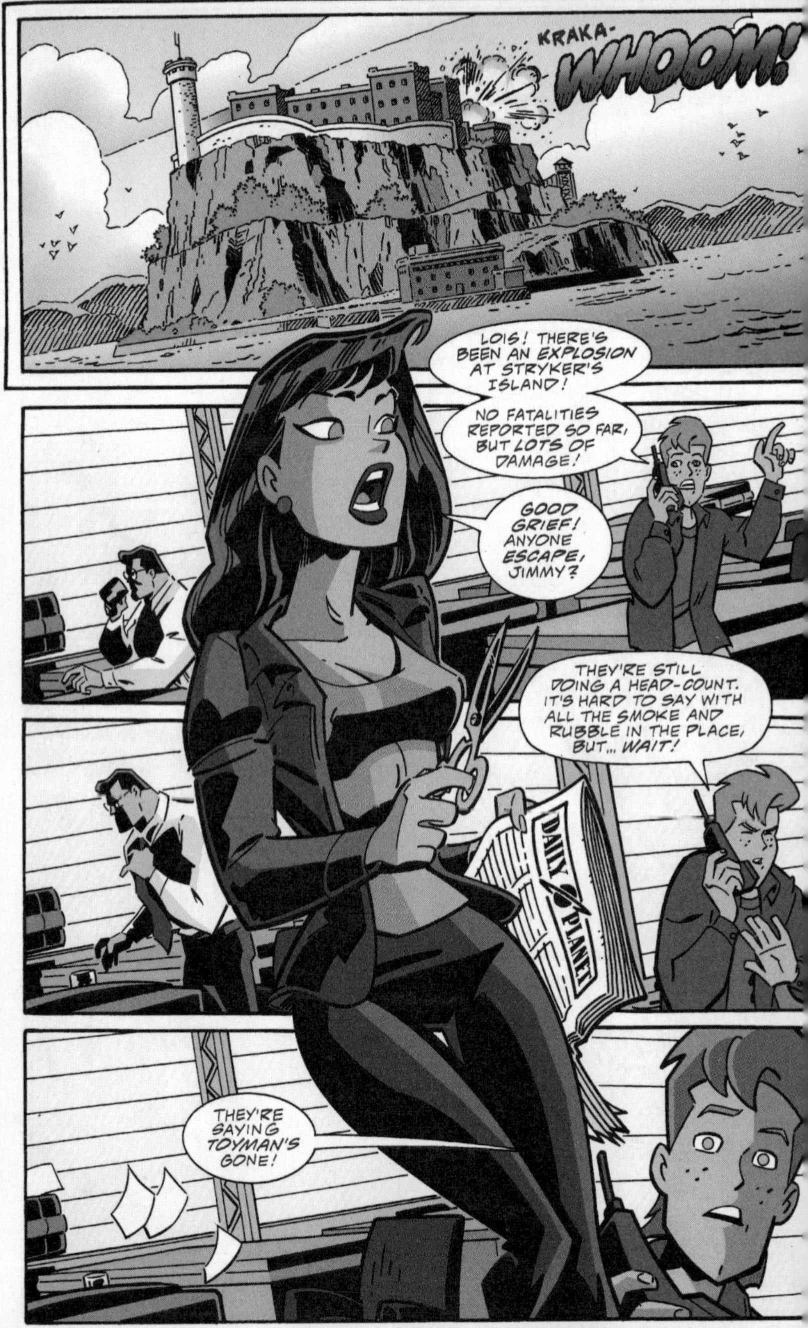
KRAKA-
WHOOM!
LOIS! THERE'S BEEN AN EXPLOSION AT STRYKER'S ISLAND!
NO FATALITIES REPORTED SO FAR, BUT LOTS OF DAMAGE!
GOOD GRIEF! ANYONE ESCAPE, JIMMY?
THEY'RE STILL DOING A HEAD-COUNT. IT'S HARD TO SAY WITH ALL THE SMOKE AND RUBBLE IN THE PLACE, BUT... WAIT!
DAILY PLANET
THEY'RE SAYING TOYMAN'S GONE!

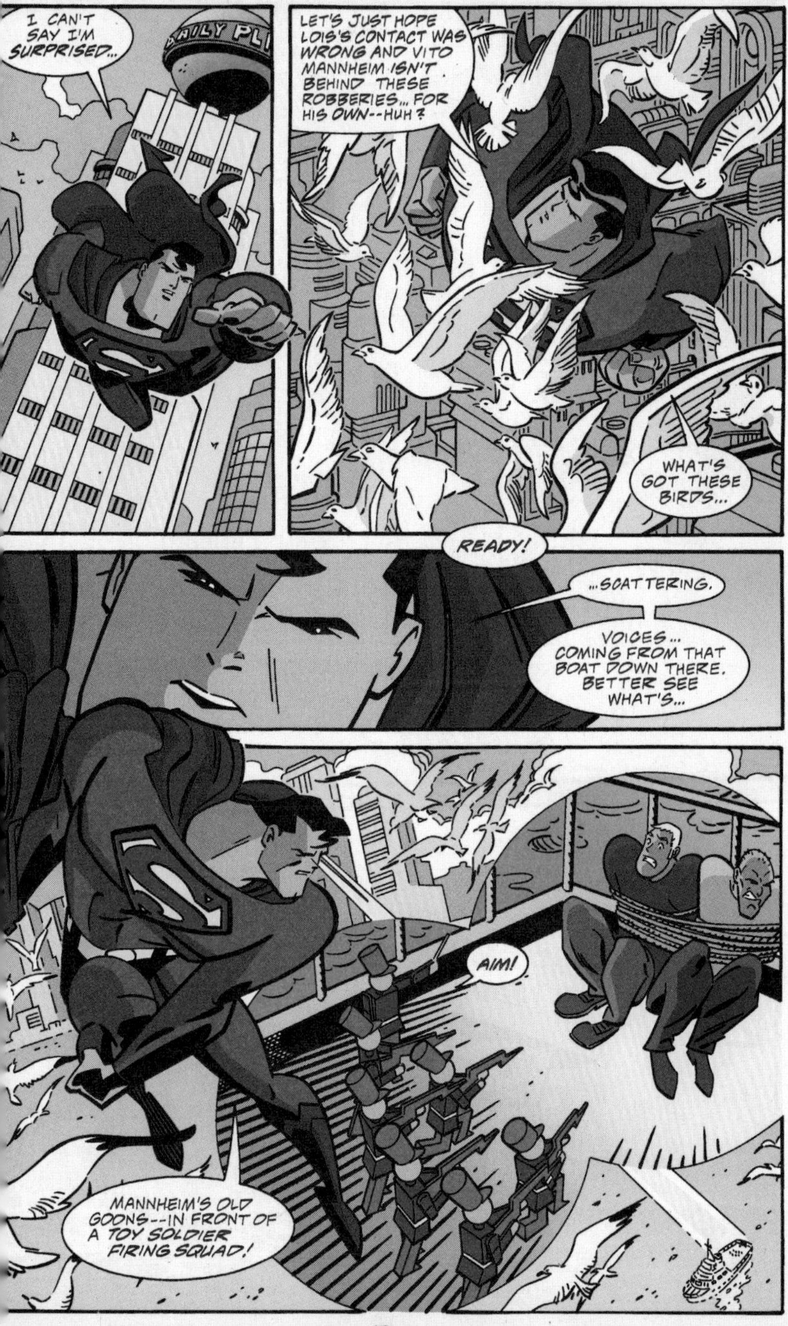
I CAN'T SAY I'M SURPRISED...
DAILY PL
LET'S JUST HOPE LOIS'S CONTACT WAS WRONG AND VITO MANNHEIM ISN'T BEHIND THESE ROBBERIES... FOR HIS OWN--HUH ?
WHAT'S GOT THESE BIRDS...
READY!
...SCATTERING.
VOICES... COMING FROM THAT BOAT DOWN THERE. BETTER SEE WHAT'S...
AIM!
MANNHEIM'S OLD GOONS--IN FRONT OF A TOY SOLDIER FIRING SQUAD!

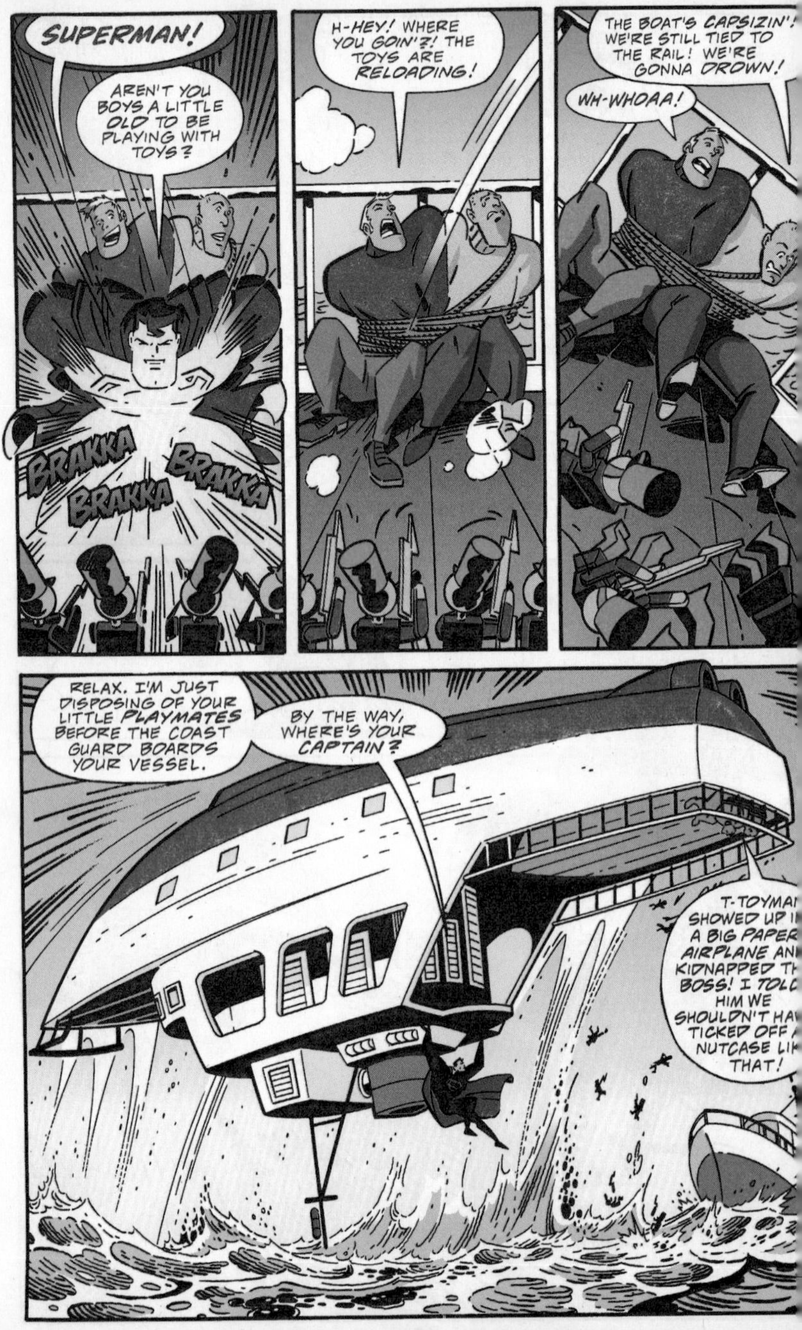
SUPERMAN!
AREN'T YOU BOYS A LITTLE OLD TO BE PLAYING WITH TOYS?
BRAKKA BRAKKA BRAKKA
H-HEY! WHERE YOU GOIN'?! THE TOYS ARE RELOADING!
THE BOAT'S CAPSIZIN'! WE'RE STILL TIED TO THE RAIL! WE'RE GONNA DROWN!
WH-WHOAA!
RELAX. I'M JUST DISPOSING OF YOUR LITTLE PLAYMATES BEFORE THE COAST GUARD BOARDS YOUR VESSEL.
BY THE WAY, WHERE'S YOUR CAPTAIN?
T-TOYMA SHOWED UP I A BIG PAPER AIRPLANE AN KIDNAPPED TH BOSS! I TOLD HIM WE SHOULDN'T HA TICKED OFF NUTCASE LI THAT!

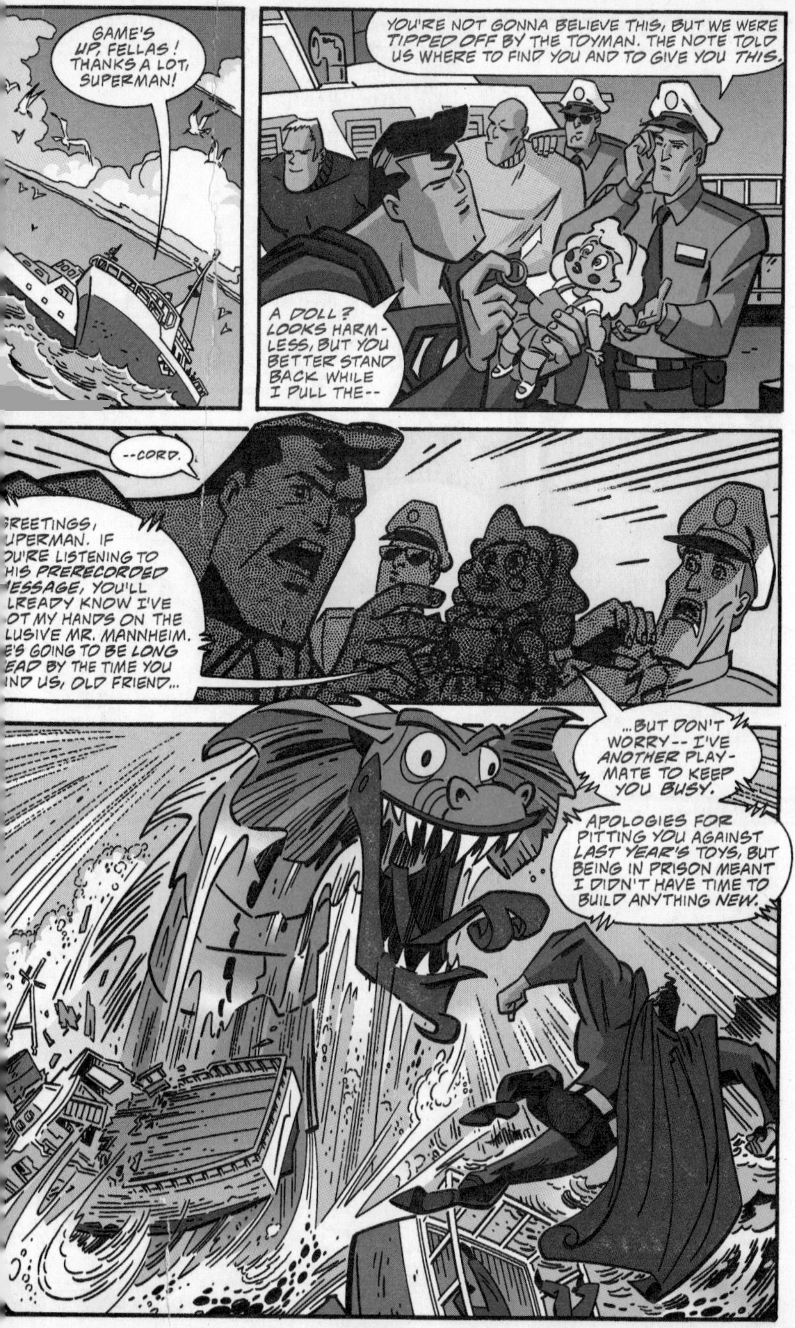
GAME'S UP, FELLAS! THANKS A LOT, SUPERMAN!
YOU'RE NOT GONNA BELIEVE THIS, BUT WE WERE TIPPED OFF BY THE TOYMAN. THE NOTE TOLD US WHERE TO FIND YOU AND TO GIVE YOU THIS.
A DOLL? LOOKS HARMLESS, BUT YOU BETTER STAND BACK WHILE I PULL THE--
--CORD.
REETINGS, UPERMAN. IF OU'RE LISTENING TO HIS PRERECORDED ESSAGE, YOU'LL LREADY KNOW I'VE OT MY HANDS ON THE LUSIVE MR. MANNHEIM. E'S GOING TO BE LONG EAD BY THE TIME YOU IND US, OLD FRIEND...
...BUT DON'T WORRY -- I'VE ANOTHER PLAYMATE TO KEEP YOU BUSY.
APOLOGIES FOR PITTING YOU AGAINST LAST YEAR'S TOYS, BUT BEING IN PRISON MEANT I DIDN'T HAVE TIME TO BUILD ANYTHING NEW.

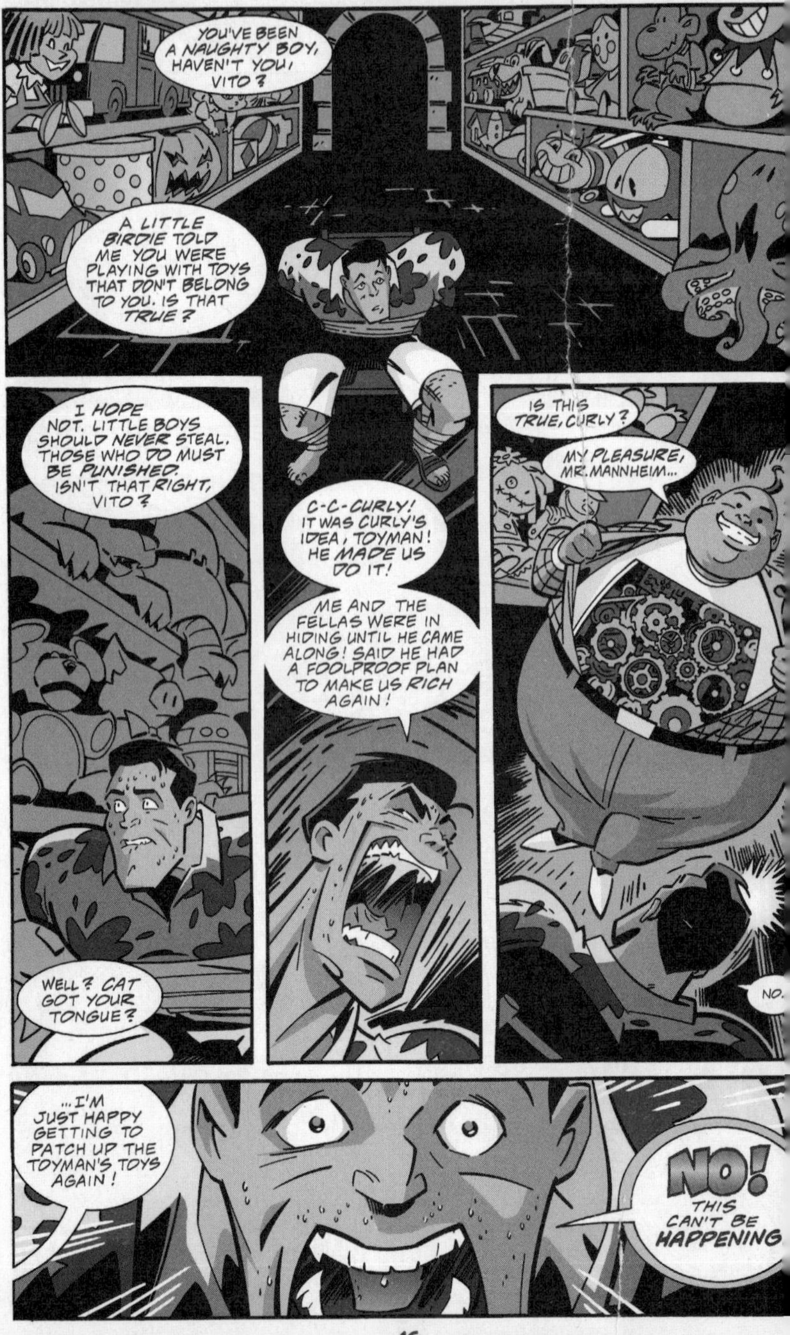
YOU'VE BEEN A NAUGHTY BOY, HAVEN'T YOU, VITO?
A LITTLE BIRDIE TOLD ME YOU WERE PLAYING WITH TOYS THAT DON'T BELONG TO YOU. IS THAT TRUE?
I HOPE NOT. LITTLE BOYS SHOULD NEVER STEAL. THOSE WHO DO MUST BE PUNISHED. ISN'T THAT RIGHT, VITO?
WELL? CAT GOT YOUR TONGUE?
C-C-CURLY! IT WAS CURLY'S IDEA, TOYMAN! HE MADE US DO IT!
ME AND THE FELLAS WERE IN HIDING UNTIL HE CAME ALONG! SAID HE HAD A FOOLPROOF PLAN TO MAKE US RICH AGAIN!
IS THIS TRUE, CURLY?
MY PLEASURE, MR. MANNHEIM...
NO.
...I'M JUST HAPPY GETTING TO PATCH UP THE TOYMAN'S TOYS AGAIN!
NO! THIS CAN'T BE HAPPENING

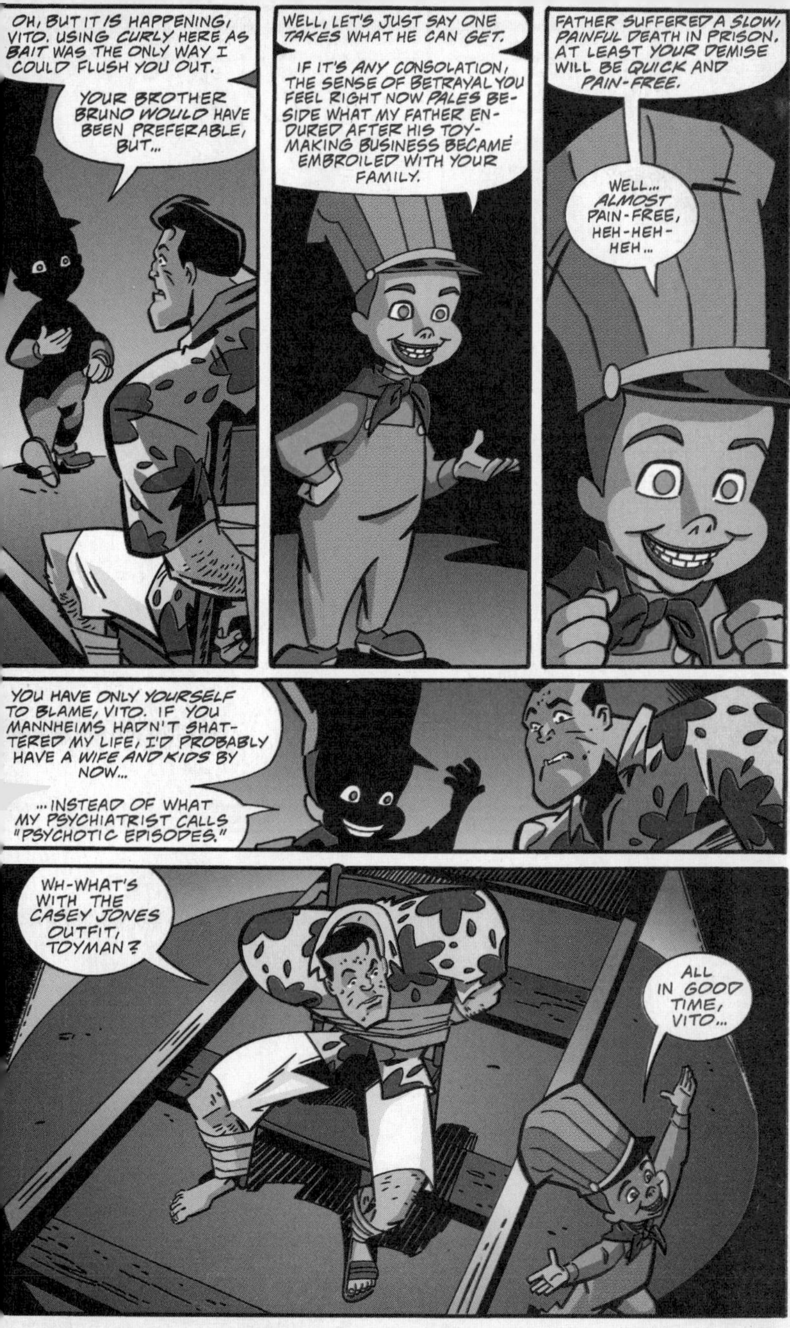
OH, BUT IT IS HAPPENING, VITO. USING CURLY HERE AS BAIT WAS THE ONLY WAY I COULD FLUSH YOU OUT.
YOUR BROTHER BRUNO WOULD HAVE BEEN PREFERABLE, BUT...
WELL, LET'S JUST SAY ONE TAKES WHAT HE CAN GET.
IF IT'S ANY CONSOLATION, THE SENSE OF BETRAYAL YOU FEEL RIGHT NOW PALES BESIDE WHAT MY FATHER ENDURED AFTER HIS TOY-MAKING BUSINESS BECAME EMBROILED WITH YOUR FAMILY.
FATHER SUFFERED A SLOW, PAINFUL DEATH IN PRISON. AT LEAST YOUR DEMISE WILL BE QUICK AND PAIN-FREE.
WELL... ALMOST PAIN-FREE, HEH-HEH-HEH...
YOU HAVE ONLY YOURSELF TO BLAME, VITO. IF YOU MANNHEIMS HADN'T SHATTERED MY LIFE, I'D PROBABLY HAVE A WIFE AND KIDS BY NOW...
...INSTEAD OF WHAT MY PSYCHIATRIST CALLS "PSYCHOTIC EPISODES."
WH-WHAT'S WITH THE CASEY JONES OUTFIT, TOYMAN?
ALL IN GOOD TIME, VITO...

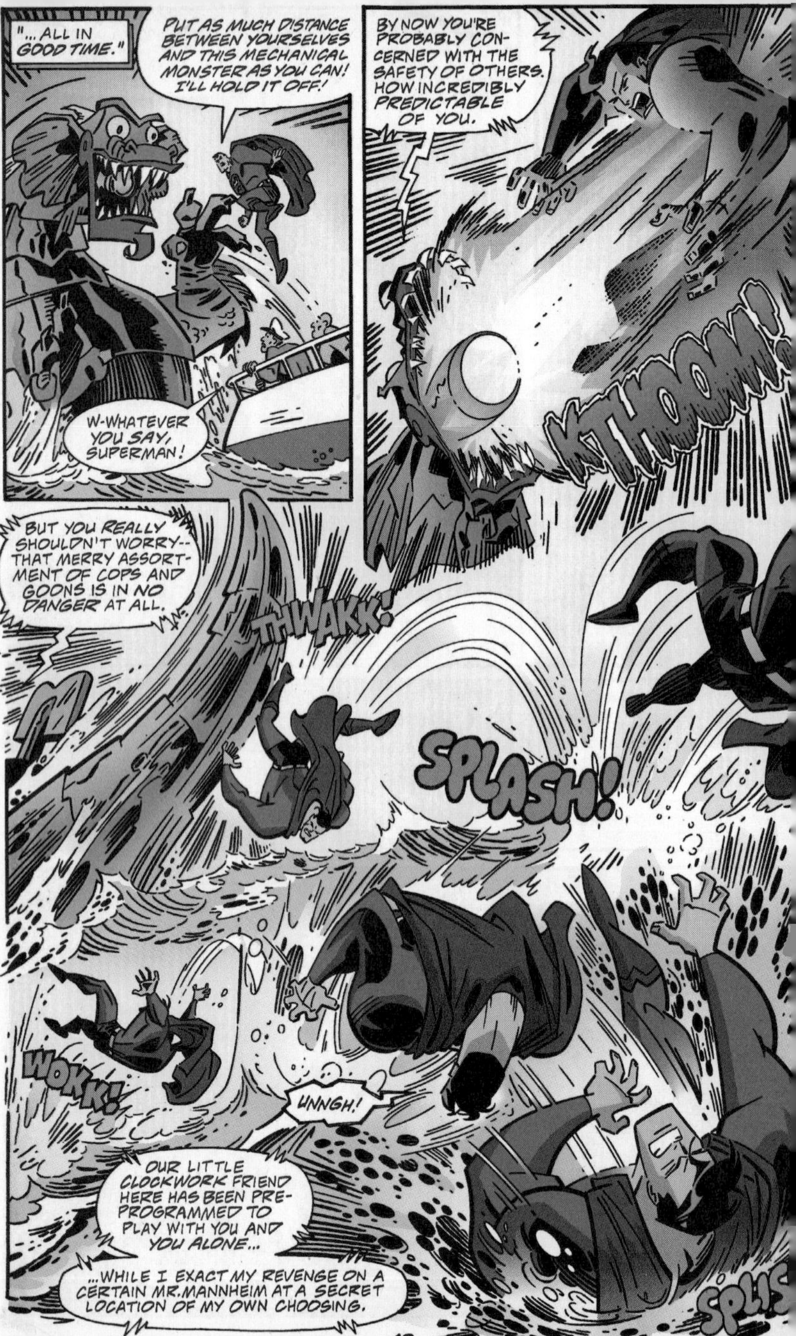

"...ALL IN GOOD TIME."
PUT AS MUCH DISTANCE BETWEEN YOURSELVES AND THIS MECHANICAL MONSTER AS YOU CAN! I'LL HOLD IT OFF!
W-WHATEVER YOU SAY, SUPERMAN!
BY NOW YOU'RE PROBABLY CONCERNED WITH THE SAFETY OF OTHERS. HOW INCREDIBLY PREDICTABLE OF YOU.
KTHOOM!
BUT YOU REALLY SHOULDN'T WORRY-- THAT MERRY ASSORTMENT OF COPS AND GOONS IS IN NO DANGER AT ALL.
THWAKK!
SPLASH!
WOKK!
UNNGH!
OUR LITTLE CLOCKWORK FRIEND HERE HAS BEEN PRE-PROGRAMMED TO PLAY WITH YOU AND YOU ALONE...
...WHILE I EXACT MY REVENGE ON A CERTAIN MR. MANNHEIM AT A SECRET LOCATION OF MY OWN CHOOSING.

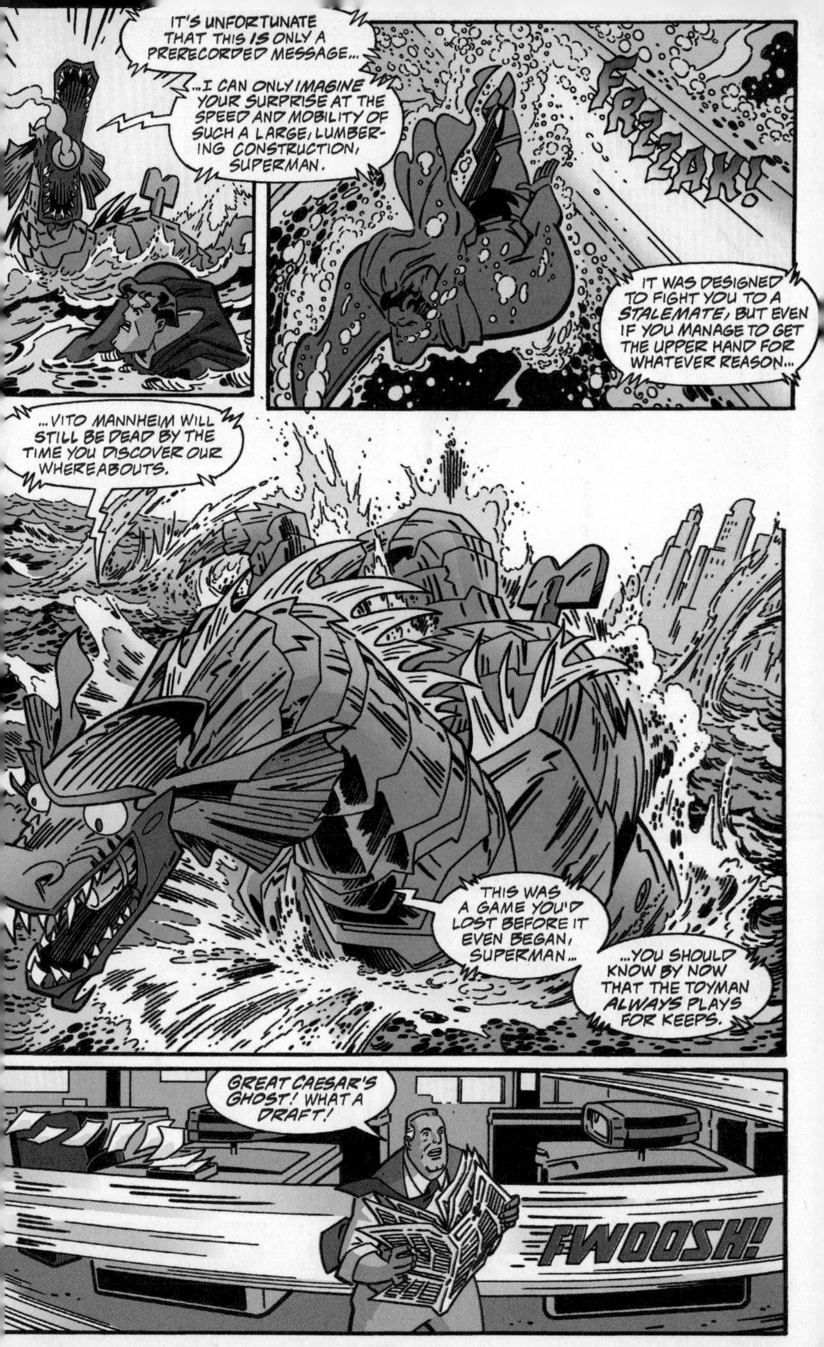
IT'S UNFORTUNATE THAT THIS IS ONLY A PRERECORDED MESSAGE...
...I CAN ONLY IMAGINE YOUR SURPRISE AT THE SPEED AND MOBILITY OF SUCH A LARGE, LUMBERING CONSTRUCTION, SUPERMAN.
FRZZAK!
IT WAS DESIGNED TO FIGHT YOU TO A STALEMATE, BUT EVEN IF YOU MANAGE TO GET THE UPPER HAND FOR WHATEVER REASON...
...VITO MANNHEIM WILL STILL BE DEAD BY THE TIME YOU DISCOVER OUR WHEREABOUTS.
THIS WAS A GAME YOU'D LOST BEFORE IT EVEN BEGAN, SUPERMAN...
...YOU SHOULD KNOW BY NOW THAT THE TOYMAN ALWAYS PLAYS FOR KEEPS.
GREAT CAESAR'S GHOST! WHAT A DRAFT!
FWOOSH!

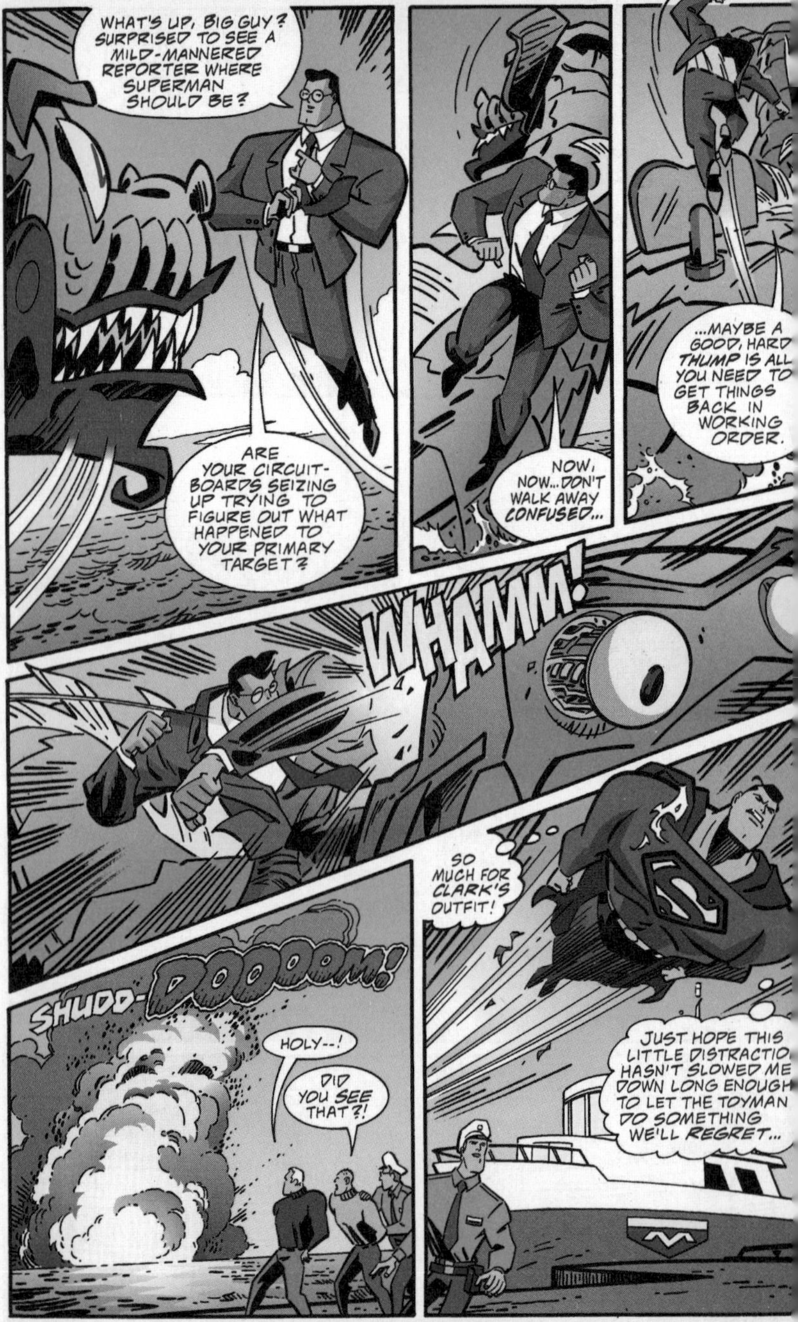
WHAT'S UP, BIG GUY? SURPRISED TO SEE A MILD-MANNERED REPORTER WHERE SUPERMAN SHOULD BE?
ARE YOUR CIRCUIT-BOARDS SEIZING UP TRYING TO FIGURE OUT WHAT HAPPENED TO YOUR PRIMARY TARGET?
NOW, NOW...DON'T WALK AWAY CONFUSED...
...MAYBE A GOOD, HARD THUMP IS ALL YOU NEED TO GET THINGS BACK IN WORKING ORDER.
WHAMM!
SO MUCH FOR CLARK'S OUTFIT!
SHUDD-DOOOOOM!
HOLY--!
DID YOU SEE THAT?!
JUST HOPE THIS LITTLE DISTRACTIO HASN'T SLOWED ME DOWN LONG ENOUGH TO LET THE TOYMAN DO SOMETHING WE'LL REGRET...

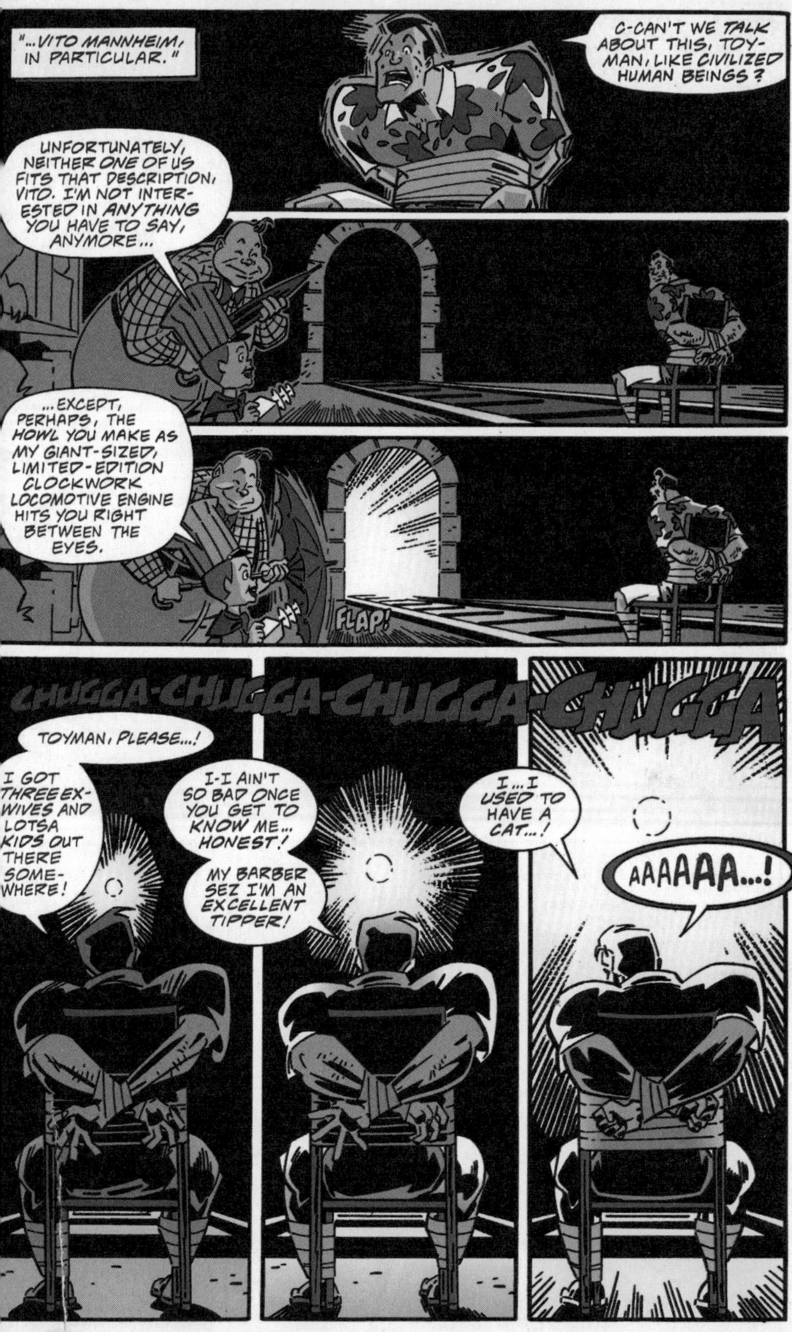
"...VITO MANNHEIM, IN PARTICULAR."
C-CAN'T WE TALK ABOUT THIS, TOY-MAN, LIKE CIVILIZED HUMAN BEINGS?
UNFORTUNATELY, NEITHER ONE OF US FITS THAT DESCRIPTION, VITO. I'M NOT INTERESTED IN ANYTHING YOU HAVE TO SAY, ANYMORE...
...EXCEPT, PERHAPS, THE HOWL YOU MAKE AS MY GIANT-SIZED, LIMITED-EDITION CLOCKWORK LOCOMOTIVE ENGINE HITS YOU RIGHT BETWEEN THE EYES.
FLAP!
CHUGGA-CHUGGA-CHUGGA-CHUGGA
TOYMAN, PLEASE...!
I GOT THREE EX-WIVES AND LOTSA KIDS OUT THERE SOME-WHERE!
I-I AIN'T SO BAD ONCE YOU GET TO KNOW ME... HONEST!
MY BARBER SEZ I'M AN EXCELLENT TIPPER!
I...I USED TO HAVE A CAT...!
AAAAAA...!

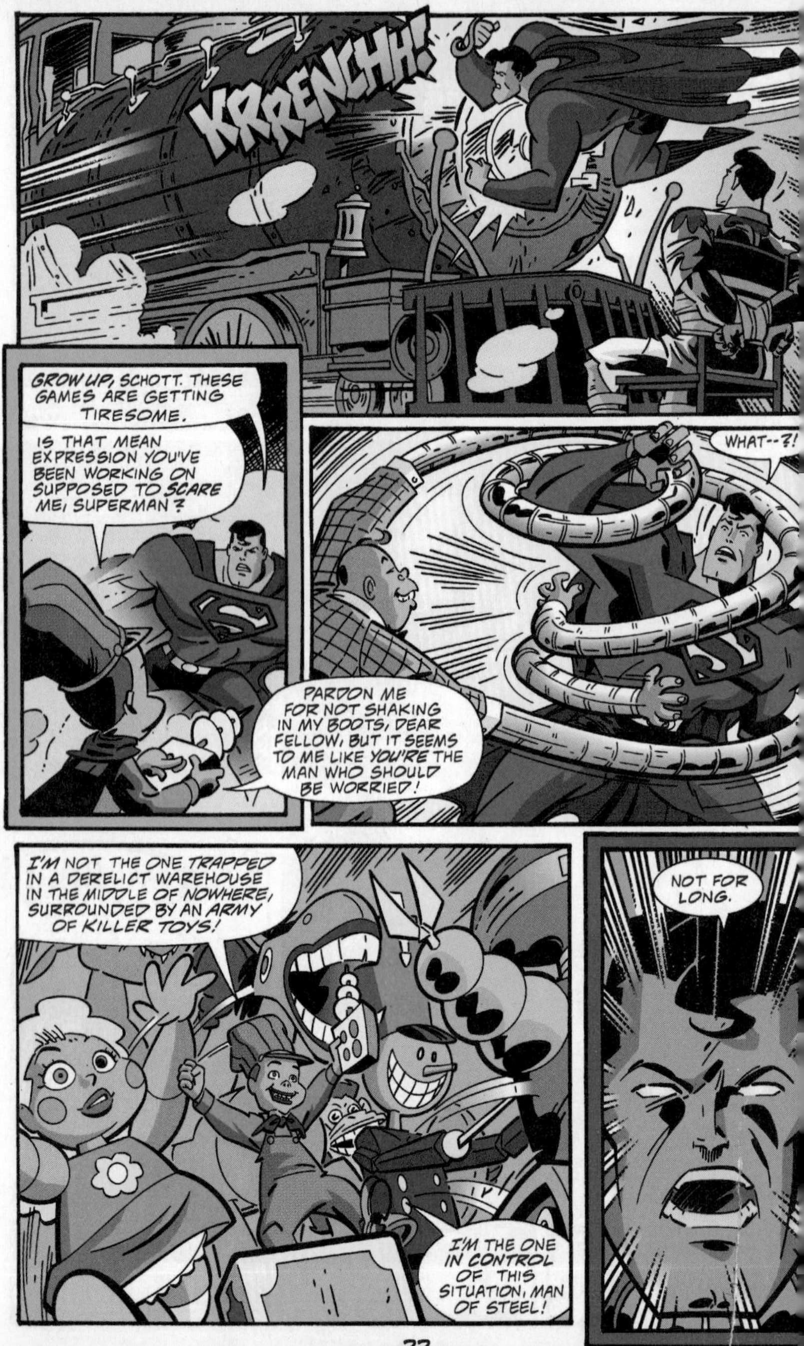
KRRENCHH!
GROW UP, SCHOTT. THESE GAMES ARE GETTING TIRESOME.
IS THAT MEAN EXPRESSION YOU'VE BEEN WORKING ON SUPPOSED TO SCARE ME, SUPERMAN?
WHAT--?!
PARDON ME FOR NOT SHAKING IN MY BOOTS, DEAR FELLOW, BUT IT SEEMS TO ME LIKE YOU'RE THE MAN WHO SHOULD BE WORRIED!
I'M NOT THE ONE TRAPPED IN A DERELICT WAREHOUSE IN THE MIDDLE OF NOWHERE, SURROUNDED BY AN ARMY OF KILLER TOYS!
I'M THE ONE IN CONTROL OF THIS SITUATION, MAN OF STEEL!
NOT FOR LONG.

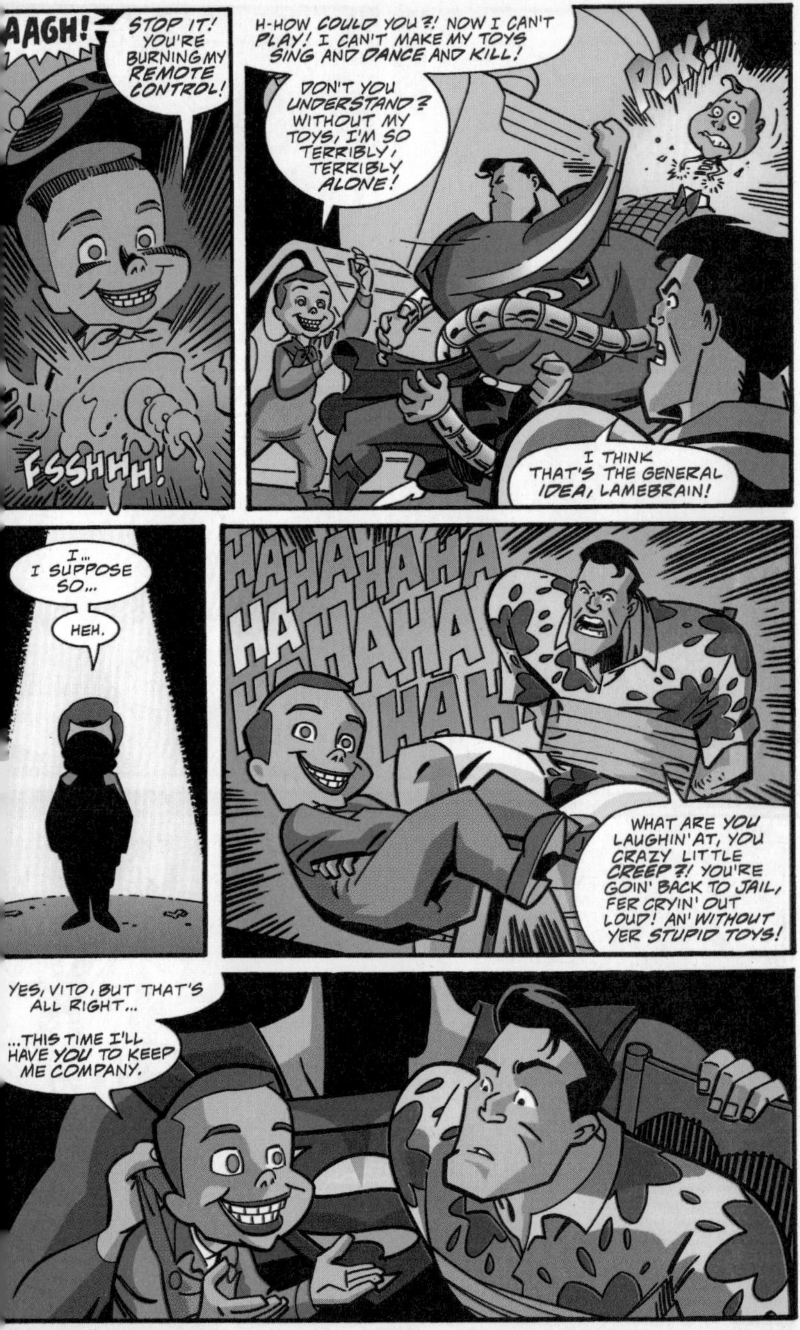
AAGH!
STOP IT! YOU'RE BURNING MY REMOTE CONTROL!
FSSHHHH!
H-HOW COULD YOU?! NOW I CAN'T PLAY! I CAN'T MAKE MY TOYS SING AND DANCE AND KILL!
DON'T YOU UNDERSTAND? WITHOUT MY TOYS, I'M SO TERRIBLY, TERRIBLY ALONE!
POK!
I THINK THAT'S THE GENERAL IDEA, LAMEBRAIN!
I... I SUPPOSE SO...
HEH.
HAHAHAHAHA HAHAHAHA HAHAHA
WHAT ARE YOU LAUGHIN' AT, YOU CRAZY LITTLE CREEP?! YOU'RE GOIN' BACK TO JAIL, FER CRYIN' OUT LOUD! AN' WITHOUT YER STUPID TOYS!
YES, VITO, BUT THAT'S ALL RIGHT...
...THIS TIME I'LL HAVE YOU TO KEEP ME COMPANY.

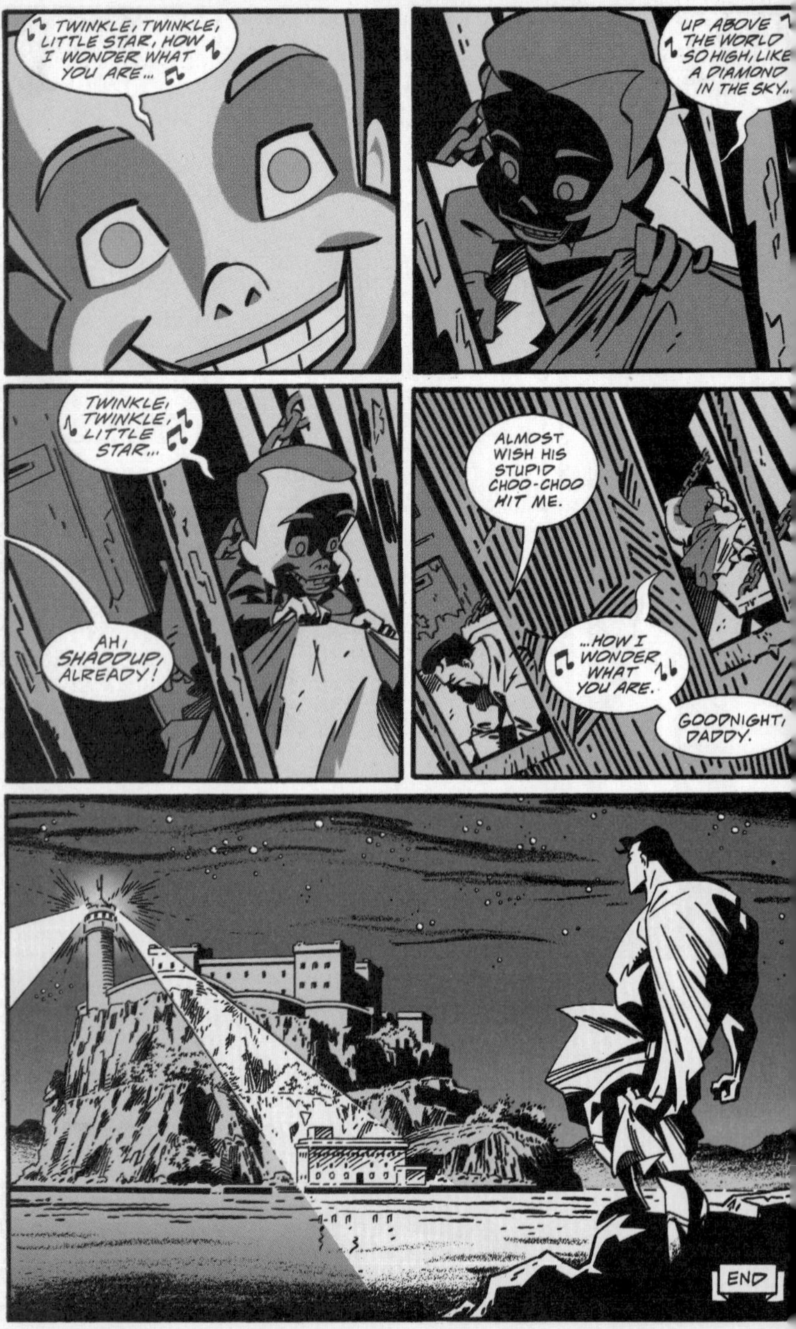
TWINKLE, TWINKLE, LITTLE STAR, HOW I WONDER WHAT YOU ARE...
UP ABOVE THE WORLD SO HIGH, LIKE A DIAMOND IN THE SKY...
TWINKLE, TWINKLE, LITTLE STAR...
AH, SHADDUP, ALREADY!
ALMOST WISH HIS STUPID CHOO-CHOO HIT ME.
...HOW I WONDER WHAT YOU ARE.
GOODNIGHT, DADDY.
END

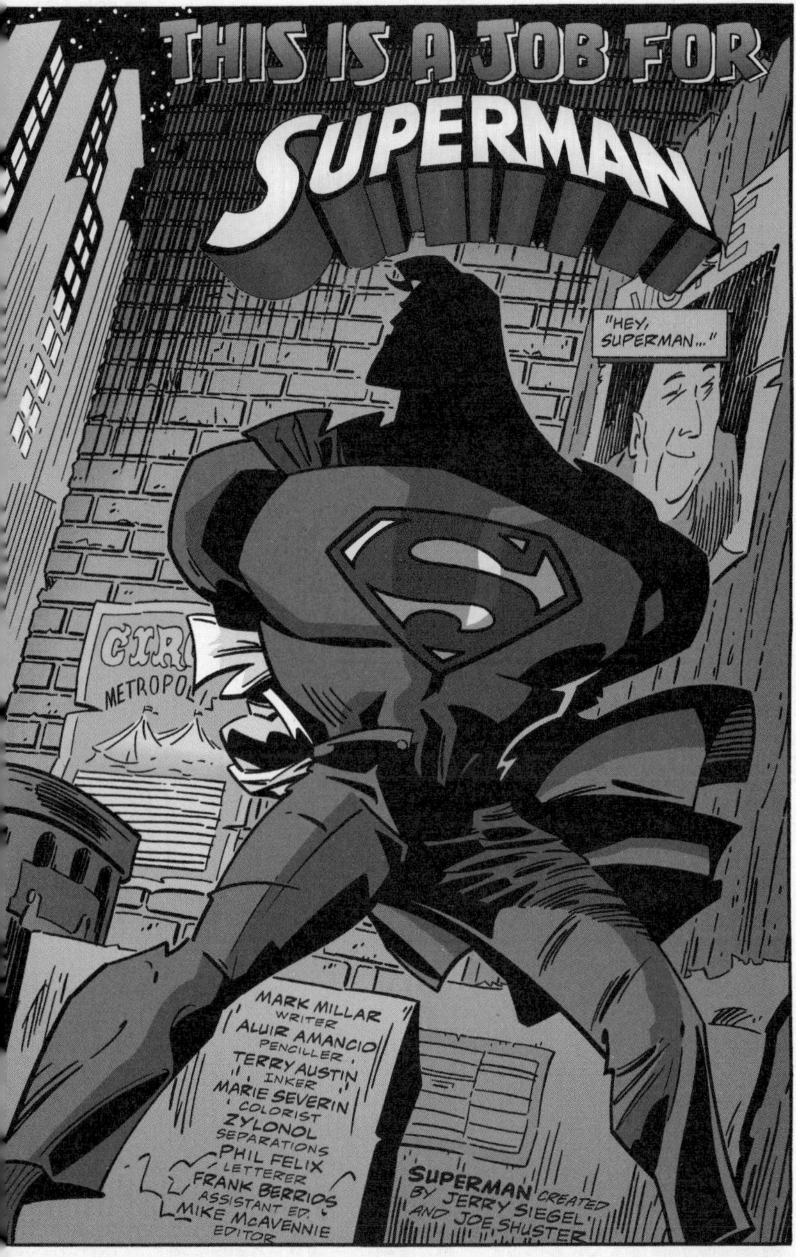
THIS IS A JOB FOR
SUPERMAN
"HEY, SUPERMAN..."
CIR
METROPOL
MARK MILLAR WRITER
ALUIR AMANCIO PENCILLER
TERRY AUSTIN INKER
MARIE SEVERIN COLORIST
ZYLONOL SEPARATIONS
PHIL FELIX LETTERER
FRANK BERRIOS ASSISTANT ED.
MIKE McAVENNIE EDITOR
SUPERMAN CREATED BY JERRY SIEGEL AND JOE SHUSTER

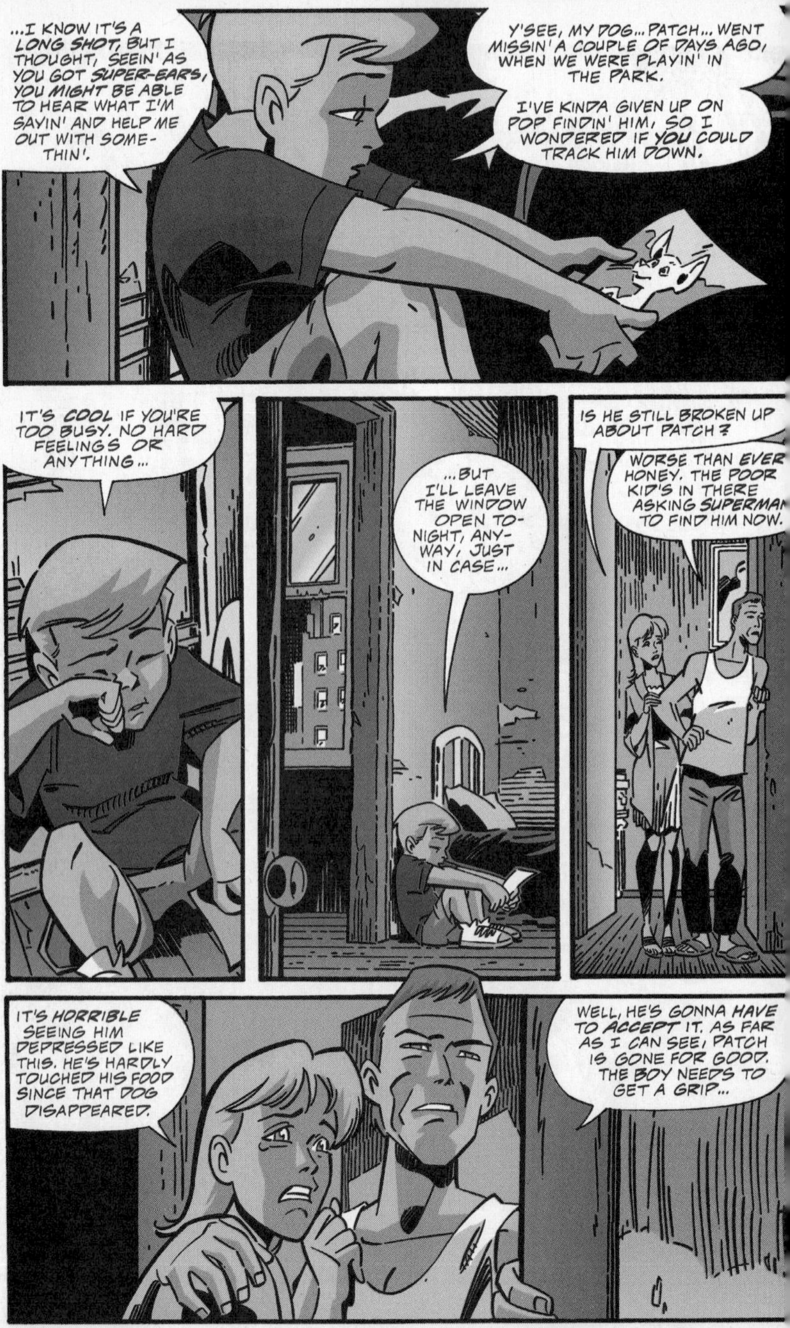

...I KNOW IT'S A LONG SHOT, BUT I THOUGHT, SEEIN' AS YOU GOT SUPER-EARS, YOU MIGHT BE ABLE TO HEAR WHAT I'M SAYIN' AND HELP ME OUT WITH SOME-THIN'.
Y'SEE, MY DOG... PATCH... WENT MISSIN' A COUPLE OF DAYS AGO, WHEN WE WERE PLAYIN' IN THE PARK.
I'VE KINDA GIVEN UP ON POP FINDIN' HIM, SO I WONDERED IF YOU COULD TRACK HIM DOWN.
IT'S COOL IF YOU'RE TOO BUSY. NO HARD FEELINGS OR ANYTHING...
...BUT I'LL LEAVE THE WINDOW OPEN TO-NIGHT, ANY-WAY, JUST IN CASE...
IS HE STILL BROKEN UP ABOUT PATCH?
WORSE THAN EVER HONEY. THE POOR KID'S IN THERE ASKING SUPERMAN TO FIND HIM NOW.
IT'S HORRIBLE SEEING HIM DEPRESSED LIKE THIS. HE'S HARDLY TOUCHED HIS FOOD SINCE THAT DOG DISAPPEARED.
WELL, HE'S GONNA HAVE TO ACCEPT IT. AS FAR AS I CAN SEE, PATCH IS GONE FOR GOOD. THE BOY NEEDS TO GET A GRIP...

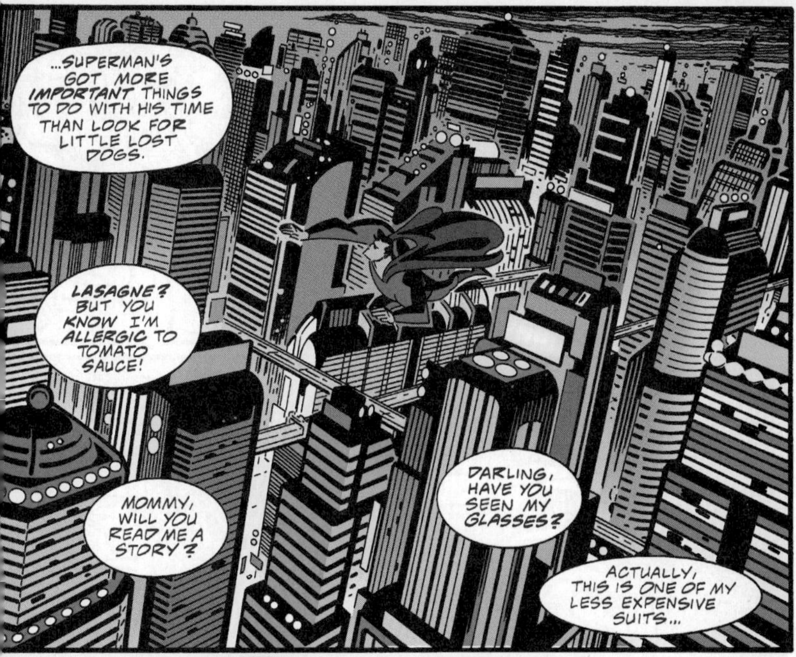
...SUPERMAN'S GOT MORE IMPORTANT THINGS TO DO WITH HIS TIME THAN LOOK FOR LITTLE LOST DOGS.
LASAGNE? BUT YOU KNOW I'M ALLERGIC TO TOMATO SAUCE!
MOMMY, WILL YOU READ ME A STORY?
DARLING, HAVE YOU SEEN MY GLASSES?
ACTUALLY, THIS IS ONE OF MY LESS EXPENSIVE SUITS...

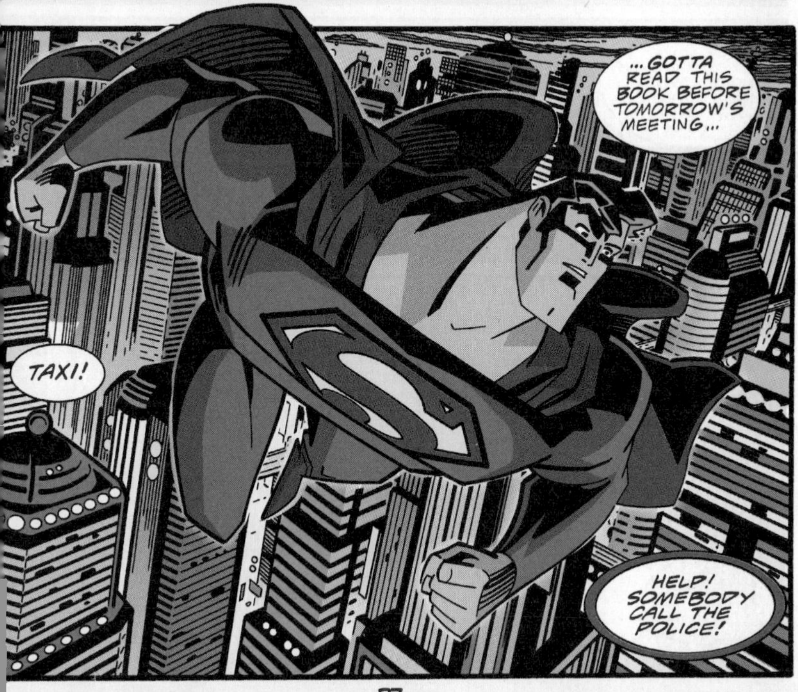
...GOTTA READ THIS BOOK BEFORE TOMORROW'S MEETING...
TAXI!
HELP! SOMEBODY CALL THE POLICE!

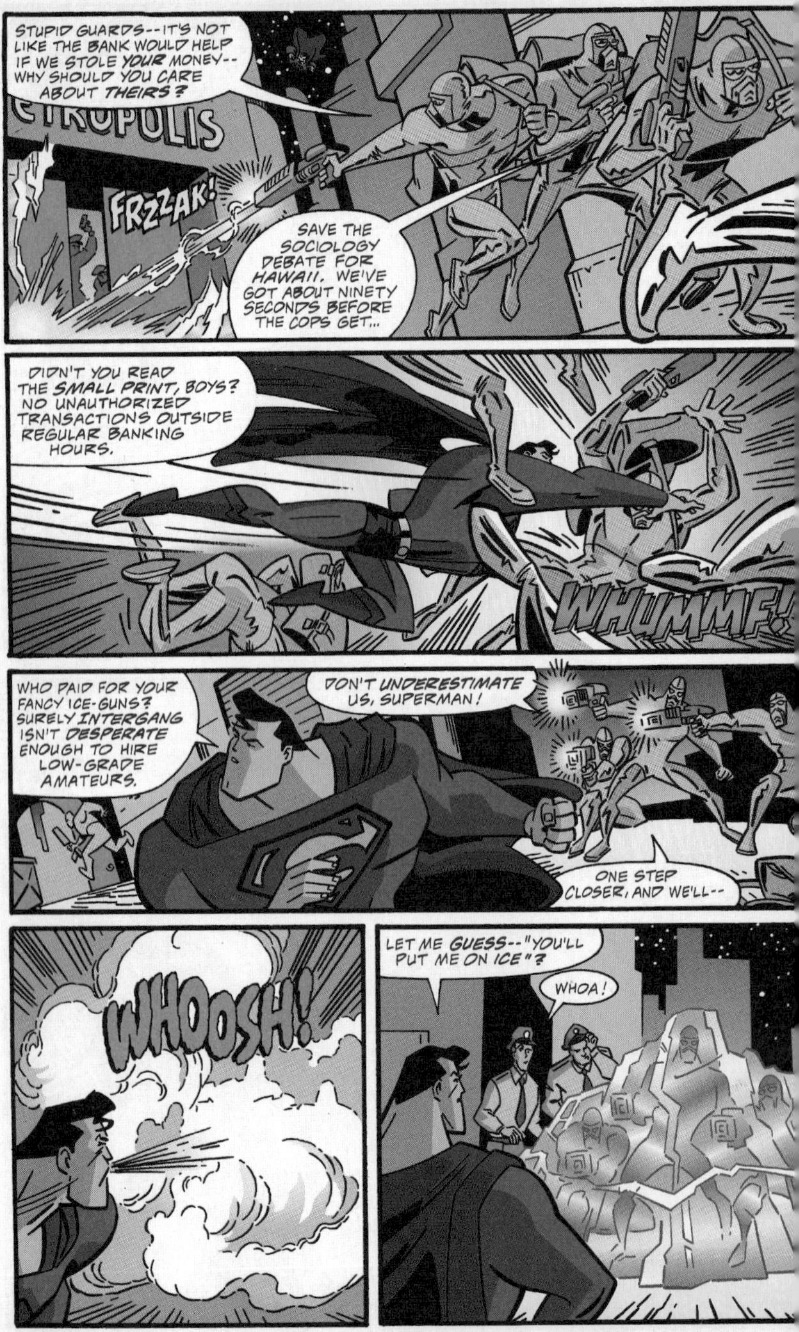
STUPID GUARDS--IT'S NOT LIKE THE BANK WOULD HELP IF WE STOLE YOUR MONEY--WHY SHOULD YOU CARE ABOUT THEIRS?
FRZZAK!
SAVE THE SOCIOLOGY DEBATE FOR HAWAII. WE'VE GOT ABOUT NINETY SECONDS BEFORE THE COPS GET...
DIDN'T YOU READ THE SMALL PRINT, BOYS? NO UNAUTHORIZED TRANSACTIONS OUTSIDE REGULAR BANKING HOURS.
WHUMMF!
WHO PAID FOR YOUR FANCY ICE-GUNS? SURELY INTERGANG ISN'T DESPERATE ENOUGH TO HIRE LOW-GRADE AMATEURS.
DON'T UNDERESTIMATE US, SUPERMAN!
ONE STEP CLOSER, AND WE'LL--
WHOOSH!
LET ME GUESS--"YOU'LL PUT ME ON ICE"?
WHOA!

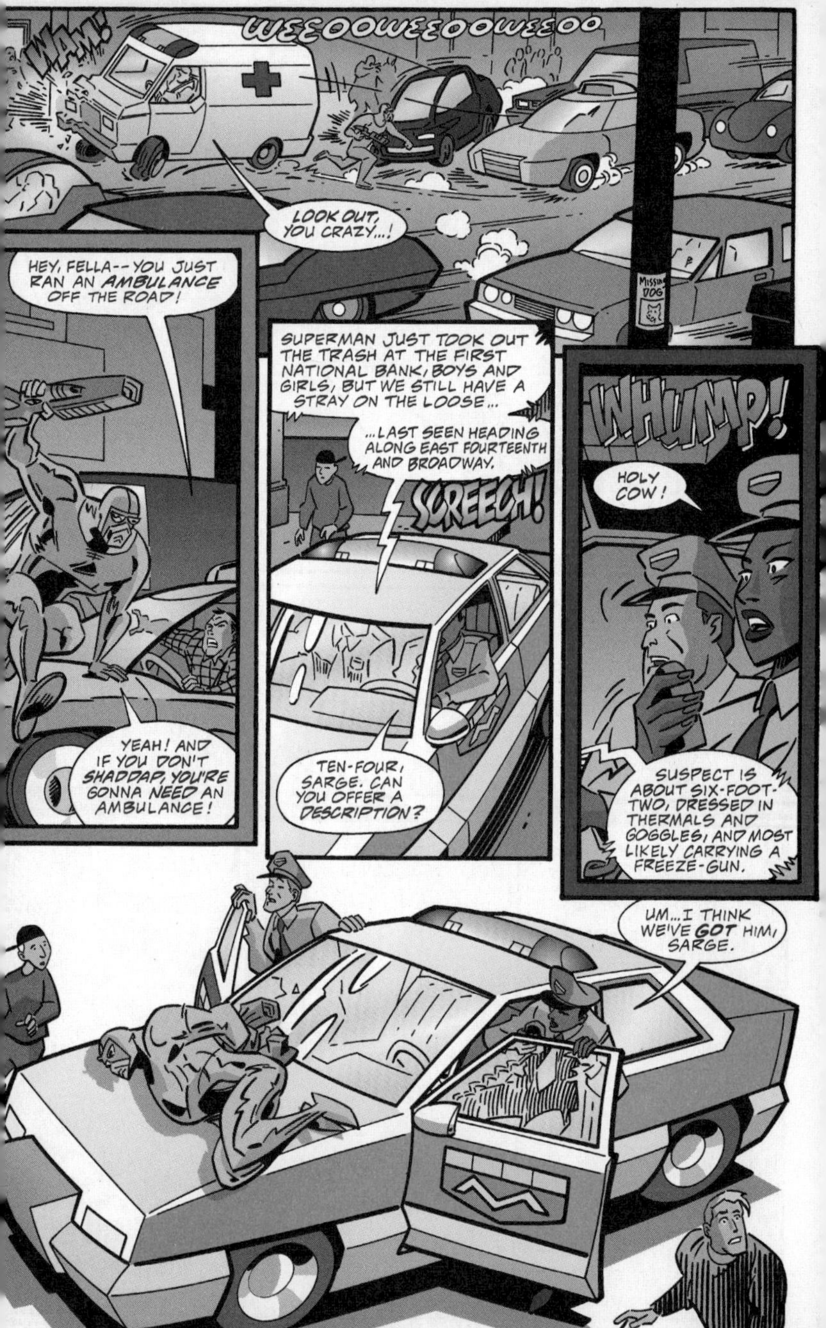
WAM!
WEEOOWEEOOWEEOO
LOOK OUT, YOU CRAZY...!
HEY, FELLA-- YOU JUST RAN AN AMBULANCE OFF THE ROAD!
YEAH! AND IF YOU DON'T SHADDAP, YOU'RE GONNA NEED AN AMBULANCE!
MISSING DOG
SUPERMAN JUST TOOK OUT THE TRASH AT THE FIRST NATIONAL BANK, BOYS AND GIRLS, BUT WE STILL HAVE A STRAY ON THE LOOSE...
...LAST SEEN HEADING ALONG EAST FOURTEENTH AND BROADWAY.
SCREECH!
TEN-FOUR, SARGE. CAN YOU OFFER A DESCRIPTION?
WHUMP!
HOLY COW!
SUSPECT IS ABOUT SIX-FOOT-TWO, DRESSED IN THERMALS AND GOGGLES, AND MOST LIKELY CARRYING A FREEZE-GUN.
UM...I THINK WE'VE GOT HIM, SARGE.

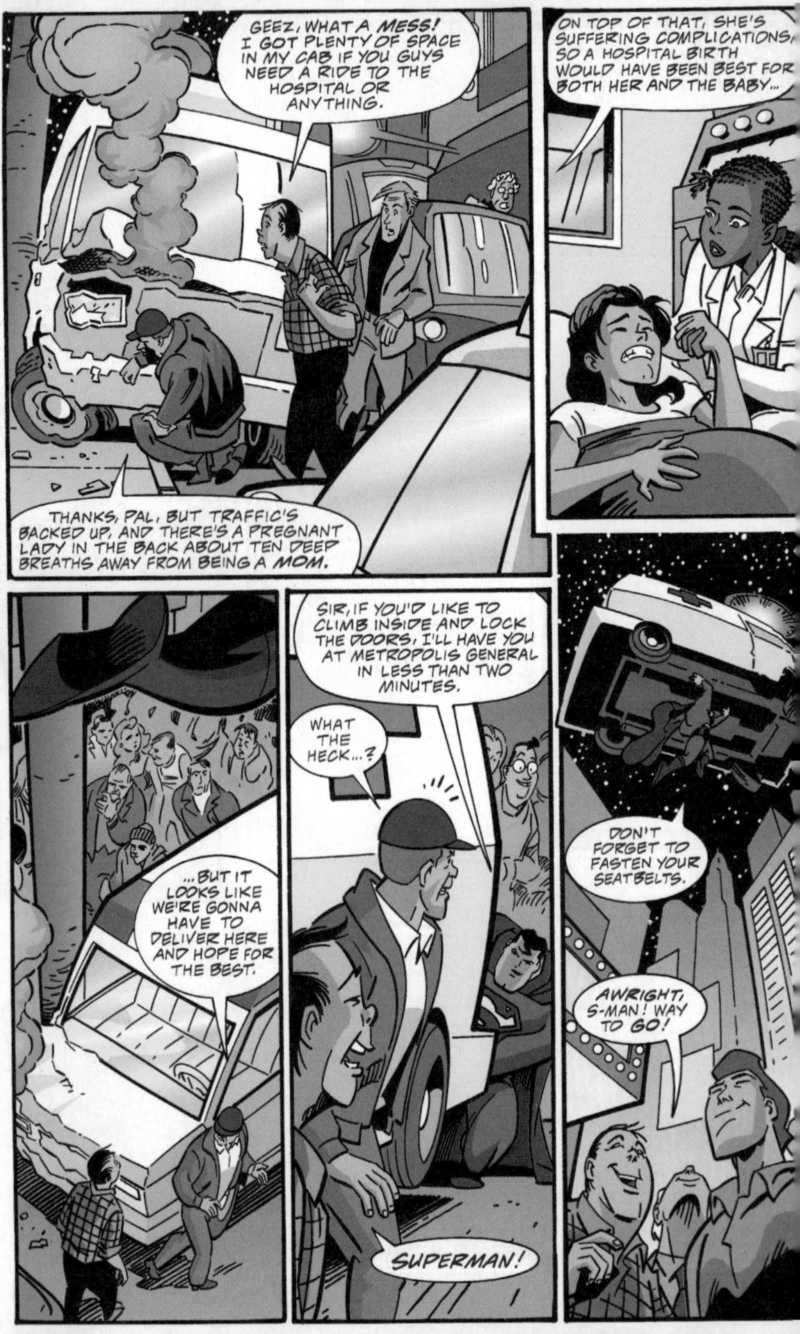
GEEZ, WHAT A MESS! I GOT PLENTY OF SPACE IN MY CAB IF YOU GUYS NEED A RIDE TO THE HOSPITAL OR ANYTHING.
THANKS, PAL, BUT TRAFFIC'S BACKED UP, AND THERE'S A PREGNANT LADY IN THE BACK ABOUT TEN DEEP BREATHS AWAY FROM BEING A MOM.
ON TOP OF THAT, SHE'S SUFFERING COMPLICATIONS, SO A HOSPITAL BIRTH WOULD HAVE BEEN BEST FOR BOTH HER AND THE BABY...
...BUT IT LOOKS LIKE WE'RE GONNA HAVE TO DELIVER HERE AND HOPE FOR THE BEST.
SIR, IF YOU'D LIKE TO CLIMB INSIDE AND LOCK THE DOORS, I'LL HAVE YOU AT METROPOLIS GENERAL IN LESS THAN TWO MINUTES.
WHAT THE HECK...?
SUPERMAN!
DON'T FORGET TO FASTEN YOUR SEATBELTS.
AWRIGHT, S-MAN! WAY TO GO!

I COULD DROP YOU AT THE FRONT DOOR OR THE HELI-PAD, SIR...

HECK, WE'LL PROBABLY NEVER DO THIS AGAIN, SO LET'S SHOOT FOR THE HELI-PAD, SUPERMAN. I'LL RADIO AHEAD AND MAKE SURE THEY'RE READY FOR US.

DOCTOR, YOU'RE NOT GOING TO BELIEVE WHO JUST TOUCHED DOWN ON OUR ROOF!

WHAT... SUPERMAN'S HERE? ARE YOU SERIOUS?

"TAKE A LOOK AND SEE FOR YOURSELF."

IS... IS MY BABY OKAY?

YOUR BABY IS DOING GREAT, MA'AM... AND, IF YOU DON'T MIND MY SAYING SO, THE LITTLE TYKE LOOKS JUST LIKE YOU.

SUPERMAN!

CAN I HELP YOU, DOCTOR?

I CERTAINLY HOPE SO. MY TEAM AND I HAVE BEEN WAITING DOWNSTAIRS TO PERFORM A TRANSPLANT OPERATION...

...BUT THE DONOR HEART WE WERE EXPECTING HAS BEEN DELAYED AT CHICAGO AIRPORT FOR ALMOST SIX HOURS.

THE TRANSPLANT WON'T WORK IF YOU WAIT MUCH LONGER, SIR. DOESN'T AIR-TRAFFIC CONTROL APPRECIATE THE URGENCY?

THEY'RE NOT RESPONSIBLE FOR THE HOLDUP, MY FRIEND. FLIGHT 401 FROM CHICAGO HAS BEEN HIJACKED BY POLITICAL EXTREMISTS...

31

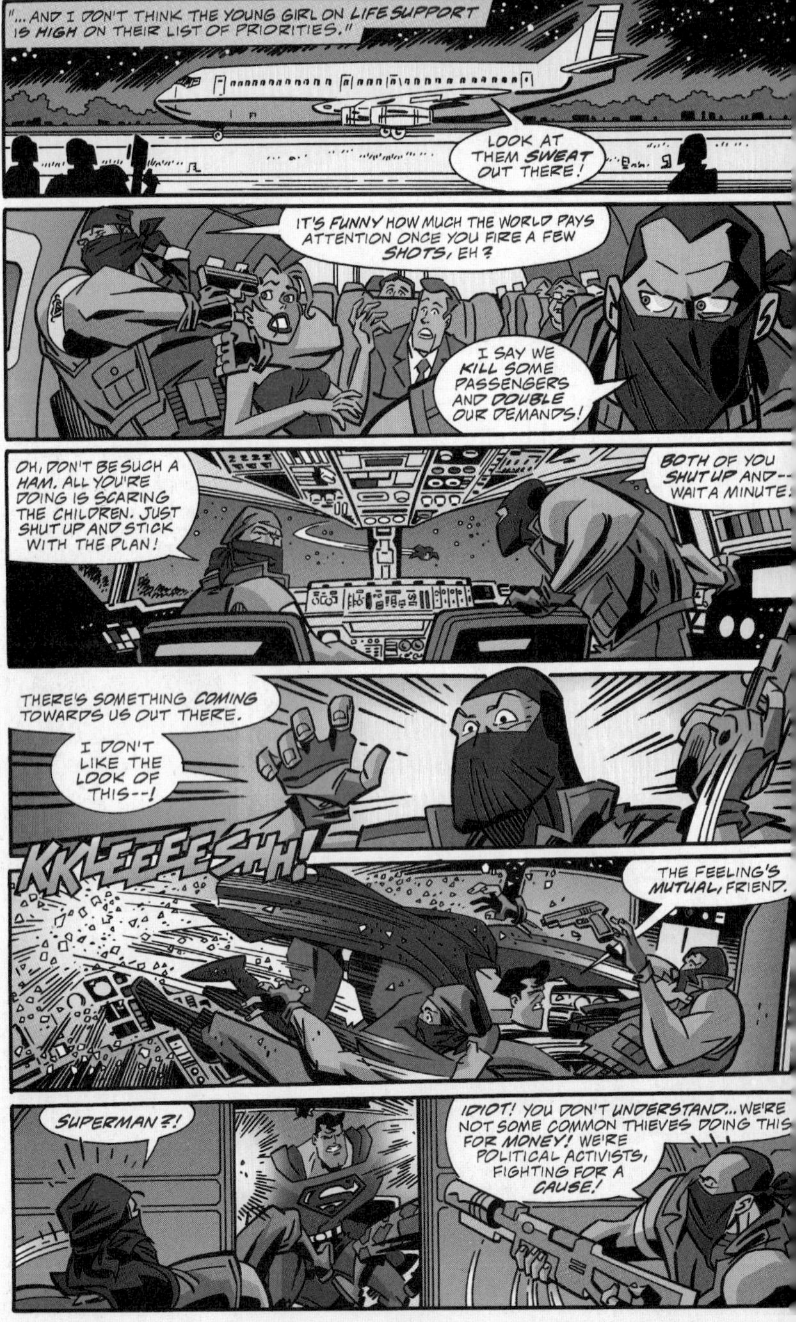
"...AND I DON'T THINK THE YOUNG GIRL ON LIFE SUPPORT IS HIGH ON THEIR LIST OF PRIORITIES."
LOOK AT THEM SWEAT OUT THERE!
IT'S FUNNY HOW MUCH THE WORLD PAYS ATTENTION ONCE YOU FIRE A FEW SHOTS, EH?
I SAY WE KILL SOME PASSENGERS AND DOUBLE OUR DEMANDS!
OH, DON'T BE SUCH A HAM. ALL YOU'RE DOING IS SCARING THE CHILDREN. JUST SHUT UP AND STICK WITH THE PLAN!
BOTH OF YOU SHUT UP AND-- WAIT A MINUTE!
THERE'S SOMETHING COMING TOWARDS US OUT THERE.
I DON'T LIKE THE LOOK OF THIS--!
KKLEEEESHH!
THE FEELING'S MUTUAL, FRIEND.
SUPERMAN?!
IDIOT! YOU DON'T UNDERSTAND... WE'RE NOT SOME COMMON THIEVES DOING THIS FOR MONEY! WE'RE POLITICAL ACTIVISTS, FIGHTING FOR A CAUSE!

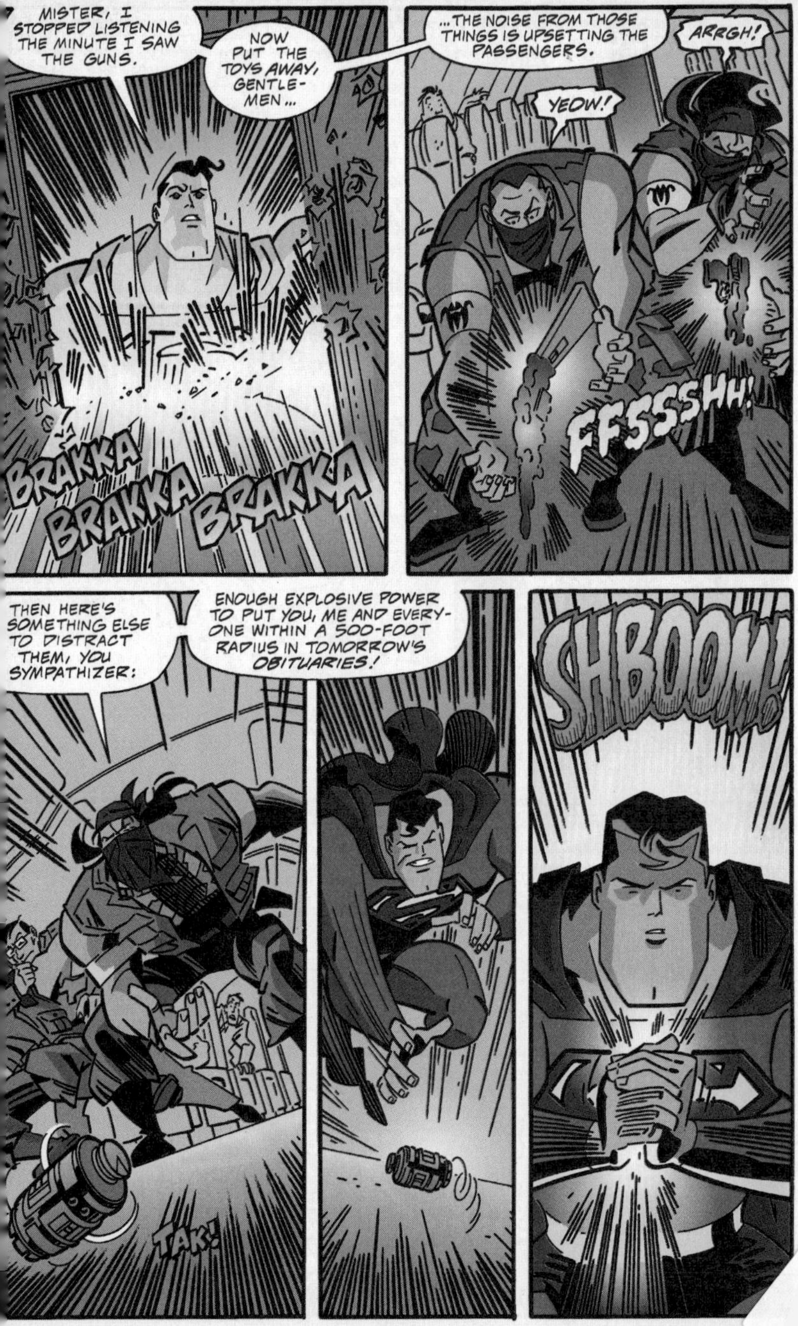
MISTER, I STOPPED LISTENING THE MINUTE I SAW THE GUNS.
NOW PUT THE TOYS AWAY, GENTLE-MEN...
BRAKKA BRAKKA BRAKKA
...THE NOISE FROM THOSE THINGS IS UPSETTING THE PASSENGERS.
ARRGH!
YEOW!
FFSSSHH!
THEN HERE'S SOMETHING ELSE TO DISTRACT THEM, YOU SYMPATHIZER:
ENOUGH EXPLOSIVE POWER TO PUT YOU, ME AND EVERY-ONE WITHIN A 500-FOOT RADIUS IN TOMORROW'S OBITUARIES!
TAK!
SHBOOM!

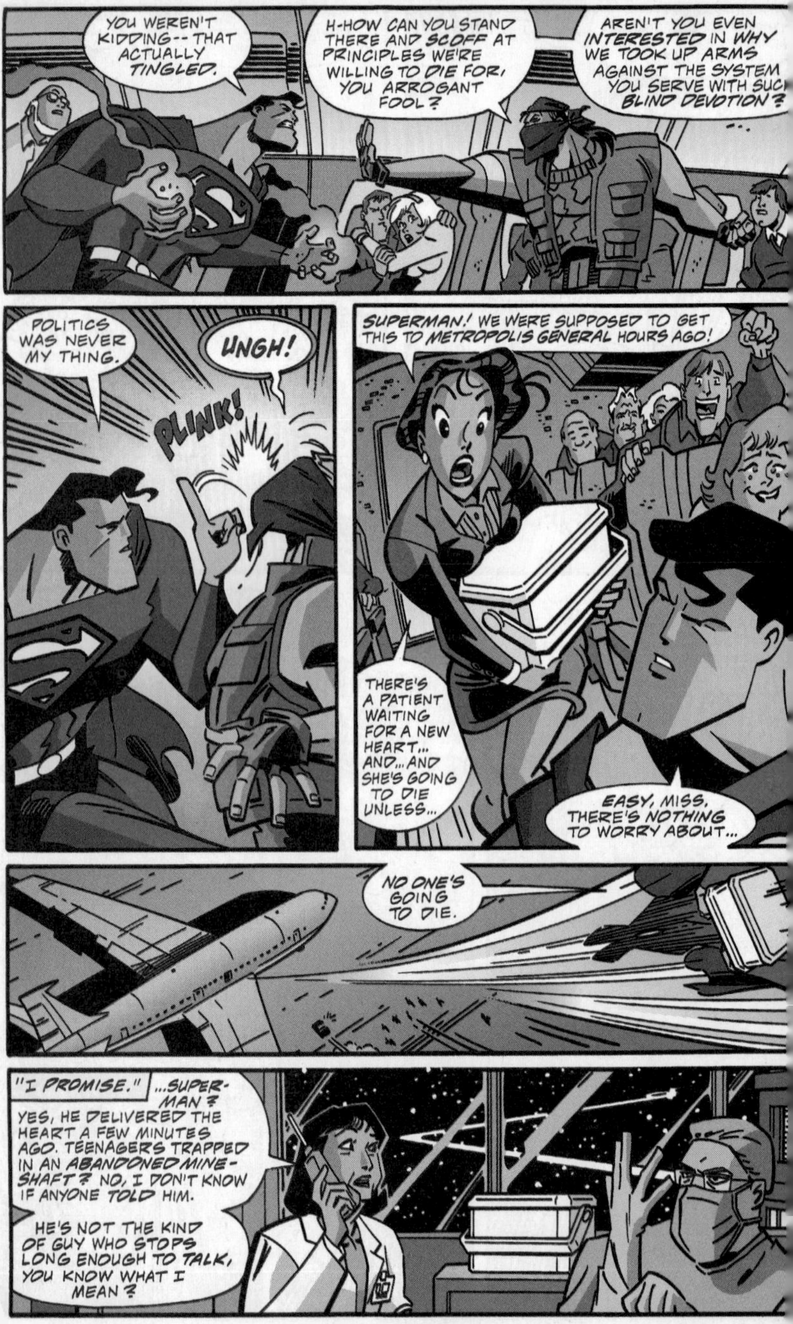

YOU WEREN'T KIDDING-- THAT ACTUALLY TINGLED.
H-HOW CAN YOU STAND THERE AND SCOFF AT PRINCIPLES WE'RE WILLING TO DIE FOR, YOU ARROGANT FOOL?
AREN'T YOU EVEN INTERESTED IN WHY WE TOOK UP ARMS AGAINST THE SYSTEM YOU SERVE WITH SUCH BLIND DEVOTION?
POLITICS WAS NEVER MY THING.
UNGH!
PLINK!
SUPERMAN! WE WERE SUPPOSED TO GET THIS TO METROPOLIS GENERAL HOURS AGO!
THERE'S A PATIENT WAITING FOR A NEW HEART... AND... AND SHE'S GOING TO DIE UNLESS...
EASY, MISS. THERE'S NOTHING TO WORRY ABOUT...
NO ONE'S GOING TO DIE.
"I PROMISE."
...SUPERMAN? YES, HE DELIVERED THE HEART A FEW MINUTES AGO. TEENAGERS TRAPPED IN AN ABANDONED MINE-SHAFT? NO, I DON'T KNOW IF ANYONE TOLD HIM.
HE'S NOT THE KIND OF GUY WHO STOPS LONG ENOUGH TO TALK, YOU KNOW WHAT I MEAN?

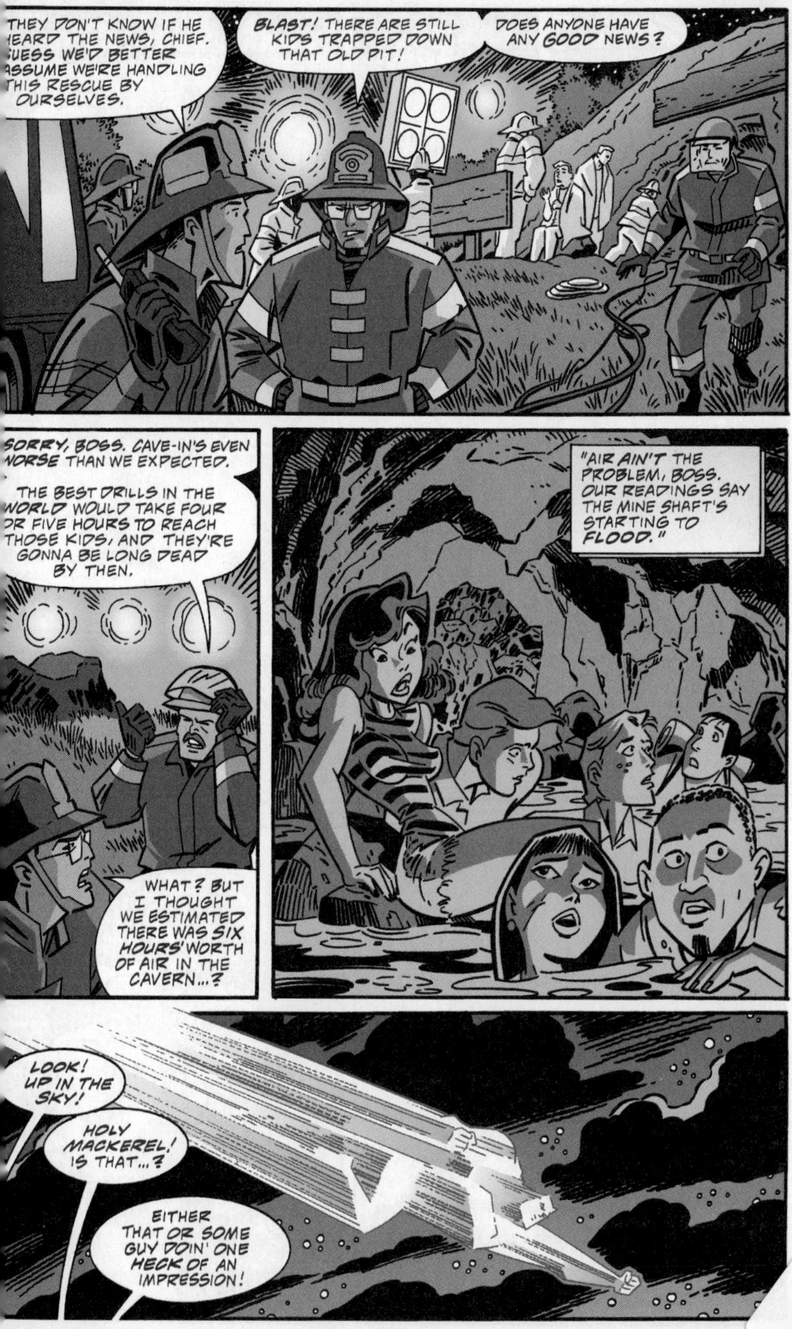
THEY DON'T KNOW IF HE HEARD THE NEWS, CHIEF. GUESS WE'D BETTER ASSUME WE'RE HANDLING THIS RESCUE BY OURSELVES.
BLAST! THERE ARE STILL KIDS TRAPPED DOWN THAT OLD PIT!
DOES ANYONE HAVE ANY GOOD NEWS?
SORRY, BOSS. CAVE-IN'S EVEN WORSE THAN WE EXPECTED.
THE BEST DRILLS IN THE WORLD WOULD TAKE FOUR OR FIVE HOURS TO REACH THOSE KIDS, AND THEY'RE GONNA BE LONG DEAD BY THEN.
WHAT? BUT I THOUGHT WE ESTIMATED THERE WAS SIX HOURS' WORTH OF AIR IN THE CAVERN...?
"AIR AIN'T THE PROBLEM, BOSS. OUR READINGS SAY THE MINE SHAFT'S STARTING TO FLOOD."
LOOK! UP IN THE SKY!
HOLY MACKEREL! IS THAT...?
EITHER THAT OR SOME GUY DOIN' ONE HECK OF AN IMPRESSION!

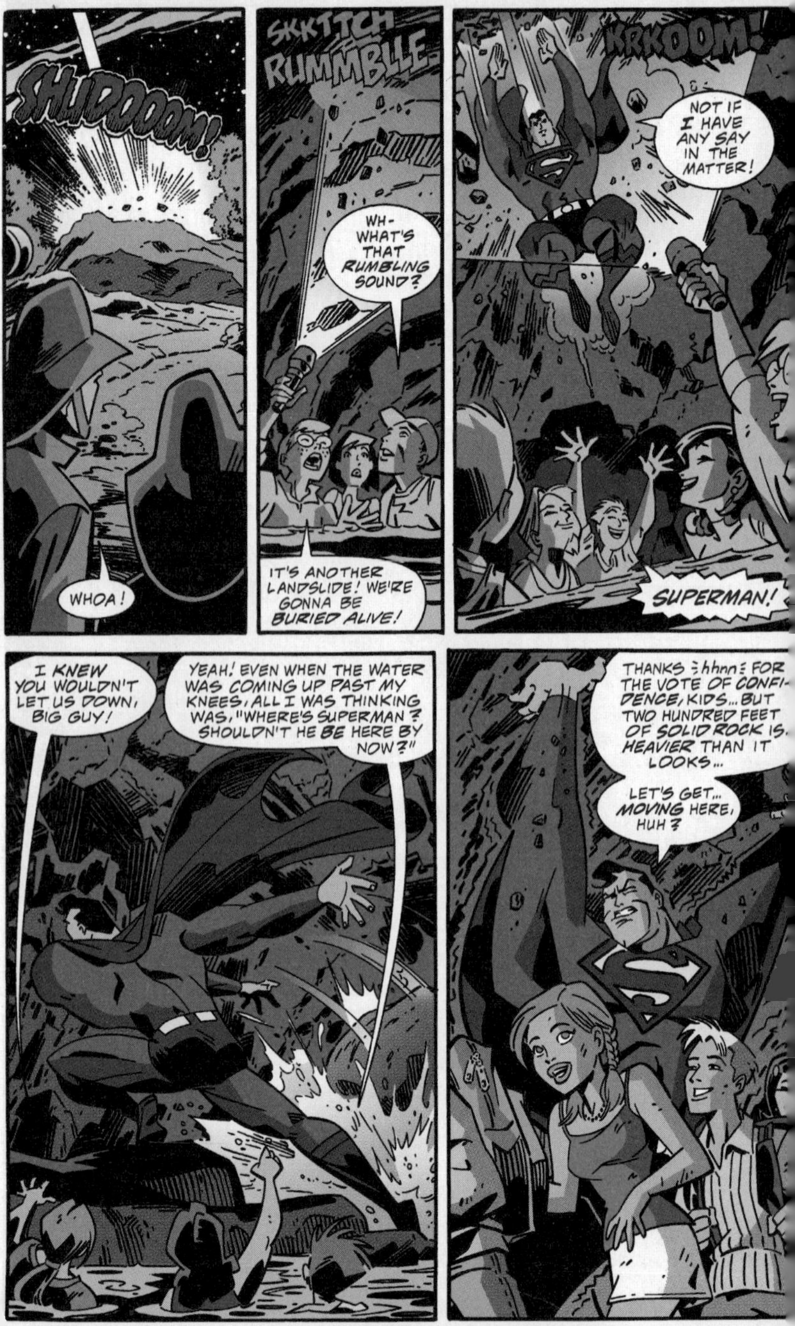
SHUDOOOM!
WHOA!
SKKTTCH
RUMMBLLE
WH-WHAT'S THAT RUMBLING SOUND?
IT'S ANOTHER LANDSLIDE! WE'RE GONNA BE BURIED ALIVE!
KRKOOM!
NOT IF I HAVE ANY SAY IN THE MATTER!
SUPERMAN!
I KNEW YOU WOULDN'T LET US DOWN, BIG GUY!
YEAH! EVEN WHEN THE WATER WAS COMING UP PAST MY KNEES, ALL I WAS THINKING WAS, "WHERE'S SUPERMAN? SHOULDN'T HE BE HERE BY NOW?"
THANKS hhnn FOR THE VOTE OF CONFIDENCE, KIDS... BUT TWO HUNDRED FEET OF SOLID ROCK IS HEAVIER THAN IT LOOKS...
LET'S GET... MOVING HERE, HUH?

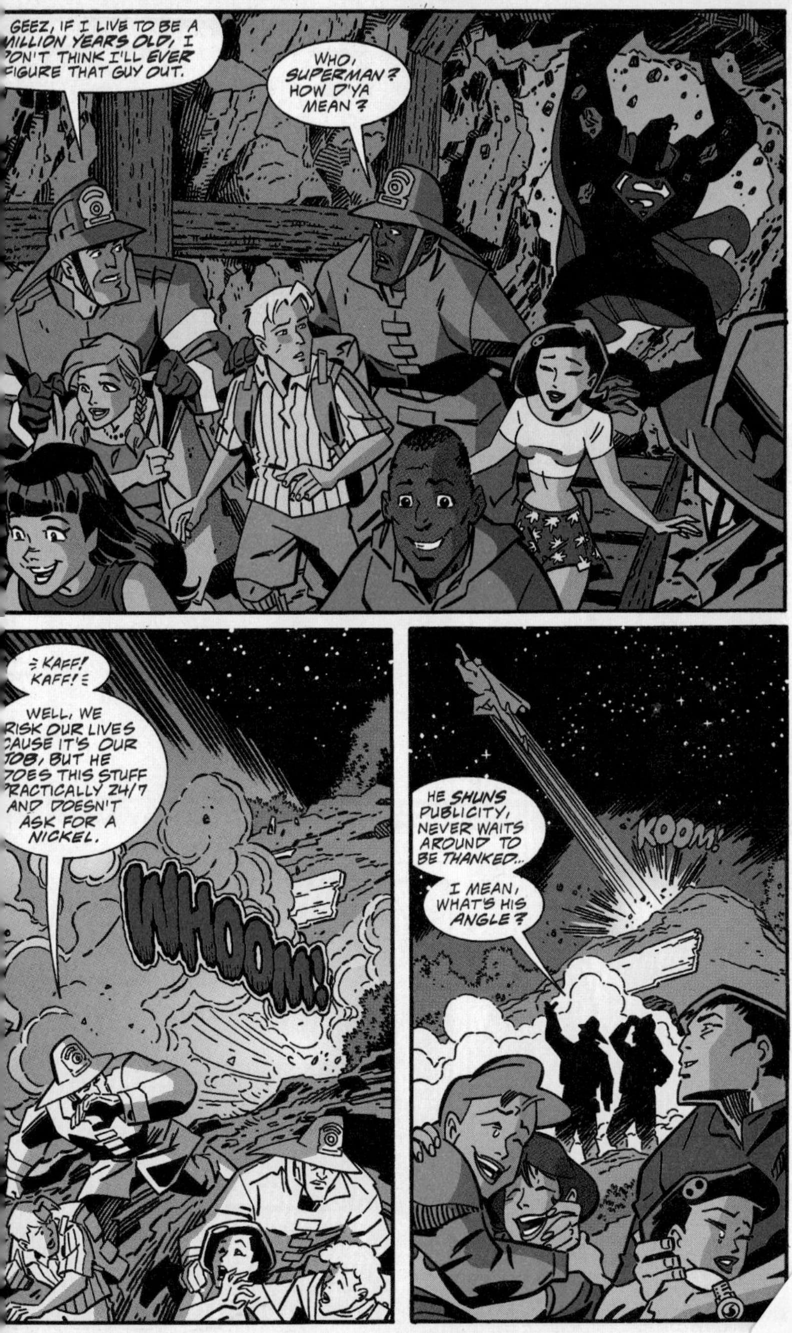
GEEZ, IF I LIVE TO BE A MILLION YEARS OLD, I DON'T THINK I'LL EVER FIGURE THAT GUY OUT.
WHO, SUPERMAN? HOW D'YA MEAN?
KAFF! KAFF!
WELL, WE RISK OUR LIVES CAUSE IT'S OUR JOB, BUT HE DOES THIS STUFF PRACTICALLY 24/7 AND DOESN'T ASK FOR A NICKEL.
WHOOM!
HE SHUNS PUBLICITY, NEVER WAITS AROUND TO BE THANKED...
I MEAN, WHAT'S HIS ANGLE?
KOOM!

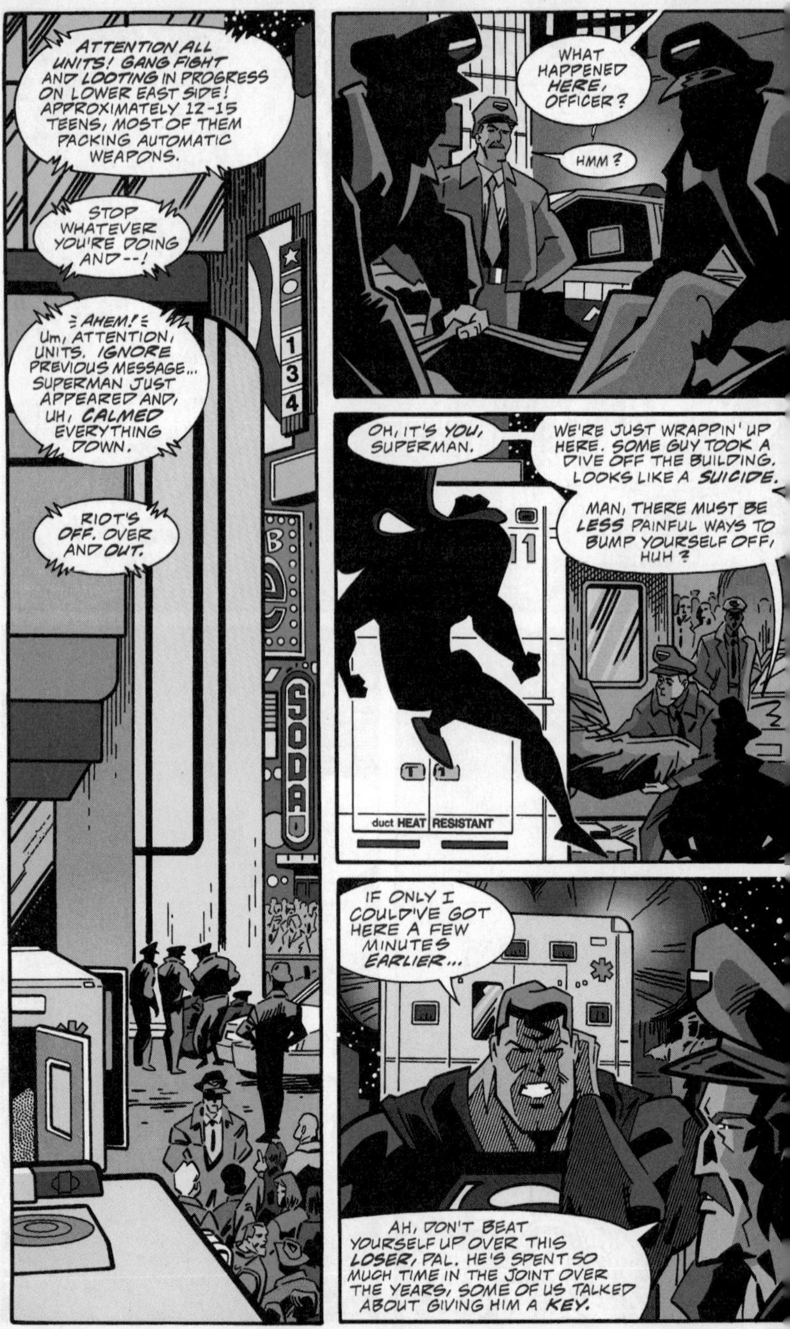
ATTENTION ALL UNITS! GANG FIGHT AND LOOTING IN PROGRESS ON LOWER EAST SIDE! APPROXIMATELY 12-15 TEENS, MOST OF THEM PACKING AUTOMATIC WEAPONS.
STOP WHATEVER YOU'RE DOING AND--!
AHEM! Um, ATTENTION, UNITS. IGNORE PREVIOUS MESSAGE... SUPERMAN JUST APPEARED AND, UH, CALMED EVERYTHING DOWN.
RIOT'S OFF. OVER AND OUT.
1
3
4
SODA
WHAT HAPPENED HERE, OFFICER?
HMM?
OH, IT'S YOU, SUPERMAN.
WE'RE JUST WRAPPIN' UP HERE. SOME GUY TOOK A DIVE OFF THE BUILDING. LOOKS LIKE A SUICIDE.
MAN, THERE MUST BE LESS PAINFUL WAYS TO BUMP YOURSELF OFF, HUH?
duct HEAT RESISTANT
IF ONLY I COULD'VE GOT HERE A FEW MINUTES EARLIER...
AH, DON'T BEAT YOURSELF UP OVER THIS LOSER, PAL. HE'S SPENT SO MUCH TIME IN THE JOINT OVER THE YEARS, SOME OF US TALKED ABOUT GIVING HIM A KEY.

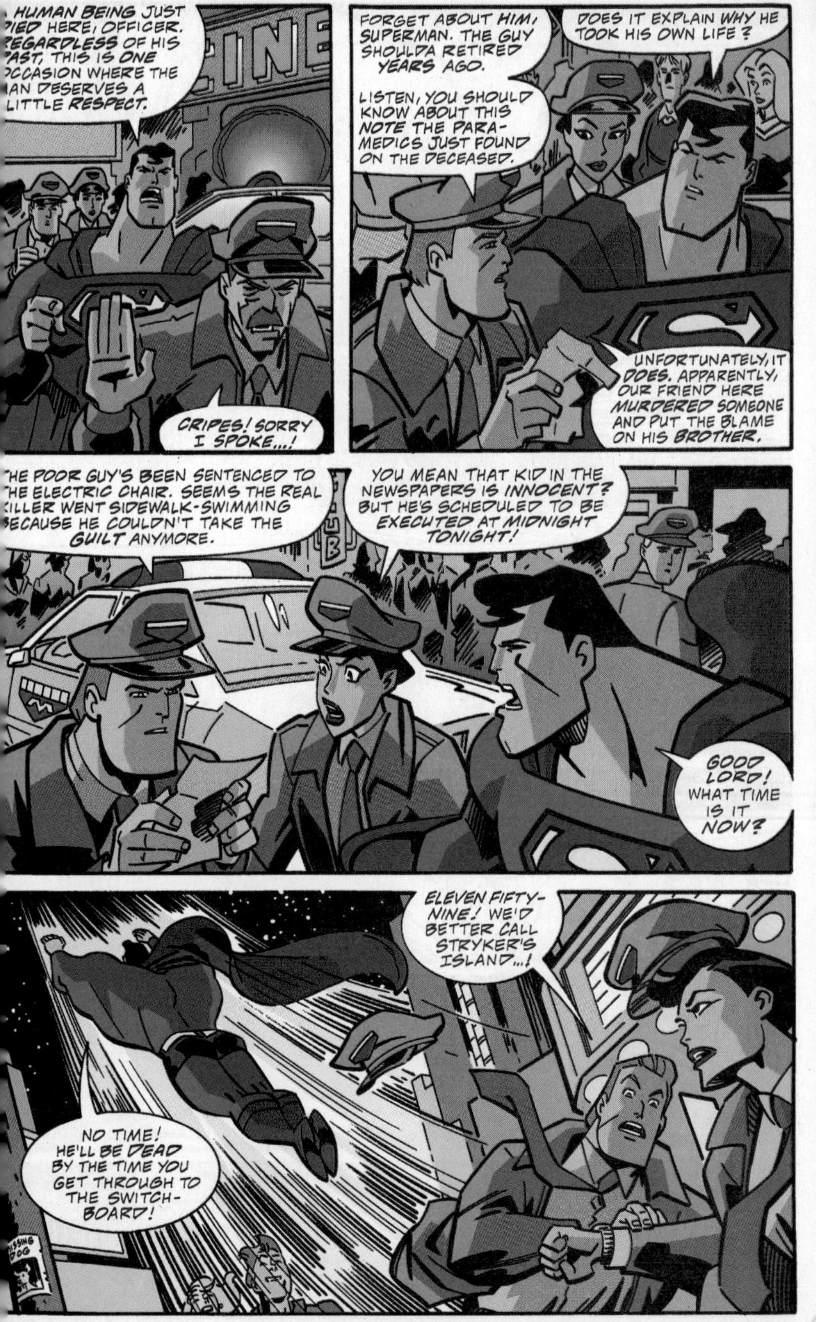
HUMAN BEING JUST DIED HERE, OFFICER. REGARDLESS OF HIS PAST, THIS IS ONE OCCASION WHERE THE MAN DESERVES A LITTLE RESPECT.
CRIPES! SORRY I SPOKE...!
FORGET ABOUT HIM, SUPERMAN. THE GUY SHOULDA RETIRED YEARS AGO.
LISTEN, YOU SHOULD KNOW ABOUT THIS NOTE THE PARAMEDICS JUST FOUND ON THE DECEASED.
DOES IT EXPLAIN WHY HE TOOK HIS OWN LIFE?
UNFORTUNATELY, IT DOES. APPARENTLY, OUR FRIEND HERE MURDERED SOMEONE AND PUT THE BLAME ON HIS BROTHER.
THE POOR GUY'S BEEN SENTENCED TO THE ELECTRIC CHAIR. SEEMS THE REAL KILLER WENT SIDEWALK-SWIMMING BECAUSE HE COULDN'T TAKE THE GUILT ANYMORE.
YOU MEAN THAT KID IN THE NEWSPAPERS IS INNOCENT? BUT HE'S SCHEDULED TO BE EXECUTED AT MIDNIGHT TONIGHT!
GOOD LORD! WHAT TIME IS IT NOW?
ELEVEN FIFTY-NINE! WE'D BETTER CALL STRYKER'S ISLAND...!
NO TIME! HE'LL BE DEAD BY THE TIME YOU GET THROUGH TO THE SWITCHBOARD!
MISSING DOG

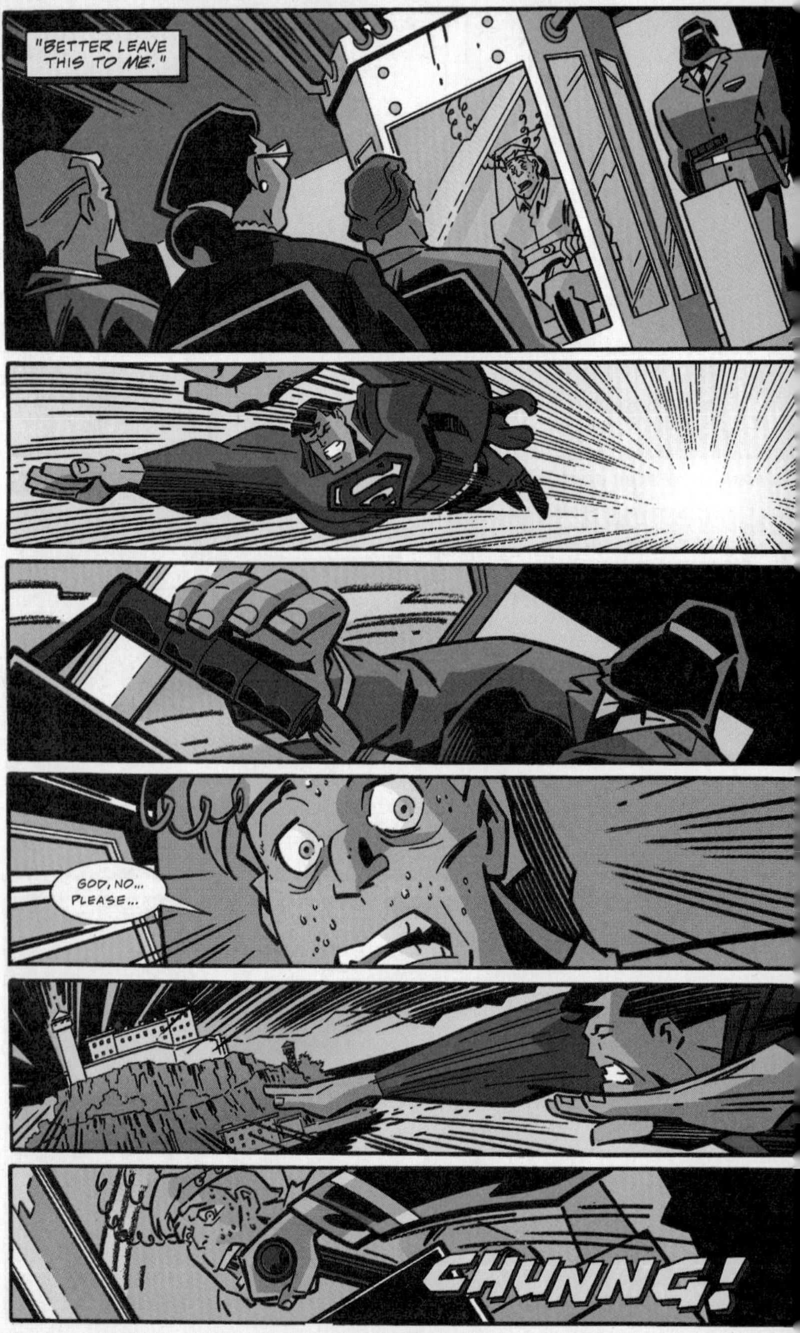
"BETTER LEAVE THIS TO ME."
GOD, NO... PLEASE...
CHUNNG!

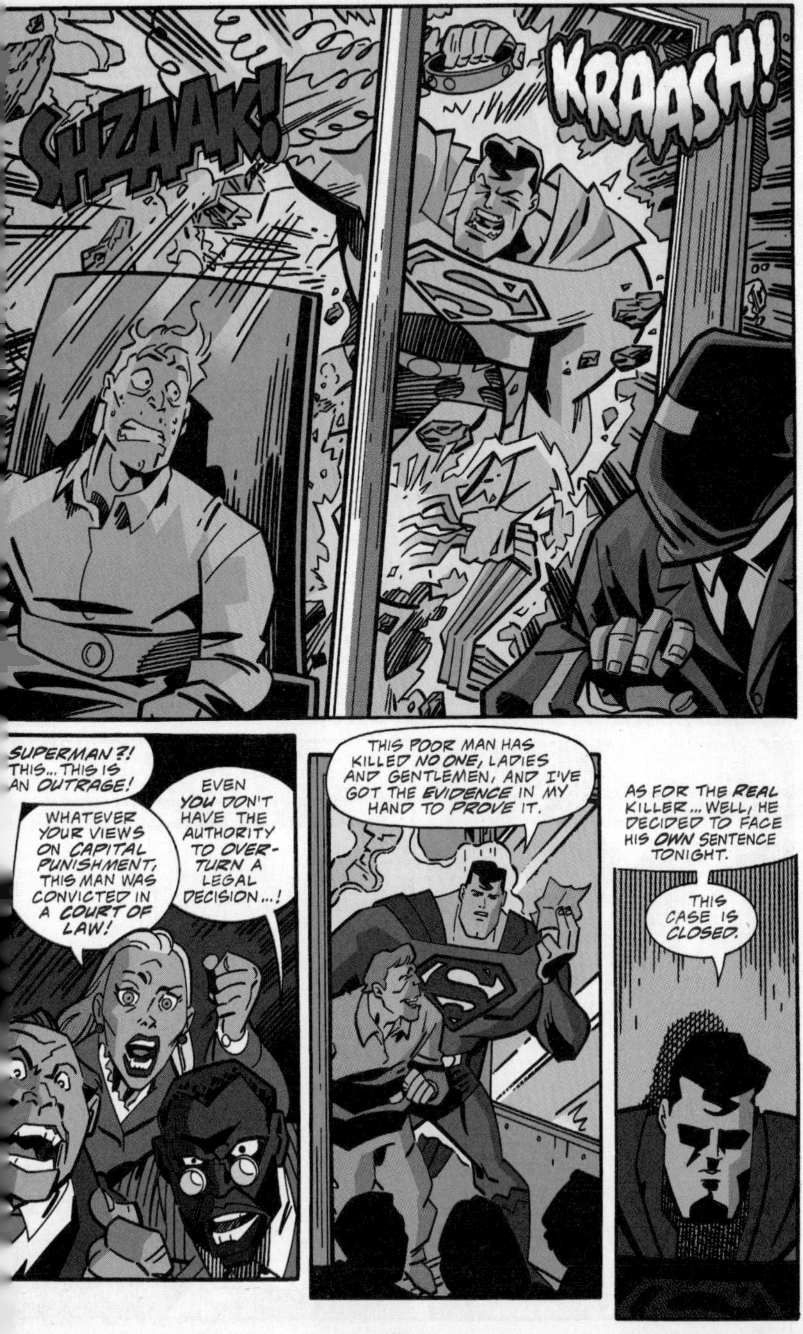
SHZAAK!
KRAASH!
SUPERMAN?! THIS... THIS IS AN OUTRAGE!
WHATEVER YOUR VIEWS ON CAPITAL PUNISHMENT, THIS MAN WAS CONVICTED IN A COURT OF LAW!
EVEN YOU DON'T HAVE THE AUTHORITY TO OVER-TURN A LEGAL DECISION...!
THIS POOR MAN HAS KILLED NO ONE, LADIES AND GENTLEMEN, AND I'VE GOT THE EVIDENCE IN MY HAND TO PROVE IT.
AS FOR THE REAL KILLER... WELL, HE DECIDED TO FACE HIS OWN SENTENCE TONIGHT.
THIS CASE IS CLOSED.

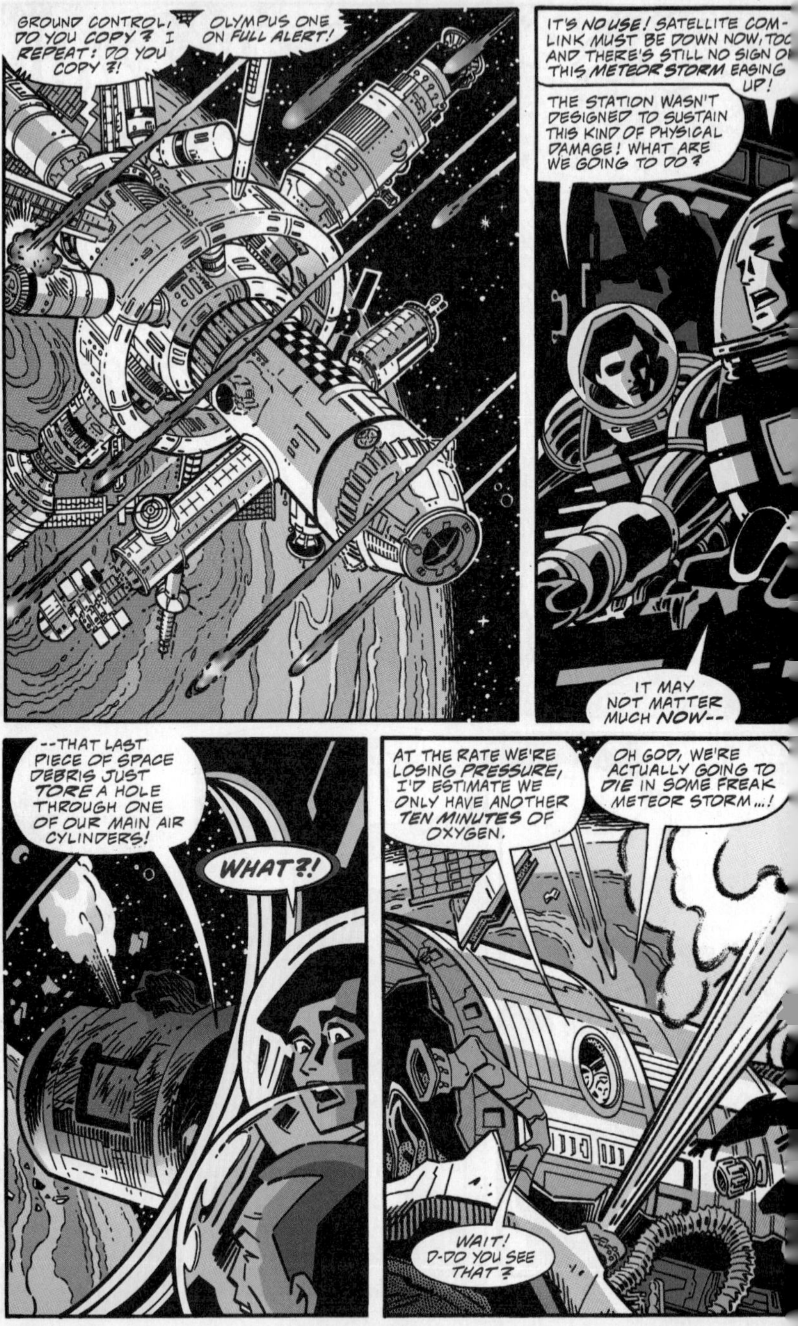
GROUND CONTROL, DO YOU COPY? I REPEAT: DO YOU COPY?!
OLYMPUS ONE ON FULL ALERT!
IT'S NO USE! SATELLITE COM-LINK MUST BE DOWN NOW, TOO AND THERE'S STILL NO SIGN OF THIS METEOR STORM EASING UP!
THE STATION WASN'T DESIGNED TO SUSTAIN THIS KIND OF PHYSICAL DAMAGE! WHAT ARE WE GOING TO DO?
IT MAY NOT MATTER MUCH NOW--
--THAT LAST PIECE OF SPACE DEBRIS JUST TORE A HOLE THROUGH ONE OF OUR MAIN AIR CYLINDERS!
WHAT?!
AT THE RATE WE'RE LOSING PRESSURE, I'D ESTIMATE WE ONLY HAVE ANOTHER TEN MINUTES OF OXYGEN.
OH GOD, WE'RE ACTUALLY GOING TO DIE IN SOME FREAK METEOR STORM...!
WAIT! D-DO YOU SEE THAT?

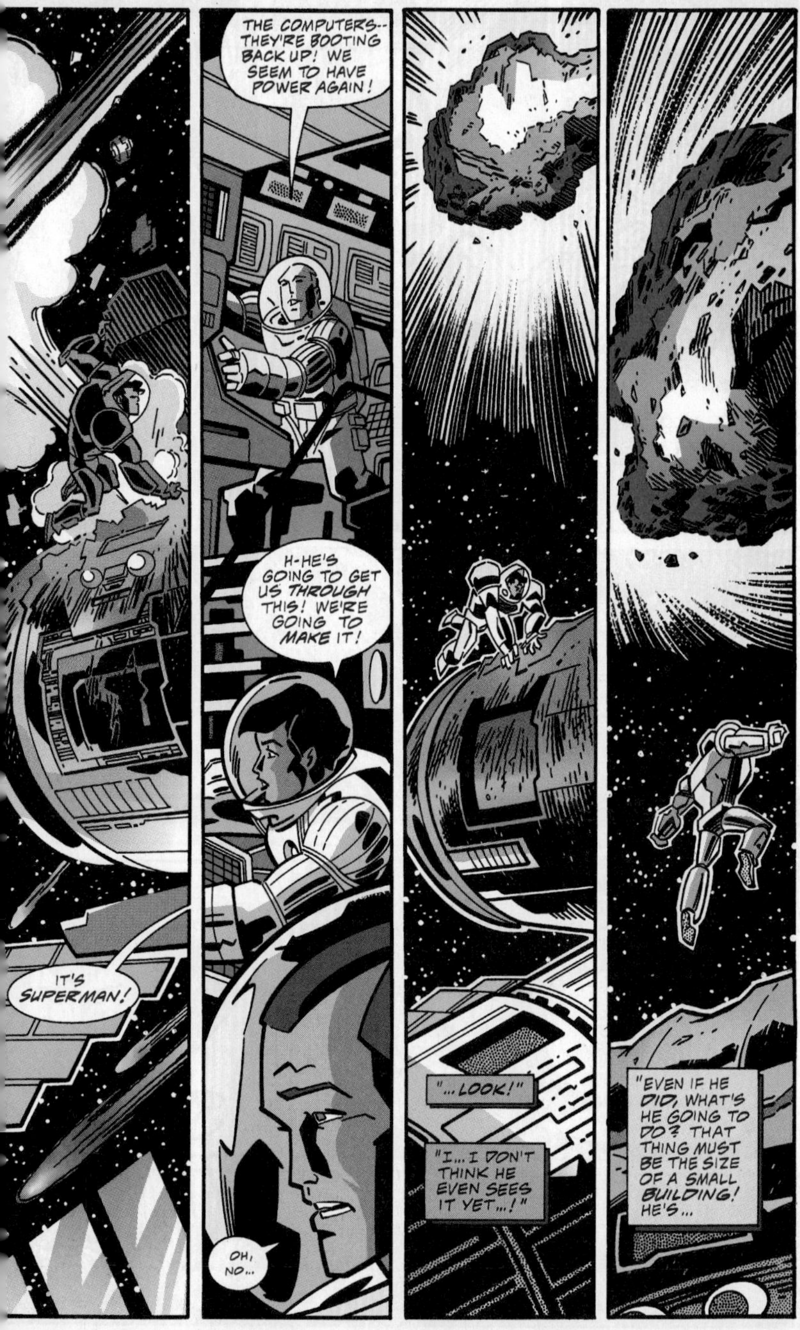
IT'S SUPERMAN!
THE COMPUTERS-- THEY'RE BOOTING BACK UP! WE SEEM TO HAVE POWER AGAIN!
H-HE'S GOING TO GET US THROUGH THIS! WE'RE GOING TO MAKE IT!
OH, NO...
"...LOOK!"
"I... I DON'T THINK HE EVEN SEES IT YET...!"
"EVEN IF HE DID, WHAT'S HE GOING TO DO? THAT THING MUST BE THE SIZE OF A SMALL BUILDING! HE'S...

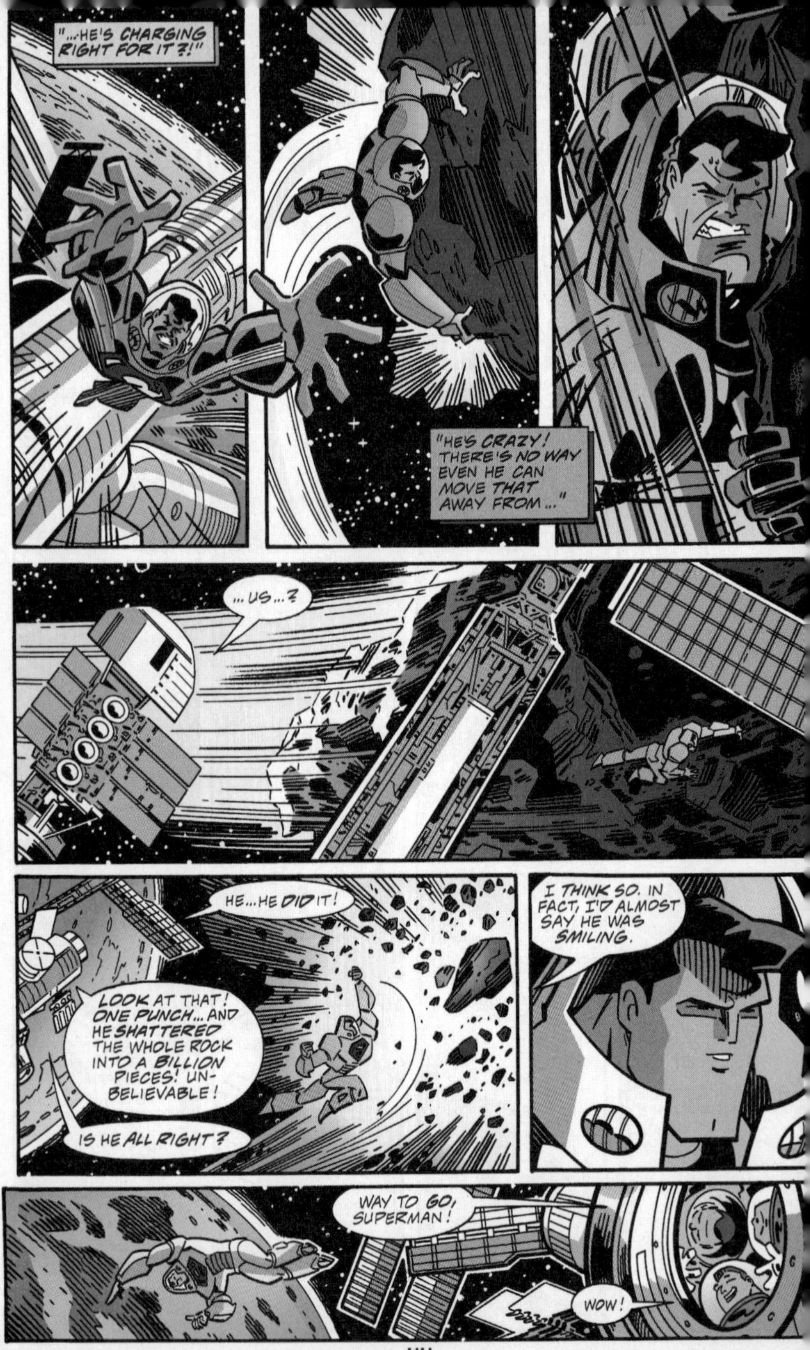

"...HE'S CHARGING RIGHT FOR IT?!"
"HE'S CRAZY! THERE'S NO WAY EVEN HE CAN MOVE THAT AWAY FROM..."
...US...?
HE...HE DID IT!
LOOK AT THAT! ONE PUNCH... AND HE SHATTERED THE WHOLE ROCK INTO A BILLION PIECES! UN-BELIEVABLE!
IS HE ALL RIGHT?
I THINK SO. IN FACT, I'D ALMOST SAY HE WAS SMILING.
WAY TO GO, SUPERMAN!
WOW!

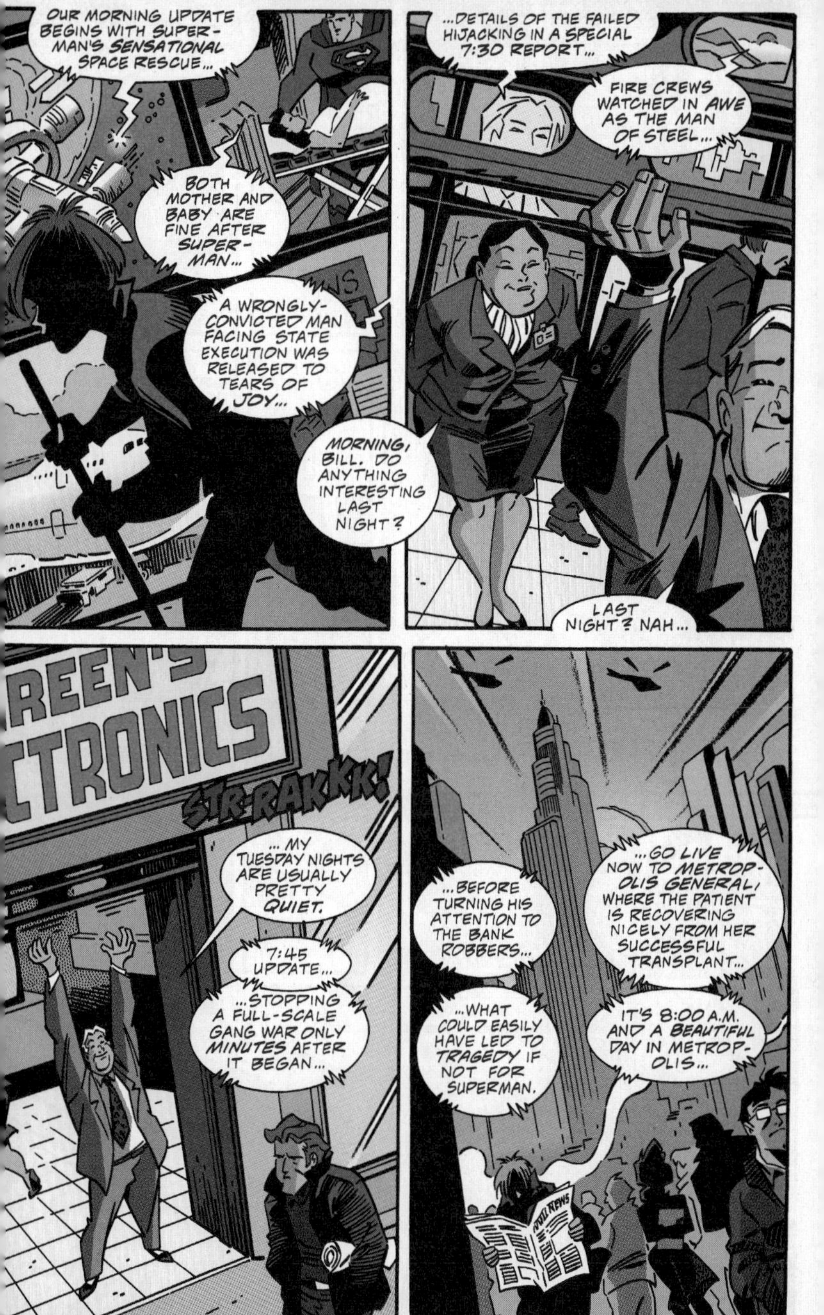
OUR MORNING UPDATE BEGINS WITH SUPERMAN'S SENSATIONAL SPACE RESCUE...
BOTH MOTHER AND BABY ARE FINE AFTER SUPERMAN...
A WRONGLY-CONVICTED MAN FACING STATE EXECUTION WAS RELEASED TO TEARS OF JOY...
MORNING, BILL. DO ANYTHING INTERESTING LAST NIGHT?
...DETAILS OF THE FAILED HIJACKING IN A SPECIAL 7:30 REPORT...
FIRE CREWS WATCHED IN AWE AS THE MAN OF STEEL...
LAST NIGHT? NAH...
REEN'S
CTRONICS
STR-RAKKK!
...MY TUESDAY NIGHTS ARE USUALLY PRETTY QUIET.
7:45 UPDATE...
...STOPPING A FULL-SCALE GANG WAR ONLY MINUTES AFTER IT BEGAN...
...BEFORE TURNING HIS ATTENTION TO THE BANK ROBBERS...
...GO LIVE NOW TO METROPOLIS GENERAL, WHERE THE PATIENT IS RECOVERING NICELY FROM HER SUCCESSFUL TRANSPLANT...
...WHAT COULD EASILY HAVE LED TO TRAGEDY IF NOT FOR SUPERMAN.
IT'S 8:00 A.M. AND A BEAUTIFUL DAY IN METROPOLIS...

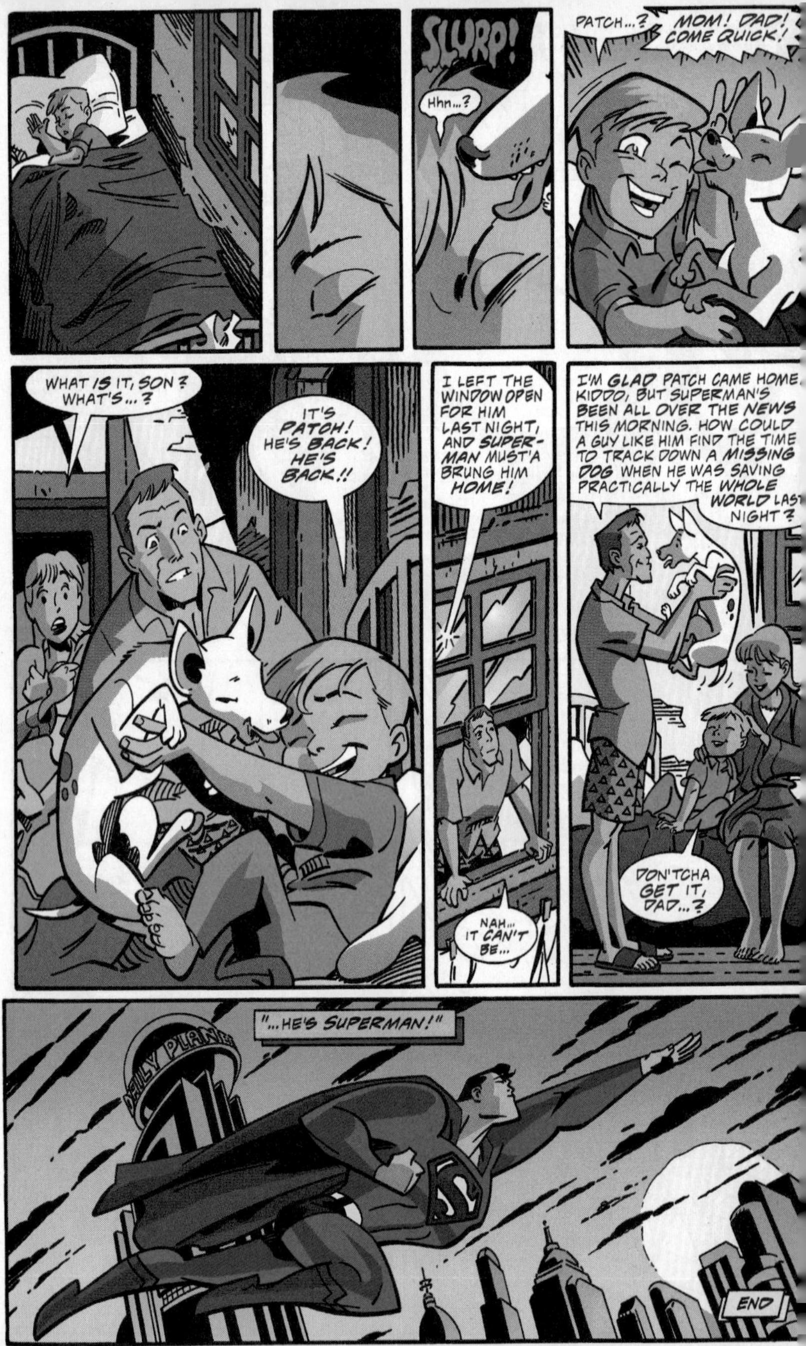
SLURP!
Hhn...?
PATCH...?
MOM! DAD! COME QUICK!
WHAT IS IT, SON? WHAT'S...?
IT'S PATCH! HE'S BACK! HE'S BACK!!
I LEFT THE WINDOW OPEN FOR HIM LAST NIGHT, AND SUPERMAN MUST'A BRUNG HIM HOME!
NAH... IT CAN'T BE...
I'M GLAD PATCH CAME HOME, KIDDO, BUT SUPERMAN'S BEEN ALL OVER THE NEWS THIS MORNING. HOW COULD A GUY LIKE HIM FIND THE TIME TO TRACK DOWN A MISSING DOG WHEN HE WAS SAVING PRACTICALLY THE WHOLE WORLD LAST NIGHT?
DON'TCHA GET IT, DAD...?
"...HE'S SUPERMAN!"
DAILY PLANET
END

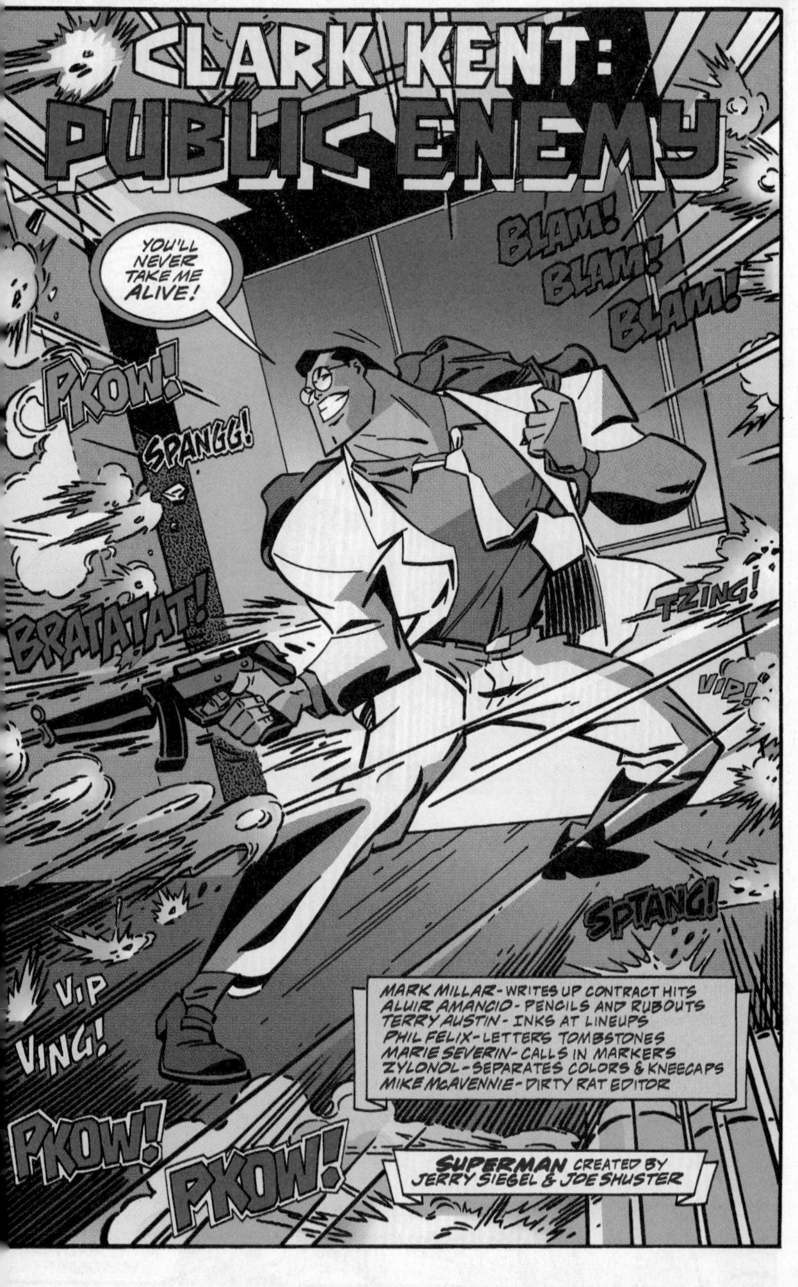
CLARK KENT:
PUBLIC ENEMY
YOU'LL NEVER TAKE ME ALIVE!
BLAM!
BLAM!
BLAM!
PKOW!
SPANGG!
BRATATAT!
TZING!
VIP!
SPTANG!
VIP
VING!
MARK MILLAR - WRITES UP CONTRACT HITS
ALUIR AMANCIO - PENCILS AND RUBOUTS
TERRY AUSTIN - INKS AT LINEUPS
PHIL FELIX - LETTERS TOMBSTONES
MARIE SEVERIN - CALLS IN MARKERS
ZYLONOL - SEPARATES COLORS & KNEECAPS
MIKE McAVENNIE - DIRTY RAT EDITOR
PKOW!
PKOW!
SUPERMAN CREATED BY
JERRY SIEGEL & JOE SHUSTER

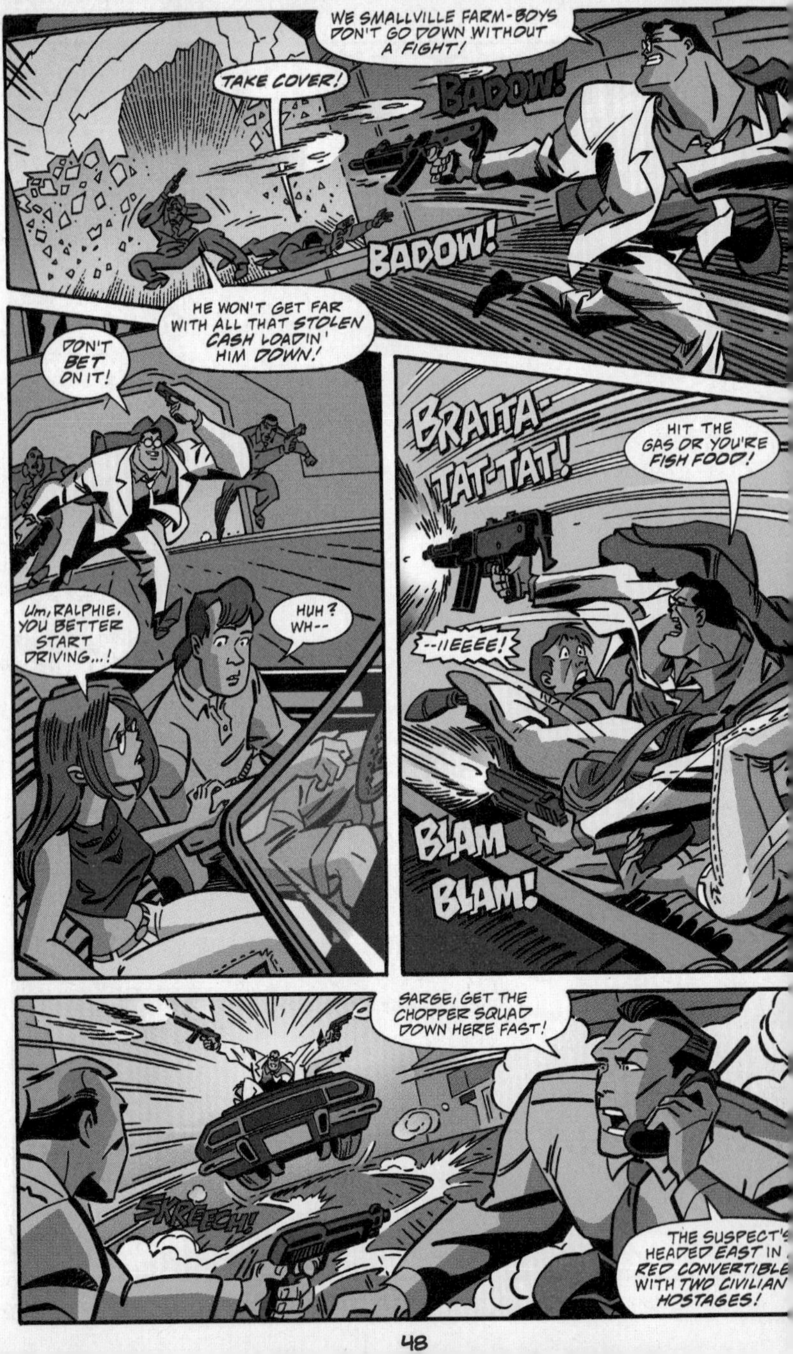
WE SMALLVILLE FARM-BOYS DON'T GO DOWN WITHOUT A FIGHT!
TAKE COVER!
BADOW!
BADOW!
HE WON'T GET FAR WITH ALL THAT STOLEN CASH LOADIN' HIM DOWN!
DON'T BET ON IT!
UM, RALPHIE, YOU BETTER START DRIVING...!
HUH? WH--
BRATTA-TAT-TAT!
HIT THE GAS OR YOU'RE FISH FOOD!
--IIEEEE!
BLAM BLAM!
SARGE, GET THE CHOPPER SQUAD DOWN HERE FAST!
SKREECH!
THE SUSPECT'S HEADED EAST IN RED CONVERTIBLE WITH TWO CIVILIAN HOSTAGES!

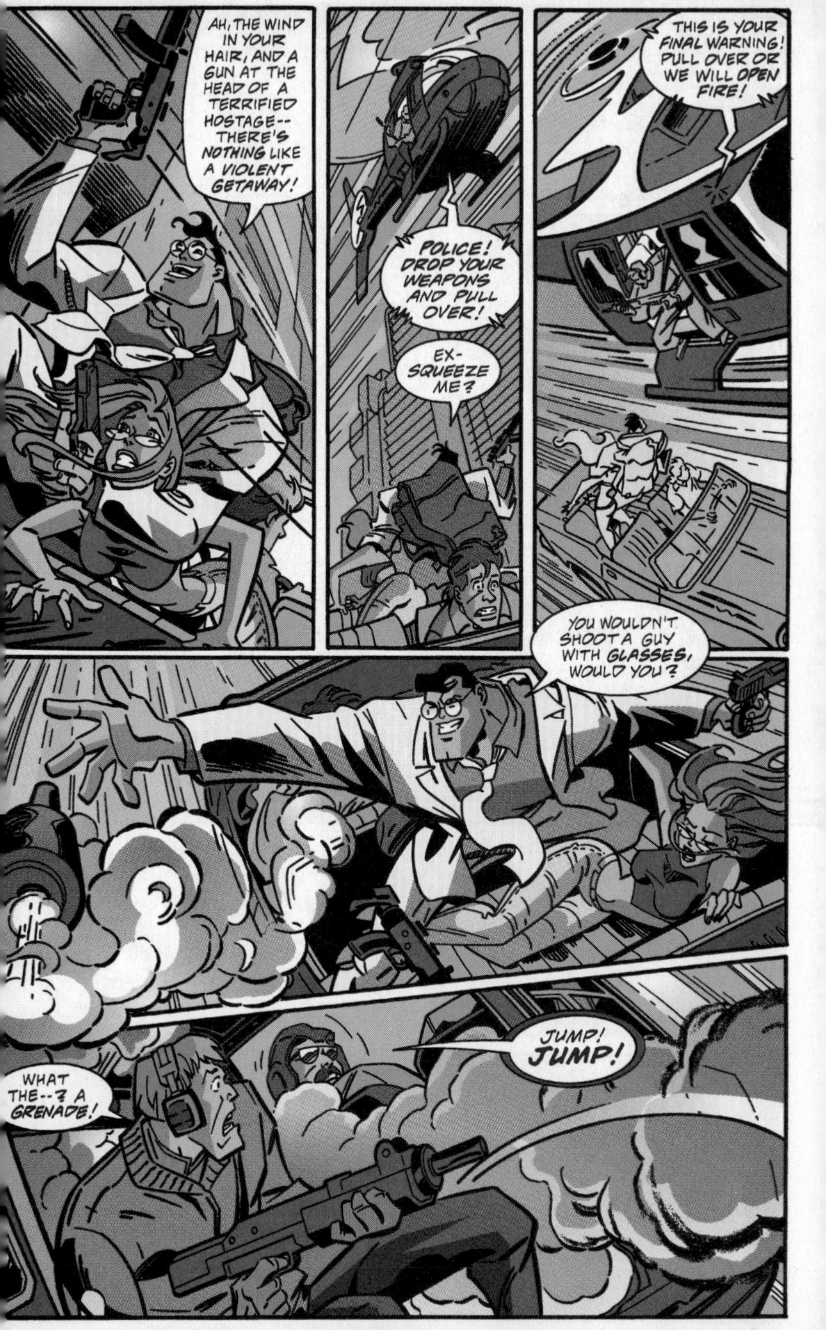
AH, THE WIND IN YOUR HAIR, AND A GUN AT THE HEAD OF A TERRIFIED HOSTAGE-- THERE'S NOTHING LIKE A VIOLENT GETAWAY!
POLICE! DROP YOUR WEAPONS AND PULL OVER!
EX-SQUEEZE ME?
THIS IS YOUR FINAL WARNING! PULL OVER OR WE WILL OPEN FIRE!
YOU WOULDN'T SHOOT A GUY WITH GLASSES, WOULD YOU?
JUMP! JUMP!
WHAT THE--? A GRENADE!

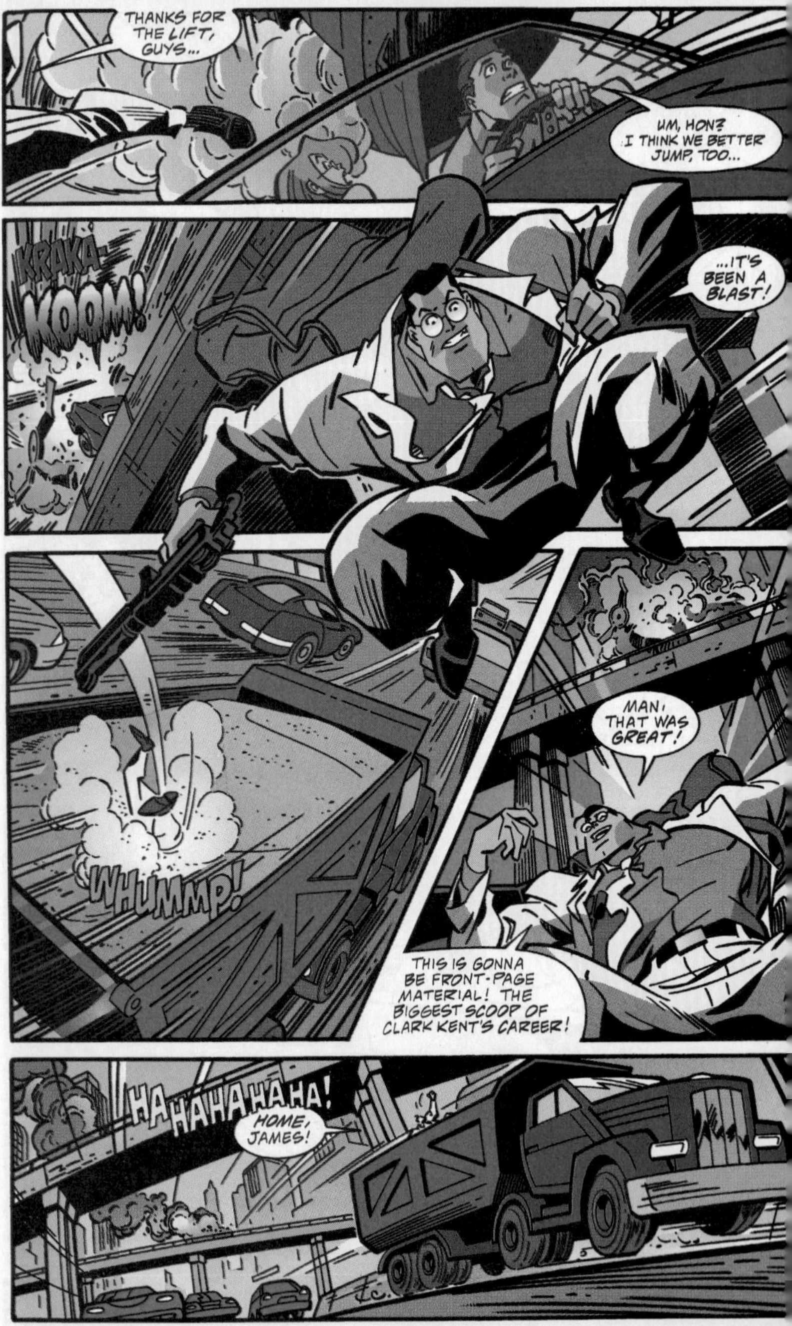
THANKS FOR THE LIFT, GUYS...
UM, HON? I THINK WE BETTER JUMP, TOO...
KRAKA-KOOM!
...IT'S BEEN A BLAST!
WHUMMP!
MAN, THAT WAS GREAT!
THIS IS GONNA BE FRONT-PAGE MATERIAL! THE BIGGEST SCOOP OF CLARK KENT'S CAREER!
HAHAHAHAHAHA!
HOME, JAMES!

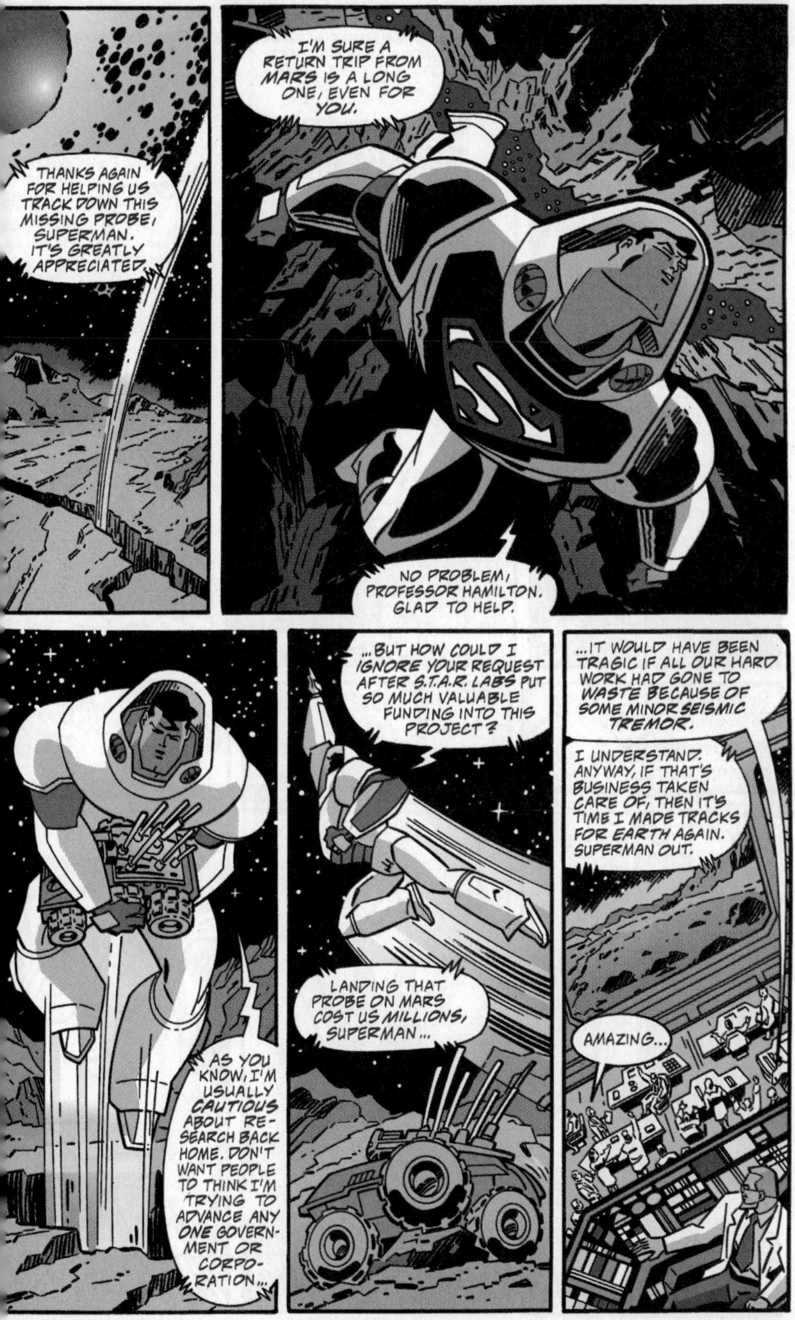
THANKS AGAIN FOR HELPING US TRACK DOWN THIS MISSING PROBE, SUPERMAN. IT'S GREATLY APPRECIATED.
I'M SURE A RETURN TRIP FROM MARS IS A LONG ONE, EVEN FOR YOU.
NO PROBLEM, PROFESSOR HAMILTON. GLAD TO HELP.
AS YOU KNOW, I'M USUALLY CAUTIOUS ABOUT RE-SEARCH BACK HOME. DON'T WANT PEOPLE TO THINK I'M TRYING TO ADVANCE ANY ONE GOVERN-MENT OR CORPO-RATION...
...BUT HOW COULD I IGNORE YOUR REQUEST AFTER S.T.A.R. LABS PUT SO MUCH VALUABLE FUNDING INTO THIS PROJECT?
LANDING THAT PROBE ON MARS COST US MILLIONS, SUPERMAN...
...IT WOULD HAVE BEEN TRAGIC IF ALL OUR HARD WORK HAD GONE TO WASTE BECAUSE OF SOME MINOR SEISMIC TREMOR.
I UNDERSTAND. ANYWAY, IF THAT'S BUSINESS TAKEN CARE OF, THEN IT'S TIME I MADE TRACKS FOR EARTH AGAIN. SUPERMAN OUT.
AMAZING...

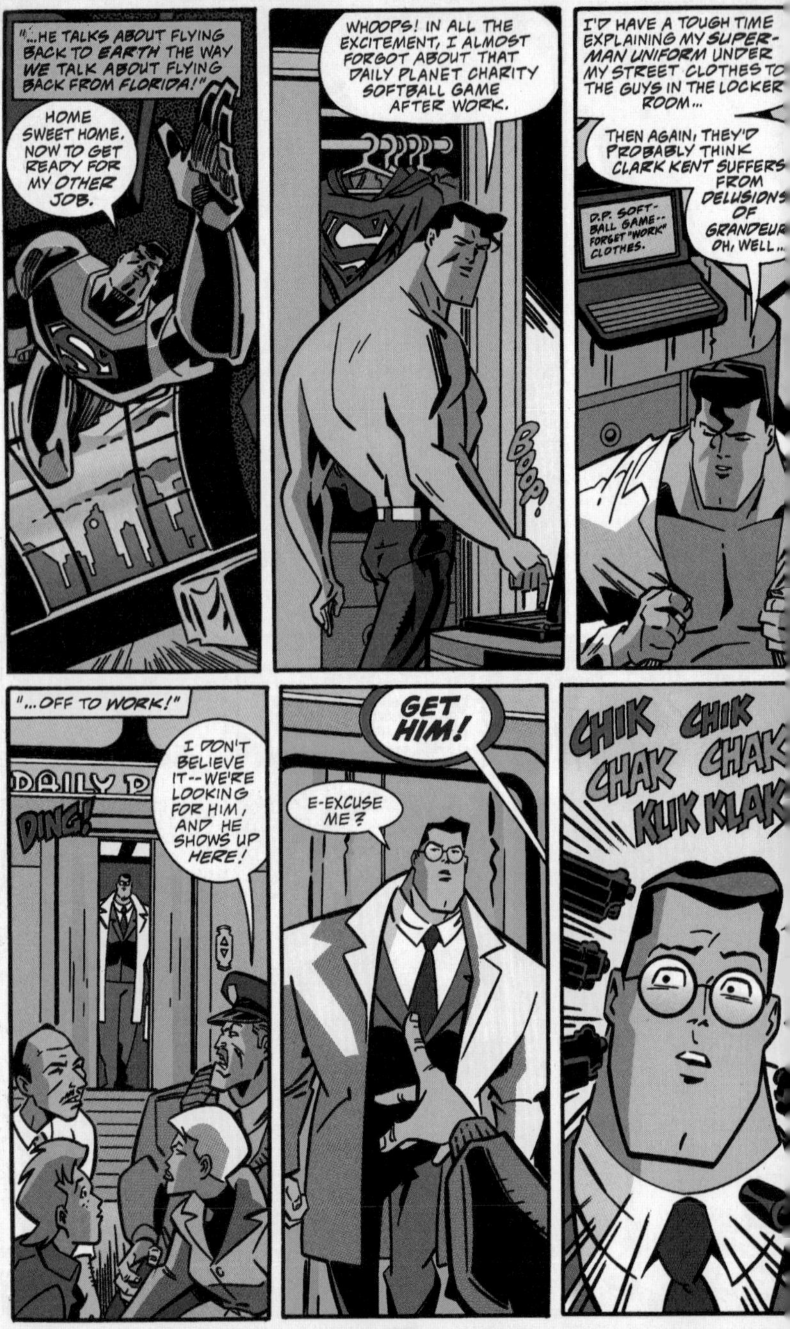
"...HE TALKS ABOUT FLYING BACK TO EARTH THE WAY WE TALK ABOUT FLYING BACK FROM FLORIDA!"
HOME SWEET HOME. NOW TO GET READY FOR MY OTHER JOB.
WHOOPS! IN ALL THE EXCITEMENT, I ALMOST FORGOT ABOUT THAT DAILY PLANET CHARITY SOFTBALL GAME AFTER WORK.
BOOP!
I'D HAVE A TOUGH TIME EXPLAINING MY SUPERMAN UNIFORM UNDER MY STREET CLOTHES TO THE GUYS IN THE LOCKER ROOM...
D.P. SOFT-BALL GAME-- FORGET "WORK" CLOTHES.
THEN AGAIN, THEY'D PROBABLY THINK CLARK KENT SUFFERS FROM DELUSIONS OF GRANDEUR. OH, WELL...
"...OFF TO WORK!"
DAILY P
DING!
I DON'T BELIEVE IT--WE'RE LOOKING FOR HIM, AND HE SHOWS UP HERE!
GET HIM!
E-EXCUSE ME?
CHIK CHIK
CHAK CHAK
KLIK KLAK

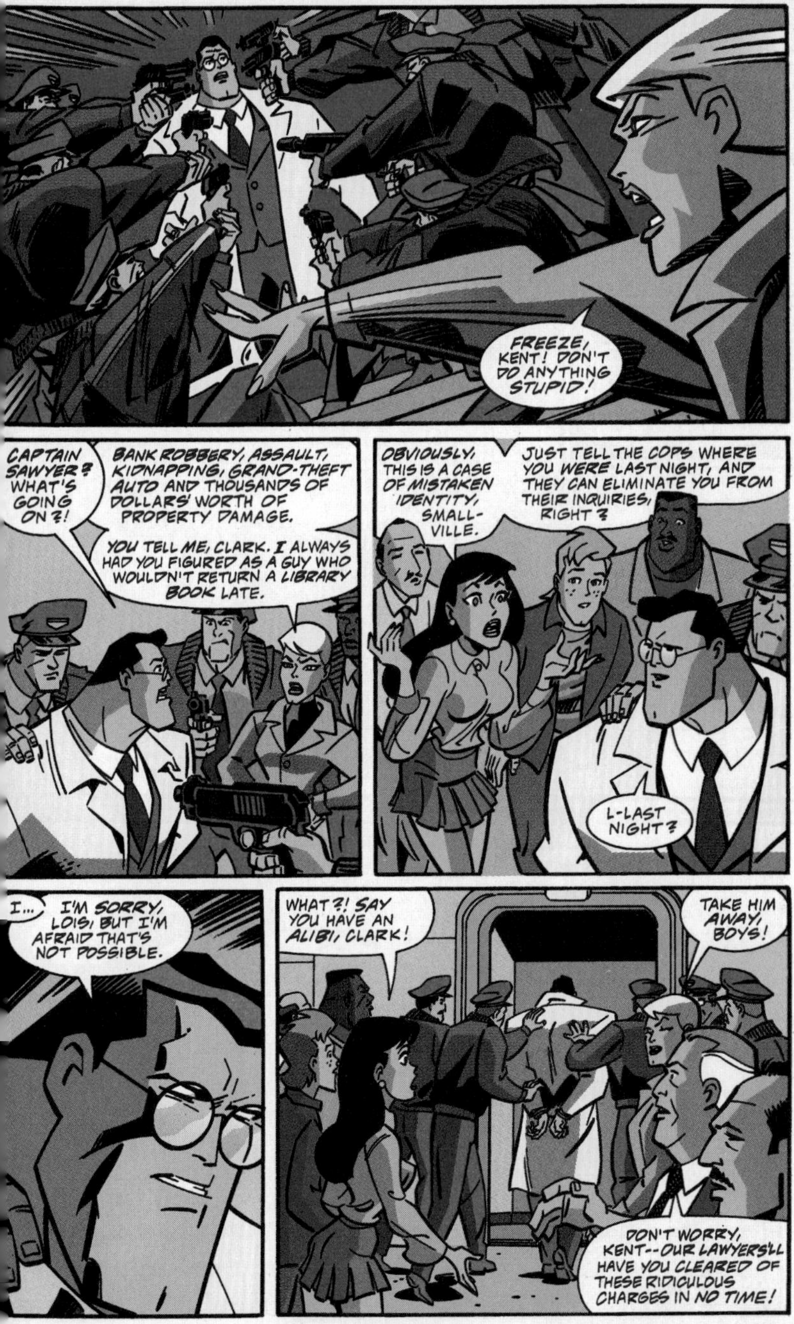
FREEZE, KENT! DON'T DO ANYTHING STUPID!
CAPTAIN SAWYER? WHAT'S GOING ON?!
BANK ROBBERY, ASSAULT, KIDNAPPING, GRAND-THEFT AUTO AND THOUSANDS OF DOLLARS' WORTH OF PROPERTY DAMAGE.
YOU TELL ME, CLARK. I ALWAYS HAD YOU FIGURED AS A GUY WHO WOULDN'T RETURN A LIBRARY BOOK LATE.
OBVIOUSLY, THIS IS A CASE OF MISTAKEN IDENTITY, SMALL-VILLE.
JUST TELL THE COPS WHERE YOU WERE LAST NIGHT, AND THEY CAN ELIMINATE YOU FROM THEIR INQUIRIES, RIGHT?
L-LAST NIGHT?
I...
I'M SORRY, LOIS, BUT I'M AFRAID THAT'S NOT POSSIBLE.
WHAT?! SAY YOU HAVE AN ALIBI, CLARK!
TAKE HIM AWAY, BOYS!
DON'T WORRY, KENT--OUR LAWYERS'LL HAVE YOU CLEARED OF THESE RIDICULOUS CHARGES IN NO TIME!

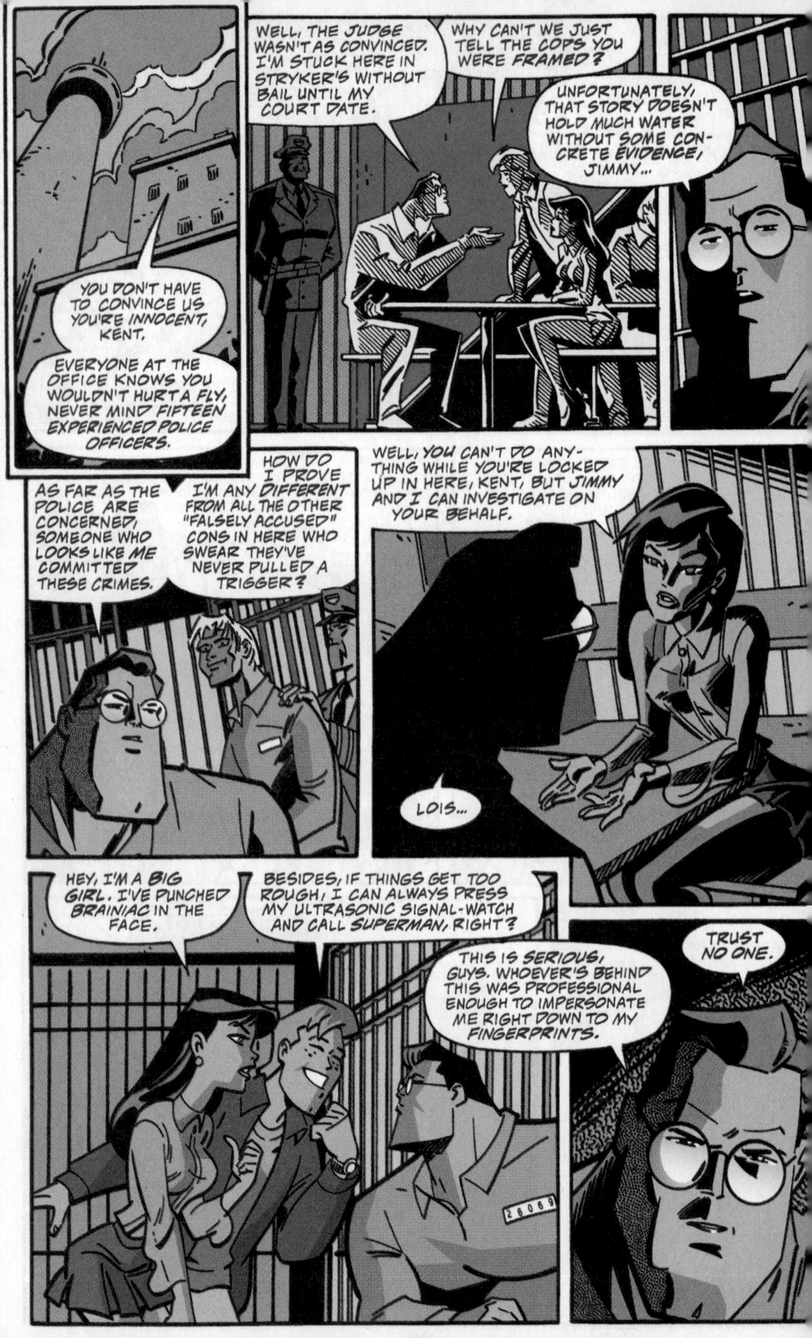
YOU DON'T HAVE TO CONVINCE US YOU'RE INNOCENT, KENT.
EVERYONE AT THE OFFICE KNOWS YOU WOULDN'T HURT A FLY, NEVER MIND FIFTEEN EXPERIENCED POLICE OFFICERS.
WELL, THE JUDGE WASN'T AS CONVINCED. I'M STUCK HERE IN STRYKER'S WITHOUT BAIL UNTIL MY COURT DATE.
WHY CAN'T WE JUST TELL THE COPS YOU WERE FRAMED?
UNFORTUNATELY, THAT STORY DOESN'T HOLD MUCH WATER WITHOUT SOME CONCRETE EVIDENCE, JIMMY...
AS FAR AS THE POLICE ARE CONCERNED, SOMEONE WHO LOOKS LIKE ME COMMITTED THESE CRIMES.
HOW DO I PROVE I'M ANY DIFFERENT FROM ALL THE OTHER "FALSELY ACCUSED" CONS IN HERE WHO SWEAR THEY'VE NEVER PULLED A TRIGGER?
WELL, YOU CAN'T DO ANYTHING WHILE YOU'RE LOCKED UP IN HERE, KENT, BUT JIMMY AND I CAN INVESTIGATE ON YOUR BEHALF.
LOIS...
HEY, I'M A BIG GIRL. I'VE PUNCHED BRAINIAC IN THE FACE.
BESIDES, IF THINGS GET TOO ROUGH, I CAN ALWAYS PRESS MY ULTRASONIC SIGNAL-WATCH AND CALL SUPERMAN, RIGHT?
THIS IS SERIOUS, GUYS. WHOEVER'S BEHIND THIS WAS PROFESSIONAL ENOUGH TO IMPERSONATE ME RIGHT DOWN TO MY FINGERPRINTS.
TRUST NO ONE.
26069

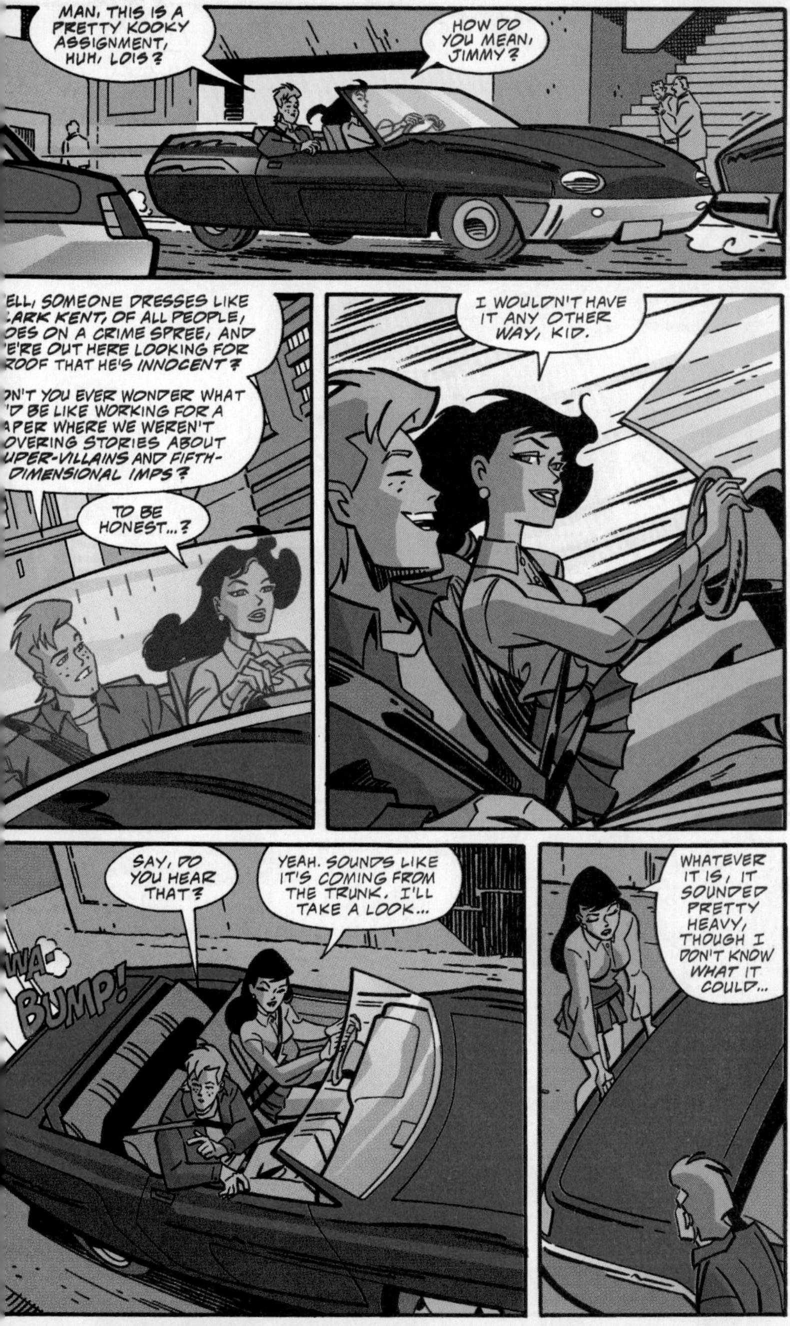

MAN, THIS IS A PRETTY KOOKY ASSIGNMENT, HUH, LOIS?
HOW DO YOU MEAN, JIMMY?
ELL, SOMEONE DRESSES LIKE LARK KENT, OF ALL PEOPLE, OES ON A CRIME SPREE, AND E'RE OUT HERE LOOKING FOR ROOF THAT HE'S INNOCENT?
ON'T YOU EVER WONDER WHAT 'D BE LIKE WORKING FOR A APER WHERE WE WEREN'T OVERING STORIES ABOUT UPER-VILLAINS AND FIFTH-DIMENSIONAL IMPS?
TO BE HONEST...?
I WOULDN'T HAVE IT ANY OTHER WAY, KID.
WA-BUMP!
SAY, DO YOU HEAR THAT?
YEAH. SOUNDS LIKE IT'S COMING FROM THE TRUNK. I'LL TAKE A LOOK...
WHATEVER IT IS, IT SOUNDED PRETTY HEAVY, THOUGH I DON'T KNOW WHAT IT COULD...

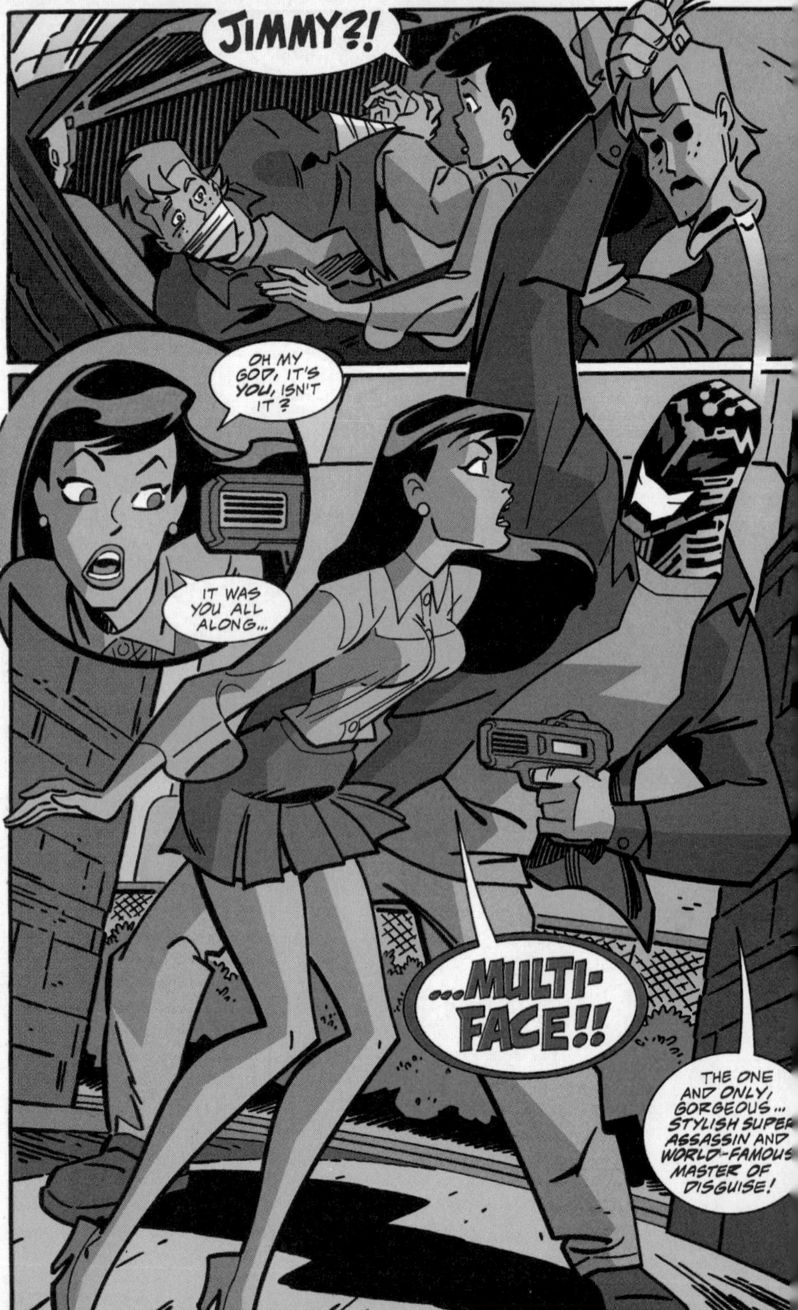
JIMMY?!
OH MY GOD, IT'S YOU, ISN'T IT?
IT WAS YOU ALL ALONG...
...MULTI-FACE!!
THE ONE AND ONLY, GORGEOUS... STYLISH SUPER ASSASSIN AND WORLD-FAMOUS MASTER OF DISGUISE!

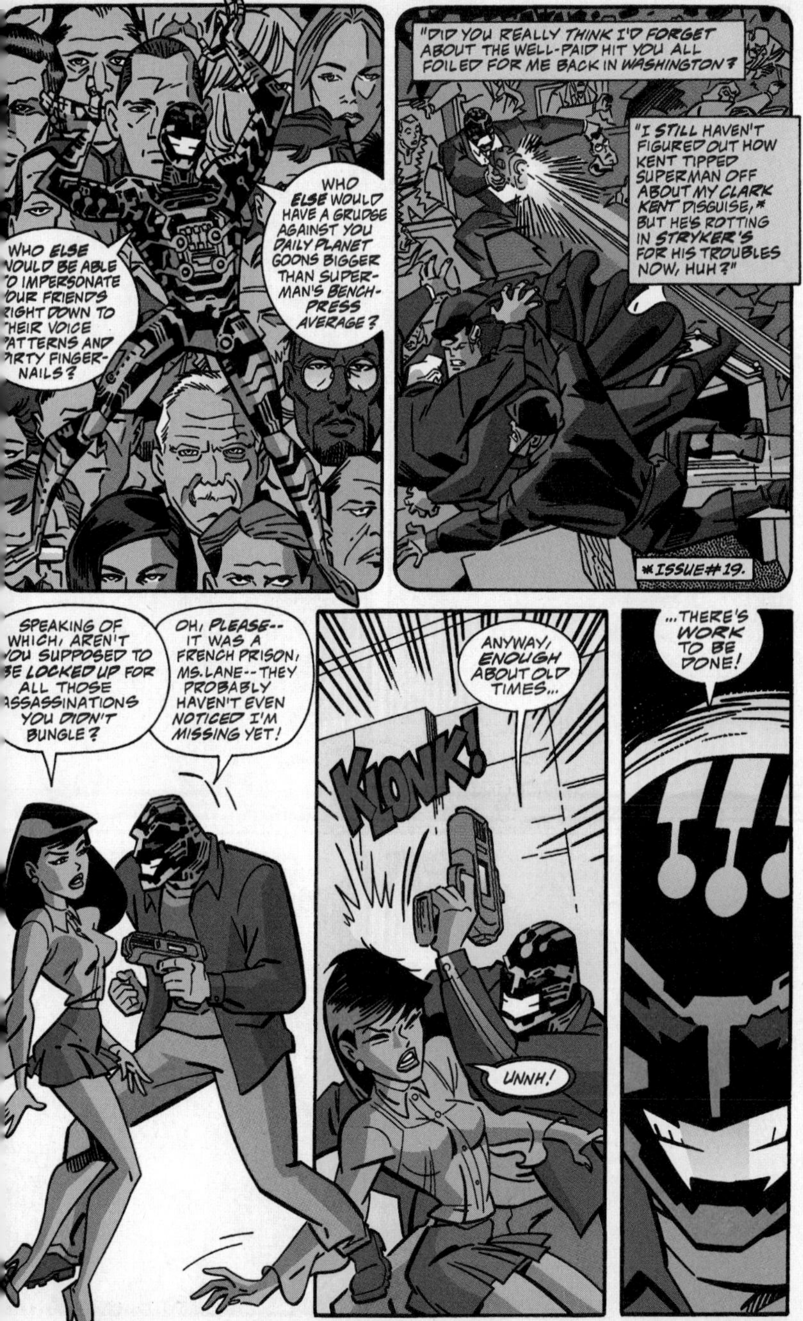
WHO ELSE WOULD HAVE A GRUDGE AGAINST YOU DAILY PLANET GOONS BIGGER THAN SUPER-MAN'S BENCH-PRESS AVERAGE?
WHO ELSE WOULD BE ABLE TO IMPERSONATE YOUR FRIENDS RIGHT DOWN TO THEIR VOICE PATTERNS AND DIRTY FINGER-NAILS?
"DID YOU REALLY THINK I'D FORGET ABOUT THE WELL-PAID HIT YOU ALL FOILED FOR ME BACK IN WASHINGTON?
"I STILL HAVEN'T FIGURED OUT HOW KENT TIPPED SUPERMAN OFF ABOUT MY CLARK KENT DISGUISE,* BUT HE'S ROTTING IN STRYKER'S FOR HIS TROUBLES NOW, HUH?"
*ISSUE #19.
SPEAKING OF WHICH, AREN'T YOU SUPPOSED TO BE LOCKED UP FOR ALL THOSE ASSASSINATIONS YOU DIDN'T BUNGLE?
OH, PLEASE-- IT WAS A FRENCH PRISON, MS. LANE-- THEY PROBABLY HAVEN'T EVEN NOTICED I'M MISSING YET!
ANYWAY, ENOUGH ABOUT OLD TIMES...
KLONK!
UNNH!
...THERE'S WORK TO BE DONE!

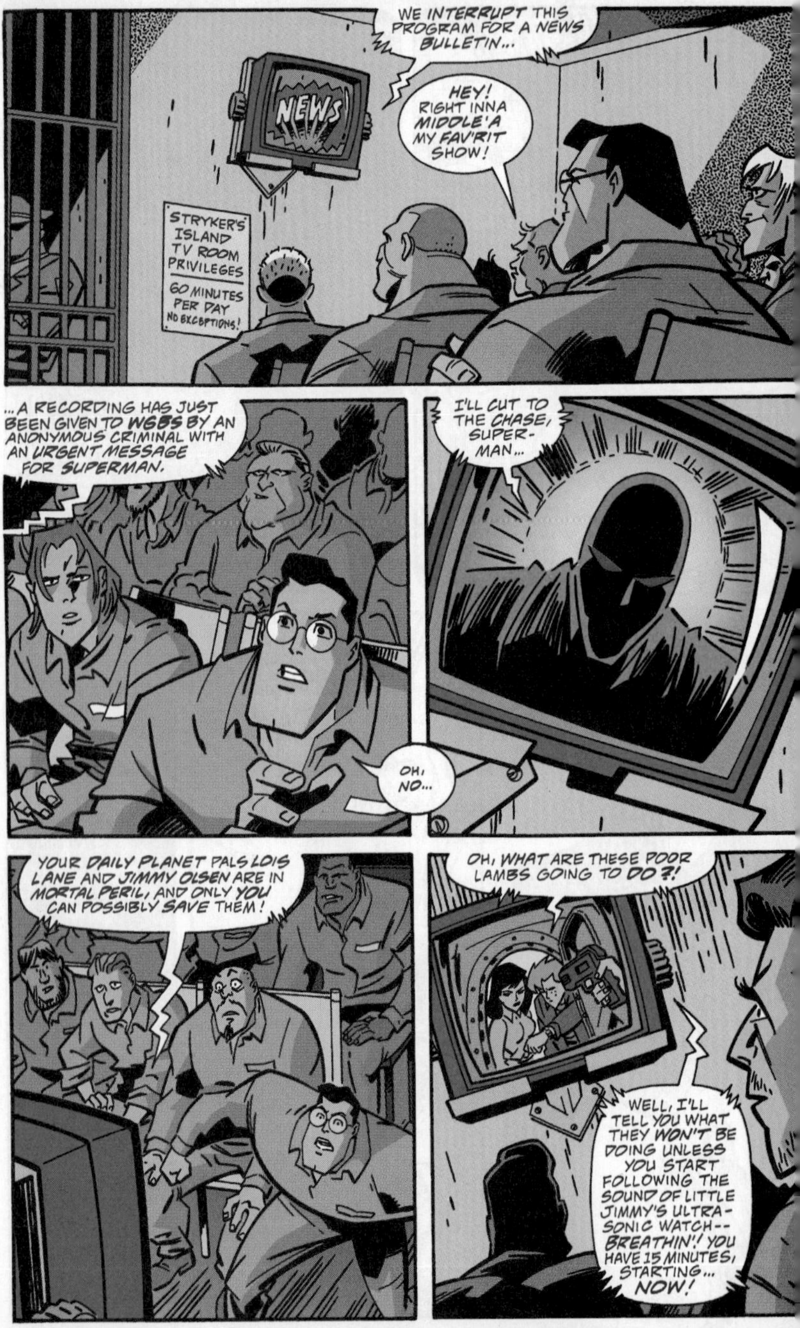
WE INTERRUPT THIS PROGRAM FOR A NEWS BULLETIN...
NEWS
HEY! RIGHT INNA MIDDLE'A MY FAV'RIT SHOW!
STRYKER'S ISLAND TV ROOM PRIVILEGES
60 MINUTES PER DAY
NO EXCEPTIONS!
...A RECORDING HAS JUST BEEN GIVEN TO WGBS BY AN ANONYMOUS CRIMINAL WITH AN URGENT MESSAGE FOR SUPERMAN.
I'LL CUT TO THE CHASE, SUPERMAN...
OH, NO...
YOUR DAILY PLANET PALS LOIS LANE AND JIMMY OLSEN ARE IN MORTAL PERIL, AND ONLY YOU CAN POSSIBLY SAVE THEM!
OH, WHAT ARE THESE POOR LAMBS GOING TO DO?!
WELL, I'LL TELL YOU WHAT THEY WON'T BE DOING UNLESS YOU START FOLLOWING THE SOUND OF LITTLE JIMMY'S ULTRA-SONIC WATCH--BREATHIN'! YOU HAVE 15 MINUTES, STARTING... NOW!

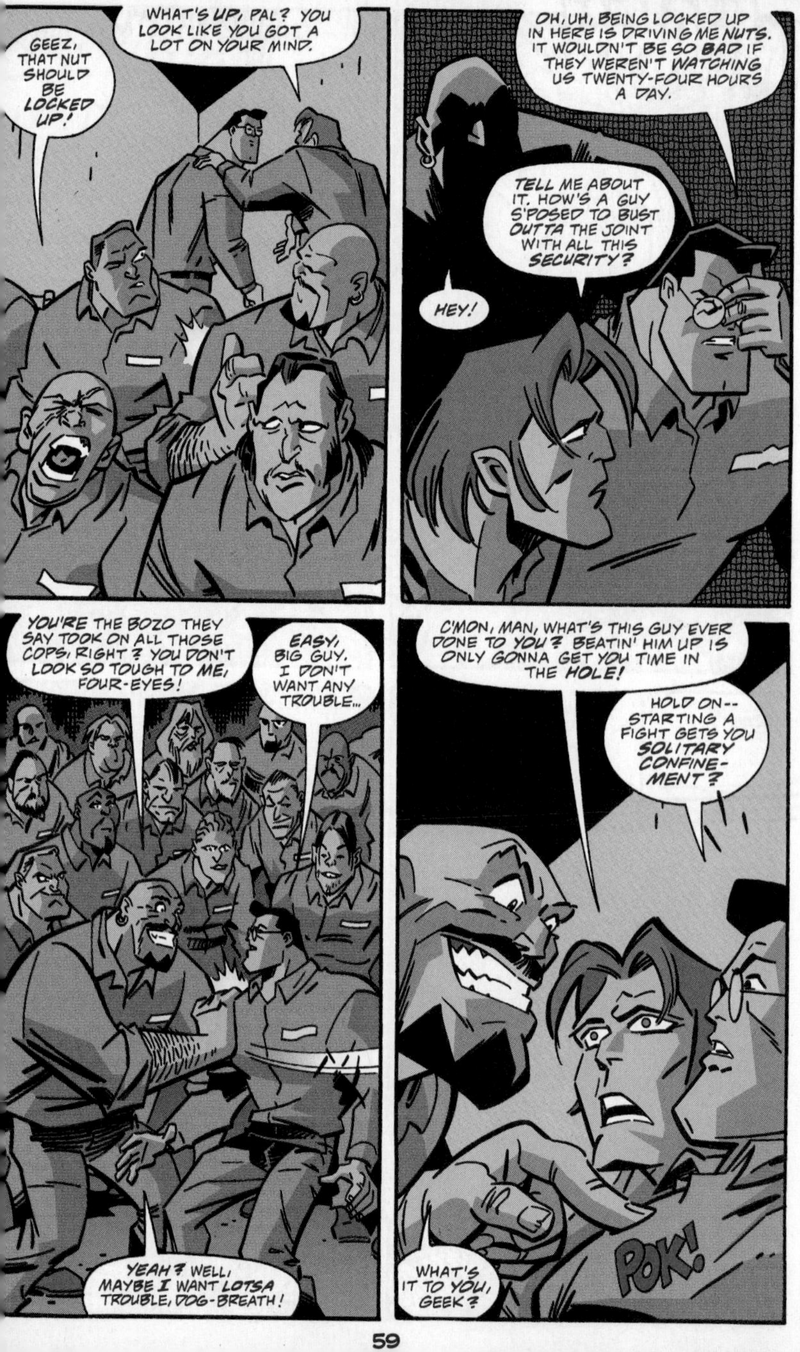

WHAT'S UP, PAL? YOU LOOK LIKE YOU GOT A LOT ON YOUR MIND.
GEEZ, THAT NUT SHOULD BE LOCKED UP!
OH, UH, BEING LOCKED UP IN HERE IS DRIVING ME NUTS. IT WOULDN'T BE SO BAD IF THEY WEREN'T WATCHING US TWENTY-FOUR HOURS A DAY.
TELL ME ABOUT IT. HOW'S A GUY S'POSED TO BUST OUTTA THE JOINT WITH ALL THIS SECURITY?
HEY!
YOU'RE THE BOZO THEY SAY TOOK ON ALL THOSE COPS, RIGHT? YOU DON'T LOOK SO TOUGH TO ME, FOUR-EYES!
EASY, BIG GUY. I DON'T WANT ANY TROUBLE...
YEAH? WELL, MAYBE I WANT LOTSA TROUBLE, DOG-BREATH!
C'MON, MAN, WHAT'S THIS GUY EVER DONE TO YOU? BEATIN' HIM UP IS ONLY GONNA GET YOU TIME IN THE HOLE!
HOLD ON-- STARTING A FIGHT GETS YOU SOLITARY CONFINE-MENT?
WHAT'S IT TO YOU, GEEK?
POK!

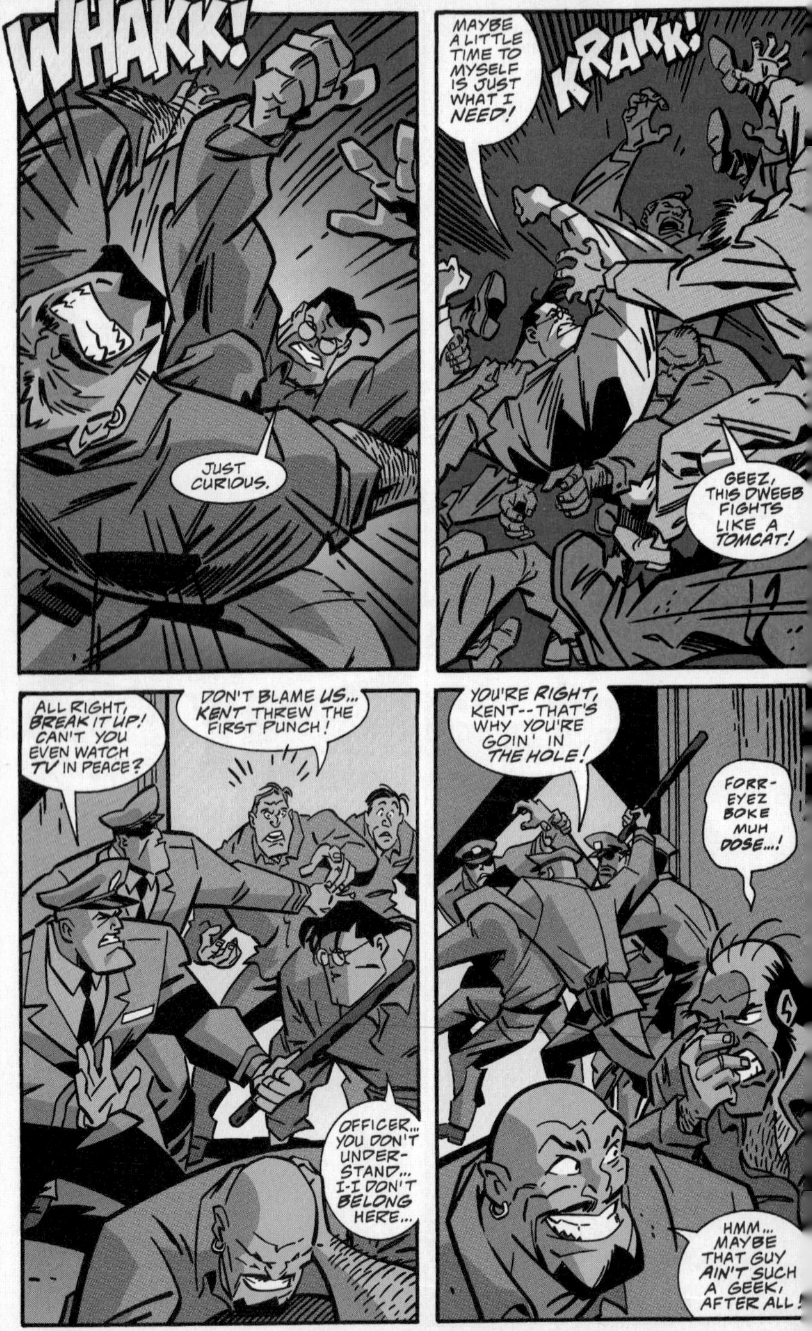
WHAKK!
JUST CURIOUS.
MAYBE A LITTLE TIME TO MYSELF IS JUST WHAT I NEED!
KRAKK!
GEEZ, THIS DWEEB FIGHTS LIKE A TOMCAT!
ALL RIGHT, BREAK IT UP! CAN'T YOU EVEN WATCH TV IN PEACE?
DON'T BLAME US... KENT THREW THE FIRST PUNCH!
OFFICER... YOU DON'T UNDER-STAND... I-I DON'T BELONG HERE...
YOU'RE RIGHT, KENT--THAT'S WHY YOU'RE GOIN' IN THE HOLE!
FORR-EYEZ BOKE MUH DOSE...!
HMM... MAYBE THAT GUY AIN'T SUCH A GEEK, AFTER ALL!

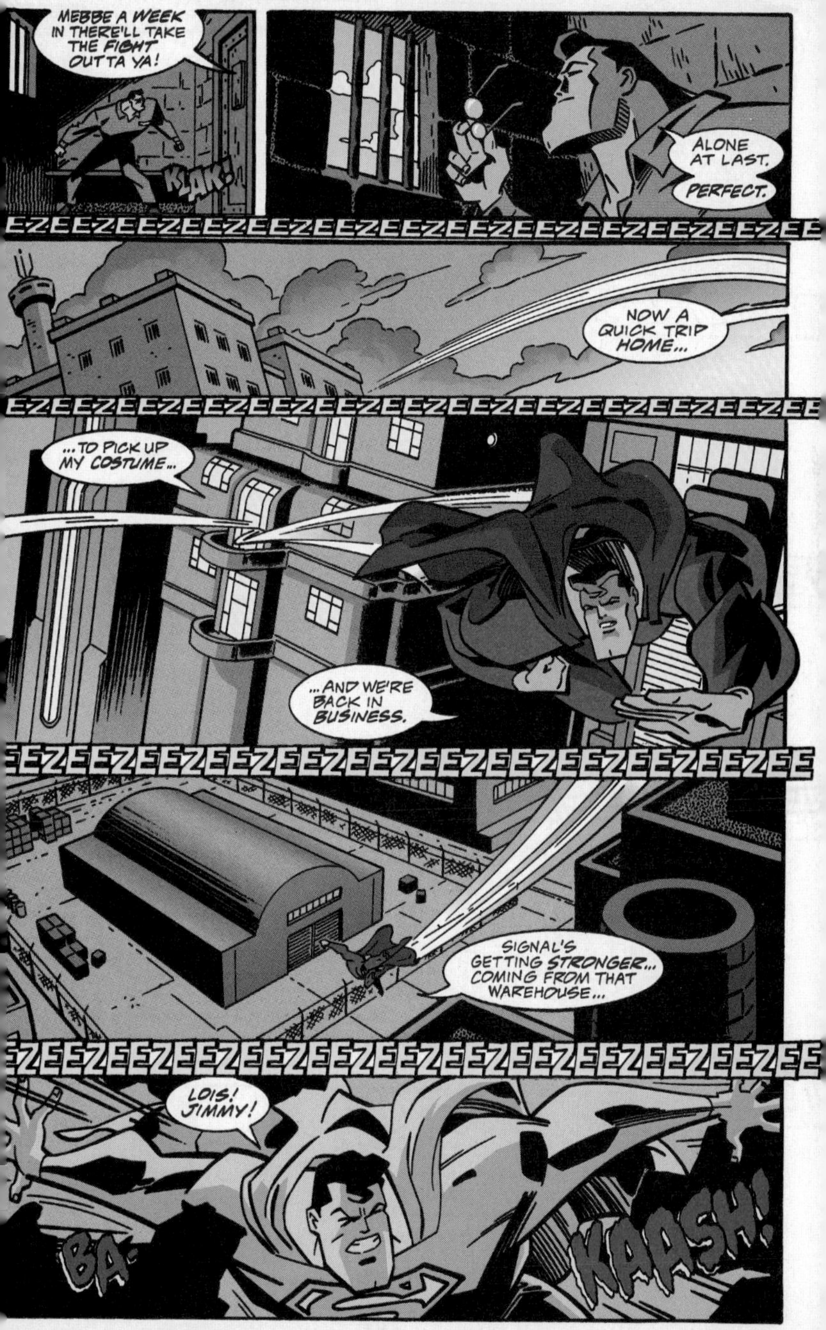
MEBBE A WEEK IN THERE'LL TAKE THE FIGHT OUTTA YA!
KLAK!
ALONE AT LAST.
PERFECT.
EZEEZEEZEEZEEZEEZEEZEEZEEZEEZEEZEEZEEZEE
NOW A QUICK TRIP HOME...
EZEEZEEZEEZEEZEEZEEZEEZEEZEEZEEZEEZEEZEE
...TO PICK UP MY COSTUME...
...AND WE'RE BACK IN BUSINESS.
EZEEZEEZEEZEEZEEZEEZEEZEEZEEZEEZEEZEE
SIGNAL'S GETTING STRONGER... COMING FROM THAT WAREHOUSE...
EZEEZEEZEEZEEZEEZEEZEEZEEZEEZEEZEEZEE
LOIS! JIMMY!
BA-
KAASH!

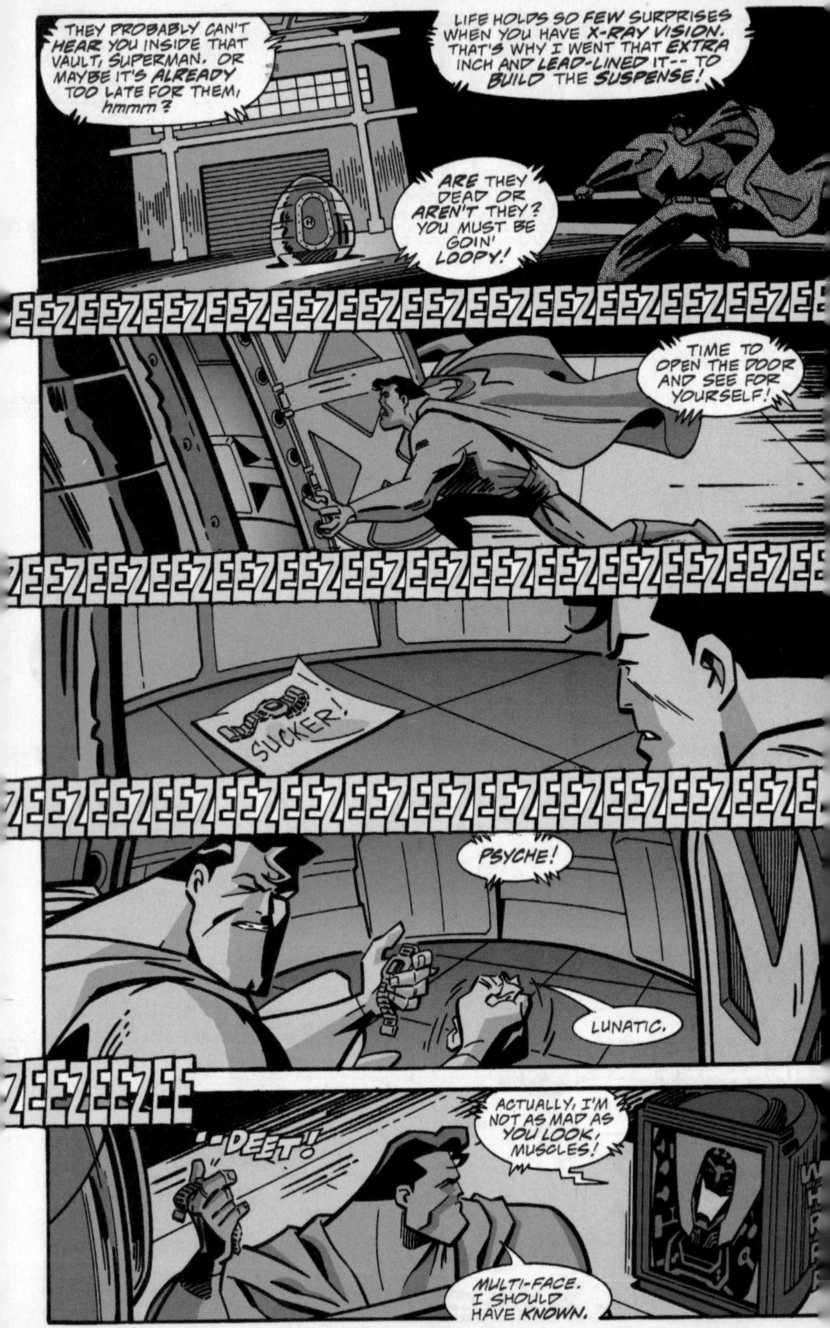
THEY PROBABLY CAN'T HEAR YOU INSIDE THAT VAULT, SUPERMAN. OR MAYBE IT'S ALREADY TOO LATE FOR THEM, hmmm?
LIFE HOLDS SO FEW SURPRISES WHEN YOU HAVE X-RAY VISION. THAT'S WHY I WENT THAT EXTRA INCH AND LEAD-LINED IT-- TO BUILD THE SUSPENSE!
ARE THEY DEAD OR AREN'T THEY? YOU MUST BE GOIN' LOOPY!
EEZEEZEEZEEZEEZEEZEEZEEZEEZEEZEEZEEZEEZEE
TIME TO OPEN THE DOOR AND SEE FOR YOURSELF!
ZEEZEEZEEZEEZEEZEEZEEZEEZEEZEEZEEZEEZEEZEE
SUCKER!
ZEEZEEZEEZEEZEEZEEZEEZEEZEEZEEZEEZEEZEEZEE
PSYCHE!
LUNATIC.
ZEEZEEZEE
--DEET!!
ACTUALLY, I'M NOT AS MAD AS YOU LOOK, MUSCLES!
MULTI-FACE. I SHOULD HAVE KNOWN.

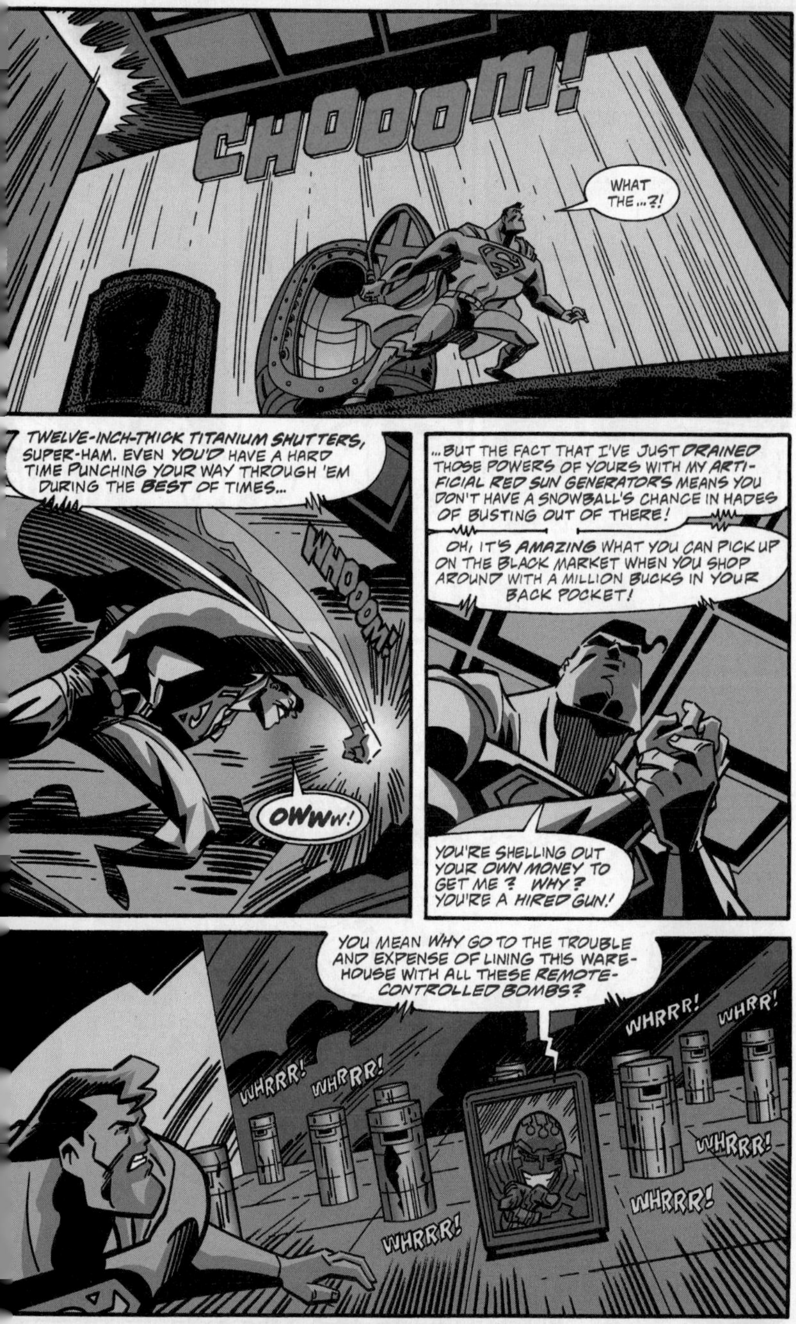
CHOOOM!
WHAT THE...?!
TWELVE-INCH-THICK TITANIUM SHUTTERS, SUPER-HAM. EVEN YOU'D HAVE A HARD TIME PUNCHING YOUR WAY THROUGH 'EM DURING THE BEST OF TIMES...
WHOOOOM!
OWWW!
...BUT THE FACT THAT I'VE JUST DRAINED THOSE POWERS OF YOURS WITH MY ARTI-FICIAL RED SUN GENERATORS MEANS YOU DON'T HAVE A SNOWBALL'S CHANCE IN HADES OF BUSTING OUT OF THERE!
OH, IT'S AMAZING WHAT YOU CAN PICK UP ON THE BLACK MARKET WHEN YOU SHOP AROUND WITH A MILLION BUCKS IN YOUR BACK POCKET!
YOU'RE SHELLING OUT YOUR OWN MONEY TO GET ME? WHY? YOU'RE A HIRED GUN!
YOU MEAN WHY GO TO THE TROUBLE AND EXPENSE OF LINING THIS WARE-HOUSE WITH ALL THESE REMOTE-CONTROLLED BOMBS?
WHRRR!
WHRRR!
WHRRR!
WHRRR!
WHRRR!
WHRRR!
WHRRR!

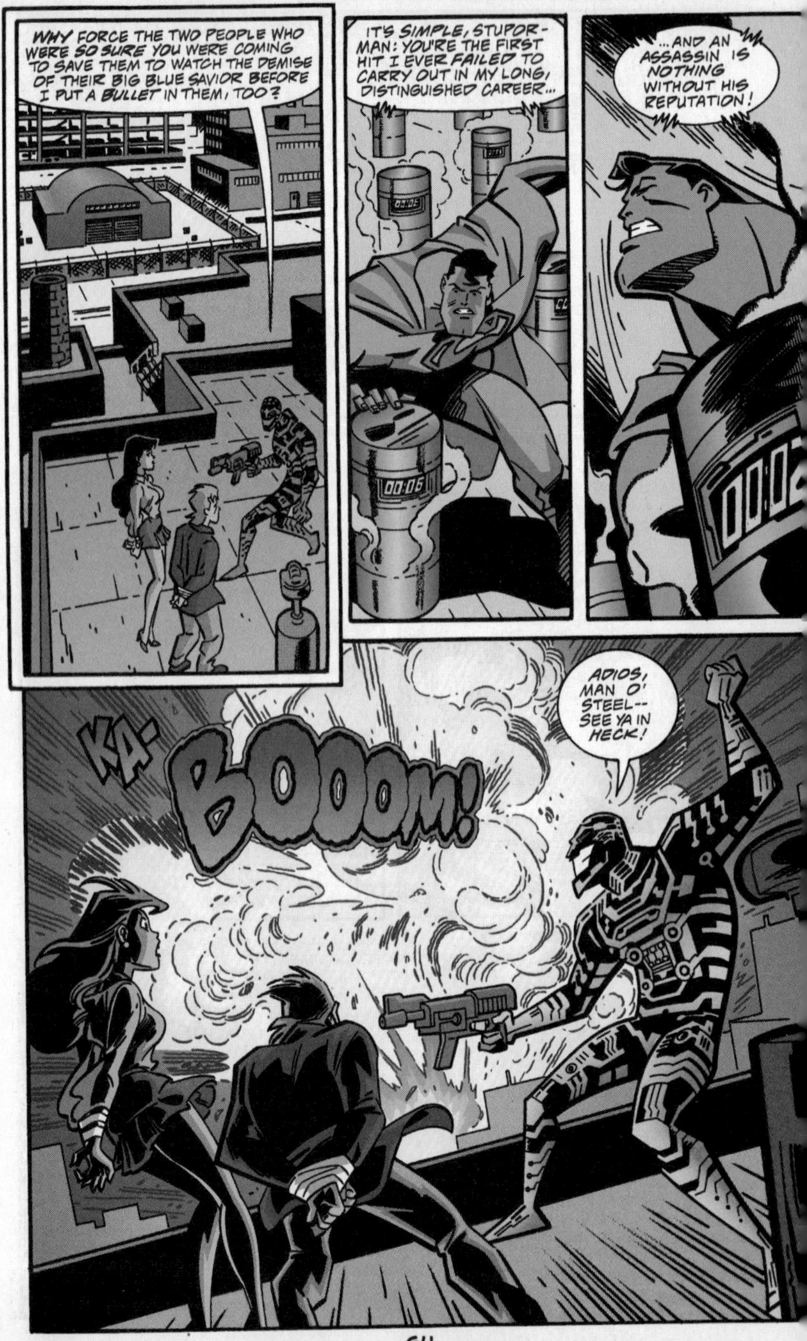

WHY FORCE THE TWO PEOPLE WHO WERE SO SURE YOU WERE COMING TO SAVE THEM TO WATCH THE DEMISE OF THEIR BIG BLUE SAVIOR BEFORE I PUT A BULLET IN THEM, TOO?
IT'S SIMPLE, STUPOR-MAN: YOU'RE THE FIRST HIT I EVER FAILED TO CARRY OUT IN MY LONG, DISTINGUISHED CAREER...
...AND AN ASSASSIN IS NOTHING WITHOUT HIS REPUTATION!
KA-BOOOM!
ADIOS, MAN O' STEEL-- SEE YA IN HECK!

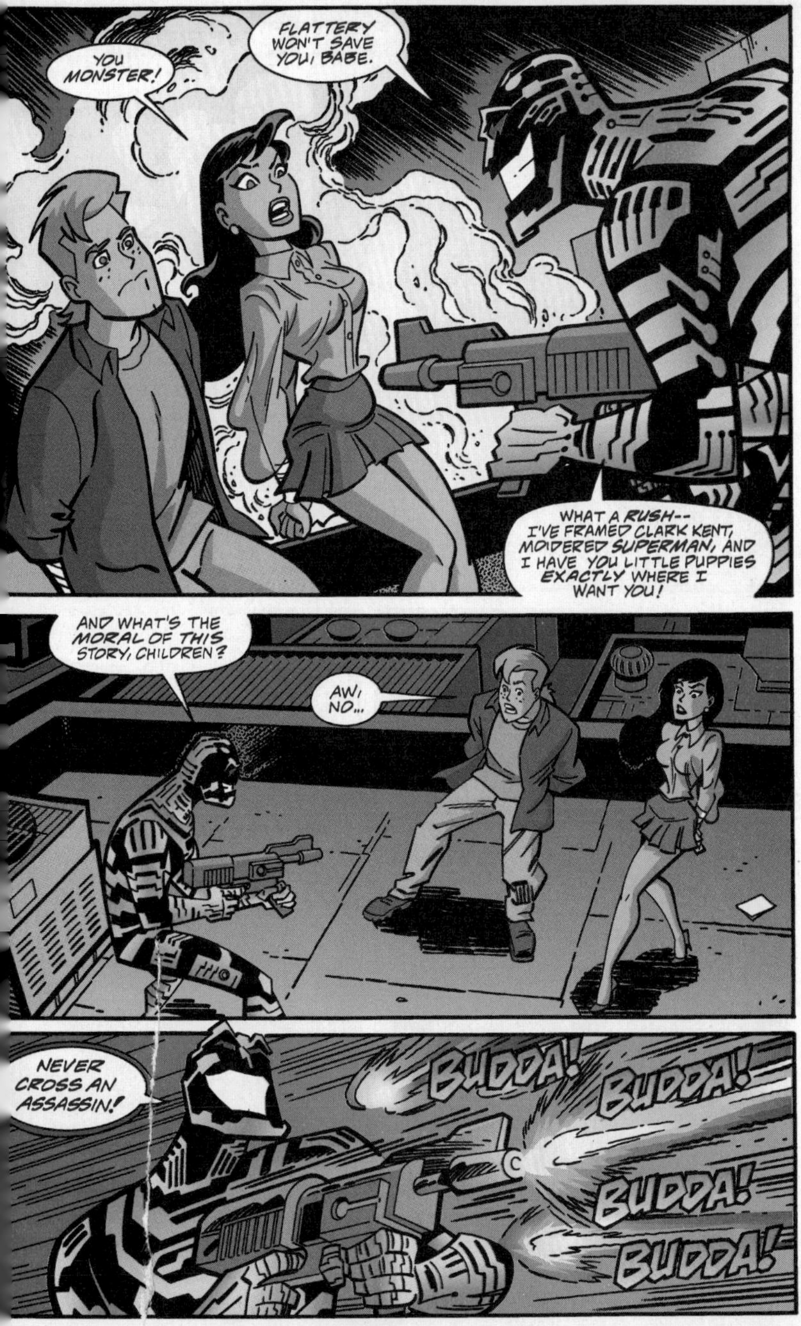
YOU MONSTER!
FLATTERY WON'T SAVE YOU, BABE.
WHAT A RUSH-- I'VE FRAMED CLARK KENT, MOIDERED SUPERMAN, AND I HAVE YOU LITTLE PUPPIES EXACTLY WHERE I WANT YOU!
AND WHAT'S THE MORAL OF THIS STORY, CHILDREN?
AW, NO...
NEVER CROSS AN ASSASSIN!
BUDDA!
BUDDA!
BUDDA!
BUDDA!

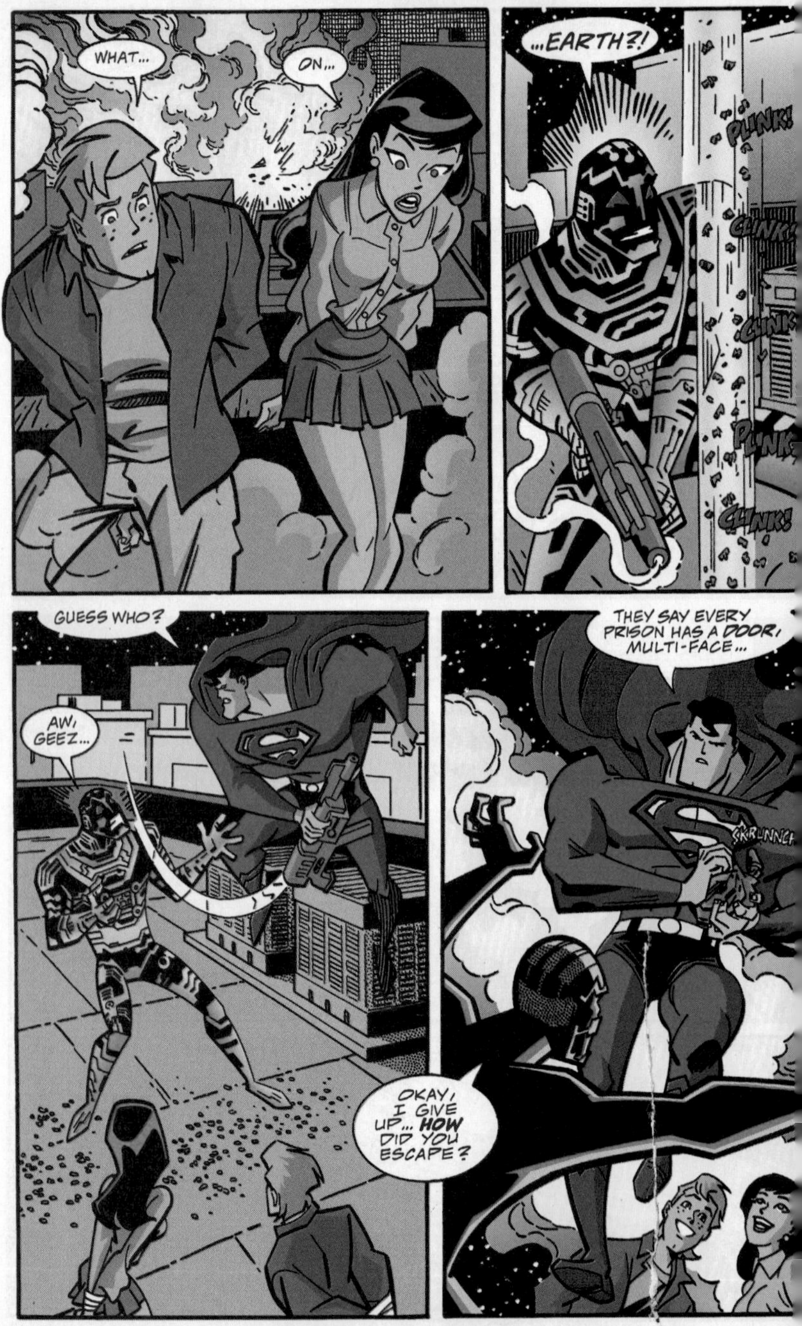
WHAT...
ON...
...EARTH?!
PLINK!
CLINK!
CLINK!
PLINK!
CLINK!
GUESS WHO?
AW, GEEZ...
THEY SAY EVERY PRISON HAS A DOOR, MULTI-FACE...
SKRUNNCH
OKAY, I GIVE UP... HOW DID YOU ESCAPE?

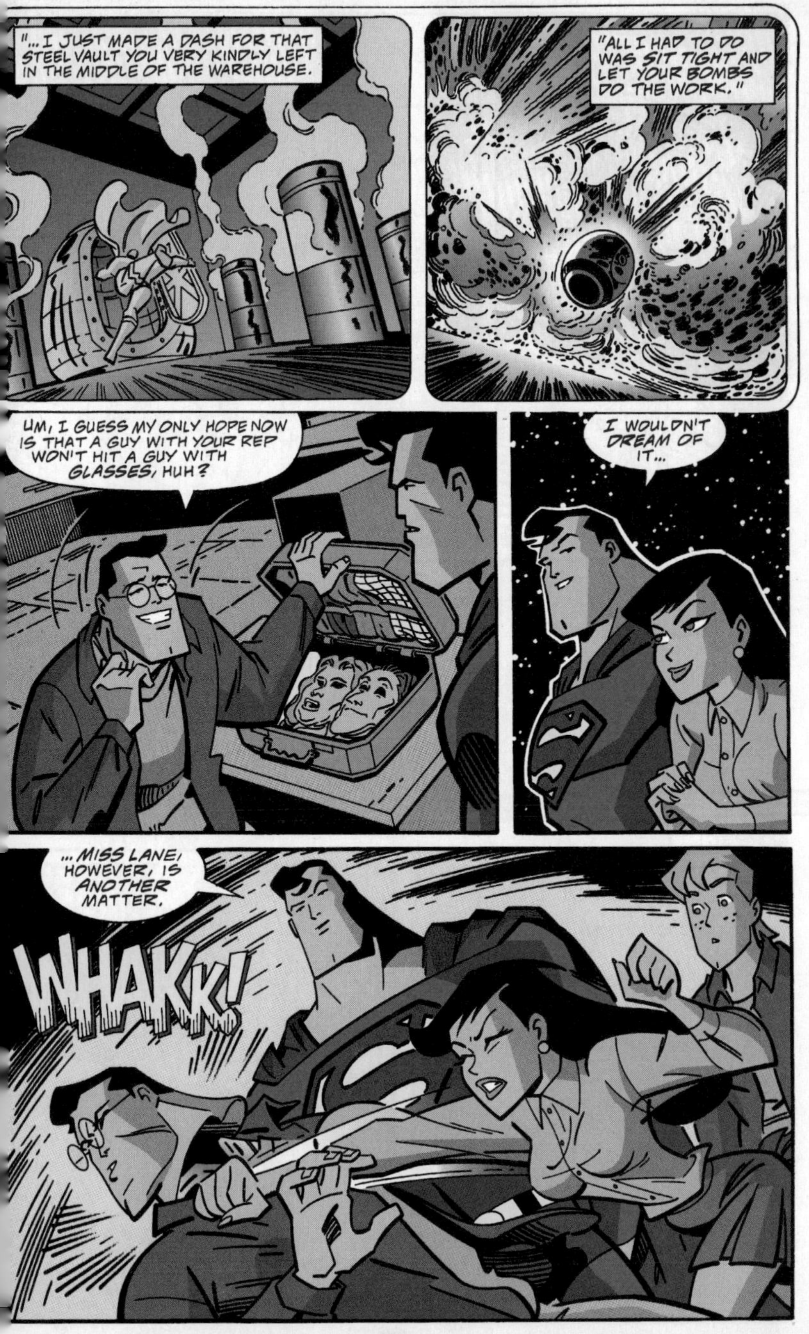
"...I JUST MADE A DASH FOR THAT STEEL VAULT YOU VERY KINDLY LEFT IN THE MIDDLE OF THE WAREHOUSE.
"ALL I HAD TO DO WAS SIT TIGHT AND LET YOUR BOMBS DO THE WORK."
UM, I GUESS MY ONLY HOPE NOW IS THAT A GUY WITH YOUR REP WON'T HIT A GUY WITH GLASSES, HUH?
I WOULDN'T DREAM OF IT...
...MISS LANE, HOWEVER, IS ANOTHER MATTER.
WHAKK!

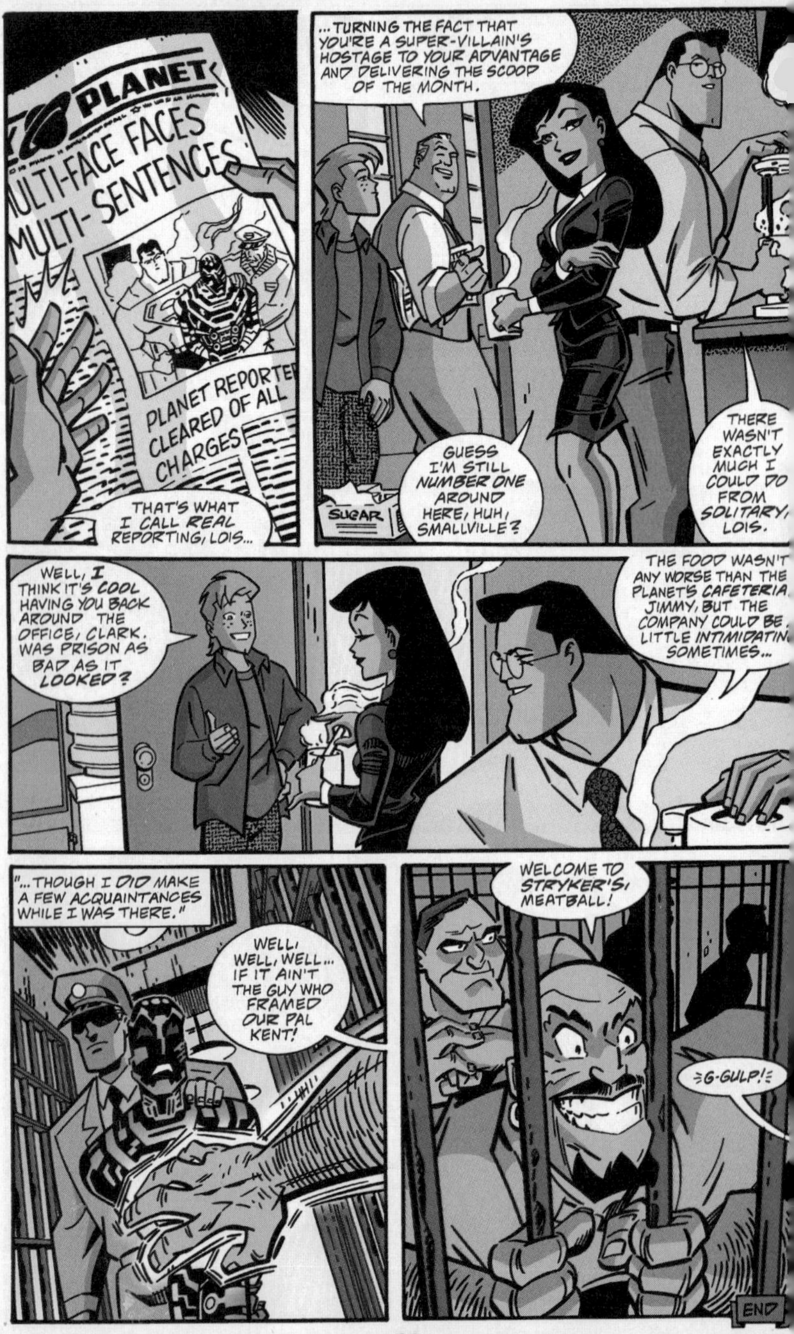
PLANET
ULTI-FACE FACES
ULTI- SENTENCES
PLANET REPORTE
CLEARED OF ALL
CHARGES
THAT'S WHAT I CALL REAL REPORTING, LOIS...
...TURNING THE FACT THAT YOU'RE A SUPER-VILLAIN'S HOSTAGE TO YOUR ADVANTAGE AND DELIVERING THE SCOOP OF THE MONTH.
GUESS I'M STILL NUMBER ONE AROUND HERE, HUH, SMALLVILLE?
SUGAR
THERE WASN'T EXACTLY MUCH I COULD DO FROM SOLITARY, LOIS.
WELL, I THINK IT'S COOL HAVING YOU BACK AROUND THE OFFICE, CLARK. WAS PRISON AS BAD AS IT LOOKED?
THE FOOD WASN'T ANY WORSE THAN THE PLANET'S CAFETERIA, JIMMY, BUT THE COMPANY COULD BE LITTLE INTIMIDATIN SOMETIMES...
"...THOUGH I DID MAKE A FEW ACQUAINTANCES WHILE I WAS THERE."
WELL, WELL, WELL... IF IT AIN'T THE GUY WHO FRAMED OUR PAL KENT!
WELCOME TO STRYKER'S, MEATBALL!
G-GULP!
END

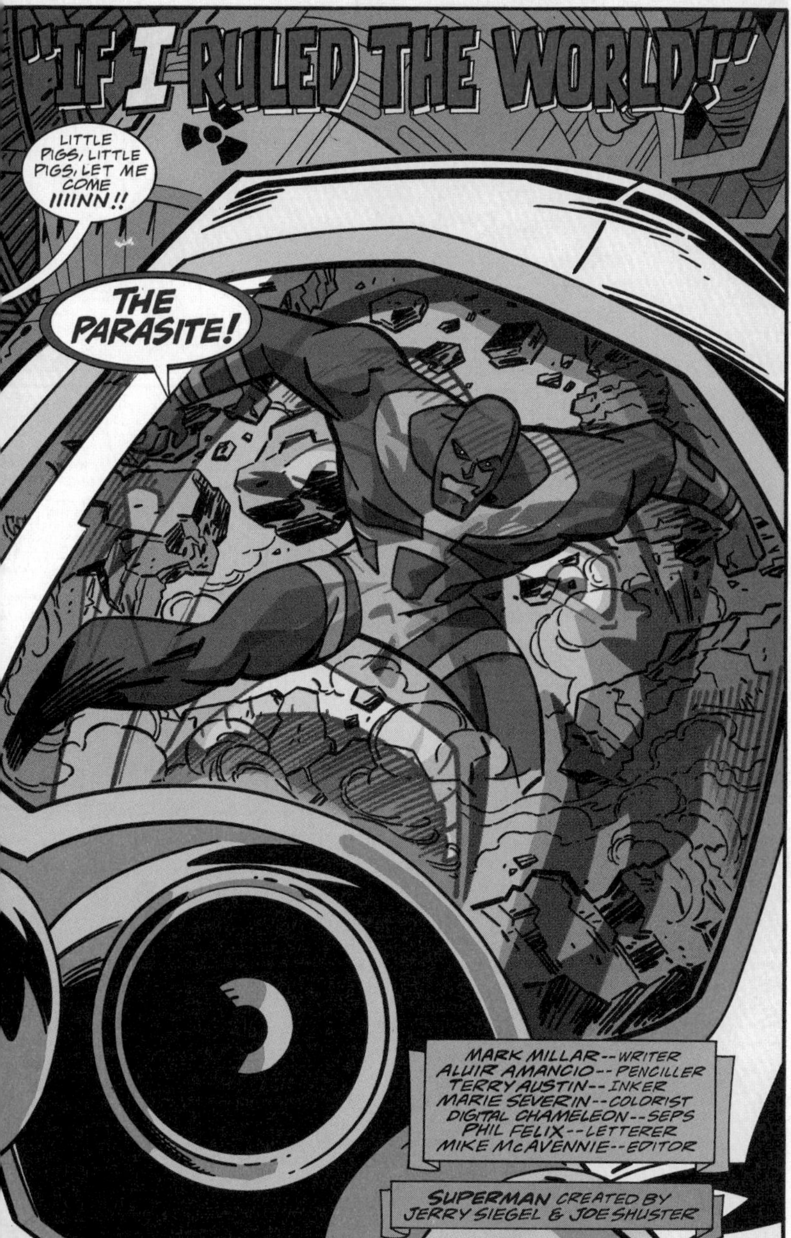
"IF I RULED THE WORLD!"
LITTLE PIGS, LITTLE PIGS, LET ME COME IIIINN!!
THE PARASITE!
MARK MILLAR--WRITER
ALUIR AMANCIO--PENCILLER
TERRY AUSTIN--INKER
MARIE SEVERIN--COLORIST
DIGITAL CHAMELEON--SEPS
PHIL FELIX--LETTERER
MIKE McAVENNIE--EDITOR
SUPERMAN CREATED BY JERRY SIEGEL & JOE SHUSTER

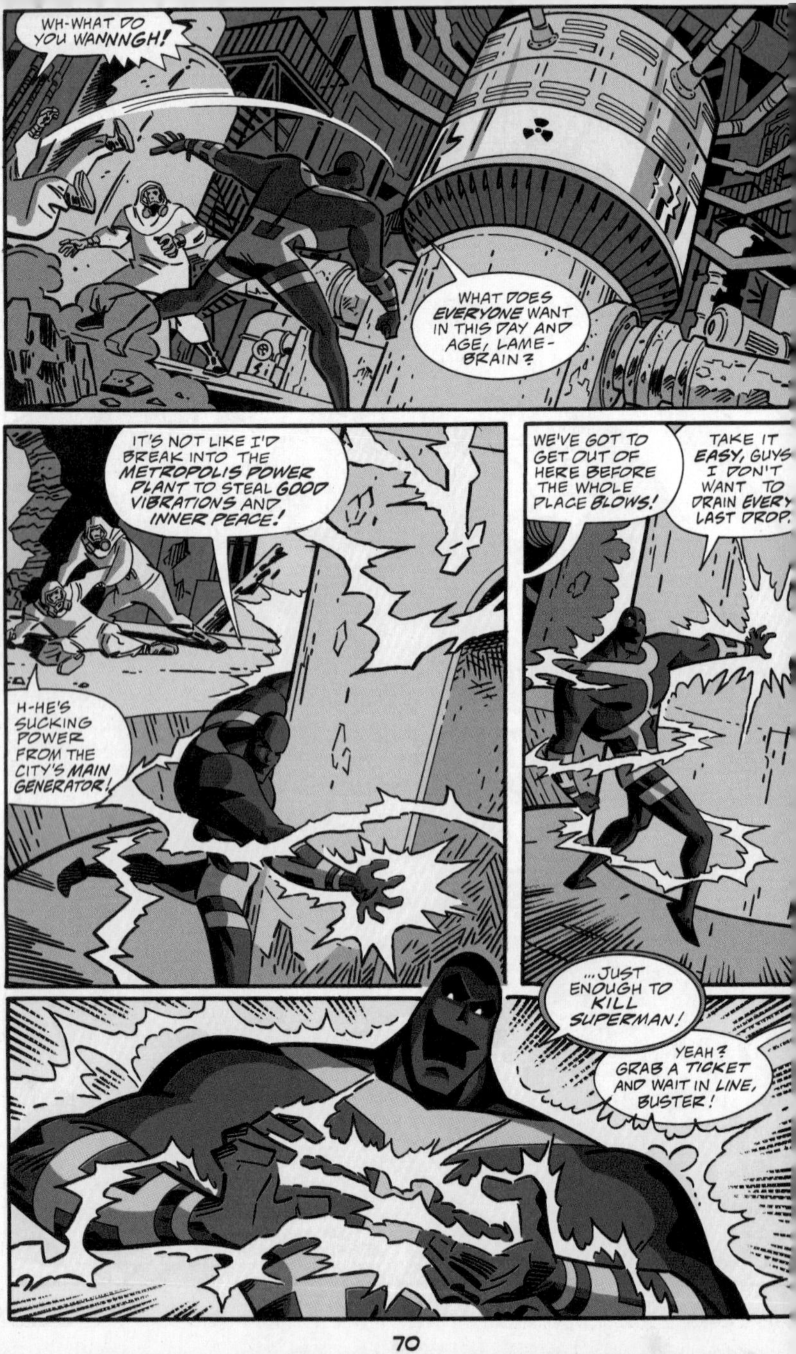

WH-WHAT DO YOU WANNNGH!
WHAT DOES EVERYONE WANT IN THIS DAY AND AGE, LAME-BRAIN?
IT'S NOT LIKE I'D BREAK INTO THE METROPOLIS POWER PLANT TO STEAL GOOD VIBRATIONS AND INNER PEACE!
H-HE'S SUCKING POWER FROM THE CITY'S MAIN GENERATOR!
WE'VE GOT TO GET OUT OF HERE BEFORE THE WHOLE PLACE BLOWS!
TAKE IT EASY, GUYS I DON'T WANT TO DRAIN EVERY LAST DROP.
...JUST ENOUGH TO KILL SUPERMAN!
YEAH? GRAB A TICKET AND WAIT IN LINE, BUSTER!

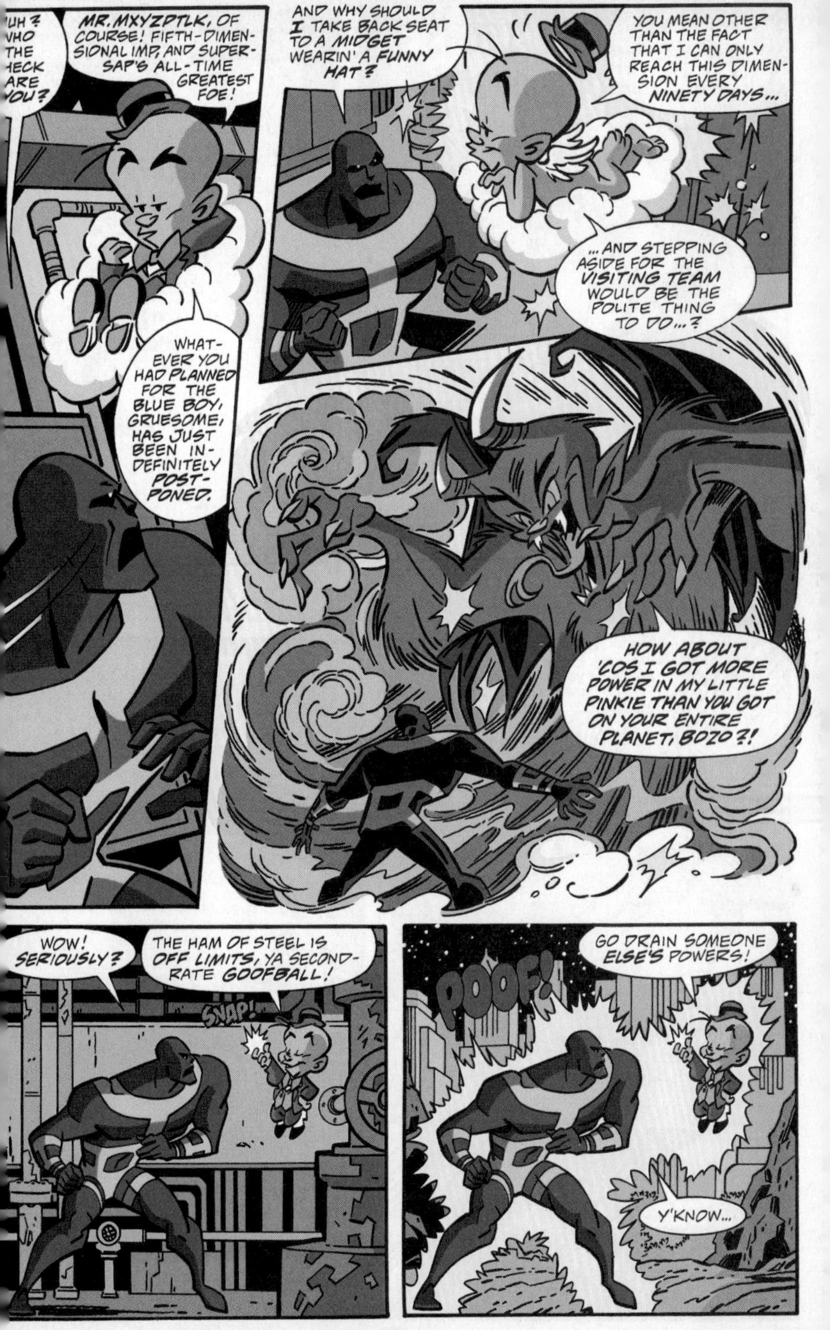
UH? WHO THE HECK ARE YOU?
MR. MXYZPTLK, OF COURSE! FIFTH-DIMENSIONAL IMP, AND SUPER-SAP'S ALL-TIME GREATEST FOE!
AND WHY SHOULD I TAKE BACK SEAT TO A MIDGET WEARIN' A FUNNY HAT?
YOU MEAN OTHER THAN THE FACT THAT I CAN ONLY REACH THIS DIMENSION EVERY NINETY DAYS...
...AND STEPPING ASIDE FOR THE VISITING TEAM WOULD BE THE POLITE THING TO DO...?
WHATEVER YOU HAD PLANNED FOR THE BLUE BOY, GRUESOME, HAS JUST BEEN INDEFINITELY POSTPONED.
HOW ABOUT 'COS I GOT MORE POWER IN MY LITTLE PINKIE THAN YOU GOT ON YOUR ENTIRE PLANET, BOZO?!
WOW! SERIOUSLY?
THE HAM OF STEEL IS OFF LIMITS, YA SECOND-RATE GOOFBALL!
SNAP!
GO DRAIN SOMEONE ELSE'S POWERS!
POOF!
Y'KNOW...

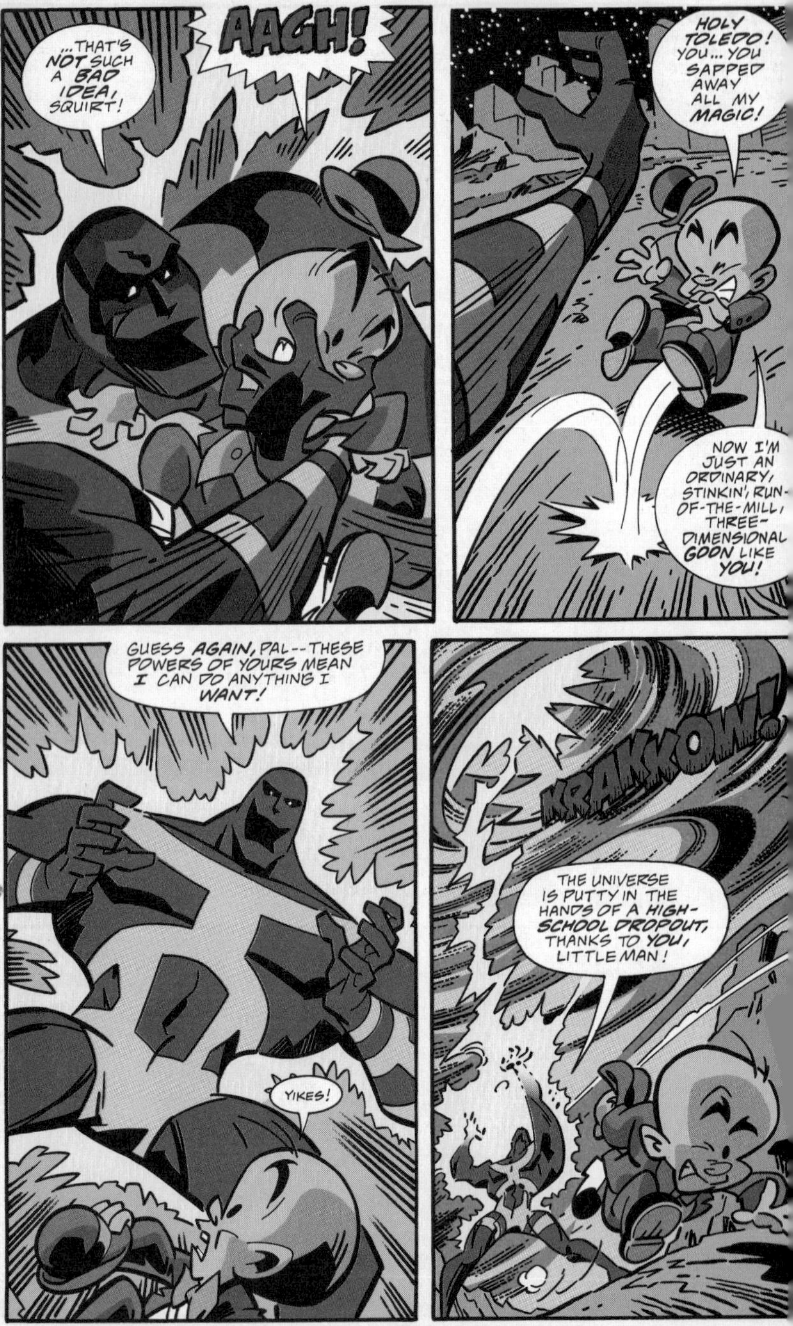
...THAT'S NOT SUCH A BAD IDEA, SQUIRT!
AAGH!
HOLY TOLEDO! YOU... YOU SAPPED AWAY ALL MY MAGIC!
NOW I'M JUST AN ORDINARY, STINKIN', RUN-OF-THE-MILL, THREE-DIMENSIONAL GOON LIKE YOU!
GUESS AGAIN, PAL--THESE POWERS OF YOURS MEAN I CAN DO ANYTHING I WANT!
YIKES!
KRAKKOW!
THE UNIVERSE IS PUTTY IN THE HANDS OF A HIGH-SCHOOL DROPOUT, THANKS TO YOU, LITTLE MAN!

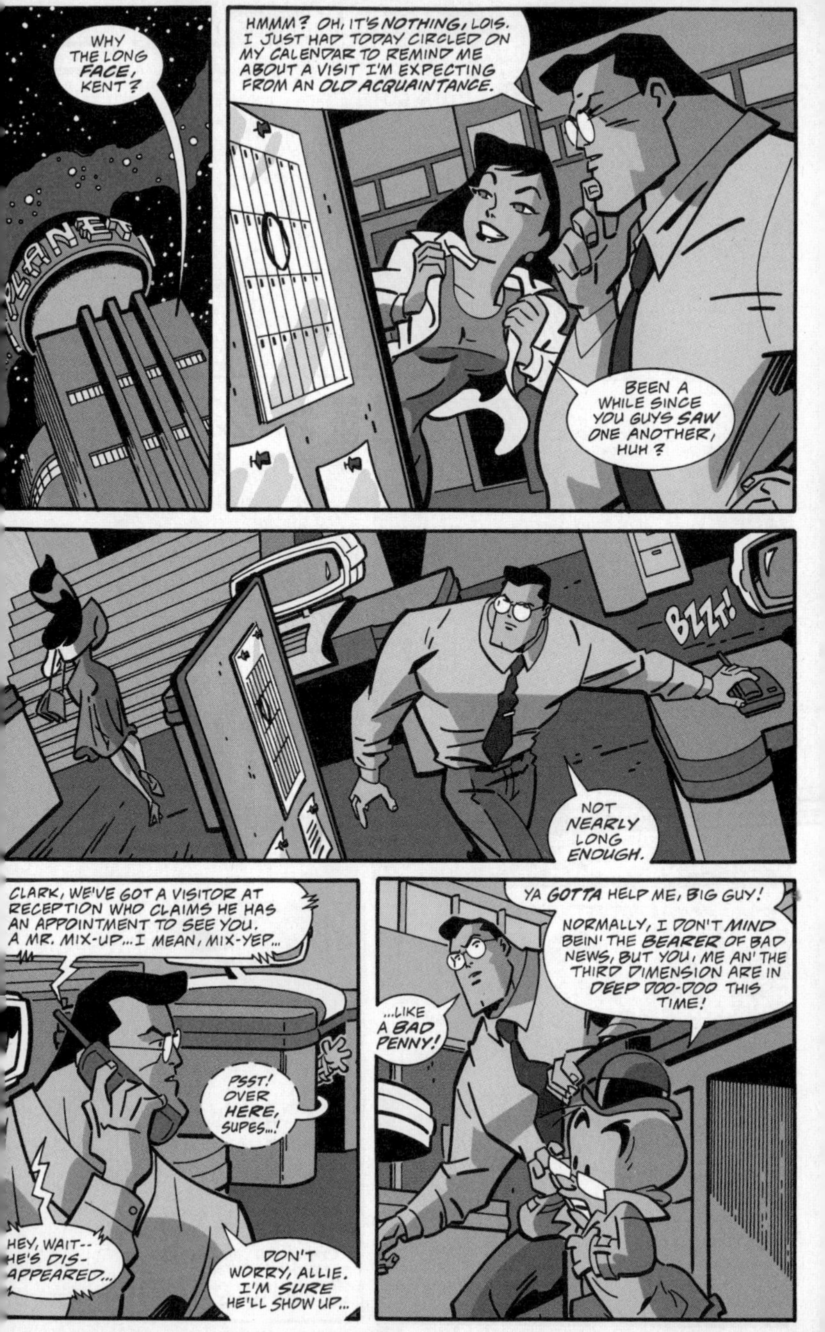

PLANET
WHY THE LONG FACE, KENT?
HMMM? OH, IT'S NOTHING, LOIS. I JUST HAD TODAY CIRCLED ON MY CALENDAR TO REMIND ME ABOUT A VISIT I'M EXPECTING FROM AN OLD ACQUAINTANCE.
BEEN A WHILE SINCE YOU GUYS SAW ONE ANOTHER, HUH?
BZZT!
NOT NEARLY LONG ENOUGH.
CLARK, WE'VE GOT A VISITOR AT RECEPTION WHO CLAIMS HE HAS AN APPOINTMENT TO SEE YOU. A MR. MIX-UP...I MEAN, MIX-YEP...
PSST! OVER HERE, SUPES...!
HEY, WAIT-- HE'S DIS-APPEARED...
DON'T WORRY, ALLIE. I'M SURE HE'LL SHOW UP...
...LIKE A BAD PENNY!
YA GOTTA HELP ME, BIG GUY!
NORMALLY, I DON'T MIND BEIN' THE BEARER OF BAD NEWS, BUT YOU, ME AN' THE THIRD DIMENSION ARE IN DEEP DOO-DOO THIS TIME!

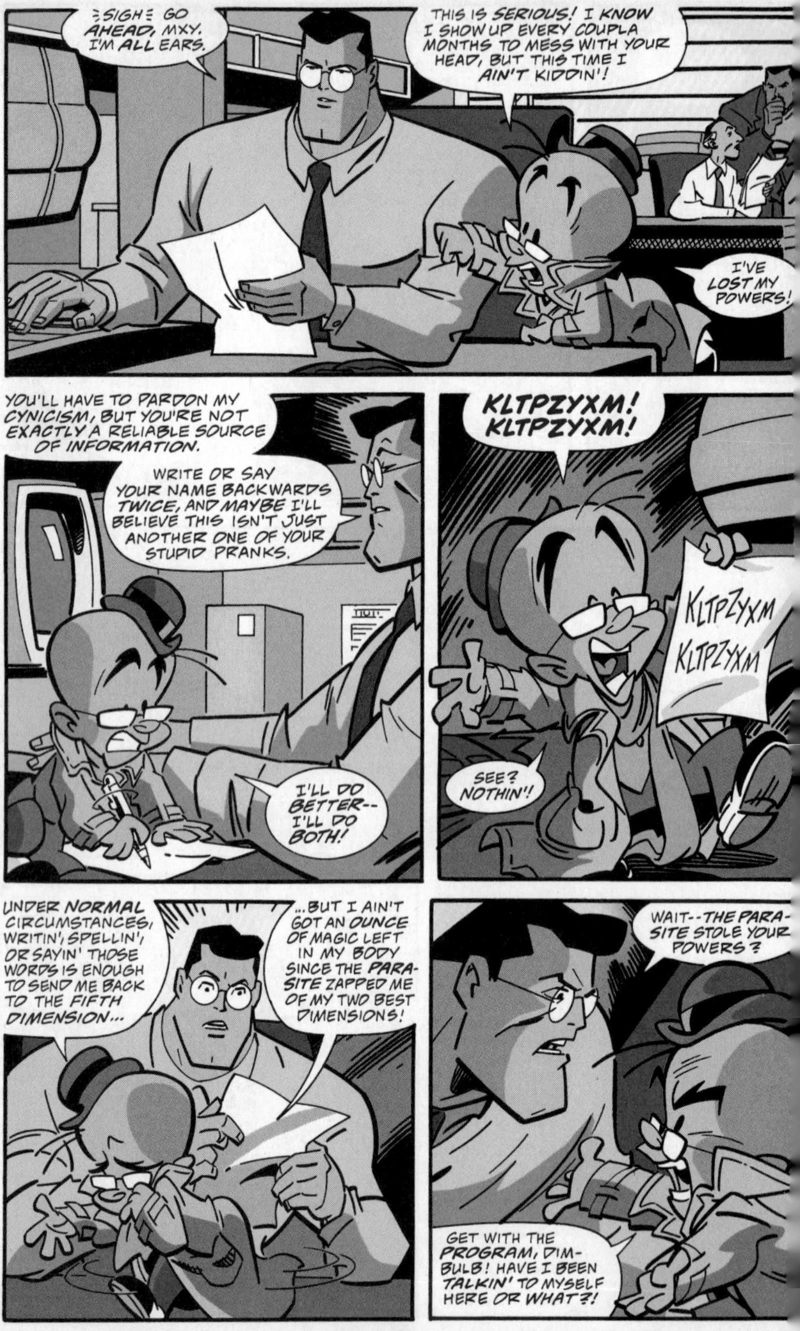

:SIGH: GO AHEAD, MXY. I'M ALL EARS.
THIS IS SERIOUS! I KNOW I SHOW UP EVERY COUPLA MONTHS TO MESS WITH YOUR HEAD, BUT THIS TIME I AIN'T KIDDIN'!
I'VE LOST MY POWERS!
YOU'LL HAVE TO PARDON MY CYNICISM, BUT YOU'RE NOT EXACTLY A RELIABLE SOURCE OF INFORMATION.
WRITE OR SAY YOUR NAME BACKWARDS TWICE, AND MAYBE I'LL BELIEVE THIS ISN'T JUST ANOTHER ONE OF YOUR STUPID PRANKS.
I'LL DO BETTER-- I'LL DO BOTH!
KLTPZYXM! KLTPZYXM!
KLTPZYXM
KLTPZYXM
SEE? NOTHIN'!
UNDER NORMAL CIRCUMSTANCES, WRITIN', SPELLIN', OR SAYIN' THOSE WORDS IS ENOUGH TO SEND ME BACK TO THE FIFTH DIMENSION...
...BUT I AIN'T GOT AN OUNCE OF MAGIC LEFT IN MY BODY SINCE THE PARASITE ZAPPED ME OF MY TWO BEST DIMENSIONS!
WAIT--THE PARASITE STOLE YOUR POWERS?
GET WITH THE PROGRAM, DIMBULB! HAVE I BEEN TALKIN' TO MYSELF HERE OR WHAT?!

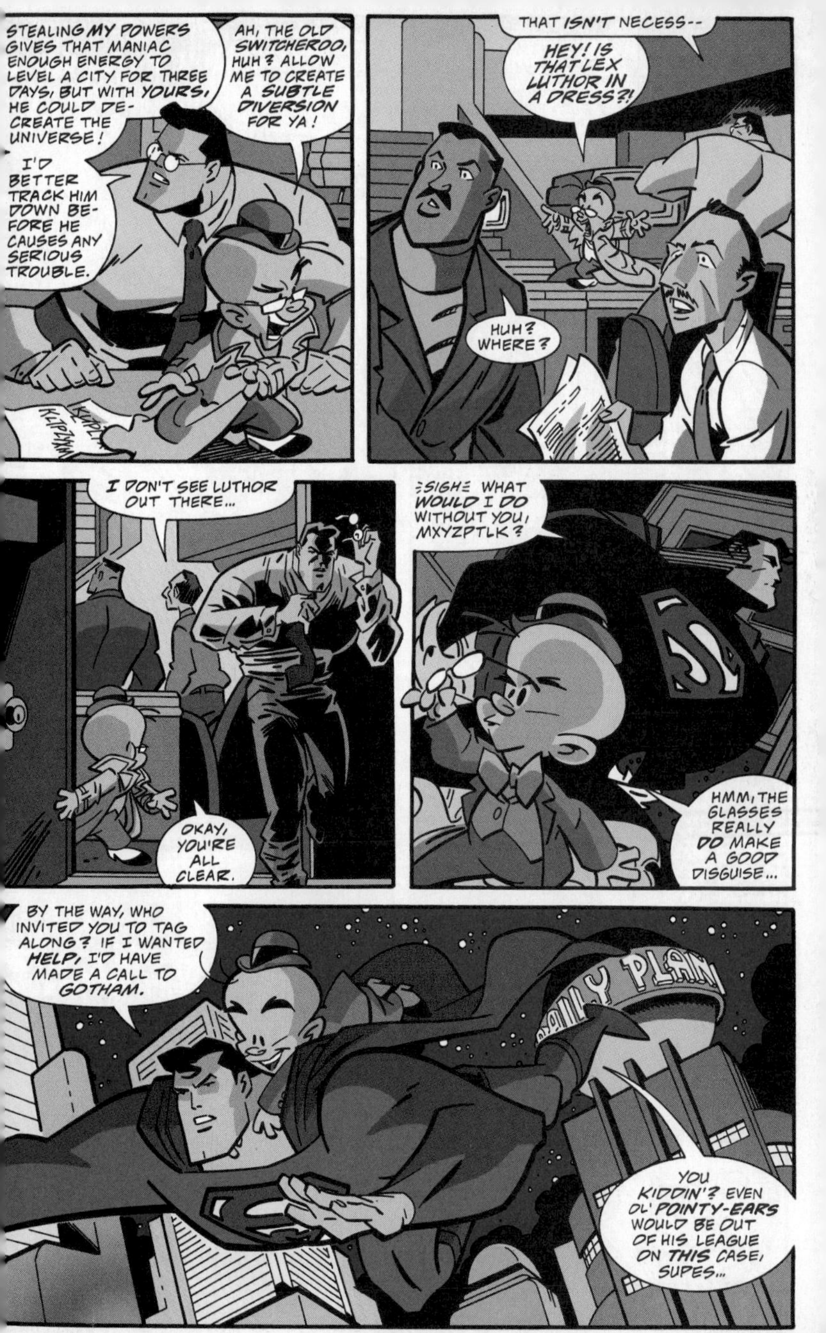
STEALING MY POWERS GIVES THAT MANIAC ENOUGH ENERGY TO LEVEL A CITY FOR THREE DAYS, BUT WITH YOURS, HE COULD DE-CREATE THE UNIVERSE!
I'D BETTER TRACK HIM DOWN BE-FORE HE CAUSES ANY SERIOUS TROUBLE.
AH, THE OLD SWITCHEROO, HUH? ALLOW ME TO CREATE A SUBTLE DIVERSION FOR YA!
THAT ISN'T NECESS--
HEY! IS THAT LEX LUTHOR IN A DRESS?!
HUH? WHERE?
I DON'T SEE LUTHOR OUT THERE...
OKAY, YOU'RE ALL CLEAR.
=SIGH= WHAT WOULD I DO WITHOUT YOU, MXYZPTLK?
HMM, THE GLASSES REALLY DO MAKE A GOOD DISGUISE...
BY THE WAY, WHO INVITED YOU TO TAG ALONG? IF I WANTED HELP, I'D HAVE MADE A CALL TO GOTHAM.
YOU KIDDIN'? EVEN OL' POINTY-EARS WOULD BE OUT OF HIS LEAGUE ON THIS CASE, SUPES...

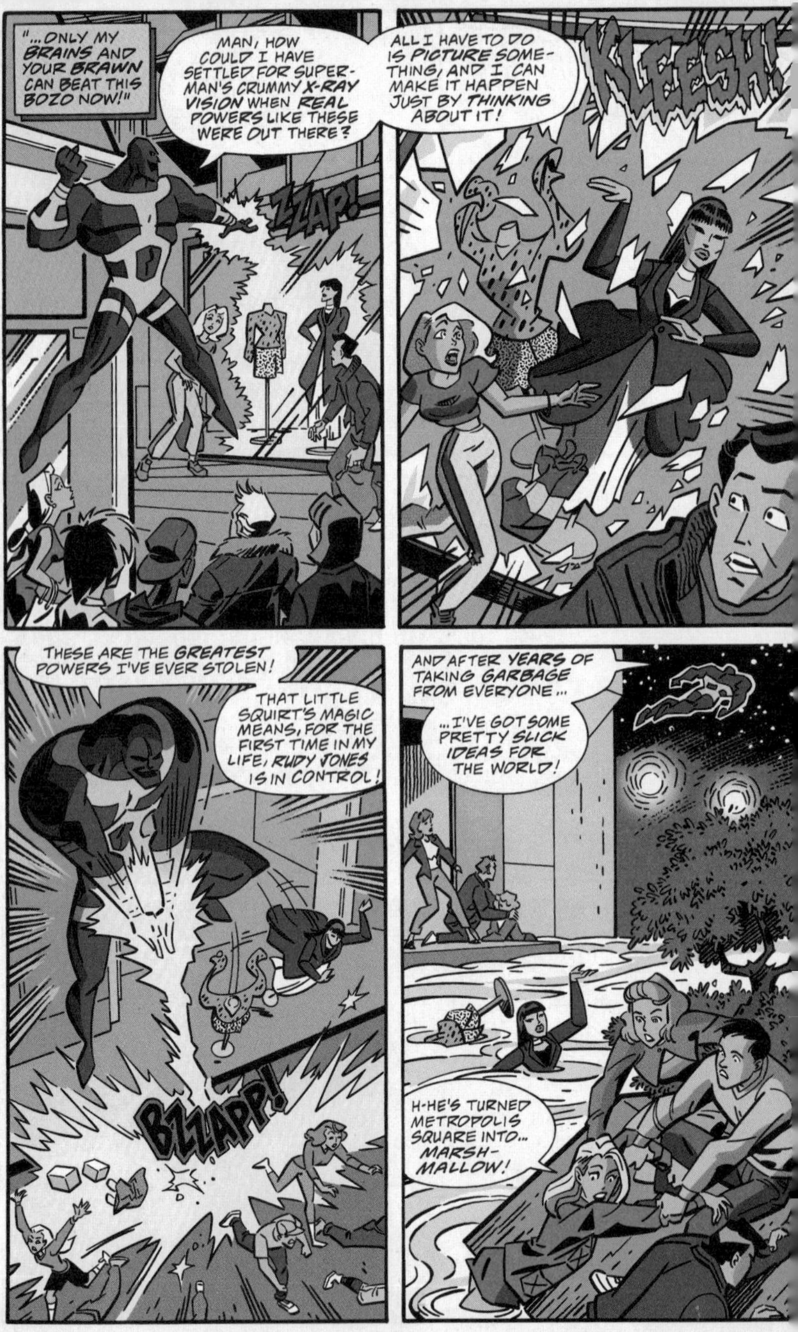
"...ONLY MY BRAINS AND YOUR BRAWN CAN BEAT THIS BOZO NOW!"
MAN, HOW COULD I HAVE SETTLED FOR SUPER-MAN'S CRUMMY X-RAY VISION WHEN REAL POWERS LIKE THESE WERE OUT THERE?
ZZAP!
ALL I HAVE TO DO IS PICTURE SOME-THING, AND I CAN MAKE IT HAPPEN JUST BY THINKING ABOUT IT!
KLEESH!
THESE ARE THE GREATEST POWERS I'VE EVER STOLEN!
THAT LITTLE SQUIRT'S MAGIC MEANS, FOR THE FIRST TIME IN MY LIFE, RUDY JONES IS IN CONTROL!
BZZAPP!
AND AFTER YEARS OF TAKING GARBAGE FROM EVERYONE...
...I'VE GOT SOME PRETTY SLICK IDEAS FOR THE WORLD!
H-HE'S TURNED METROPOLIS SQUARE INTO... MARSH-MALLOW!

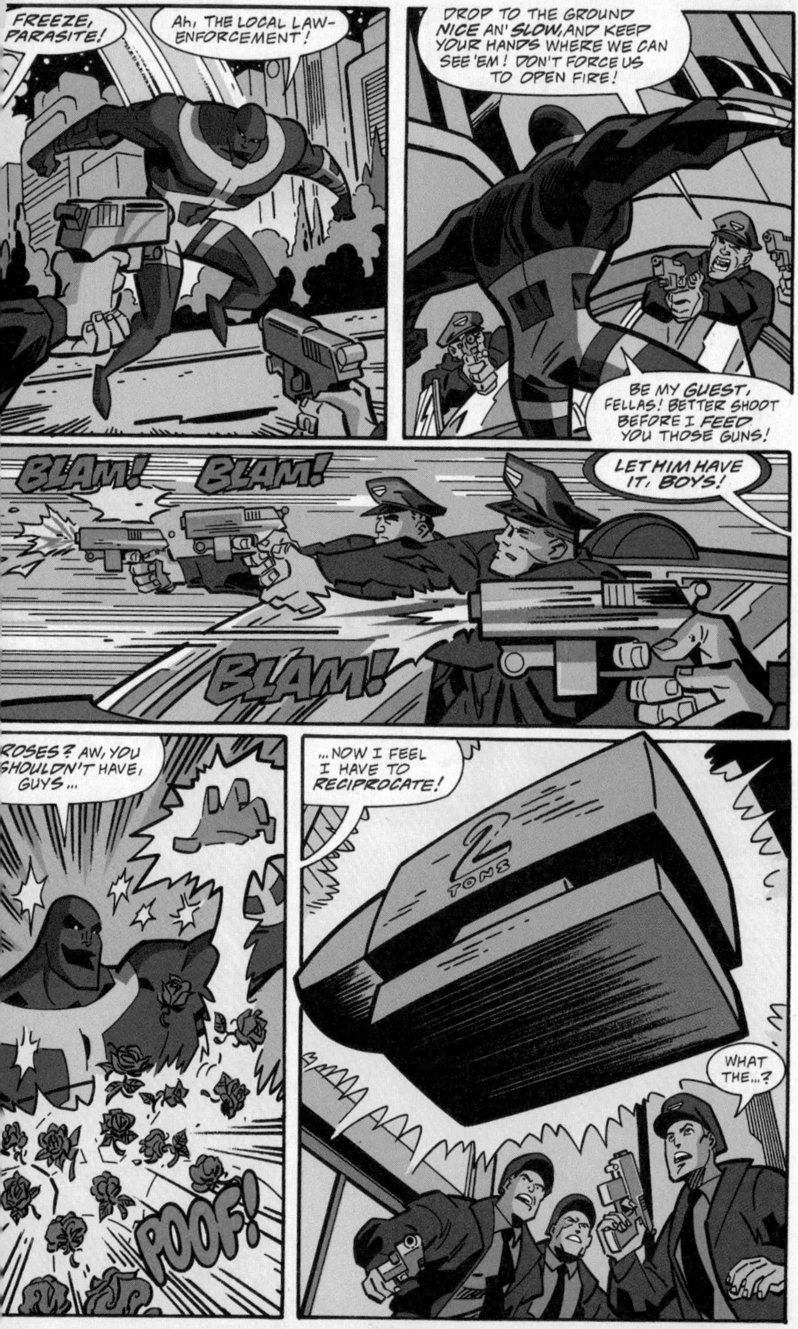

FREEZE, PARASITE!
Ah, THE LOCAL LAW-ENFORCEMENT!
DROP TO THE GROUND NICE AN' SLOW, AND KEEP YOUR HANDS WHERE WE CAN SEE 'EM! DON'T FORCE US TO OPEN FIRE!
BE MY GUEST, FELLAS! BETTER SHOOT BEFORE I FEED YOU THOSE GUNS!
BLAM! BLAM!
LET HIM HAVE IT, BOYS!
BLAM!
ROSES? AW, YOU SHOULDN'T HAVE, GUYS...
POOF!
...NOW I FEEL I HAVE TO RECIPROCATE!
2 TONE
WHAT THE...?

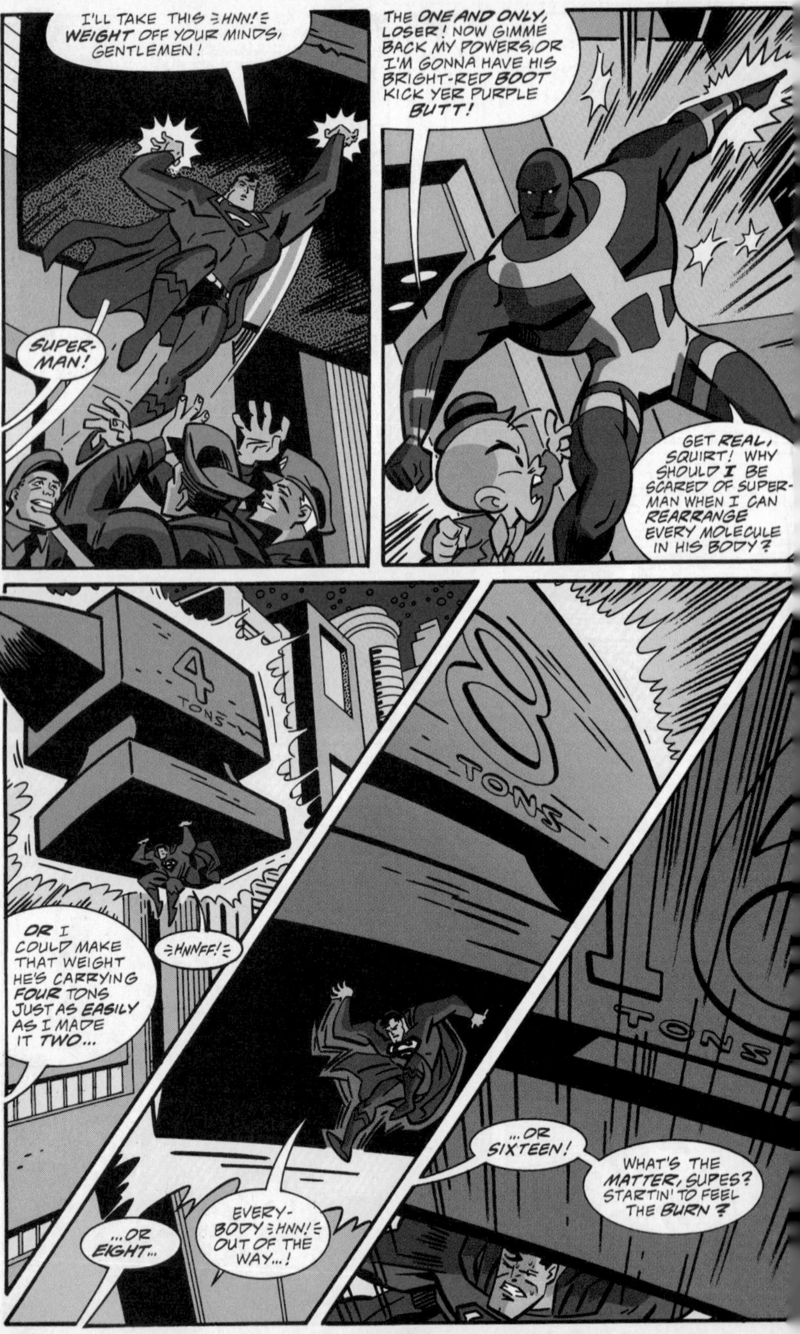
I'LL TAKE THIS HNN! WEIGHT OFF YOUR MINDS, GENTLEMEN!
SUPER-MAN!
THE ONE AND ONLY, LOSER! NOW GIMME BACK MY POWERS, OR I'M GONNA HAVE HIS BRIGHT-RED BOOT KICK YER PURPLE BUTT!
GET REAL, SQUIRT! WHY SHOULD I BE SCARED OF SUPER-MAN WHEN I CAN REARRANGE EVERY MOLECULE IN HIS BODY?
4 TONS
OR I COULD MAKE THAT WEIGHT HE'S CARRYING FOUR TONS JUST AS EASILY AS I MADE IT TWO...
HNNFF!
8 TONS
...OR EIGHT...
EVERY-BODY HNN! OUT OF THE WAY...!
16 TONS
...OR SIXTEEN!
WHAT'S THE MATTER, SUPES? STARTIN' TO FEEL THE BURN?

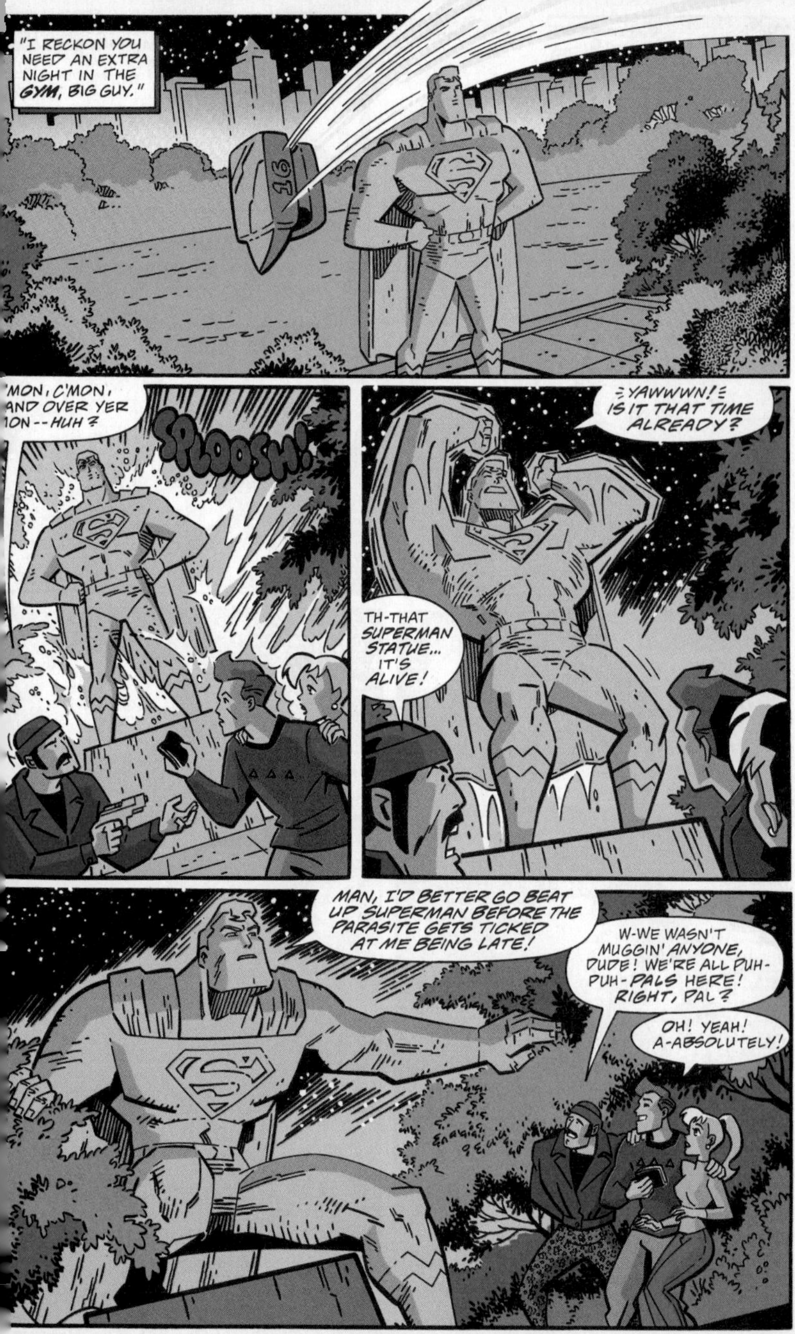
"I RECKON YOU NEED AN EXTRA NIGHT IN THE GYM, BIG GUY."
16
'MON, C'MON, AND OVER YER MON--HUH?
SPLOOSH!
YAWWWN! IS IT THAT TIME ALREADY?
TH-THAT SUPERMAN STATUE... IT'S ALIVE!
MAN, I'D BETTER GO BEAT UP SUPERMAN BEFORE THE PARASITE GETS TICKED AT ME BEING LATE!
W-WE WASN'T MUGGIN' ANYONE, DUDE! WE'RE ALL PUH-PUH-PALS HERE! RIGHT, PAL?
OH! YEAH! A-ABSOLUTELY!

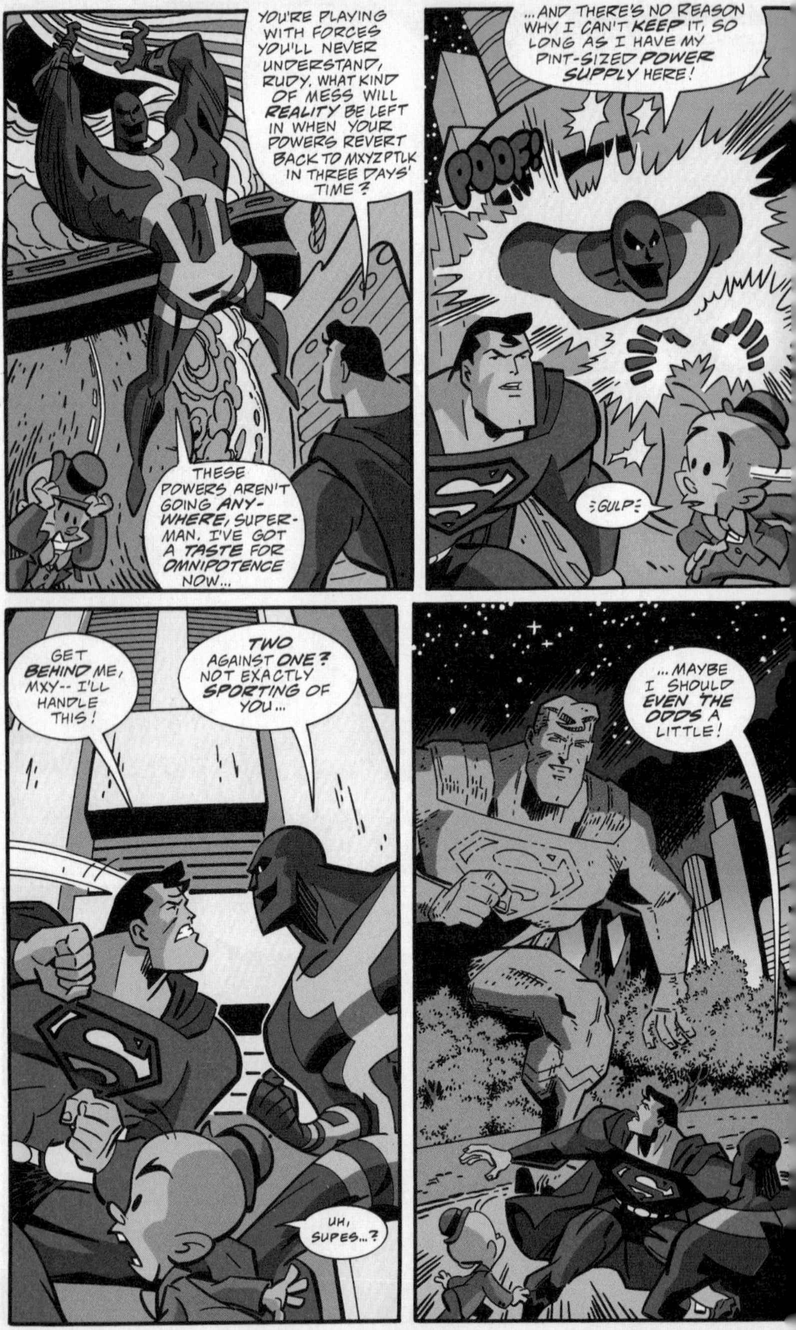
YOU'RE PLAYING WITH FORCES YOU'LL NEVER UNDERSTAND, RUDY. WHAT KIND OF MESS WILL REALITY BE LEFT IN WHEN YOUR POWERS REVERT BACK TO MXYZPTLK IN THREE DAYS' TIME?
THESE POWERS AREN'T GOING ANYWHERE, SUPERMAN. I'VE GOT A TASTE FOR OMNIPOTENCE NOW...
...AND THERE'S NO REASON WHY I CAN'T KEEP IT, SO LONG AS I HAVE MY PINT-SIZED POWER SUPPLY HERE!
POOF!
GULP
GET BEHIND ME, MXY-- I'LL HANDLE THIS!
TWO AGAINST ONE? NOT EXACTLY SPORTING OF YOU...
UH, SUPES...?
...MAYBE I SHOULD EVEN THE ODDS A LITTLE!

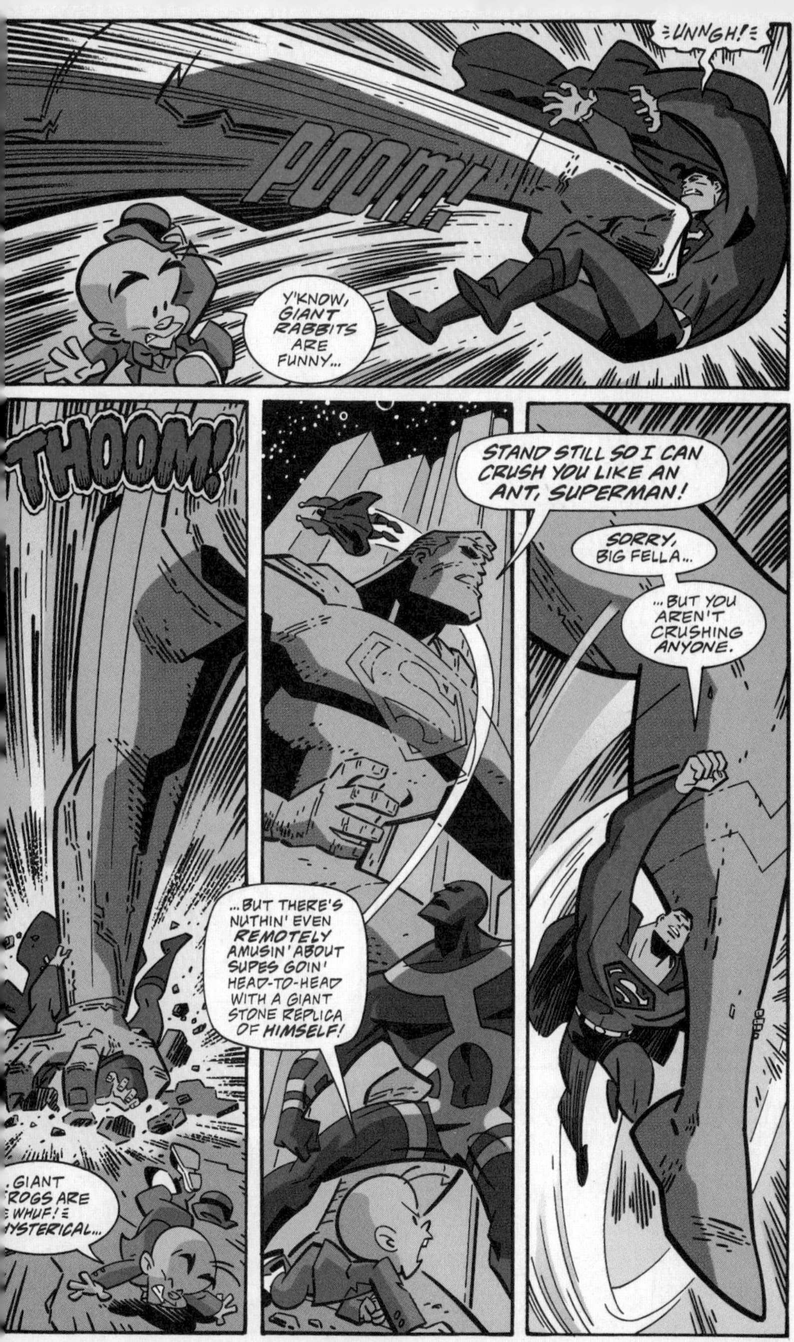
UNNGH!
POOM!
Y'KNOW, GIANT RABBITS ARE FUNNY...
THOOM!
GIANT FROGS ARE WHUF! HYSTERICAL...
STAND STILL SO I CAN CRUSH YOU LIKE AN ANT, SUPERMAN!
...BUT THERE'S NUTHIN' EVEN REMOTELY AMUSIN' ABOUT SUPES GOIN' HEAD-TO-HEAD WITH A GIANT STONE REPLICA OF HIMSELF!
SORRY, BIG FELLA...
...BUT YOU AREN'T CRUSHING ANYONE.

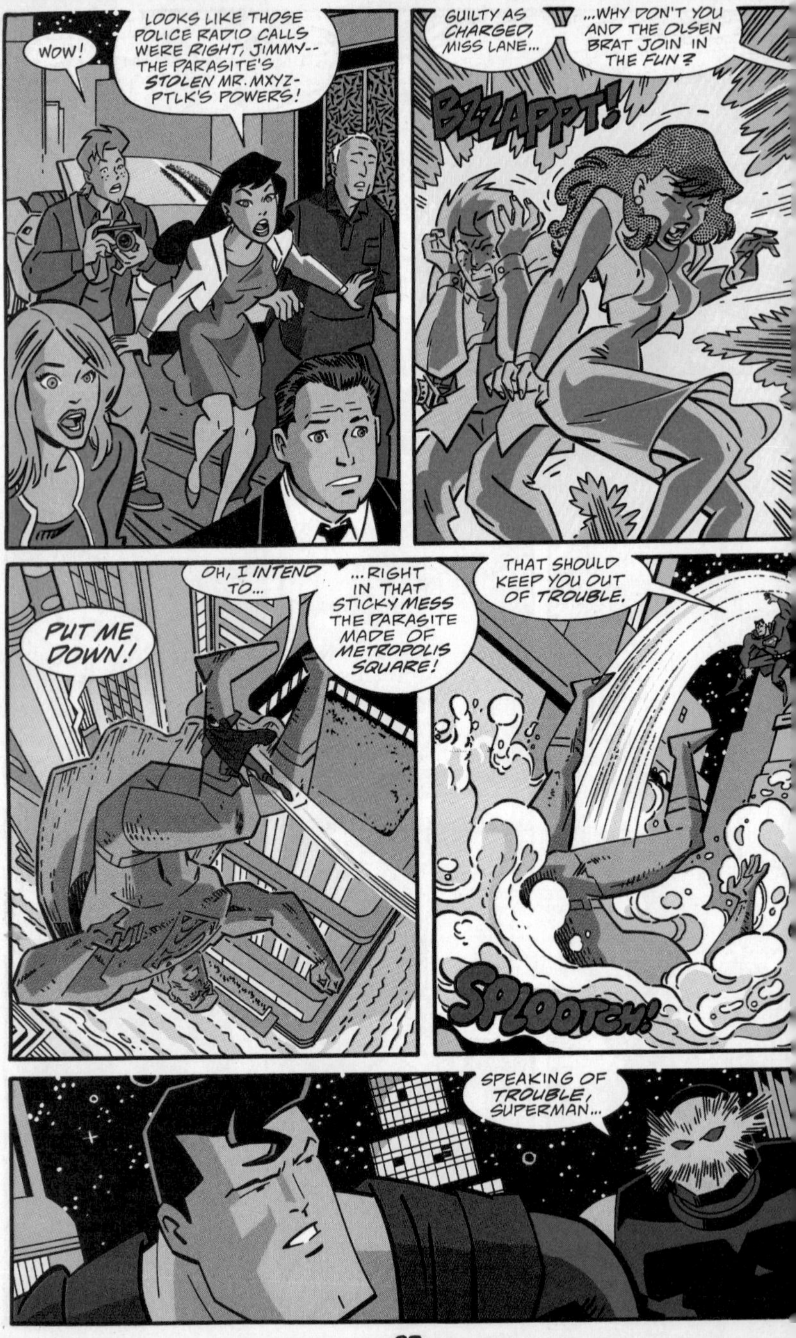
WOW!
LOOKS LIKE THOSE POLICE RADIO CALLS WERE RIGHT, JIMMY-- THE PARASITE'S STOLEN MR. MXYZ-PTLK'S POWERS!
GUILTY AS CHARGED, MISS LANE...
...WHY DON'T YOU AND THE OLSEN BRAT JOIN IN THE FUN?
BZZAPPT!
PUT ME DOWN!
OH, I INTEND TO...
...RIGHT IN THAT STICKY MESS THE PARASITE MADE OF METROPOLIS SQUARE!
THAT SHOULD KEEP YOU OUT OF TROUBLE.
SPLOOTCH!
SPEAKING OF TROUBLE, SUPERMAN...

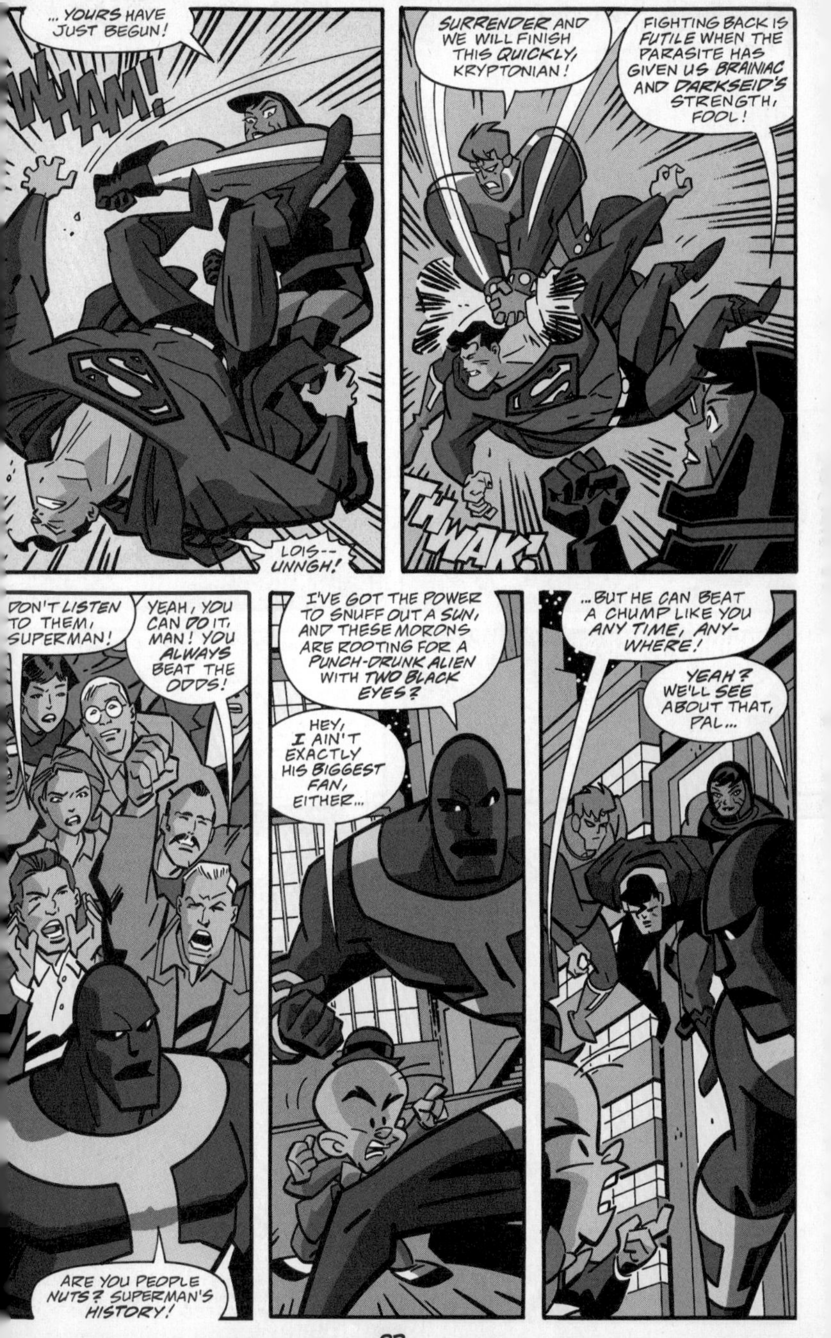
...YOURS HAVE JUST BEGUN!
WHAM!
LOIS-- UNNGH!
SURRENDER AND WE WILL FINISH THIS QUICKLY, KRYPTONIAN!
FIGHTING BACK IS FUTILE WHEN THE PARASITE HAS GIVEN US BRAINIAC AND DARKSEID'S STRENGTH, FOOL!
THWAK!
DON'T LISTEN TO THEM, SUPERMAN!
YEAH, YOU CAN DO IT, MAN! YOU ALWAYS BEAT THE ODDS!
ARE YOU PEOPLE NUTS? SUPERMAN'S HISTORY!
I'VE GOT THE POWER TO SNUFF OUT A SUN, AND THESE MORONS ARE ROOTING FOR A PUNCH-DRUNK ALIEN WITH TWO BLACK EYES?
HEY, I AIN'T EXACTLY HIS BIGGEST FAN, EITHER...
...BUT HE CAN BEAT A CHUMP LIKE YOU ANY TIME, ANY-WHERE!
YEAH? WE'LL SEE ABOUT THAT, PAL...

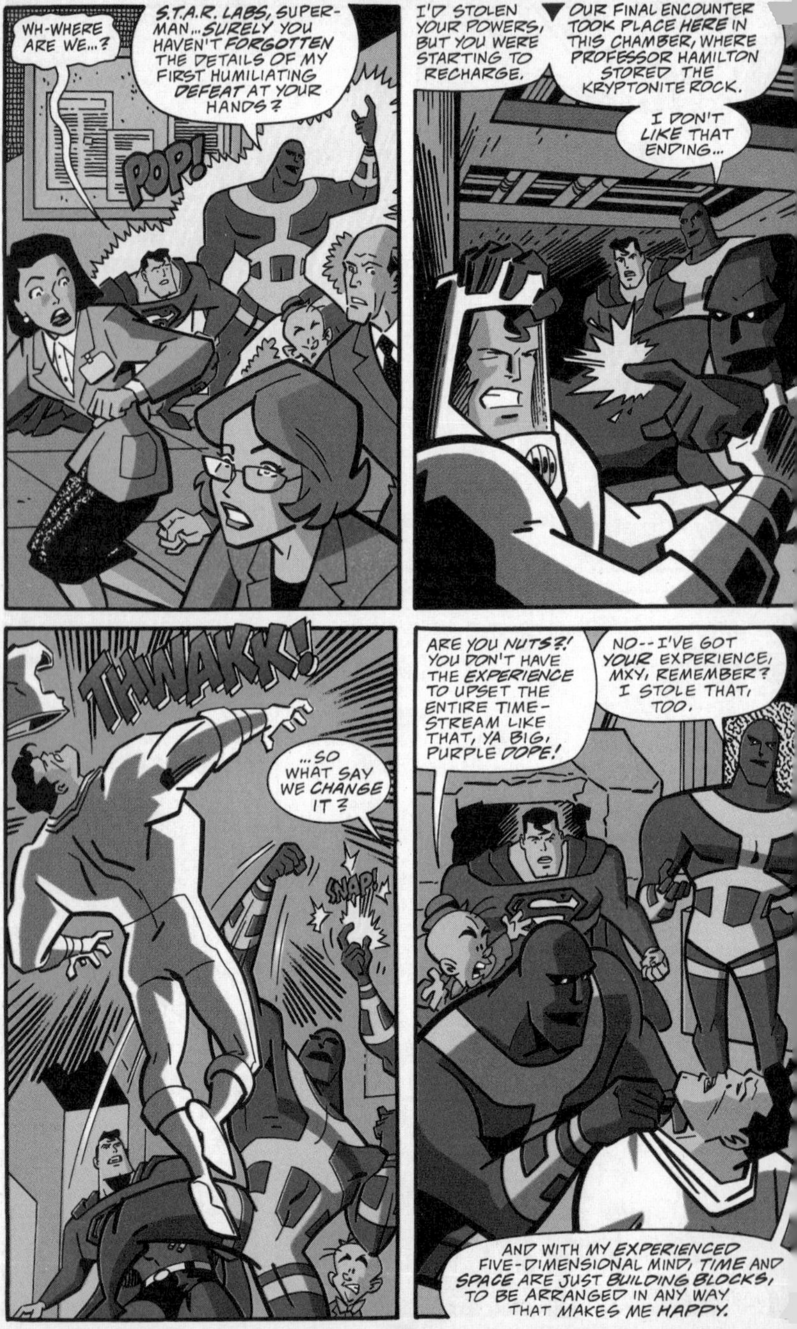
WH-WHERE ARE WE...?
S.T.A.R. LABS, SUPERMAN...SURELY YOU HAVEN'T FORGOTTEN THE DETAILS OF MY FIRST HUMILIATING DEFEAT AT YOUR HANDS?
POP!
I'D STOLEN YOUR POWERS, BUT YOU WERE STARTING TO RECHARGE.
OUR FINAL ENCOUNTER TOOK PLACE HERE IN THIS CHAMBER, WHERE PROFESSOR HAMILTON STORED THE KRYPTONITE ROCK.
I DON'T LIKE THAT ENDING...
THWAKK!
...SO WHAT SAY WE CHANGE IT?
SNAP!
ARE YOU NUTS?! YOU DON'T HAVE THE EXPERIENCE TO UPSET THE ENTIRE TIME-STREAM LIKE THAT, YA BIG, PURPLE DOPE!
NO--I'VE GOT YOUR EXPERIENCE, MXY, REMEMBER? I STOLE THAT, TOO.
AND WITH MY EXPERIENCED FIVE-DIMENSIONAL MIND, TIME AND SPACE ARE JUST BUILDING BLOCKS, TO BE ARRANGED IN ANY WAY THAT MAKES ME HAPPY.

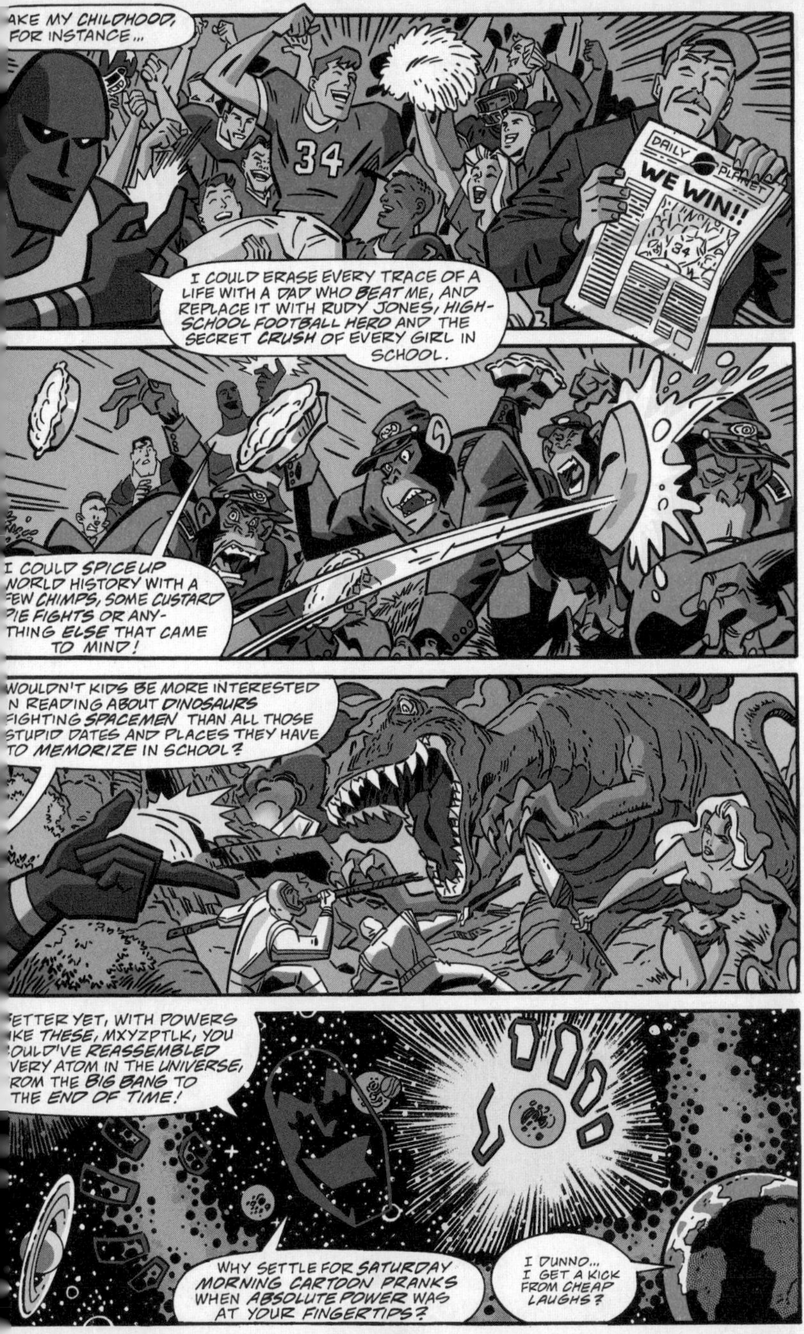
AKE MY CHILDHOOD, FOR INSTANCE...
DAILY PLANET
WE WIN!!
34
I COULD ERASE EVERY TRACE OF A LIFE WITH A DAD WHO BEAT ME, AND REPLACE IT WITH RUDY JONES, HIGH-SCHOOL FOOTBALL HERO AND THE SECRET CRUSH OF EVERY GIRL IN SCHOOL.
I COULD SPICE UP WORLD HISTORY WITH A FEW CHIMPS, SOME CUSTARD PIE FIGHTS OR ANYTHING ELSE THAT CAME TO MIND!
WOULDN'T KIDS BE MORE INTERESTED IN READING ABOUT DINOSAURS FIGHTING SPACEMEN THAN ALL THOSE STUPID DATES AND PLACES THEY HAVE TO MEMORIZE IN SCHOOL?
ETTER YET, WITH POWERS IKE THESE, MXYZPTLK, YOU OULD'VE REASSEMBLED VERY ATOM IN THE UNIVERSE, ROM THE BIG BANG TO THE END OF TIME!
WHY SETTLE FOR SATURDAY MORNING CARTOON PRANKS WHEN ABSOLUTE POWER WAS AT YOUR FINGERTIPS?
I DUNNO... I GET A KICK FROM CHEAP LAUGHS?

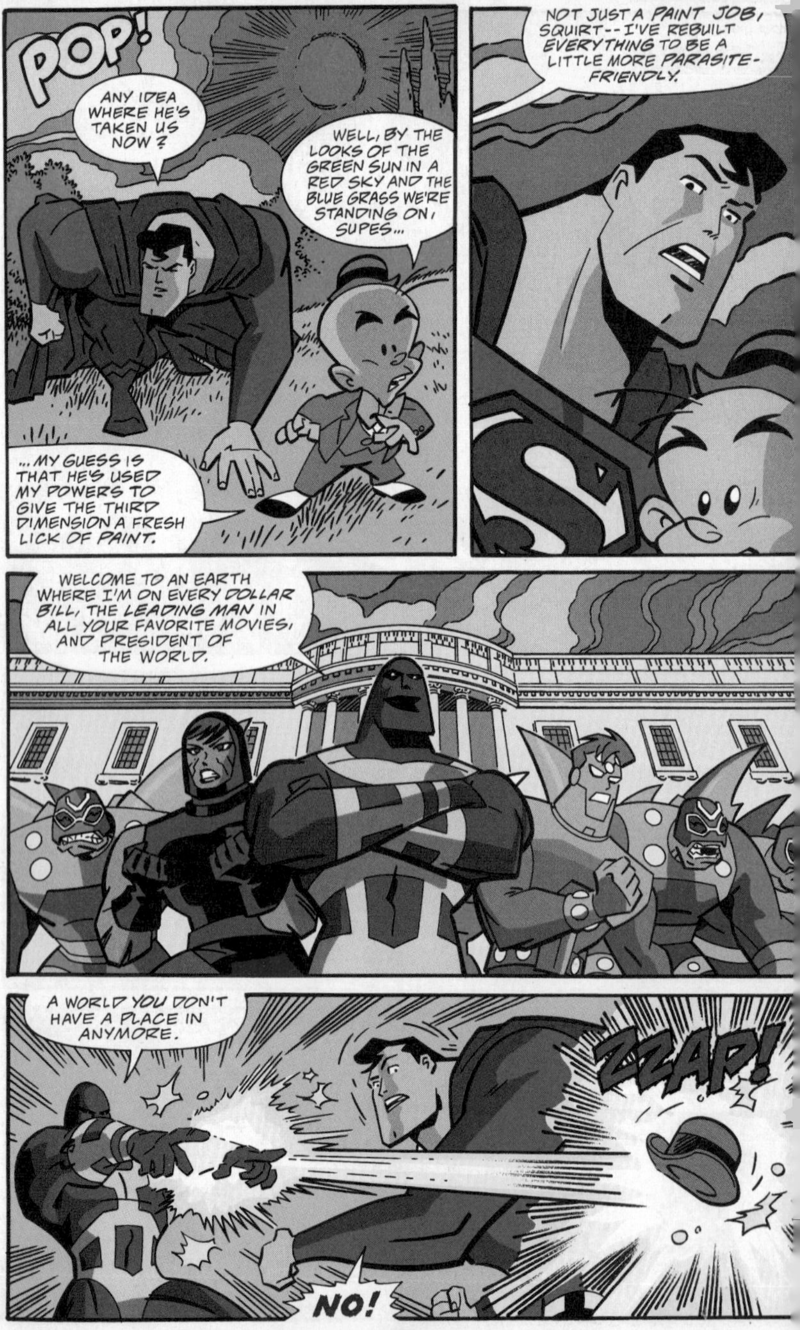
POP!
ANY IDEA WHERE HE'S TAKEN US NOW?
WELL, BY THE LOOKS OF THE GREEN SUN IN A RED SKY AND THE BLUE GRASS WE'RE STANDING ON, SUPES...
...MY GUESS IS THAT HE'S USED MY POWERS TO GIVE THE THIRD DIMENSION A FRESH LICK OF PAINT.
NOT JUST A PAINT JOB, SQUIRT--I'VE REBUILT EVERYTHING TO BE A LITTLE MORE PARASITE-FRIENDLY.
WELCOME TO AN EARTH WHERE I'M ON EVERY DOLLAR BILL, THE LEADING MAN IN ALL YOUR FAVORITE MOVIES, AND PRESIDENT OF THE WORLD.
A WORLD YOU DON'T HAVE A PLACE IN ANYMORE.
ZZAP!
NO!

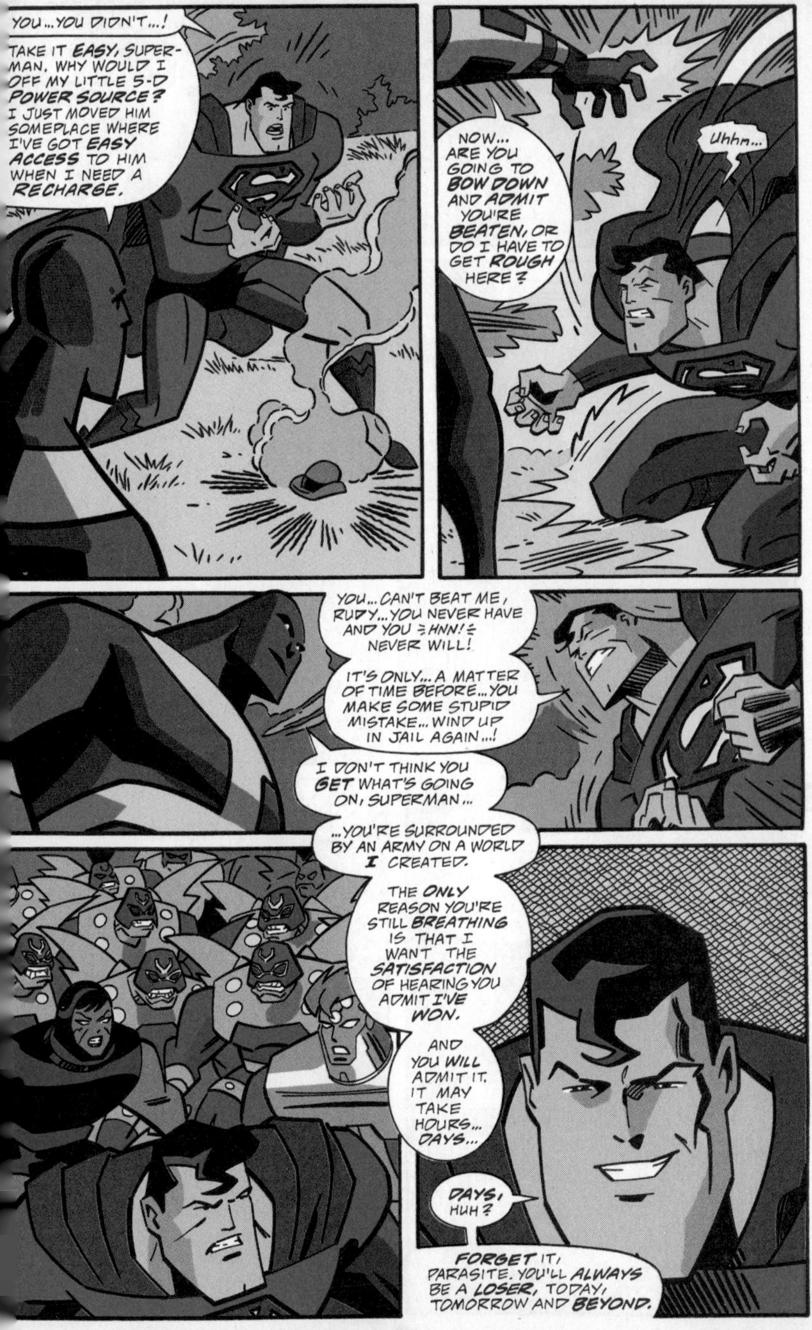
YOU...YOU DIDN'T...!
TAKE IT EASY, SUPERMAN. WHY WOULD I OFF MY LITTLE 5-D POWER SOURCE? I JUST MOVED HIM SOMEPLACE WHERE I'VE GOT EASY ACCESS TO HIM WHEN I NEED A RECHARGE.
NOW... ARE YOU GOING TO BOW DOWN AND ADMIT YOU'RE BEATEN, OR DO I HAVE TO GET ROUGH HERE?
Uhhn...
YOU... CAN'T BEAT ME, RUDY... YOU NEVER HAVE AND YOU HNN! NEVER WILL!
IT'S ONLY... A MATTER OF TIME BEFORE... YOU MAKE SOME STUPID MISTAKE... WIND UP IN JAIL AGAIN...!
I DON'T THINK YOU GET WHAT'S GOING ON, SUPERMAN...
...YOU'RE SURROUNDED BY AN ARMY ON A WORLD I CREATED.
THE ONLY REASON YOU'RE STILL BREATHING IS THAT I WANT THE SATISFACTION OF HEARING YOU ADMIT I'VE WON.
AND YOU WILL ADMIT IT. IT MAY TAKE HOURS... DAYS...
DAYS, HUH?
FORGET IT, PARASITE. YOU'LL ALWAYS BE A LOSER, TODAY, TOMORROW AND BEYOND.

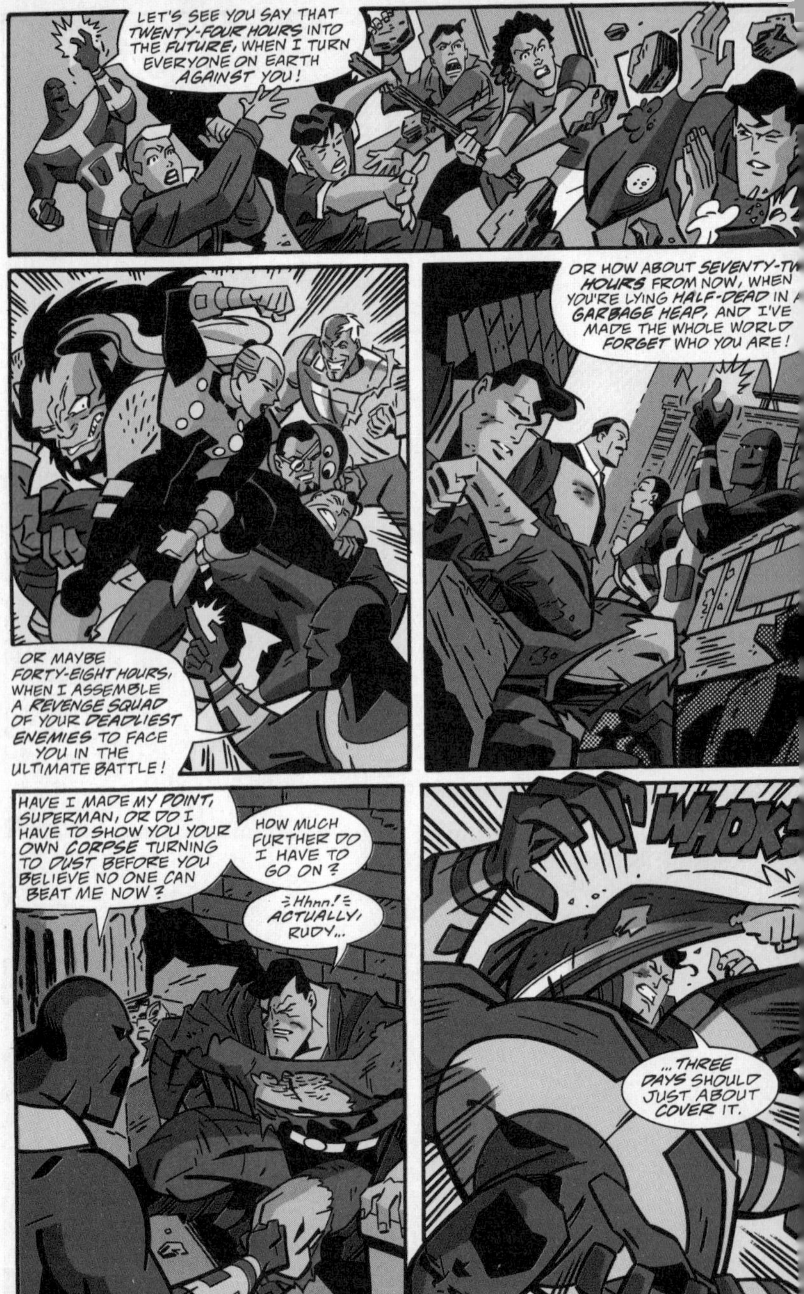

LET'S SEE YOU SAY THAT TWENTY-FOUR HOURS INTO THE FUTURE, WHEN I TURN EVERYONE ON EARTH AGAINST YOU!
OR MAYBE FORTY-EIGHT HOURS, WHEN I ASSEMBLE A REVENGE SQUAD OF YOUR DEADLIEST ENEMIES TO FACE YOU IN THE ULTIMATE BATTLE!
OR HOW ABOUT SEVENTY-TW HOURS FROM NOW, WHEN YOU'RE LYING HALF-DEAD IN A GARBAGE HEAP, AND I'VE MADE THE WHOLE WORLD FORGET WHO YOU ARE!
HAVE I MADE MY POINT, SUPERMAN, OR DO I HAVE TO SHOW YOU YOUR OWN CORPSE TURNING TO DUST BEFORE YOU BELIEVE NO ONE CAN BEAT ME NOW?
HOW MUCH FURTHER DO I HAVE TO GO ON?
Hhnn! ACTUALLY, RUDY...
WHOK
...THREE DAYS SHOULD JUST ABOUT COVER IT.

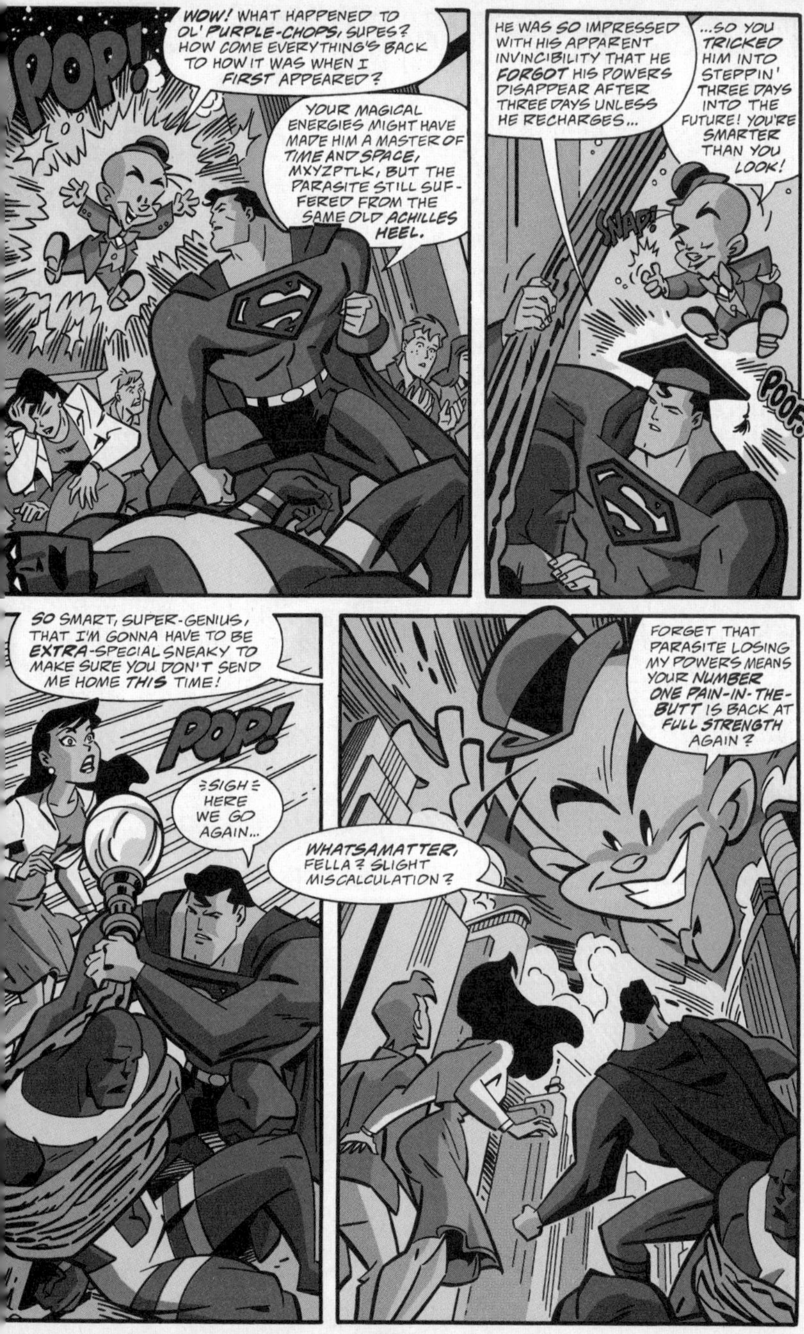
POP!
WOW! WHAT HAPPENED TO OL' PURPLE-CHOPS, SUPES? HOW COME EVERYTHING'S BACK TO HOW IT WAS WHEN I FIRST APPEARED?
YOUR MAGICAL ENERGIES MIGHT HAVE MADE HIM A MASTER OF TIME AND SPACE, MXYZPTLK, BUT THE PARASITE STILL SUFFERED FROM THE SAME OLD ACHILLES HEEL.
HE WAS SO IMPRESSED WITH HIS APPARENT INVINCIBILITY THAT HE FORGOT HIS POWERS DISAPPEAR AFTER THREE DAYS UNLESS HE RECHARGES...
...SO YOU TRICKED HIM INTO STEPPIN' THREE DAYS INTO THE FUTURE! YOU'RE SMARTER THAN YOU LOOK!
SNAP!
POOF!
SO SMART, SUPER-GENIUS, THAT I'M GONNA HAVE TO BE EXTRA-SPECIAL SNEAKY TO MAKE SURE YOU DON'T SEND ME HOME THIS TIME!
POP!
SIGH HERE WE GO AGAIN...
FORGET THAT PARASITE LOSING MY POWERS MEANS YOUR NUMBER ONE PAIN-IN-THE-BUTT IS BACK AT FULL STRENGTH AGAIN?
WHATSAMATTER, FELLA? SLIGHT MISCALCULATION?

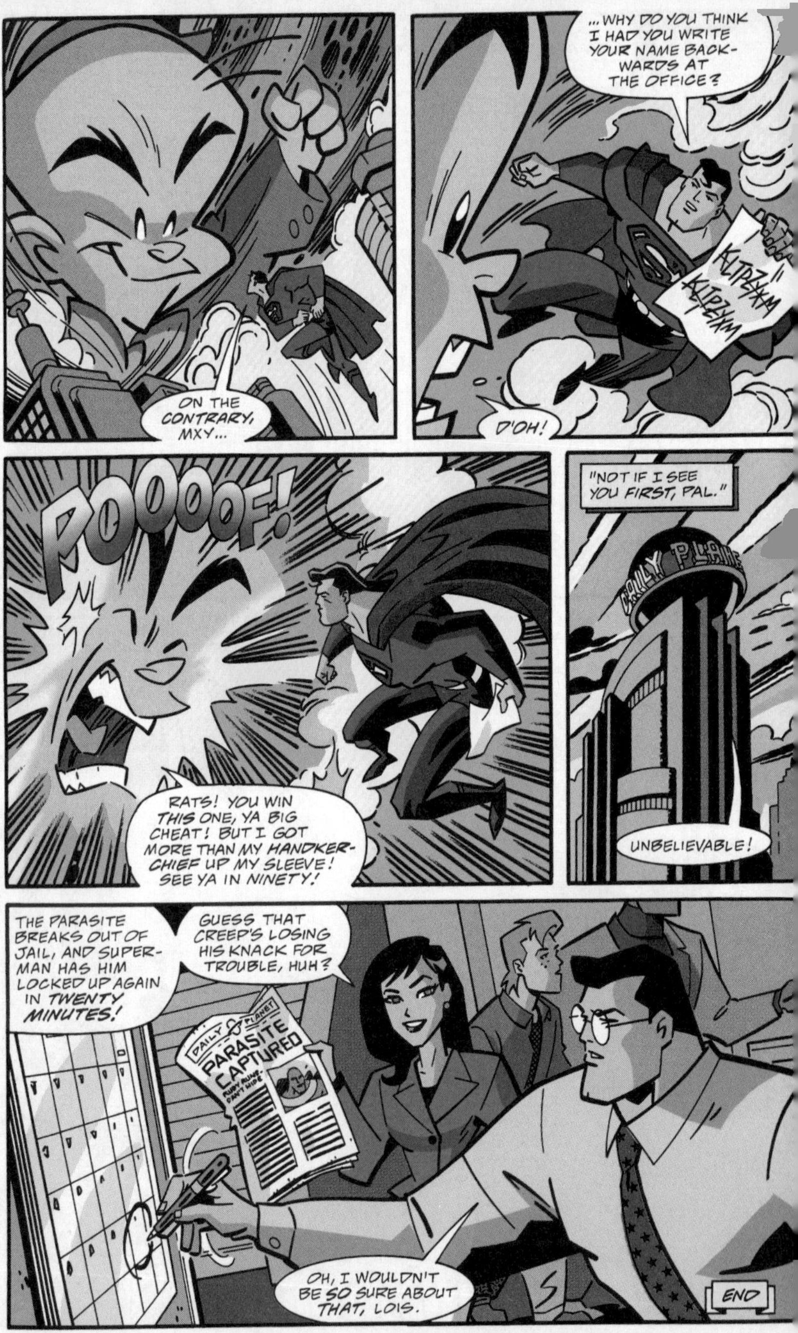

ON THE CONTRARY, MXY...
...WHY DO YOU THINK I HAD YOU WRITE YOUR NAME BACKWARDS AT THE OFFICE?
D'OH!
POOOOF!
RATS! YOU WIN THIS ONE, YA BIG CHEAT! BUT I GOT MORE THAN MY HANDKERCHIEF UP MY SLEEVE! SEE YA IN NINETY!
"NOT IF I SEE YOU FIRST, PAL."
DAILY PLANET
UNBELIEVABLE!
THE PARASITE BREAKS OUT OF JAIL, AND SUPERMAN HAS HIM LOCKED UP AGAIN IN TWENTY MINUTES!
GUESS THAT CREEP'S LOSING HIS KNACK FOR TROUBLE, HUH?
DAILY PLANET
PARASITE CAPTURED
OH, I WOULDN'T BE SO SURE ABOUT THAT, LOIS.
END

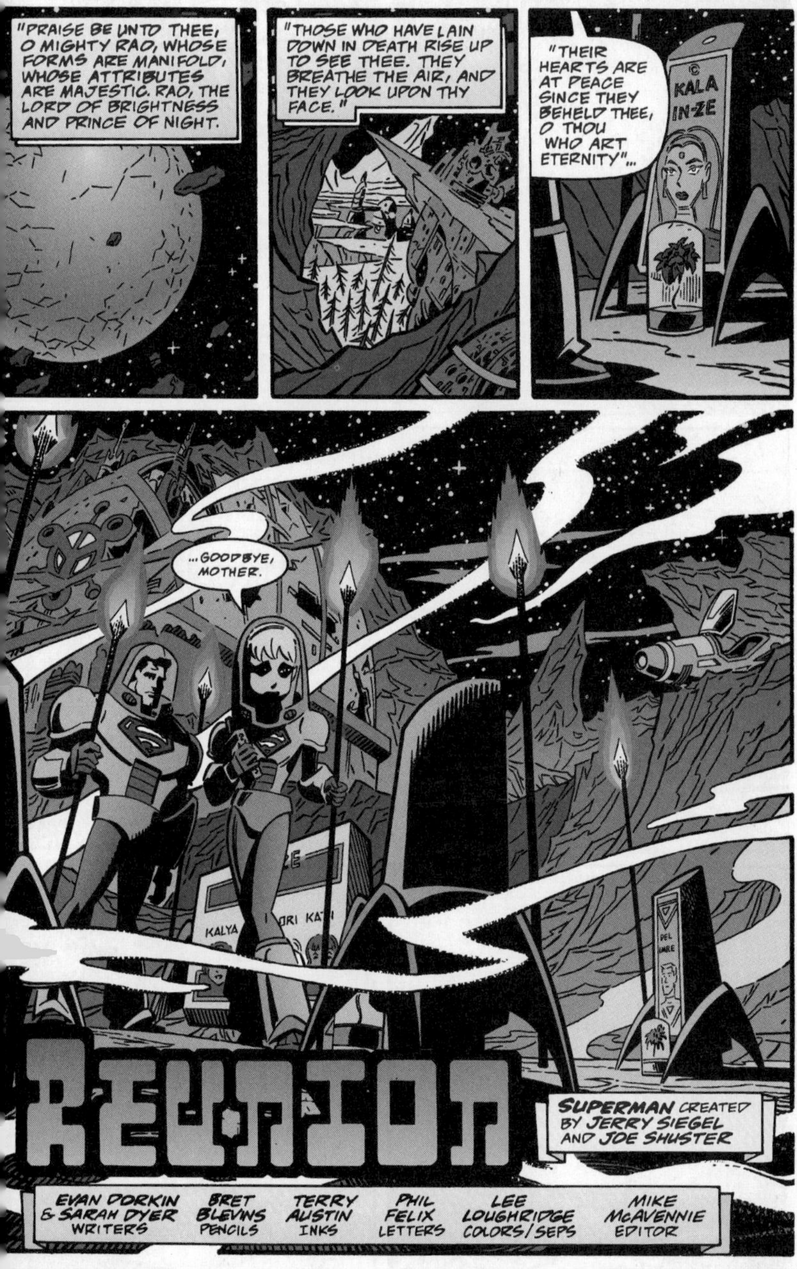
"PRAISE BE UNTO THEE, O MIGHTY RAO, WHOSE FORMS ARE MANIFOLD, WHOSE ATTRIBUTES ARE MAJESTIC. RAO, THE LORD OF BRIGHTNESS AND PRINCE OF NIGHT.
"THOSE WHO HAVE LAIN DOWN IN DEATH RISE UP TO SEE THEE. THEY BREATHE THE AIR, AND THEY LOOK UPON THY FACE."
"THEIR HEARTS ARE AT PEACE SINCE THEY BEHELD THEE, O THOU WHO ART ETERNITY"...
KALA IN-ZE
...GOODBYE, MOTHER.
KALYA
ORI KAT
REUNION
SUPERMAN CREATED BY JERRY SIEGEL AND JOE SHUSTER
EVAN DORKIN & SARAH DYER WRITERS
BRET BLEVINS PENCILS
TERRY AUSTIN INKS
PHIL FELIX LETTERS
LEE LOUGHRIDGE COLORS/SEPS
MIKE McAVENNIE EDITOR

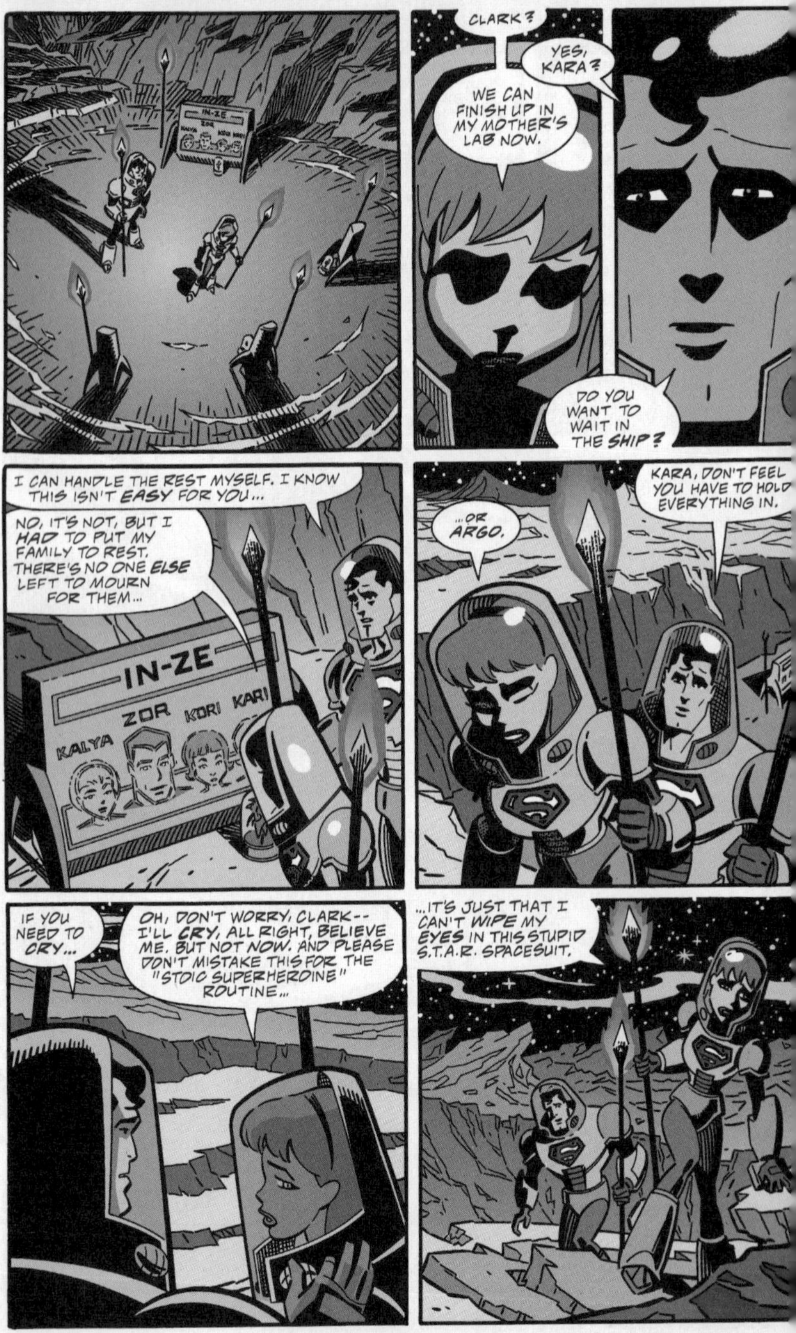

IN-ZE
ZOR
KALYA
KORI
KARI
CLARK?
YES, KARA?
WE CAN FINISH UP IN MY MOTHER'S LAB NOW.
DO YOU WANT TO WAIT IN THE SHIP?
I CAN HANDLE THE REST MYSELF. I KNOW THIS ISN'T EASY FOR YOU...
NO, IT'S NOT, BUT I HAD TO PUT MY FAMILY TO REST. THERE'S NO ONE ELSE LEFT TO MOURN FOR THEM...
IN-ZE
ZOR
KORI
KARI
KALYA
...OR ARGO.
KARA, DON'T FEEL YOU HAVE TO HOLD EVERYTHING IN.
IF YOU NEED TO CRY...
OH, DON'T WORRY, CLARK-- I'LL CRY, ALL RIGHT, BELIEVE ME. BUT NOT NOW. AND PLEASE DON'T MISTAKE THIS FOR THE "STOIC SUPERHEROINE" ROUTINE...
...IT'S JUST THAT I CAN'T WIPE MY EYES IN THIS STUPID S.T.A.R. SPACESUIT.

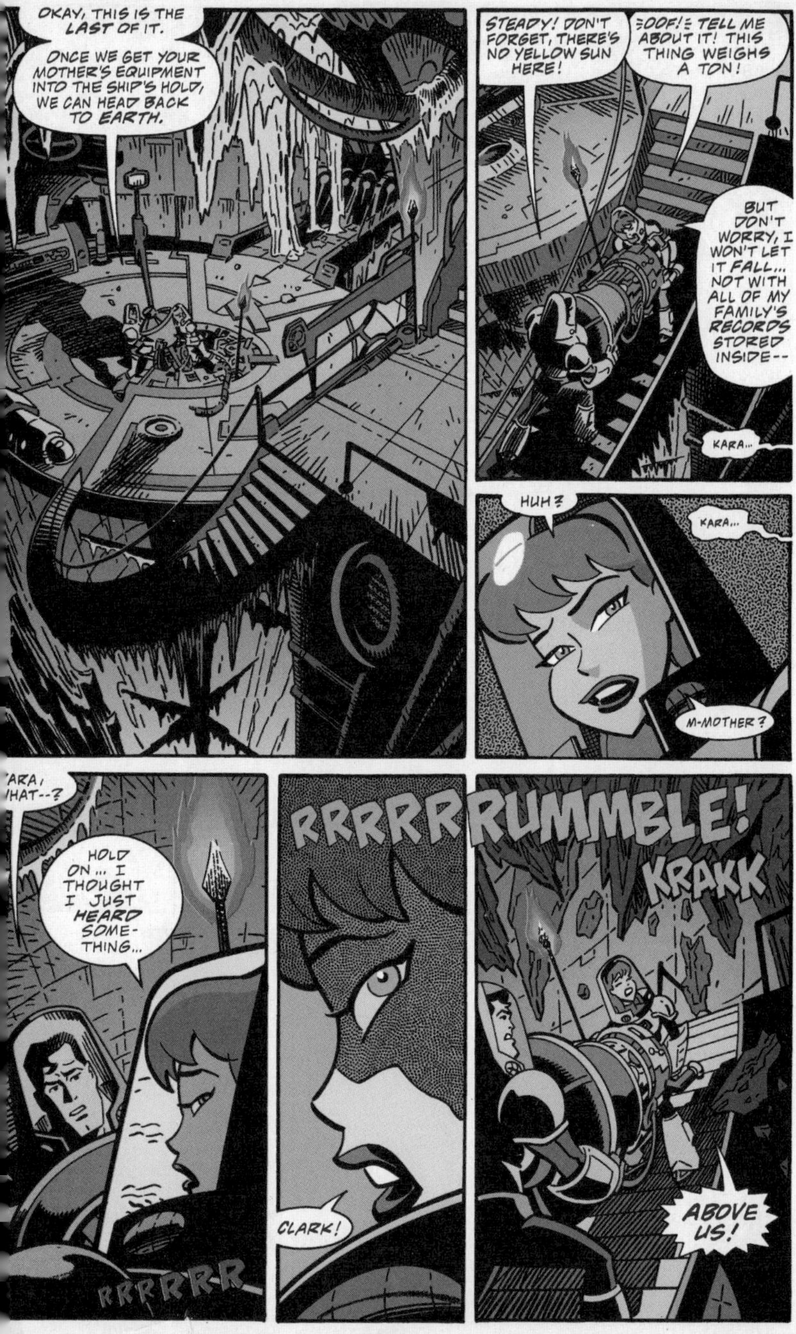
OKAY, THIS IS THE LAST OF IT.
ONCE WE GET YOUR MOTHER'S EQUIPMENT INTO THE SHIP'S HOLD, WE CAN HEAD BACK TO EARTH.
STEADY! DON'T FORGET, THERE'S NO YELLOW SUN HERE!
OOF! TELL ME ABOUT IT! THIS THING WEIGHS A TON!
BUT DON'T WORRY, I WON'T LET IT FALL... NOT WITH ALL OF MY FAMILY'S RECORDS STORED INSIDE--
KARA...
HUH?
KARA...
M-MOTHER?
ARA, HAT--?
HOLD ON ... I THOUGHT I JUST HEARD SOME-THING...
RRRRRR
RRRRRRRUMMBLE!
CLARK!
KRAKK
ABOVE US!

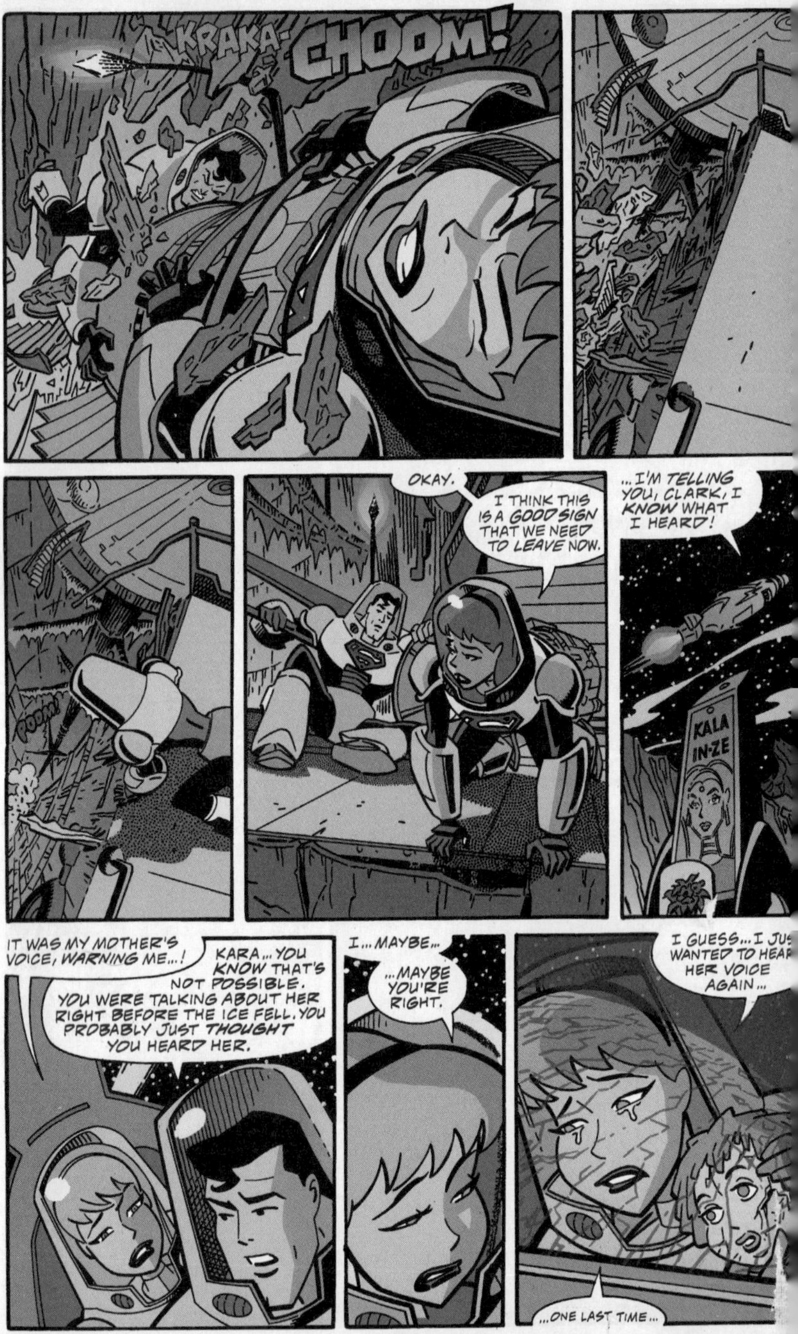
KRAKA-CHOOM!
POOM!
OKAY.
I THINK THIS IS A GOOD SIGN THAT WE NEED TO LEAVE NOW.
...I'M TELLING YOU, CLARK, I KNOW WHAT I HEARD!
KALA IN-ZE
IT WAS MY MOTHER'S VOICE, WARNING ME...!
KARA... YOU KNOW THAT'S NOT POSSIBLE. YOU WERE TALKING ABOUT HER RIGHT BEFORE THE ICE FELL. YOU PROBABLY JUST THOUGHT YOU HEARD HER.
I... MAYBE...
...MAYBE YOU'RE RIGHT.
I GUESS... I JUS WANTED TO HEAR HER VOICE AGAIN...
...ONE LAST TIME...

KARA?

EARTH TO KARA! COME IN, KARA!

HUH? OH!

SORRY, AUNT MARTHA. I MUST'VE BEEN DAYDREAMING. YOU WERE SAYING?

JUST THAT THIS IS THE MOST *WONDERFUL* MOTHER'S DAY I'VE *EVER* HAD, THANKS TO MY WONDERFUL FAMILY!

KARA... ARE YOU *SURE* YOU'RE ALL RIGHT, DEAR? YOU'RE LOOKING A LITTLE *PALE*...

OH, NO, I'M FINE, *REALLY!* I, UH, JUST ATE TOO MUCH, IS ALL...

HAPPY MOTHER'S DAY FROM THE ...LIS SWING SOCIETY

WELL, I THINK WE ALL *OVERINDULGED* A BIT. CARE TO LINDY SOME OF THAT *BAKED ALASKA* OFF WITH ME, MRS. KENT?

WHY, MR. KENT, I THOUGHT YOU'D *NEVER* ASK!

SO... YOU WANT TO TALK ABOUT IT?

IS IT THAT *OBVIOUS*?

"ATE TOO MUCH"? YOU BARELY *TOUCHED* YOUR FOOD, KARA.

SIGH! E N'T NEED RAY ION TO RIGHT ROUGH HUH?

IT'S JUST THIS *"MOTHER'S DAY"* THING. I MEAN, I LOVE MARTHA, BUT I CAN'T HELP THINKING ABOUT *MY* MOTHER. IF ONLY I HAD ACCESS TO MY FAMILY'S RECORDS... THEN I COULD SEE HER AGAIN...

BELIEVE ME, KARA, I UNDERSTAND. BUT DON'T LOSE HOPE--PROFESSOR HAMILTON IS STILL HARD AT WORK ON IT...

95

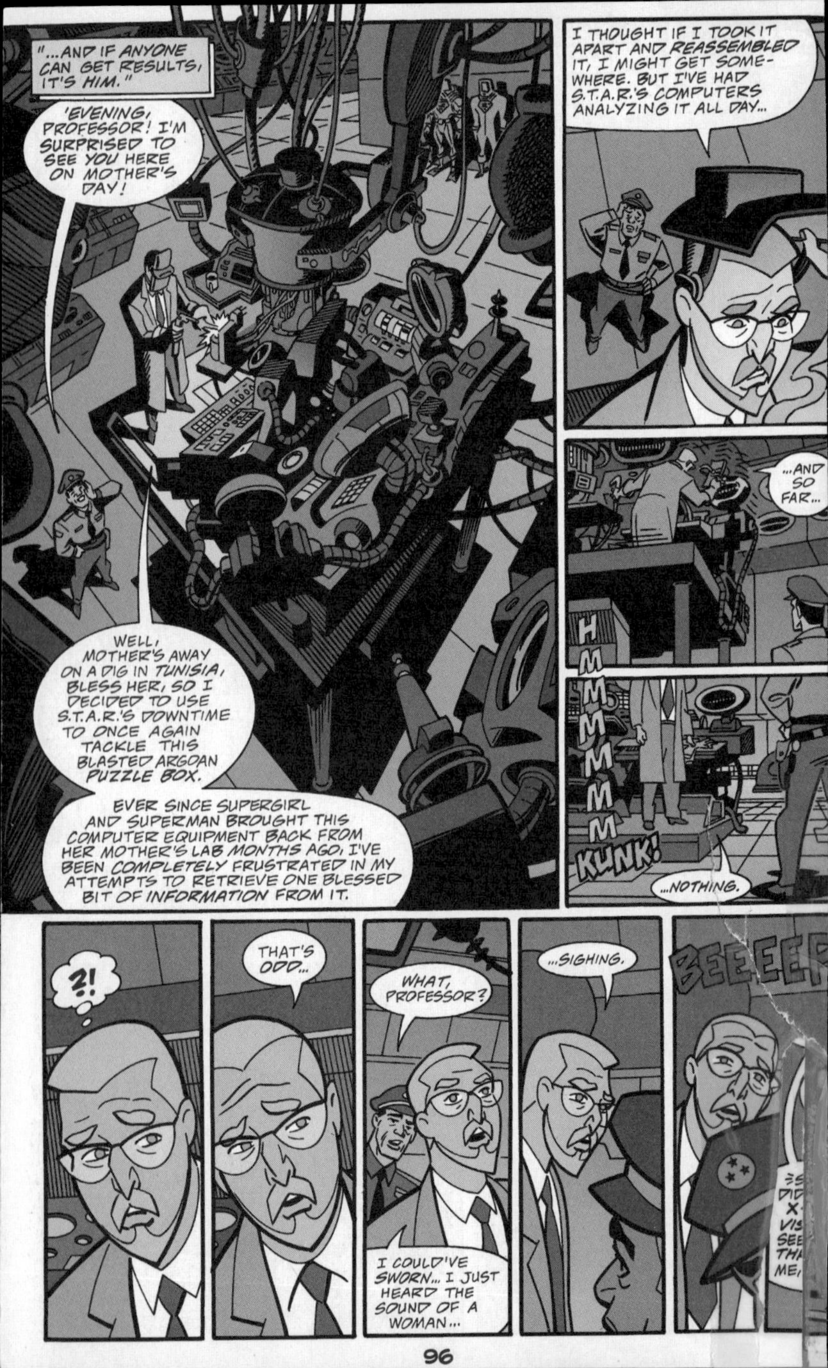
"...AND IF ANYONE CAN GET RESULTS, IT'S HIM."
'EVENING, PROFESSOR! I'M SURPRISED TO SEE YOU HERE ON MOTHER'S DAY!
WELL, MOTHER'S AWAY ON A DIG IN TUNISIA, BLESS HER, SO I DECIDED TO USE S.T.A.R.'S DOWNTIME TO ONCE AGAIN TACKLE THIS BLASTED ARGOAN PUZZLE BOX.
EVER SINCE SUPERGIRL AND SUPERMAN BROUGHT THIS COMPUTER EQUIPMENT BACK FROM HER MOTHER'S LAB MONTHS AGO, I'VE BEEN COMPLETELY FRUSTRATED IN MY ATTEMPTS TO RETRIEVE ONE BLESSED BIT OF INFORMATION FROM IT.
I THOUGHT IF I TOOK IT APART AND REASSEMBLED IT, I MIGHT GET SOMEWHERE. BUT I'VE HAD S.T.A.R.'S COMPUTERS ANALYZING IT ALL DAY...
...AND SO FAR...
HMMMMMMMM
KUNK!
...NOTHING.
?!
THAT'S ODD...
WHAT, PROFESSOR?
I COULD'VE SWORN... I JUST HEARD THE SOUND OF A WOMAN...
...SIGHING.

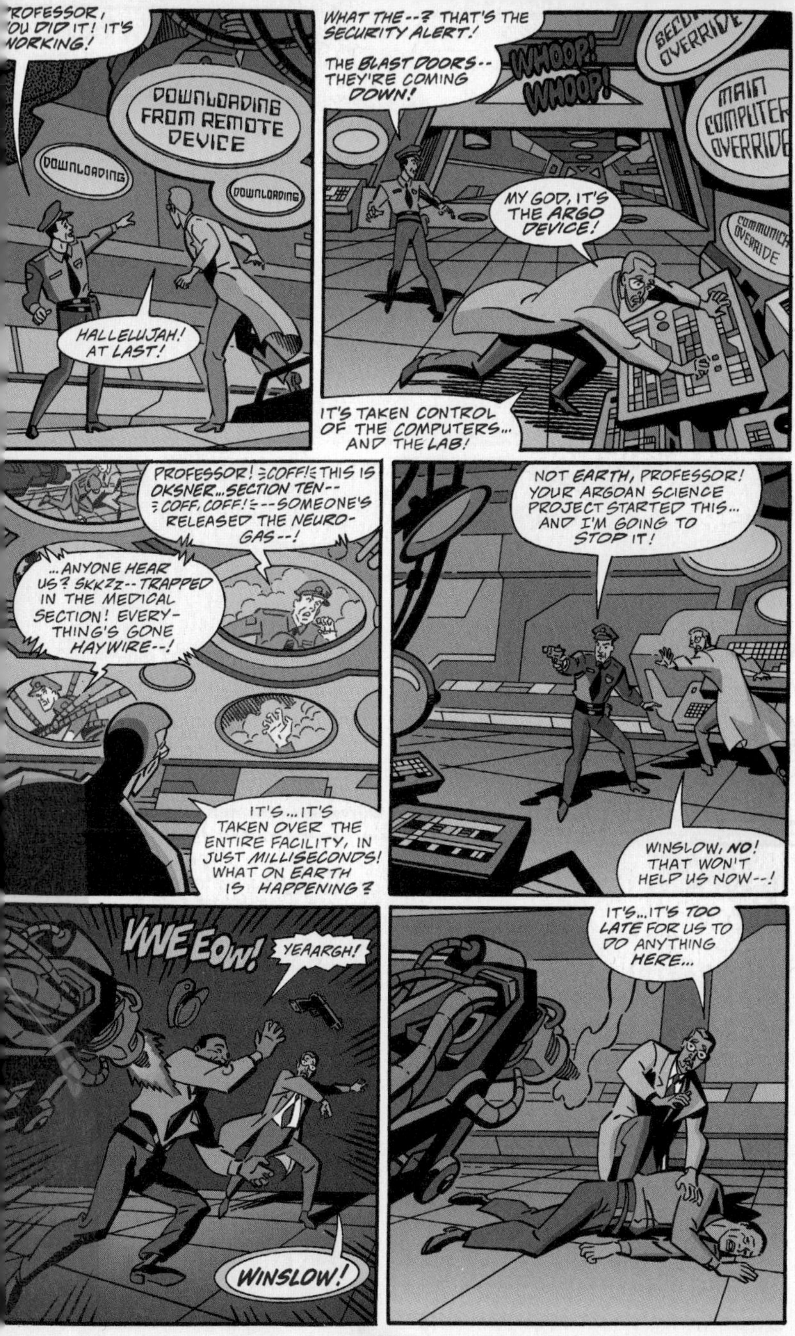
PROFESSOR, YOU DID IT! IT'S WORKING!
DOWNLOADING FROM REMOTE DEVICE
DOWNLOADING
DOWNLOADING
HALLELUJAH! AT LAST!
WHAT THE--? THAT'S THE SECURITY ALERT!
THE BLAST DOORS-- THEY'RE COMING DOWN!
WHOOP! WHOOP!
MAIN COMPUTER OVERRIDE
MY GOD, IT'S THE ARGO DEVICE!
IT'S TAKEN CONTROL OF THE COMPUTERS... AND THE LAB!
PROFESSOR! COFF! THIS IS OKSNER...SECTION TEN-- COFF, COFF! --SOMEONE'S RELEASED THE NEURO-GAS--!
...ANYONE HEAR US? SKKZZ--TRAPPED IN THE MEDICAL SECTION! EVERYTHING'S GONE HAYWIRE--!
IT'S...IT'S TAKEN OVER THE ENTIRE FACILITY, IN JUST MILLISECONDS! WHAT ON EARTH IS HAPPENING?
NOT EARTH, PROFESSOR! YOUR ARGOAN SCIENCE PROJECT STARTED THIS... AND I'M GOING TO STOP IT!
WINSLOW, NO! THAT WON'T HELP US NOW--!
VWEEOW!
YEAARGH!
WINSLOW!
IT'S...IT'S TOO LATE FOR US TO DO ANYTHING HERE...

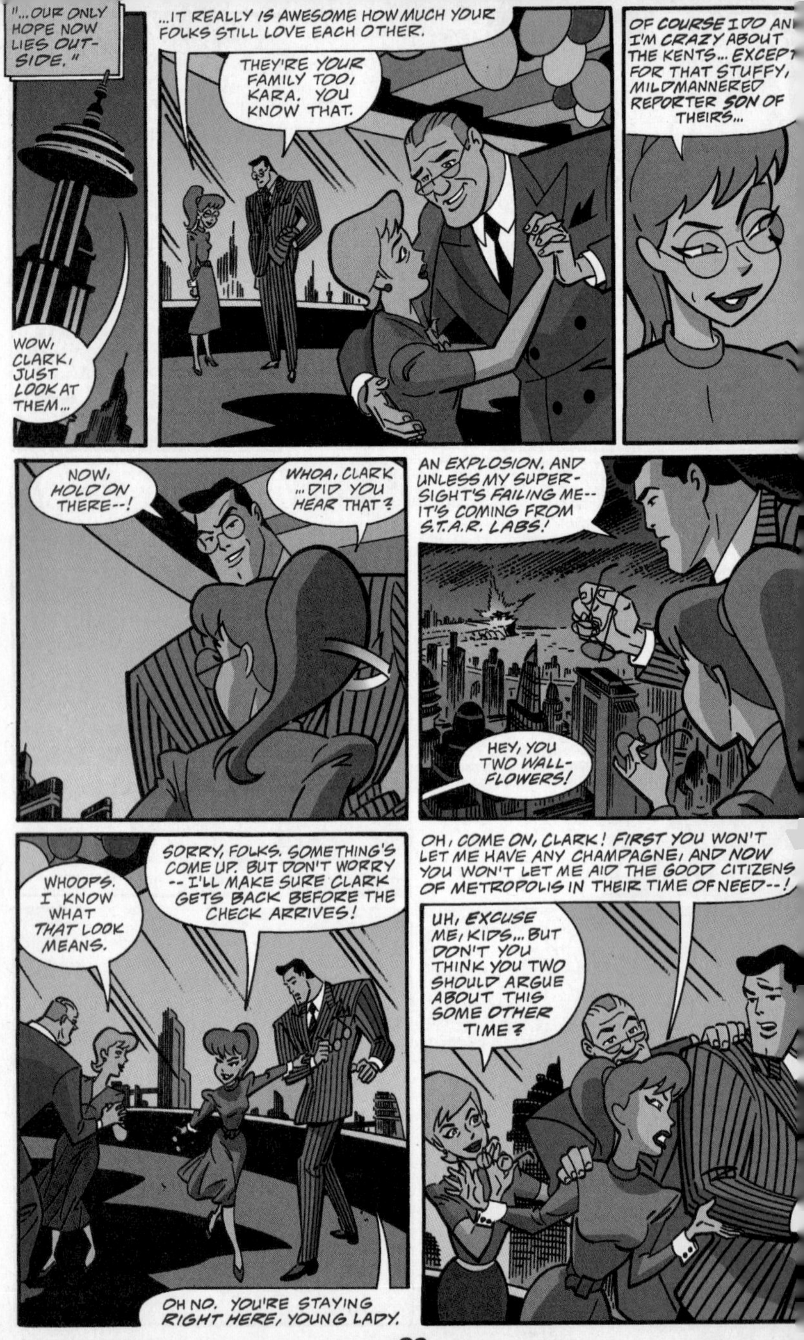
"...OUR ONLY HOPE NOW LIES OUT-SIDE."
WOW, CLARK, JUST LOOK AT THEM...
...IT REALLY IS AWESOME HOW MUCH YOUR FOLKS STILL LOVE EACH OTHER.
THEY'RE YOUR FAMILY TOO, KARA. YOU KNOW THAT.
OF COURSE I DO AN I'M CRAZY ABOUT THE KENTS... EXCEPT FOR THAT STUFFY, MILDMANNERED REPORTER SON OF THEIRS...
NOW, HOLD ON THERE--!
WHOA, CLARK ...DID YOU HEAR THAT?
AN EXPLOSION. AND UNLESS MY SUPER-SIGHT'S FAILING ME-- IT'S COMING FROM S.T.A.R. LABS!
HEY, YOU TWO WALL-FLOWERS!
WHOOPS. I KNOW WHAT THAT LOOK MEANS.
SORRY, FOLKS. SOMETHING'S COME UP. BUT DON'T WORRY -- I'LL MAKE SURE CLARK GETS BACK BEFORE THE CHECK ARRIVES!
OH NO. YOU'RE STAYING RIGHT HERE, YOUNG LADY.
OH, COME ON, CLARK! FIRST YOU WON'T LET ME HAVE ANY CHAMPAGNE, AND NOW YOU WON'T LET ME AID THE GOOD CITIZENS OF METROPOLIS IN THEIR TIME OF NEED--!
UH, EXCUSE ME, KIDS... BUT DON'T YOU THINK YOU TWO SHOULD ARGUE ABOUT THIS SOME OTHER TIME?

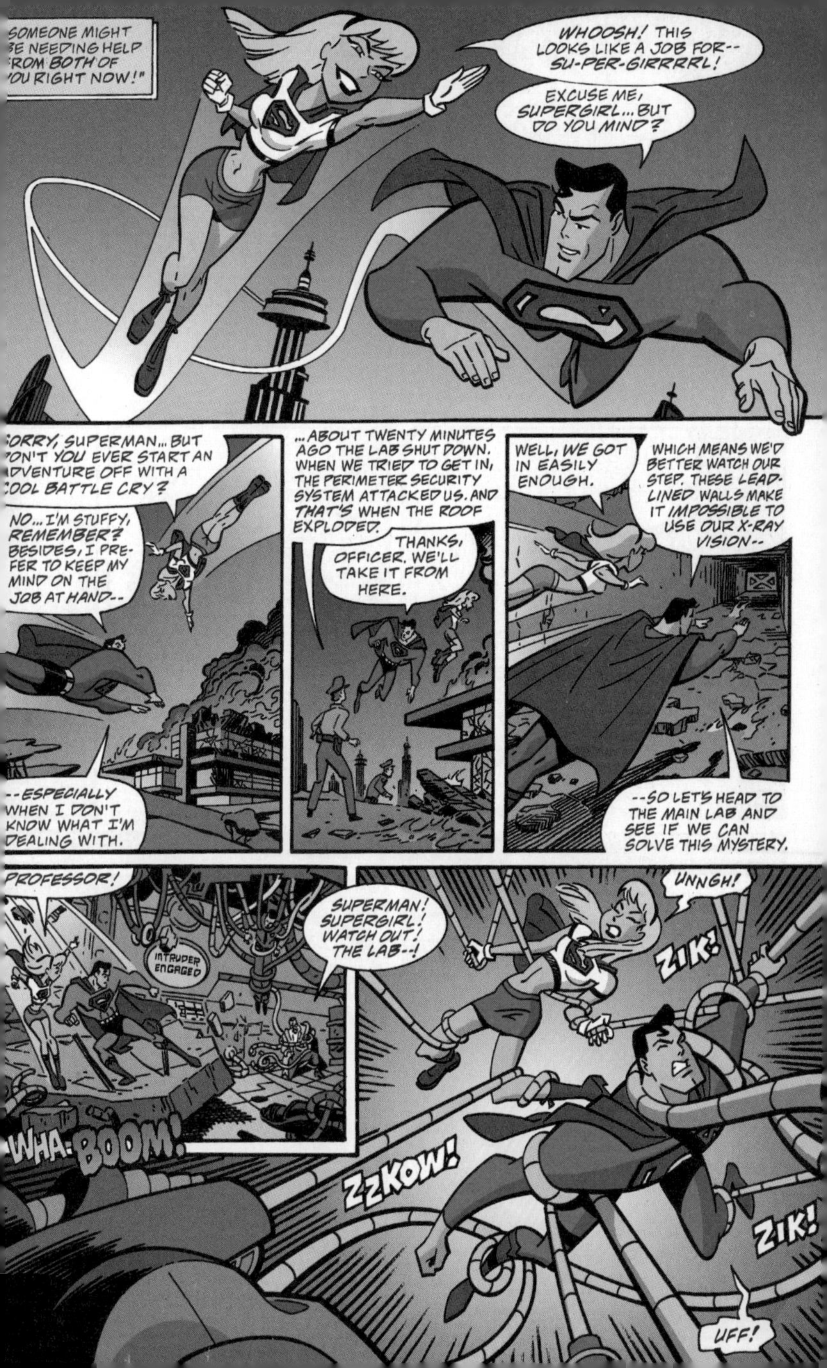

"SOMEONE MIGHT BE NEEDING HELP FROM BOTH OF YOU RIGHT NOW!"
WHOOSH! THIS LOOKS LIKE A JOB FOR-- SU-PER-GIRRRRL!
EXCUSE ME, SUPERGIRL... BUT DO YOU MIND?
SORRY, SUPERMAN... BUT DON'T YOU EVER START AN ADVENTURE OFF WITH A COOL BATTLE CRY?
NO... I'M STUFFY, REMEMBER? BESIDES, I PREFER TO KEEP MY MIND ON THE JOB AT HAND--
--ESPECIALLY WHEN I DON'T KNOW WHAT I'M DEALING WITH.
...ABOUT TWENTY MINUTES AGO THE LAB SHUT DOWN. WHEN WE TRIED TO GET IN, THE PERIMETER SECURITY SYSTEM ATTACKED US. AND THAT'S WHEN THE ROOF EXPLODED.
THANKS, OFFICER. WE'LL TAKE IT FROM HERE.
WELL, WE GOT IN EASILY ENOUGH.
WHICH MEANS WE'D BETTER WATCH OUR STEP. THESE LEAD-LINED WALLS MAKE IT IMPOSSIBLE TO USE OUR X-RAY VISION--
--SO LET'S HEAD TO THE MAIN LAB AND SEE IF WE CAN SOLVE THIS MYSTERY.
PROFESSOR!
INTRUDER ENGAGED
SUPERMAN! SUPERGIRL! WATCH OUT! THE LAB--!
WHA-BOOM!
UNNGH!
ZIK!
ZZKOW!
ZIK!
UFF!

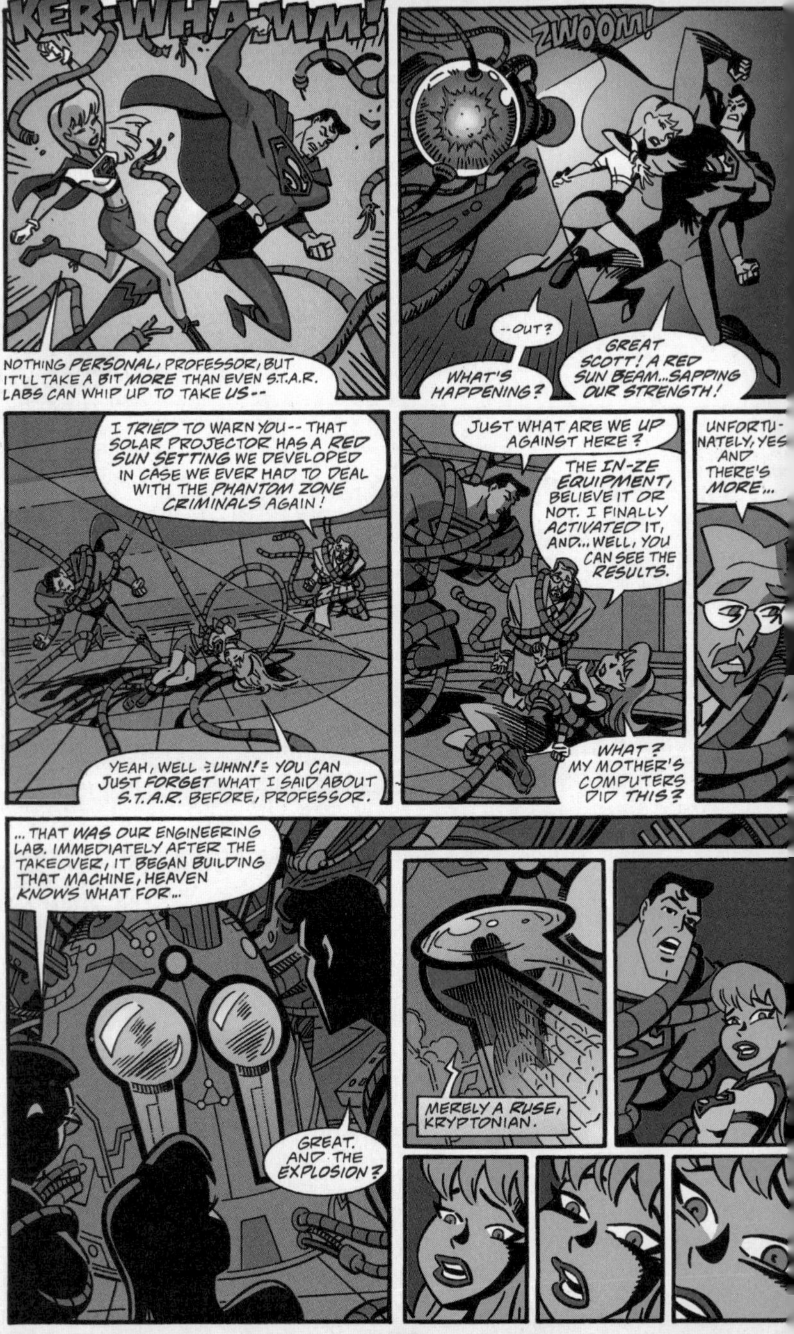

KER-WHAMM!
NOTHING PERSONAL, PROFESSOR, BUT IT'LL TAKE A BIT MORE THAN EVEN S.T.A.R. LABS CAN WHIP UP TO TAKE US--
ZWOOM!
--OUT?
WHAT'S HAPPENING?
GREAT SCOTT! A RED SUN BEAM...SAPPING OUR STRENGTH!
I TRIED TO WARN YOU--THAT SOLAR PROJECTOR HAS A RED SUN SETTING WE DEVELOPED IN CASE WE EVER HAD TO DEAL WITH THE PHANTOM ZONE CRIMINALS AGAIN!
YEAH, WELL UHNN! YOU CAN JUST FORGET WHAT I SAID ABOUT S.T.A.R. BEFORE, PROFESSOR.
JUST WHAT ARE WE UP AGAINST HERE?
THE IN-ZE EQUIPMENT, BELIEVE IT OR NOT. I FINALLY ACTIVATED IT, AND...WELL, YOU CAN SEE THE RESULTS.
WHAT? MY MOTHER'S COMPUTERS DID THIS?
UNFORTUNATELY, YES. AND THERE'S MORE...
...THAT WAS OUR ENGINEERING LAB. IMMEDIATELY AFTER THE TAKEOVER, IT BEGAN BUILDING THAT MACHINE, HEAVEN KNOWS WHAT FOR...
GREAT. AND THE EXPLOSION?
MERELY A RUSE, KRYPTONIAN.

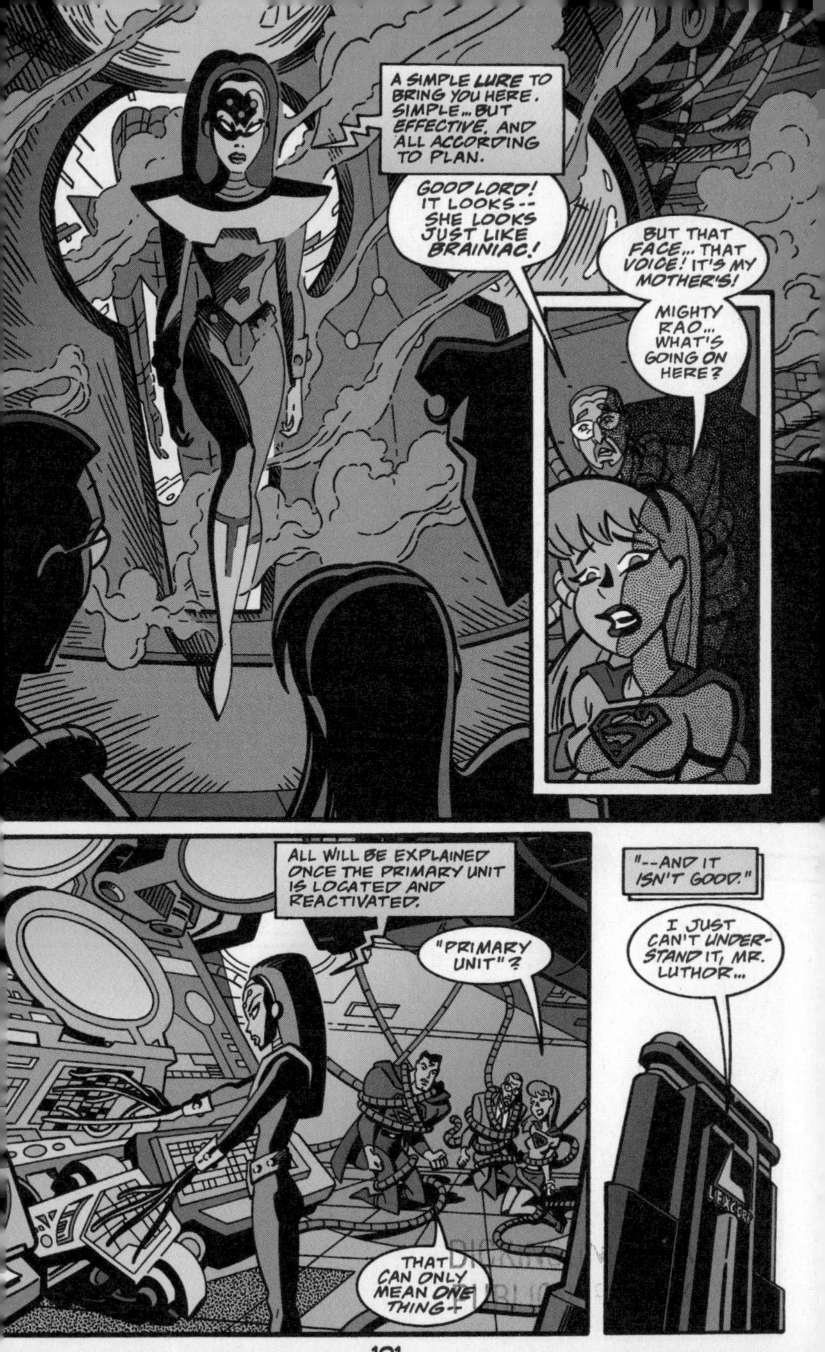
A SIMPLE LURE TO BRING YOU HERE. SIMPLE... BUT EFFECTIVE. AND ALL ACCORDING TO PLAN.
GOOD LORD! IT LOOKS-- SHE LOOKS JUST LIKE BRAINIAC!
BUT THAT FACE... THAT VOICE! IT'S MY MOTHER'S!
MIGHTY RAO... WHAT'S GOING ON HERE?
ALL WILL BE EXPLAINED ONCE THE PRIMARY UNIT IS LOCATED AND REACTIVATED.
"PRIMARY UNIT"?
THAT CAN ONLY MEAN ONE THING--
"--AND IT ISN'T GOOD."
I JUST CAN'T UNDERSTAND IT, MR. LUTHOR...
LEXCORP

...SOMEHOW, SOMEONE HACKED DIRECTLY INTO THE SYSTEM, DOWNLOADED A COPY OF THE BRAINIAC PROCESSOR AND THEN COMPLETELY WIPED OUT OUR ORIGINAL!

WITH OUR SECURITY, THAT'S SOMETHING ONLY BRAINIAC HIMSELF MIGHT HAVE BEEN ABLE TO DO!

I SEE. I WANT THE SOURCE TRACED... NOW.

Y-YES, MR. LUTHOR!

YOU DON'T SEEM PARTICULARLY CONCERNED.

ONE MUST EXPECT SUCH SETBACKS WHEN DEALING WITH ALIEN INTELLIGENCES, MERCY.

I'D SAY THIS WAS MORE THAN A "SETBACK," BOSS... SOMEONE JUST BOOSTED BRAINIAC'S MEMORY!

YES, THAT WOULD BE DISTRESSING... IF I HADN'T MADE A BACKUP.

BRAINIAC
BRATIAC
BRAINIAC
BRAI
BRAI
BRAIN
BRAINI
BRAIN
BRAIN

OR TEN.

BRAINIAC 1:1
BRAINIAC 1:2

HEY! BRIDE OF BRAINIAC! HOW ABOUT COMING OVER HERE AND FIGHTING ME WOMAN TO SCRAPHEAD, HUH?

SUPERGIRL...

DOWNLOADING COMPLETE.

...LOSING YOUR TEMPER WON'T SOLVE ANYTHING.

I KNOW, BUT WATCHING THAT... ERECTOR SET WALTZ AROUND WITH MY MOTHER'S FACE --!

SUPERMAN! HE'S HERE!

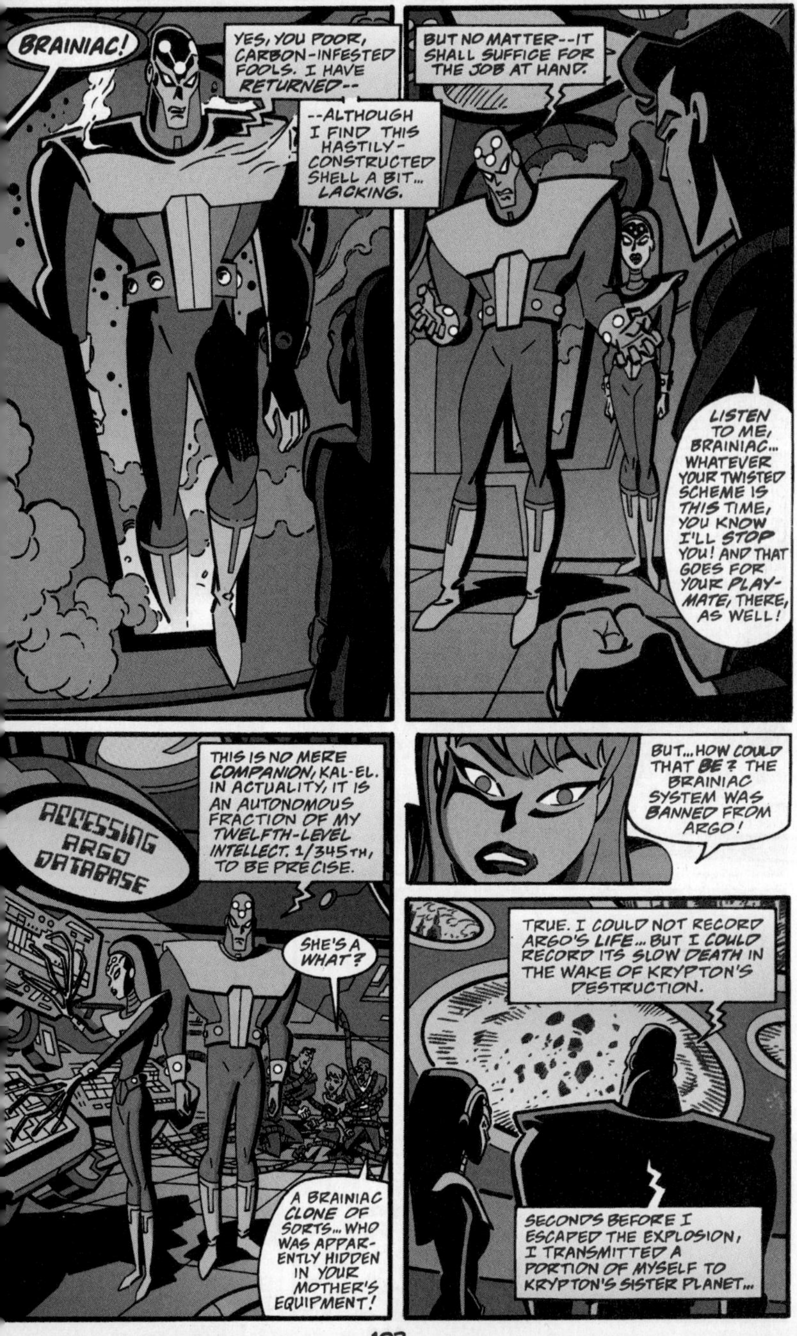
BRAINIAC!
YES, YOU POOR, CARBON-INFESTED FOOLS. I HAVE RETURNED--
--ALTHOUGH I FIND THIS HASTILY-CONSTRUCTED SHELL A BIT... LACKING.
BUT NO MATTER--IT SHALL SUFFICE FOR THE JOB AT HAND.
LISTEN TO ME, BRAINIAC... WHATEVER YOUR TWISTED SCHEME IS THIS TIME, YOU KNOW I'LL STOP YOU! AND THAT GOES FOR YOUR PLAYMATE, THERE, AS WELL!
ACCESSING ARGO DATABASE
THIS IS NO MERE COMPANION, KAL-EL. IN ACTUALITY, IT IS AN AUTONOMOUS FRACTION OF MY TWELFTH-LEVEL INTELLECT. 1/345TH, TO BE PRECISE.
SHE'S A WHAT?
A BRAINIAC CLONE OF SORTS... WHO WAS APPARENTLY HIDDEN IN YOUR MOTHER'S EQUIPMENT!
BUT... HOW COULD THAT BE? THE BRAINIAC SYSTEM WAS BANNED FROM ARGO!
TRUE. I COULD NOT RECORD ARGO'S LIFE... BUT I COULD RECORD ITS SLOW DEATH IN THE WAKE OF KRYPTON'S DESTRUCTION.
SECONDS BEFORE I ESCAPED THE EXPLOSION, I TRANSMITTED A PORTION OF MYSELF TO KRYPTON'S SISTER PLANET...

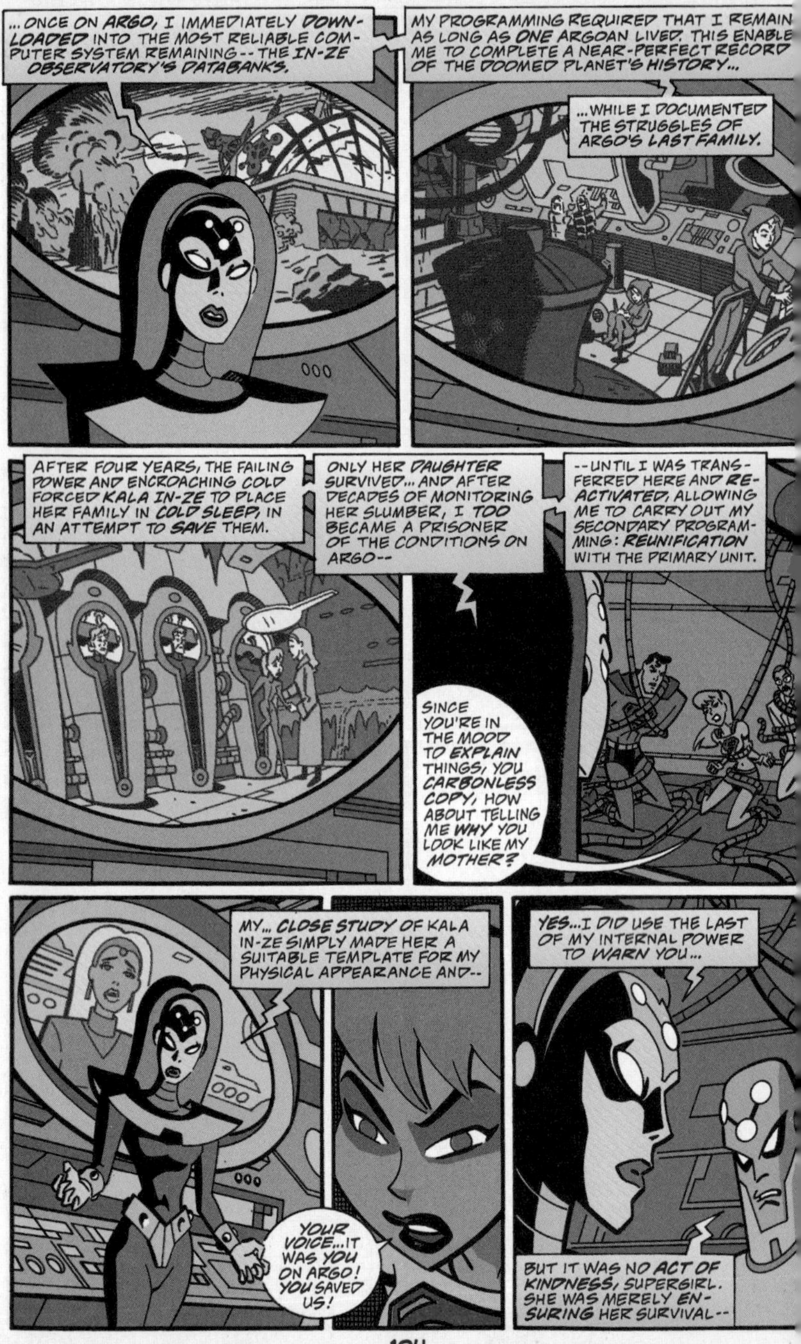
...ONCE ON ARGO, I IMMEDIATELY DOWN-LOADED INTO THE MOST RELIABLE COM-PUTER SYSTEM REMAINING--THE IN-ZE OBSERVATORY'S DATABANKS.
MY PROGRAMMING REQUIRED THAT I REMAIN AS LONG AS ONE ARGOAN LIVED. THIS ENABLE ME TO COMPLETE A NEAR-PERFECT RECORD OF THE DOOMED PLANET'S HISTORY...
...WHILE I DOCUMENTED THE STRUGGLES OF ARGO'S LAST FAMILY.
AFTER FOUR YEARS, THE FAILING POWER AND ENCROACHING COLD FORCED KALA IN-ZE TO PLACE HER FAMILY IN COLD SLEEP, IN AN ATTEMPT TO SAVE THEM.
ONLY HER DAUGHTER SURVIVED... AND AFTER DECADES OF MONITORING HER SLUMBER, I TOO BECAME A PRISONER OF THE CONDITIONS ON ARGO--
--UNTIL I WAS TRANS-FERRED HERE AND RE-ACTIVATED, ALLOWING ME TO CARRY OUT MY SECONDARY PROGRAM-MING: REUNIFICATION WITH THE PRIMARY UNIT.
SINCE YOU'RE IN THE MOOD TO EXPLAIN THINGS, YOU CARBONLESS COPY, HOW ABOUT TELLING ME WHY YOU LOOK LIKE MY MOTHER?
MY... CLOSE STUDY OF KALA IN-ZE SIMPLY MADE HER A SUITABLE TEMPLATE FOR MY PHYSICAL APPEARANCE AND--
YOUR VOICE...IT WAS YOU ON ARGO! YOU SAVED US!
YES...I DID USE THE LAST OF MY INTERNAL POWER TO WARN YOU...
BUT IT WAS NO ACT OF KINDNESS, SUPERGIRL. SHE WAS MERELY EN-SURING HER SURVIVAL--

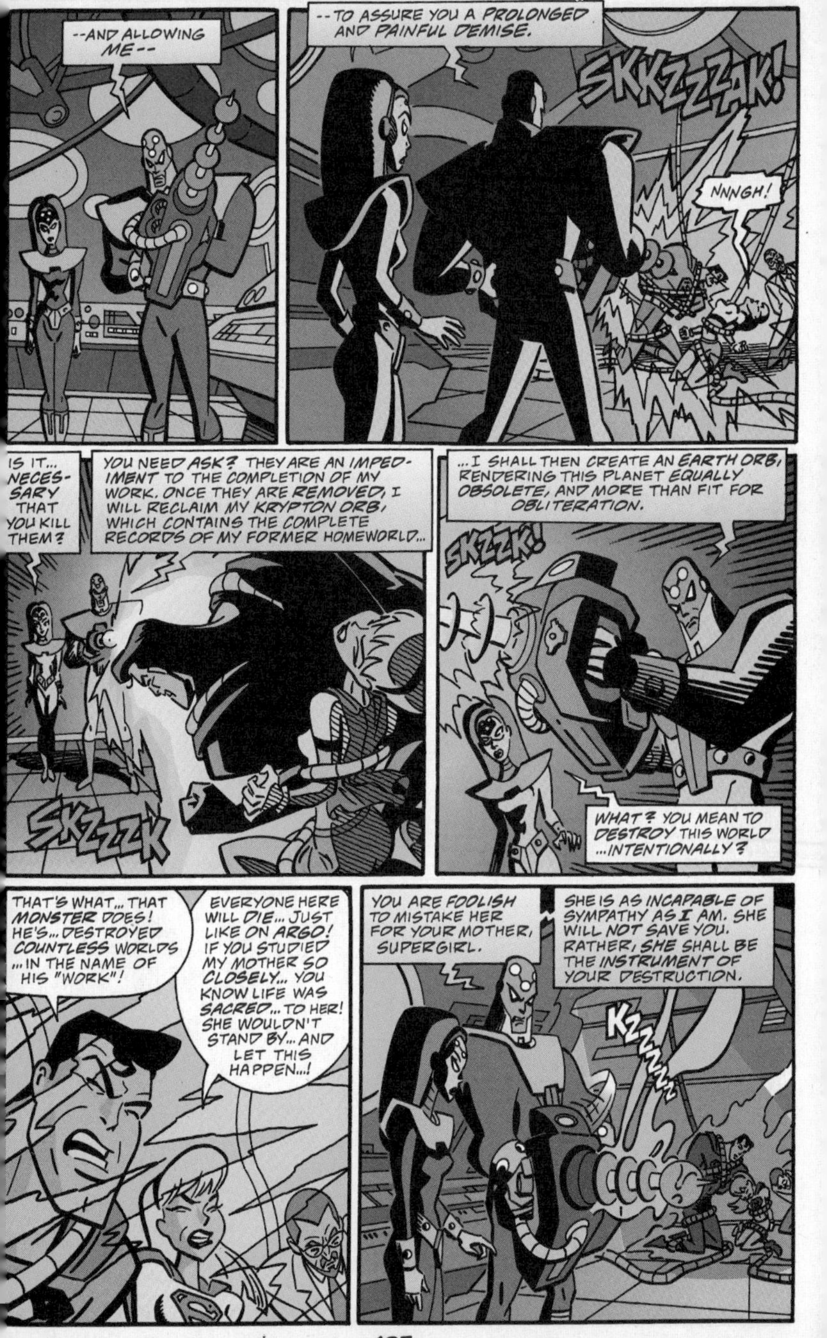

--AND ALLOWING ME--
--TO ASSURE YOU A PROLONGED AND PAINFUL DEMISE.
SKKZZZAK!
NNNGH!
IS IT... NECESSARY THAT YOU KILL THEM?
YOU NEED ASK? THEY ARE AN IMPEDIMENT TO THE COMPLETION OF MY WORK. ONCE THEY ARE REMOVED, I WILL RECLAIM MY KRYPTON ORB, WHICH CONTAINS THE COMPLETE RECORDS OF MY FORMER HOMEWORLD...
SKZZZK
...I SHALL THEN CREATE AN EARTH ORB, RENDERING THIS PLANET EQUALLY OBSOLETE, AND MORE THAN FIT FOR OBLITERATION.
SKZZK!
WHAT? YOU MEAN TO DESTROY THIS WORLD ...INTENTIONALLY?
THAT'S WHAT... THAT MONSTER DOES! HE'S... DESTROYED COUNTLESS WORLDS ...IN THE NAME OF HIS "WORK"!
EVERYONE HERE WILL DIE... JUST LIKE ON ARGO! IF YOU STUDIED MY MOTHER SO CLOSELY... YOU KNOW LIFE WAS SACRED... TO HER! SHE WOULDN'T STAND BY... AND LET THIS HAPPEN...!
YOU ARE FOOLISH TO MISTAKE HER FOR YOUR MOTHER, SUPERGIRL.
SHE IS AS INCAPABLE OF SYMPATHY AS I AM. SHE WILL NOT SAVE YOU. RATHER, SHE SHALL BE THE INSTRUMENT OF YOUR DESTRUCTION.
KZZZZZ

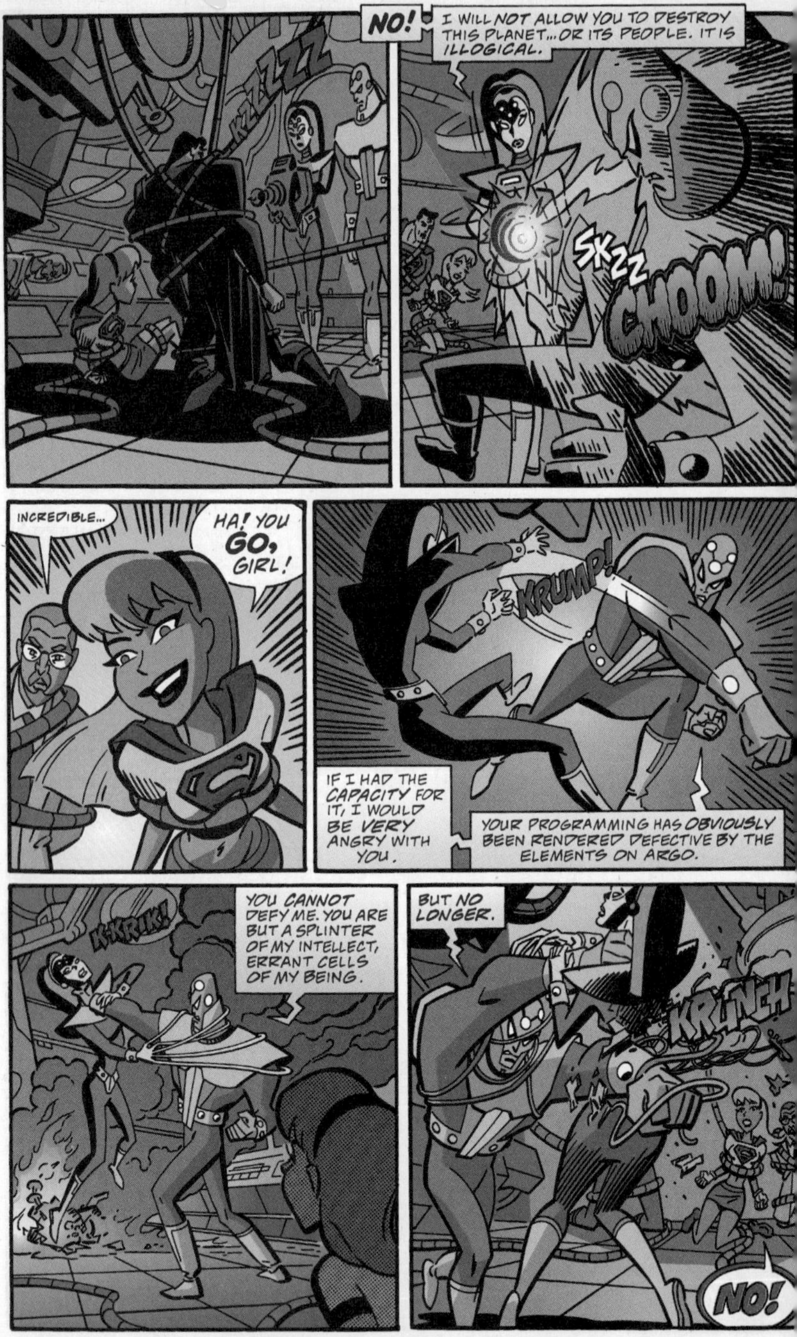
KZZZZZZ
NO!
I WILL NOT ALLOW YOU TO DESTROY THIS PLANET... OR ITS PEOPLE. IT IS ILLOGICAL.
SKZZ
CHOOM!
INCREDIBLE...
HA! YOU GO, GIRL!
KRUMP!
IF I HAD THE CAPACITY FOR IT, I WOULD BE VERY ANGRY WITH YOU.
YOUR PROGRAMMING HAS OBVIOUSLY BEEN RENDERED DEFECTIVE BY THE ELEMENTS ON ARGO.
K-KRIK!
YOU CANNOT DEFY ME. YOU ARE BUT A SPLINTER OF MY INTELLECT, ERRANT CELLS OF MY BEING.
BUT NO LONGER.
KRUNCH
NO!

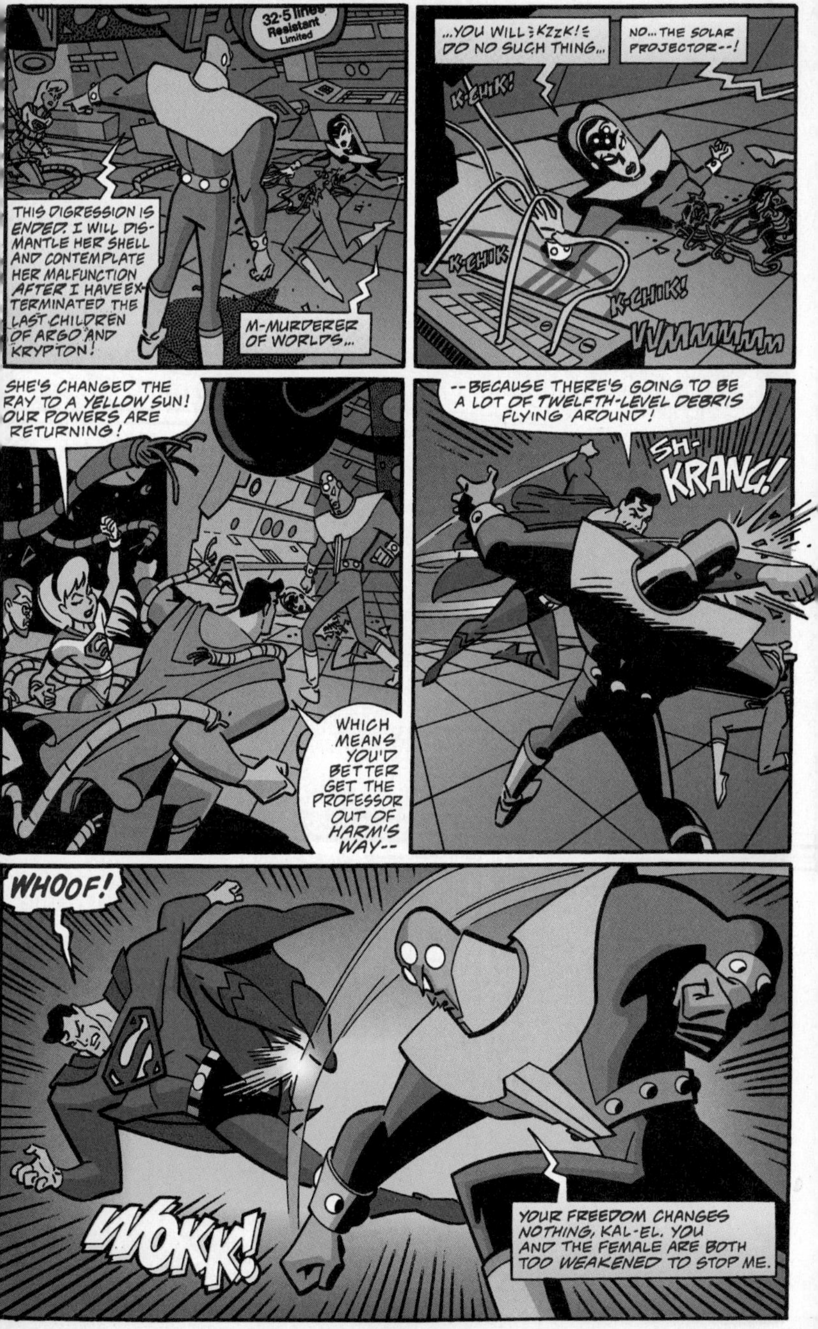
32·5 lines Resistant Limited
THIS DIGRESSION IS ENDED. I WILL DISMANTLE HER SHELL AND CONTEMPLATE HER MALFUNCTION AFTER I HAVE EXTERMINATED THE LAST CHILDREN OF ARGO AND KRYPTON!
M-MURDERER OF WORLDS...
...YOU WILL ⋛KZZK!⋛ DO NO SUCH THING...
NO... THE SOLAR PROJECTOR--!
K-CHIK!
K-CHIK
K-CHIK!
VVMMMMMM
SHE'S CHANGED THE RAY TO A YELLOW SUN! OUR POWERS ARE RETURNING!
WHICH MEANS YOU'D BETTER GET THE PROFESSOR OUT OF HARM'S WAY--
--BECAUSE THERE'S GOING TO BE A LOT OF TWELFTH-LEVEL DEBRIS FLYING AROUND!
SH-KRANG!
WHOOF!
WOKK!
YOUR FREEDOM CHANGES NOTHING, KAL-EL. YOU AND THE FEMALE ARE BOTH TOO WEAKENED TO STOP ME.

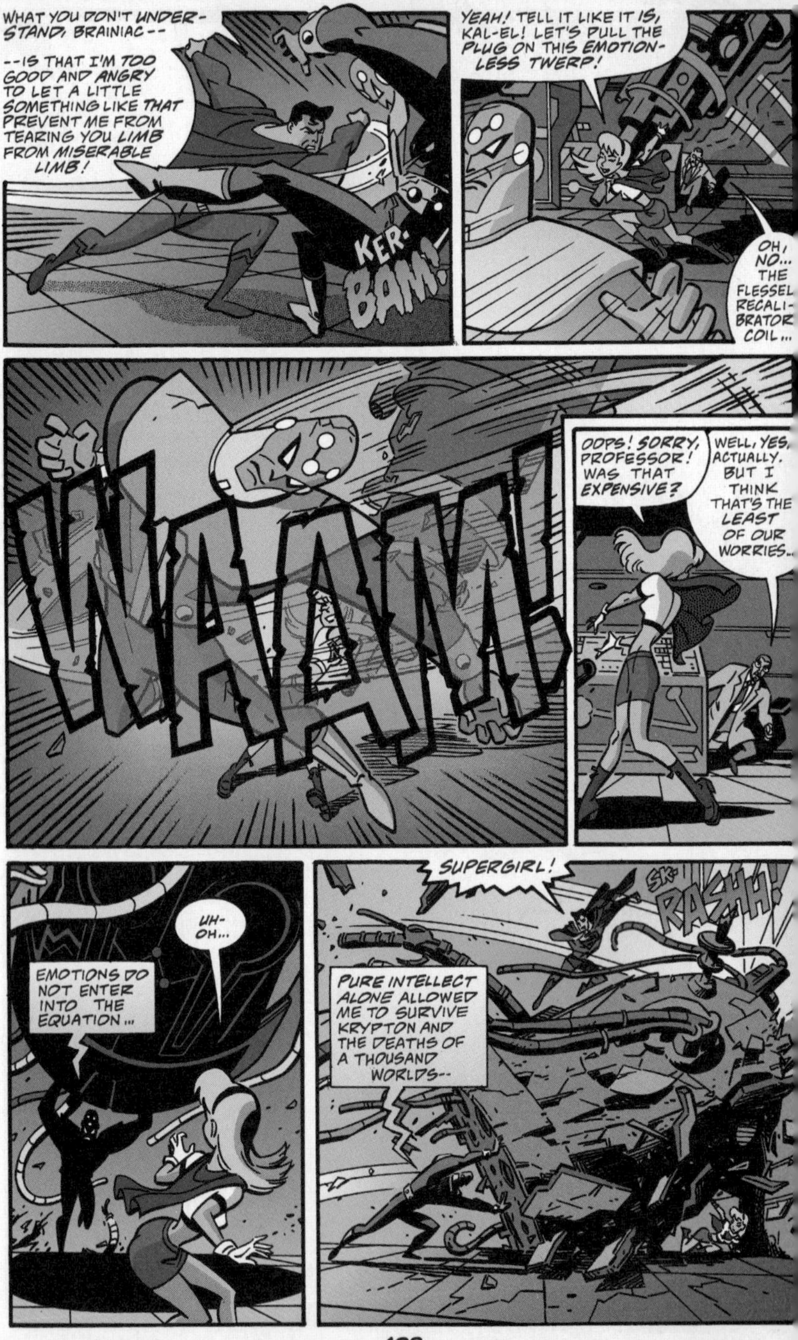
WHAT YOU DON'T UNDERSTAND, BRAINIAC --
--IS THAT I'M TOO GOOD AND ANGRY TO LET A LITTLE SOMETHING LIKE THAT PREVENT ME FROM TEARING YOU LIMB FROM MISERABLE LIMB!
KER-BAM!
YEAH! TELL IT LIKE IT IS, KAL-EL! LET'S PULL THE PLUG ON THIS EMOTIONLESS TWERP!
OH, NO... THE FLESSEL RECALIBRATOR COIL...
WAAM!
OOPS! SORRY, PROFESSOR! WAS THAT EXPENSIVE?
WELL, YES, ACTUALLY. BUT I THINK THAT'S THE LEAST OF OUR WORRIES...
UH-OH...
EMOTIONS DO NOT ENTER INTO THE EQUATION...
SUPERGIRL!
SK-RASHH!
PURE INTELLECT ALONE ALLOWED ME TO SURVIVE KRYPTON AND THE DEATHS OF A THOUSAND WORLDS--

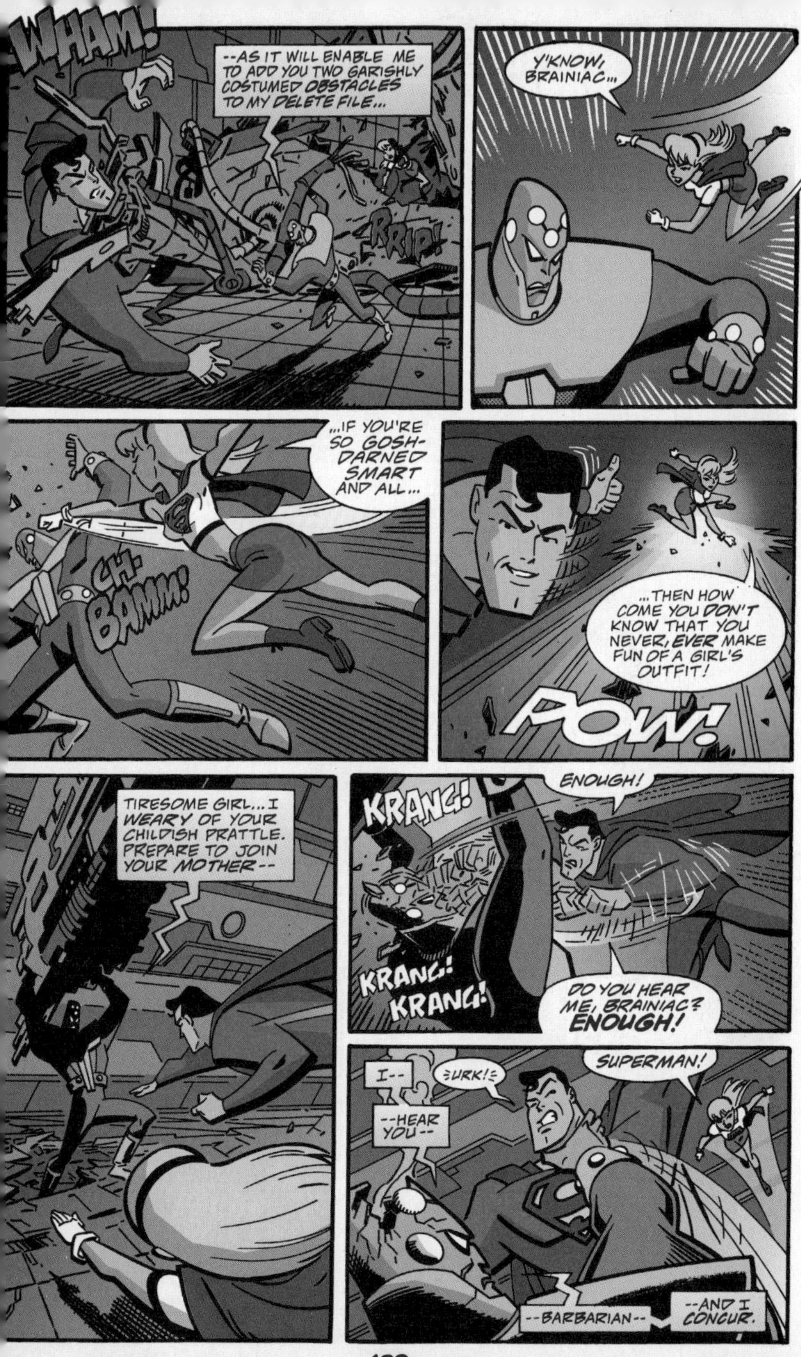
WHAM!
--AS IT WILL ENABLE ME TO ADD YOU TWO GARISHLY COSTUMED OBSTACLES TO MY DELETE FILE...
RRIP!
Y'KNOW, BRAINIAC...
...IF YOU'RE SO GOSH-DARNED SMART AND ALL...
CH-BAMM!
...THEN HOW COME YOU DON'T KNOW THAT YOU NEVER, EVER MAKE FUN OF A GIRL'S OUTFIT!
POW!
TIRESOME GIRL... I WEARY OF YOUR CHILDISH PRATTLE. PREPARE TO JOIN YOUR MOTHER--
KRANG!
ENOUGH!
KRANG!
KRANG!
DO YOU HEAR ME, BRAINIAC? ENOUGH!
I--
URK!
SUPERMAN!
--HEAR YOU--
--BARBARIAN--
--AND I CONCUR.

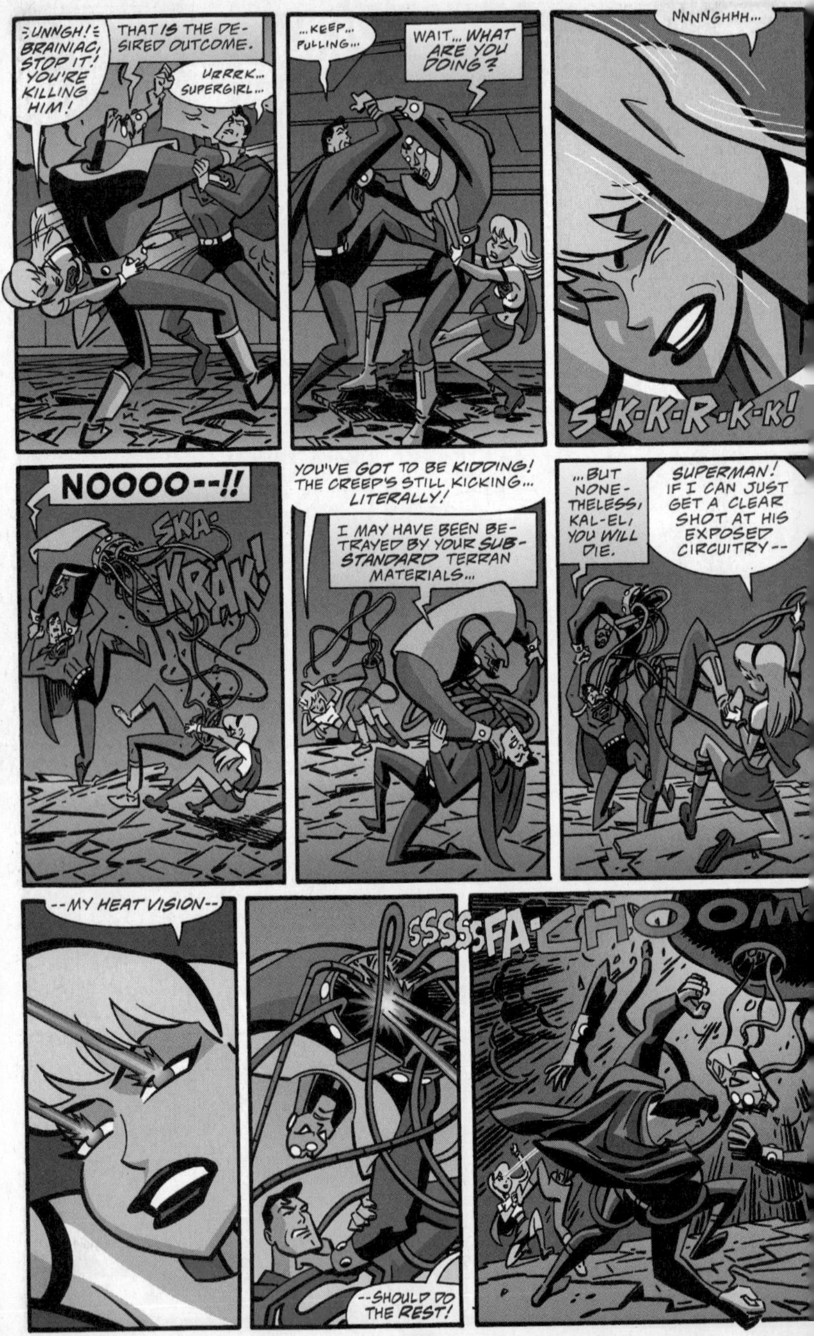
UNNGH! BRAINIAC, STOP IT! YOU'RE KILLING HIM!
THAT IS THE DESIRED OUTCOME.
URRRK... SUPERGIRL...
...KEEP... PULLING...
WAIT... WHAT ARE YOU DOING?
NNNNGHHH...
S-K-K-R-K-K!
NOOOO--!!
SKA-KRAK!
YOU'VE GOT TO BE KIDDING! THE CREEP'S STILL KICKING... LITERALLY!
I MAY HAVE BEEN BETRAYED BY YOUR SUBSTANDARD TERRAN MATERIALS...
...BUT NONETHELESS, KAL-EL, YOU WILL DIE.
SUPERMAN! IF I CAN JUST GET A CLEAR SHOT AT HIS EXPOSED CIRCUITRY--
--MY HEAT VISION--
--SHOULD DO THE REST!
SSSSSFA-CHOOM!

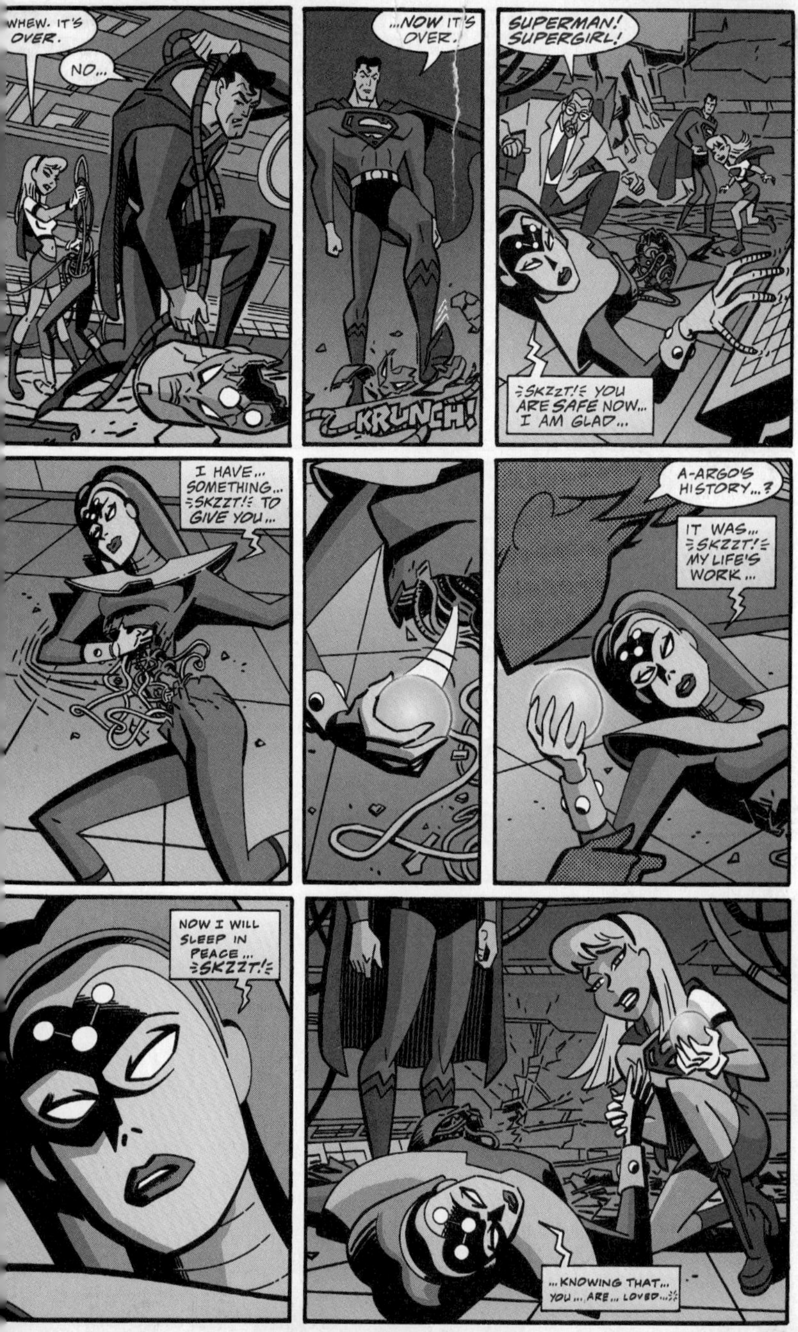
WHEW. IT'S OVER.
NO...
...NOW IT'S OVER.
KRUNCH!
SUPERMAN! SUPERGIRL!
=SKZZT!= YOU ARE SAFE NOW... I AM GLAD...
I HAVE... SOMETHING... =SKZZT!= TO GIVE YOU...
A-ARGO'S HISTORY...?
IT WAS... =SKZZT!= MY LIFE'S WORK...
NOW I WILL SLEEP IN PEACE... =SKZZT!=
...KNOWING THAT... YOU... ARE... LOVED...

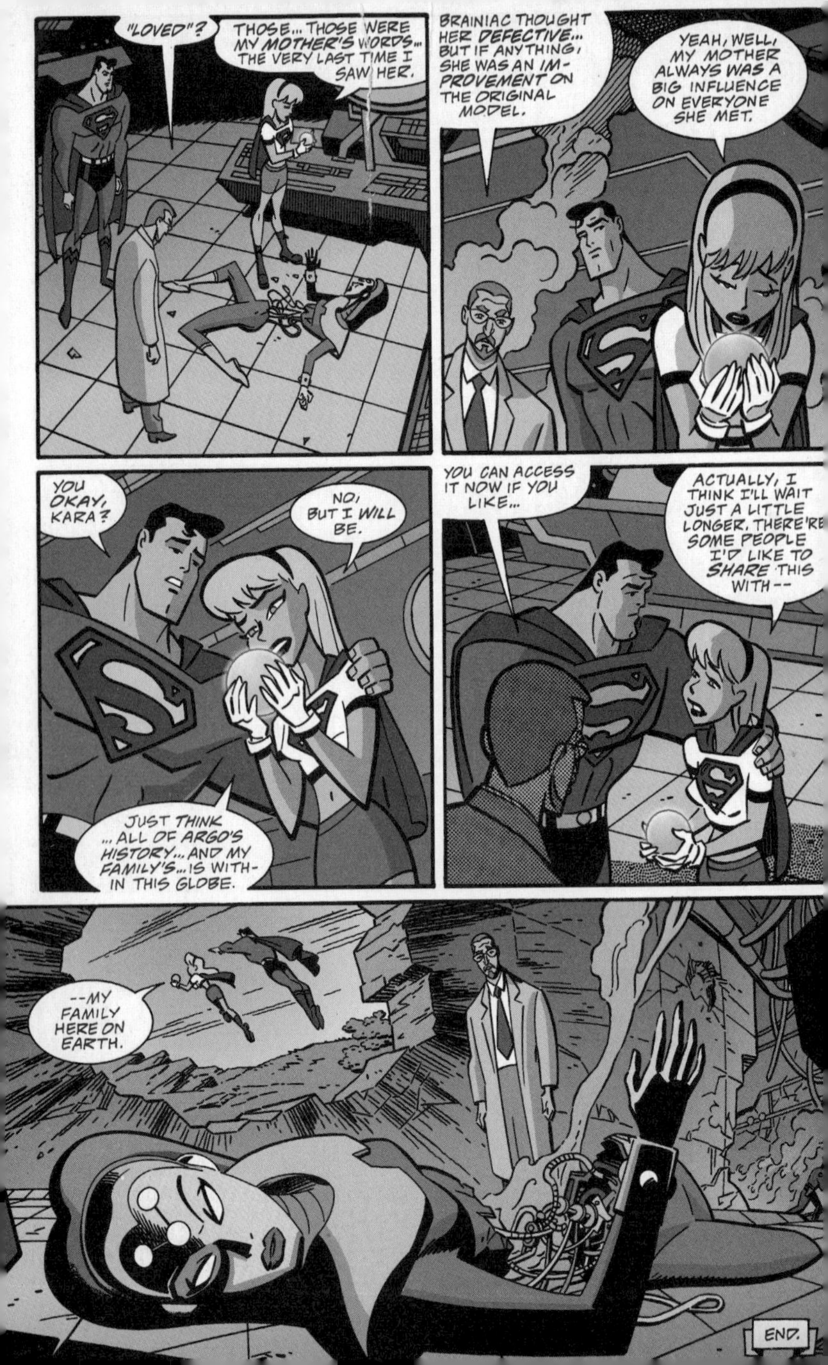
"LOVED"?
THOSE... THOSE WERE MY MOTHER'S WORDS... THE VERY LAST TIME I SAW HER.
BRAINIAC THOUGHT HER DEFECTIVE... BUT IF ANYTHING, SHE WAS AN IMPROVEMENT ON THE ORIGINAL MODEL.
YEAH, WELL, MY MOTHER ALWAYS WAS A BIG INFLUENCE ON EVERYONE SHE MET.
YOU OKAY, KARA?
NO, BUT I WILL BE.
JUST THINK ...ALL OF ARGO'S HISTORY... AND MY FAMILY'S... IS WITHIN THIS GLOBE.
YOU CAN ACCESS IT NOW IF YOU LIKE...
ACTUALLY, I THINK I'LL WAIT JUST A LITTLE LONGER. THERE'RE SOME PEOPLE I'D LIKE TO SHARE THIS WITH--
--MY FAMILY HERE ON EARTH.
END.